ABOUT THE AUTHOR

Elizabeth Lyle is the pseudonym of a
Fleet Street editor's daughter. *Cassy* is her
first full-length work and will be followed by a historical novel set in Turkey,
where Elizabeth Lyle spent many years
with her husband. She has traveled widely
and at the present lives partway up a
mountain in Andorra.

Cassy

Elizabeth Lyle

ST. MARTIN'S PRESS / NEW YORK

10 9 8 7 6 5 4 3 2 1
First Edition

Library of Congress Cataloging in Publication Data

Lyle, Elizabeth.
    Cassy.
    I. Title.
PR6062.Y477C3   1981   823'.914   81-872
ISBN 0-312-12352-3   AACR2

1

The gentleman who descended from the curricle had good looks and a fashionable air. But Cassy regarded him through the downstairs bow window with dismay. 'I can't see him. I can't,' she cried, jumping to her feet. 'You must tell him, Thea, that I am indisposed.'

'Indisposed to marry him,' Grace laughed, peeping through the casement. 'Look again at what you are refusing.' But her eldest sister had already run from the room.

'The Marquis of Allingham,' Grimble announced, impassively. The two remaining sisters of the trio studied the handsome, moody countenance with curiosity.

His Lordship looked at the pretty youngsters. The taller had smooth brown hair with golden lights in it, and the smaller, auburn ringlets. Two pairs of direct blue eyes gazed unwaveringly at him. His own softened, and the firm set of his lips relaxed into an unexpectedly attractive smile. 'I think,' he said, 'it must be your older sister I have come to see. Althea, is it not?'

'Oh no,' the older girl corrected him, shocked. 'I am Althea; she is called Lucasta.'

'I am sorry ...'

'I am not surprised that you are confused,' the younger reassured him kindly. 'Our mother was very romantical, you see, and had us christened after the ladies to whom the poet Lovelace wrote his poems. She was much attached to his verses.' She looked suddenly stricken, and, after a quick glance at his informant, the Marquis enquired matter-of-factly, 'Have you also then a name taken from the poetry of the cavalier poet?'

'I fear so. I am really Gratiana. But it has become Grace.'

'That is an improvement on the original and suits you,' he told her gravely, whereupon she coloured with pleasure and was confirmed in her original impression of him. It was a pity that she was herself but twelve years old and Thea only fourteen, else he might perhaps have offered for one of them instead.

'I understand your aunt is from home. Will you ask Miss Lucasta if she will receive me? I believe she is expecting my visit.'

'Yes, but she is – not disposed,' answered Althea quickly, as if reciting a lesson.

The gentleman raised an astonished eyebrow, and asked with a twinkle that made the girls beam back at him artlessly, 'Might she be disposed to receive me another time?'

Remembering Cassy's protestations Grace said quickly, 'It is difficult to say.'

'Yes, I can see that it must be,' he agreed sympathetically, his eyes dancing now. 'Please inform Miss Lucasta that I shall give myself the pleasure of waiting upon her on Thursday afternoon.' He directed his disarming smile at them again and bowed himself out.

The Marquis of Allingham at nine and twenty was wearied and disenchanted by being made the prey of every matchmaking mama in town, for his position, his wealth, his historic family seat near Oxford and his perfectly appointed house in Grosvenor Square. His appearance added to his aura of magnificence. But for his friends his charm lay not so much in the excellence of physique and precision of firmly moulded nose and mouth, as in a pair of light, flecked hazel eyes, full of intelligence, viewing the world with an ironic gleam that held lurking amusement.

His well-merited reputation as a rake did him, oddly enough, no disservice in the eyes of the ladies, since most of them were confident of reforming him once granted the opportunity.

His Lordship had received a ball in the shoulder during the Duke of Wellington's advance from the lines at Torres Vedras to Madrid. He had sold out on the advice of his doctor. But he had not relinquished his connection with the army, and now in 1813 was working still in some undisclosed capacity at the war department as he had done since his recovery.

He had as yet never met a female who inspired him with a desire to marry her and was aware of the fact that, as the only son of his widowed mother, it was his duty to take a wife and provide an heir. He remembered with extreme clarity one of his last conversations with his father, who had died the year before.

'Julian,' the elderly Marquis had asked him anxiously, 'is there no young woman to whom you feel particularly drawn?'

His heir's frown at the inception of yet another lecture on the debt he owed the family changed to wicked enjoyment as he rejoined: 'Why yes, sir, there is. But I doubt whether you or my mother would welcome her as your daughter-in-law any more than you would have done her predecessors.' Alone with his father, and mindful of the gentleman's past reputation in the petticoat line during the days when the King they called 'Farmer George' was still able to rule the country, he could afford to be frank.

The older man scowled and then permitted himself a half-smile at his graceless but beloved son. 'You are right. Neither your mother nor I would be grateful to see any of your pieces of muslin from Drury Lane or Covent Garden in a position which should be one of the most respected in the land.

'Furthermore these – Cyprians – I am persuaded, have no place in your heart, even when under your protection.'

'You are right of course, sir.'

'Well then, why not heed your mother's suggestions? She was herself, I confess to you, chosen for me by my family. But I soon confirmed for myself her graciousness and attractions. You must know that our union has been happy, with but a single regret, that we had only one child, yourself, and that at an age when we were unlikely to have many years before us to enjoy our grandchildren, if you ever provide legitimate progeny.'

It was perhaps on account of this exchange that the present Marquis was more amenable to his mother's efforts than she had hoped. After ignoring the caps set at him in London he consented to give serious consideration to the various belles from the surrounding shires invited to dinner at Allingham Park, or even, if he showed as much as a flicker of interest, as house guests.

But so far, much as he wished to please his mother, to whom he was devoted, he had been unable to bring himself to woo any of them. Accordingly, on impulse he had resolved to offer his hand in marriage to Lucasta Loring.

He had been seated one morning at breakfast with the Marchioness in

7

the country when he heard her give a gasp of distress as she read a letter recently arrived.

'What is it, dear?' he asked, struck by the sparkle of tears in the fine eyes so like his own.

'I am most upset, Julian. You have heard me speak of Eleanor Page and her sister, Lettice, with whom your youngest aunt, Margaret, attended that horrid seminary. They became almost like extra little sisters to me.'

'I believe so.'

'Such dear, lovely girls. They and Margaret were presented at Court at the same time.' He waited patiently while she dabbed her eyes with a wisp of lace-edged lawn. 'Eleanor and her husband, Sir James Loring, were both killed instantly when his tilbury overturned in a collision with a farm wagon.'

'How sad! I am sorry, mother. Did they have a family?'

'Indeed they did. Three young daughters, the eldest barely eighteen. Eleanor's sister-in-law from Yorkshire writes that they have been left in something approaching penury.'

'But I understood that Sir James, whom I have met at White's, was wealthy. Did he not own large estates in Leicestershire?'

'Yes, and it seems that they will all have to be sold to pay off his outstanding debts. He and Eleanor were very fashionable and expensive. Both were celebrated for their looks and gaiety. I think Eleanor was an uneconomical housekeeper, to say the least of it, though the sweetest creature. He was no manager, though a notable Corinthian in his time.'

'I know it.'

'I suspect they soon spent his fortune and her dowry and then it was all hopes and creditors.'

'Have I met the daughters?'

'You were introduced to Lucasta, the eldest, at Almack's and stood up with her once. She is a beauty and it seems expedient now that she should marry well and take her little sisters under her wing. Their aunt Lettice, who has always lived with them, has never married, though she was well-favoured and had many opportunities. She is a most cultivated person.'

'I do not have any recollection of Lucasta.'

'I did not suppose you would have. But you may accept my assurance that though she has no dowry, she has everything to recommend her in the way of looks and breeding.'

'I have no need of a rich wife. Should I marry her then, mother, and save her family?'

'Why not?' said the Marchioness simply.

Cassy had not forgotten the Marquis of Allingham, who had danced with her that one time at Almack's. She recalled him because at first, when Lady Jersey, one of the patrons, brought him up to her, and he led her on to the floor, she thought him the personification of an ideal, so straight and broad-shouldered he was, with an exciting line of mouth and nostril. But she saw his look of utter boredom, and the sweet smile that started in her eyes and lifted the corners of her lips died away, and her face became as expressionless as his – not that he noticed the change, for he stared over the top of her head. He had taken all the fun and thrill out of her first visit to the legendary Almack's. She saw him once or twice at fashionable parties after that, but as he had quite clearly forgotten it, she had no desire to remind him of her existence.

Since the news of their parents' death, not only social life, but any semblance of life as they had known it had stopped for Cassy, Thea and Grace. They were naturally prostrated with grief at their loss. Then there was a period of numbness during which nothing seemed worth while. Finally there was the legal business associated with the tragedy, in the course of which the face of their family lawyer became more and more serious.

First they were bewildered. Then they began to realise why their father had already dispensed with the horses he used to keep on the Brighton and Newmarket roads, then his hunters and finally his hacks. They understood why the small but elegant house in Lowndes Square which they had taken for the season, and still for the moment occupied, had been substituted for their large town residence. It became clear why so many of their mother's jewels turned out to be copies of the originals which she had sold in an unavailing effort to keep down the rising tide of insolvency.

They were forced to witness the auction of their Leicestershire home and lands and the unwilling exodus of the devoted servants they had known all their lives. They kept one maid, one cook and Grimble the butler, in his case as much because he refused to be dislodged as to give them countenance and provide a male about the house. Involved as he was with the family, he had suffered his own sorrow for the handsome and happy couple he had served since their marriage.

9

Miss Lettice Page, their mother's younger sister, had always lived with them and given them their lessons. She was pleasant to look at, placid, and a dear and familiar part of their lives; her presence now gave them some sense of security and continuity in a world that was falling to pieces around them.

Finally a committee formed by the loyal lawyer, Miss Page and Cassy came to the conclusion that, with everything else gone, it might be possible to retain their present rented house if a little extra could somehow be found in the way of income to supplement what remained for the girls after everything was settled, added to Aunt Letty's small private means.

The alternative, unattractive as it might be, was to accept the suggestion of their father's younger brother, now Sir Matthew Loring, to join his household in Yorkshire. The invitation was particularly kind since he was not a rich man and had one son and no less than four daughters of his own.

After the lawyer had departed, leaving them to further discussion of ways and means, Cassy looked round the parlour, thinking how tasteful and comfortable it was with their favourite pieces which they had saved from going, like the rest, under the hammer. She did not think their home looked shabby-genteel.

'We must keep it if only for the girls' sake,' Cassy declared. 'It would not be fair to Uncle Matthew to accept his offer, even if we relished the idea of being buried in Yorkshire. Thank goodness you can give them a good education, Aunt Letty. They are both incipient belles, and with their name and a respectable background, even without dowries, they should eventually make satisfactory marriages.'

'Yes, dearest, I agree. But where is that extra money to come from?'

'From me. It must.'

Miss Page looked at her eldest niece appraisingly. Then she smiled, and one could see from her dimpled, fresh cheeks and her bright blue-grey eyes that she had, like her sister, been in her day a diamond of the first water. 'Thea and Grace,' she concurred, 'have potential. But you already possess the attributes necessary to make a good match, except of course the money.'

Cassy made a comic grimace and assessed herself candidly in the long cheval glass as a marriageable commodity. Lapislazuli eyes fringed with long black lashes looked levelly back at her beneath soft golden curls. Her pretty mouth pursed, and she put her little hands on elegant hips that swelled from a tiny waist.

'Not bad, I suppose,' she decided frankly.

Miss Page laughed at her niece's expression and bowed to the inevitable. 'I think we must accept your uncle's offer of a home. You have had a London season and received a number of desirable offers of marriage, none of which appealed to you, and none of which your father would encourage you to accept, even realising his parlous financial position. I fear a romantical and not a practical disposition runs in the family.' She sighed, thinking of her own disappointed suitors and those of her sister. 'But,' she remembered with eyes suddenly damp, 'your mama was quick enough to recognise her fate when she met it in the person of your dear papa.'

'I know,' agreed Cassy, fearful of the tears that would spring to her own eyes if they expanded on the subject. 'I have not, it would seem, yet met my fate. So, aunt dear, leaving out the possibility of a marriage of convenience to a gentleman who fancied me enough to wed me without the wherewithal to buy a bonnet, and to take on the responsibility of my sisters and their future settlements, what is there left for a girl who wishes to make her way? I do not think I should easily secure a post as a governess or school teacher. I am not a scholar like you.'

Miss Page looked aghast, having had Cassy not so long ago in the schoolroom. 'No you are not, although you are quick and intelligent. I cannot see you giving instruction in the harp or pianoforte since you never would practise on those instruments yourself. Your French and German are promising though you were ever remiss about learning your irregular verbs. Your spelling is enterprising but not always accurate. Besides, you are too pretty. No sensible matron would engage a governess who outshone her own daughters and represented temptation to her husband and older sons. In any case the pay is wretched.'

Cassy laughed. 'Well then, since you are so discouraging, that profession is eliminated. What of other possibilities? Companion to an old lady? I could not bear it. Modiste or milliner? I do not sew very well either, do I, Aunt?'

'Not nearly as well as your sisters,' Miss Page agreed with feeling. 'But you have a true, pleasing singing voice and talent for elocution. You are a graceful dancer with excellent deportment like your mama; you have warmth of personality and you are a naughty mimic.' She laughed, recalling a Cassy strutting pompously and affecting the tones of one of her more self-important admirers. She also remembered the self-forgetfulness with which Cassy had, more recently, cheered her little sisters by singing them snatches of popular songs in her clear, high voice or prancing with them in an improvised ballet. 'These qualities will endear you to the right man, my love, but otherwise ...'

For a wild moment Cassy thought of a proud, dark head with cold hazel eyes and hastily banished the vision. Then she conceived the germ of an idea. But she had no intention of discussing it with her aunt until she had thought it through to its logical conclusion.

Just two days later Miss Page came into the parlour with the oddest expression on her face. It was compounded of relief, incredulity, uncertainty and amusement. She said to Cassy, 'I have had a most unexpected communication from your uncle.' Her niece waited expectantly. 'The Marquis of Allingham has asked permission, which has been granted, to pay you his addresses.'

There was a stunned silence broken by a babble of excited comment from Thea and Grace, hushed immediately by their aunt who seemed only then to have noticed their presence. She drew Cassy into the small salon, saying as they entered, 'It is gratifying and opportune that he should have fallen in love with you. He says he made your acquaintance one evening at Almack's.'

Cassy's fair skin flushed with surprise, chagrin and some other emotion she would not admit to herself, but which sprang from that look he had seemed at first glance to have had of a hero of romance. 'But, Aunt, he cannot possibly even bring my face to mind,' she objected. 'He never spoke a word except to say "thank you" after he had led me back to mama.'

'Well, you must have made more of an impression than you imagined.'

'No, I am sure he has the intention of marrying simply for the sake of the succession, and that his mother, being mama's and your friend, hearing of our plight, must have persuaded him to this course. I dare say he would not care whom he took for wife providing she be presentable and suitably connected, and that he would then keep on his mistresses. Oh, no, dearest aunt, I will not marry an arrogant, indifferent, immoral—'

Her aunt put up her hand in dissent. 'Come, Cassy! I confess he has something of a reputation as a libertine. But he is after all a bachelor, and being a desirable parti, is doubtless spoiled. But I feel sure he would forgo any other attachments after marriage. He fought for his country and was wounded in its service. I know he is a loving son, and he is extremely good-looking.'

Cassy was still pink as she rejoined. 'He cannot, I concede, be all bad. I did not know he had been a soldier, although, not being blind, I did observe his appearance. However, the points for and against him cannot signify since I do not care for him, nor he for me. I do not wish to be married out of pity and because I am well-bred. You would not either, Aunt, would you?'

'No, Cassy,' Miss Page sighed, 'I would not. It is the Yorkshire moors for us, I see, and the hope that you may meet and become enamoured of some country squire.'

2

The visit of the Marquis to Lowndes Square had occurred unexpectedly soon after the reception of the missive announcing it from Uncle Matthew in Yorkshire. Cassy's precipitate flight was as much because, unaccountably, she did not care to be seen in her grey merino gown of half mourning as that she had not yet decided how to deal with the situation.

But from her bed-chamber, which faced the square, she saw his retreating figure and the somewhat puzzled look back he gave at the house over his shoulder, before he took the reins from his tiger and flicked them at his perfectly matched greys. With a flourish of the whip he was off and Cassy descended the stairs to her sisters. 'What did the Marquis say?' she demanded of Thea.

'He said,' the girl returned conscientiously, 'It would be your elder sister I have come to see.'

Cassy sniffed. His words were proof, if any were needed, that he had no recollection of her appearance.

'Then he said he would return on Thursday afternoon.'

'Oh, jiminy!' exclaimed Cassy inelegantly.

'But he is very amiable and has such smiling eyes!' Grace insisted on giving her opinion. 'In your place I—'

'Count yourself fortunate in not being there,' her eldest sister rejoined with unusual tartness, reflecting that Grace's impression of the caller hardly tallied with her own. But with a reputation such as his he must be presumed capable of making himself engaging, even to little girls. She decided that her plan of action must be put into operation before his next visit.

14

That very evening, after the younger girls had gone to bed, she approached her aunt cautiously on the subject of the solution to their problems that she had arrived at, after great agony of mind, and with constant misgivings that she must learn to keep to herself.

'Aunt Letty,' she began in her most winning tones, 'you and mama knew Mrs Siddons, did you not?'

There was a sudden defensive look on the still comely face of the older woman. She made a visible effort as she answered, 'Yes, Cassy. Both your mama and I loved going to the play. We met a number of theatre people when we were young, the most notable of them being Sarah Siddons.'

'She must have been a wonderful actress.'

'She was – incandescent. Your parents and I were at her farewell performance two years ago when she played perhaps her greatest role, that of Lady Macbeth, at Covent Garden for the last time – such an emotional occasion! There was hardly a dry eye in the house. I wish you could have seen her.'

'So do I. Mama told us she was particularly impressive in the sleep-walking scene.'

'The way she seemed to be washing imagined blood off her hands was unforgettable. They say that Richard Brinsley Sheridan, the playwright and manager at Drury Lane where she first played the part, objected to it, but she insisted on playing the scene in her own way, on being true to her art.'

'I can believe it. She is still accepted everywhere in society, is she not, and has even received royal hospitality?'

'Yes,' Miss Page assented with sudden apprehension.

'Then she has made the stage respectable, surely?'

Aunt looked at niece with horror. Cassy's intention was beginning to be distressingly clear. 'No, dear,' she insisted emphatically, 'and if you are imagining yourself a second Sarah Siddons please divest yourself of the illusion. You have not the makings of a great tragedienne.'

Cassy had to laugh. 'No, Aunt, I did not mean that'

'Your appearance, your voice and your dancing are not advantages that are going to make you a national figure on the stage, or respectable. Mrs Siddons is one alone. On the contrary, all they are likely to achieve for you is a *carte blanche* from some buck. Is that your ambition? Do you not wish to marry?'

'You know it is not, and I do hope to marry eventually, but for love.

In the meantime I would like to help to keep this house for us all. Dearest Aunt Letty, if I changed my name and disguised myself I am sure I could earn enough in the theatre for our needs. The most I could hope for, I realise, would be small roles after, presumably, an apprenticeship in the chorus. Then when we had saved something for the future and Thea and Grace were educated I would be only too happy to retire. Please, please, ask Mrs Siddons to help me.'

'No, no, I shall not!'

'Please, please – for all of us.'

She saw the indecision on her aunt's face as she pleaded, pressing her advantage, 'After all I might find somebody in the theatre world with whom I could fall in love. Edmund Kean must be very respectable.'

'A genius rather. That is not at all the same thing. Anyway he has a wife. The younger actors and actresses are not considered respectable.'

Cassy thought she saw a shimmer of tears in her aunt's eyes but, although she was curious, she did not like to appear importunate.

'You are sure you cannot accept the handsome Marquis? You are not like to get a chance like that again.'

'Quite sure. He has after all not yet paid his addresses to me. You must tell him on Thursday that I have gone away. If he enquires further, say that I have gone to be a teacher in a select academy for young ladies. That must be unexceptionable.'

'Such falsehoods you would have me tell, Cassy! The average girl,' she added, making a final effort, 'would give anything even for a marriage of convenience with such a catch as Lord Allingham, who has had I don't know how many fine ladies on the catch for him.' Miss Page was visibly distressed.

'I know and I am sorry. But you and I are not average, are we, Aunt?'

Aunt Letty shook her head speechlessly and at length said unwillingly, 'I shall write a note to Mrs Siddons if you really insist on taking this course, and ask if she will receive us. But I cannot like it, Cassy. Say nothing to your sisters, I beg of you. Let us hope, for propriety's sake, that she does not wish to help or that your audition is unsuccessful.'

'No, Aunt, I cannot wish that. How else can I earn a decent salary? But I promise that I shall tread the boards, if given the opportunity, wearing a wig.' Her eyes shone with merriment and excitement. 'We have a splendid assortment of wigs, you know, belonging to your mother. I am not sure that dark hair will not be more becoming to me than my own colour, and it is more fashionable.' Her aunt put up her hands in sad resignation.

Miss Page told Cassy something of Sarah Siddons before the meeting that had been arranged for the following afternoon. The greatest living actress liked to tell people that she was very nearly born on the stage. Roger Kemble, her father, was an actor-manager and her mother a fine actress. She conquered London as Isabella in *The Fatal Marriage*. Her death scene was so realistic in this piece that her eight-year-old son, Henry, who had a small part, thought she had actually died and wept bitterly until she rose, to the delight of the audience, and took him in her arms.

After hearing something of her story Cassy was full of curiosity to meet the Queen of Drury Lane, as well as anxiety on her own behalf. Mrs Siddons was nearly sixty when the girl, wide-eyed, was introduced to her by Miss Page in the green-painted saloon decorated with theatrical portraits and prints of old playbills in the quiet house in Baker Street.

Her classic features were still noble and her stately figure upright and slender. But Cassy found her a little overwhelming. She had heard that for Mrs Siddons the illusion of the theatre was the stuff of reality; that the great actress's most ordinary sayings tended to come out like blank verse.

Now, having embraced her old friend, she surveyed Cassy and, to the girl's private delight, declaimed, 'Such youth, such charm, it must be served.'

However, holding Cassy's hands and directing her piercing gaze at her, she proceeded to warn her about the drawbacks of the theatrical profession. 'You would be at the mercy of bucks who frequent the Green Room. Those of them who would not wish to hurt the reputation and chances of a gently nurtured girl consider actresses fair game.'

'But, ma'am, your reputation is spotless and you are worshipped almost as a deity,' Cassy objected with vehemence.

Mrs Siddons looked pleased. 'I have perhaps carved myself a special niche, my dear, but I was protected by my husband and brother in the same profession. Now, having done my duty by uttering my dire warning, let me hear you sing.'

With a plea for permission Aunt Letty went to the piano and played the opening bars of a ballad which began:

17

My heart is like a bird
That hungers in the snow.
You have not said a word
And yet I love you so.

The words were banal, but Cassy's voice, though not strong, was sweet and true, and her expression while singing them so appealing that Mrs Siddons was more impressed than she had expected.

Miss Page broke into a sprightly rhythm now and Cassy executed a little dance she had devised herself. She pirouetted prettily, her white arms arranged so gracefully that they were like garlands.

Mrs Siddons nodded with some approval. But she laughed heartily when Cassy, somewhat breathlessly, rushed into the sleep-walking scene from *Macbeth* that the tragedienne had made so peculiarly her own. 'No, no Cassy,' she begged. 'Not that. But when you dance and sing you are a breath of spring.'

The girl, although a little disconcerted, had to smile, marvelling still at the lady's habit of turning conversation into poetry.

Sarah Siddons looked with a touch of nostalgia for her own youth at the beauty of the girl's face and figure. She might not have a great talent, but with those enchanting looks her small gift would do. She only hoped the child would keep her freshness and innocence among the many temptations to which she would inevitably be exposed in the theatre. She wondered if Letty Page had ever regretted renouncing her beau. Aloud she said, 'I shall write a billet to the committee of management at Drury Lane.'

Cassy thanked her with an expression of delight, and her aunt with one of doubt and foreboding.

Late that evening Cassy, elated yet far more apprehensive than she could admit, told Miss Page, 'You were right to say that my sisters should not be told if I am given a chance at Drury Lane. The fact of my being on the stage could do their reputations no good, and it would be putting an unfair burden on them to expect them to keep our secret.'

'Granted. But what can we say to account for your absences in such a case?'

'As far as the girls are concerned I shall be teaching elocution and dancing at a select academy for females outside London, the same one as you describe to the Marquis!' she smiled encouragingly at her anxious aunt. 'It is no use trying to persuade Thea and Grace that I am instructing my pupils in scholastic subjects, for they simply would not believe it. The Marquis has not had the same opportunity of learning my limitations. He could be led to suppose my aim to be the establishment of my own school.' She laughed at the unlikelihood of such an ambition.

'You do not, I hope, intend to sail out of this house in a black wig!'

'No, I promise you, nor to do a quick switch-over in the street. It were better for all concerned if I could lodge with John Coachman and Louise in the event of my securing employment at Drury Lane. Their house and hire service is situated, you will recall, just behind the theatre in Russell Street, and I am sure they would let me a room for a nominal sum. We should have to take them into our confidence.'

'You could trust them with your life, Cassy. You know that, although they will not approve of your becoming a player.'

'Of course I do. John would be a splended bodyguard, and it would be handy to have a hack available for hire on the premises.'

'But how we should miss you!' lamented Aunt Letty.

'And I you three. But you can depend upon it that I should be home every weekend and, after all, the productions only have limited runs.'

On the dissolution of the household their coachman had married Lady Loring's personal maid. With their combined savings the couple had bought a small home, with a good yard and stabling, and one hackney carriage. John's industry combined with their close vicinity to the theatre and to the Black Lion Tavern, meeting place for aspiring actors and managers, had resulted in their soon acquiring another conveyance and a second jarvey.

A note was delivered to Miss Page the next day bidding her accompany her niece to an audition at Drury Lane for a position in the chorus of a new burletta entitled *Up all Night*.

Cassy and her aunt took a hired carriage in much trepidation. One of Grandmama's wigs was in a hat-box, and the girl put it on during the journey while Aunt Letty held the hand mirror. The different texture and colour of hair together with an elaborate style such as Cassy had never favoured changed her appearance to a surprising degree.

'It is vastly becoming and an excellent disguise,' Miss Page was forced to admit. 'But I miss my golden girl.'

'She shall be returned to you.' Cassy gave her aunt an impulsive kiss of affection and gratitude.

19

They reported as directed to the stage manager who had read with reverence his letter from the great tragedienne. He was disposed to accept her protégée if she showed any promise, and asked the wardrobe mistress to find Cassy something to wear. She changed into a gauzy, spangled costume which reached just below her knees and a pair of the new tights or 'maillots'. She was exhilarated by the unwonted freedom of her limbs and at the same time embarrassed at showing them thus to what, she presumed, must be the management committee and sundry other interested spectators in the dim auditorium. But she knew that she must get used to this display, and was herself forced to acknowledge their shapeliness.

The dresser, a kindly grey-haired woman with years-long experience of the theatre, told her, 'The hideous masks, panniers and perukes of some years ago have been done away with, I am glad to say.' Cassy, surveying herself anxiously in the spotted mirror, was even more conscious of wearing Grandmama's wig after hearing this observation, but grateful that it both fitted and suited her so well.

She had requested the pianist to play a lively song, translated from the French, with the refrain 'and so my heart goes dancing'. She sang to the unidentified faces in the theatre as if to a full audience, with her heart in the simple sentiments and a look of radiance.

She followed the ballad with her own arrangement of a gavotte which she had performed for Sarah Siddons. After she had finished she waited tremulously.

Two gentlemen came up on to the stage. One of them, she noticed briefly, was of middle years and had mobile, comic features. But the pale face of the younger, with its deep-set dark grey eyes and the close chestnut curls on a head like that of a Greek hero, was reputed to cast females into a swoon when he so much as glanced in their direction.

Cassy did not feel like fainting, but she thought she had never seen so arresting a male countenance as that of Lord Byron, although the thought came unbidden to her mind that she preferred the harder, more virile looks of the Marquis of Allingham, however haughty and objectionable he might be. Byron said lazily, in his light voice, 'Well, Joe, she's no Taglioni. But, for her beauty at least, she's going to set the town by its ears.' He gave her a melting glance and walked languidly away with a barely discernible limp. Cassy remembered that the poet was on the management committee of Drury Lane.

The gentleman with the humorous face patted her shoulder and the stage manager said, 'Right. You have a place in the production, a three-act comic opera. Report for the rehearsal on Monday. You will find a list of times hanging in the Green Room.' His voice became stern. 'Any absence, unless through illness, or any lack of punctuality, means a forfeit of some part of your pay, which will start at five guineas weekly.'

'Oh, thank you, sir,' beamed Cassy.

He smiled now and said, 'Good luck!'

3

When Cassy emerged from the dressing-room in her street clothes her aunt hugged her and said, 'Very well done, love!' Seeing the new chorus girl's glowing satisfaction, she had not the heart to express again her own enduring disquiet and her abiding sense of guilt that she had allowed her niece to over-persuade her.

They would have liked to walk briskly the short way to the corner where John and Louise had their home and living, for the autumn afternoon was damp and chilly. But they were forced to hold their skirts up and step with care on the rough cobbles which were slippery with moisture and soiled with refuse.

'Did you realise, Cassy,' asked Miss Page as they trod gingerly, 'that the younger gentleman of the two who came on the stage after your audition was Lord Byron?'

'Yes, I did, because I recognised him from portraits I have seen. Not that I think they do him justice. Is he as wicked, I wonder, as people say?'

'I should liefer give him the benefit of the doubt. The females make fools of themselves over him. When Lady Caroline Lamb, his first great amour, met him she described him as "mad, bad and dangerous to know", and the epithets became common usage. She fell in love with him, pursued him relentlessly and then persecuted him with importunities and threats when he tired of her.'

'Foolish creature!' exclaimed Cassy. 'I blame her husband for failing to stop the liaison.'

'Ah, here is the house. I would know it was Louise's even if we had not visited her here before, for the brass door-knocker shines, and the windows and curtains are spotless.'

'In contrast with most of her neighbours! Aunt, with my five guineas weekly I shall be able to supplement the family income and still have enough to reimburse Louise if she will take me in.'

The one-time abigail welcomed the ladies with expressions of surprised delight. Then she looked at Cassy with consternation. 'Why are you wearing your grandmama's peruke, Miss Cassy?' she asked reprovingly. 'It is not at all the mode now to wear a wig.' The girl laughed and explained her peculiar circumstances and hope of finding accommodation.

Louise was, predictably, horrified at Cassy's news but nevertheless overjoyed at the prospect of having her beloved Lady Loring's first born living with her. She waved away payment saying, 'The pleasure will more than recompense for a little room and a share of our simple fare. But,' she said anxiously, 'it is not a suitable area for you, Miss Cassy dear.'

'It is its perfect suitability, Louise, as well as your chaperonage and company that I seek. I should pay for my lodgings, else I should not come.'

Louise was gratified, but her evident pleasure was still tempered with shock and much concern for Cassy. The girl was grateful that her mother's one-time maid could not know that she had chosen a stage career in preference to becoming a marchioness, or Louise would have questioned her sanity and delivered her a long lecture.

'You had better consult your husband before making any final decision about having Miss Cassy to stay,' counselled Miss Page.

'My dear ma'am, you know my John always does as I ask him.' They did know, for the coachman's wooing, with its excessive gallantries and conciliation of the capricious and personable Louise, had been a subject for amused speculation. 'Anyway', she concluded, 'my bidding this time will be just what will please him most, for you know how devoted he is to the family and was as grieved as myself when—'

'Yes, Louise, we do know and are grateful,' Aunt Letty cut in hurriedly, for they were both not sufficiently recovered from the blow of the fatal accident to their loved ones to be able easily to tolerate any unexpected reference to it.

'So far so very good,' decided a happy but overstrung Cassy on the way home. 'Now it only remains for you to dismiss the Marquis of Allingham with tact on Thursday.'

'I cannot help thinking still, my dear, that you should do him the courtesy of receiving him yourself.'

'Oh, no, Aunt. The only way to ward off his charitable proposition is for me to have departed from home already. Although he is so odiously top lofty, I do not care to reward what must be considered a kind, if cold-blooded, intention with a set-down. Moreover, if the Marquis happened to look at me instead of over my head as he did at our only encounter it is just possible he might recognise me some time on the stage, even in my gorgeous wig and greasepaint.'

So it was that, when the Marquis of Allingham called as promised, only Miss Page was at home to receive him. Before he could utter anything but a polite greeting she had stated, 'I regret that my niece, Lucasta, is not here. I believe you wished to convey your condolences to her on her sad loss, which was kind of you. I shall mention the fact to her when I see her again.'

The Marquis looked, for one of the only times since he had reached man's estate, slightly at a loss as he asked hesitantly, 'She is away – on a visit?'

'Not exactly.' Miss Page was all of a sudden overcome with the absurdity of the announcement she must make and conscious of her inability to sound convincing. 'She has gone away to be a teacher at an academy for young ladies.'

His Lordship looked much struck. He gave the patently discountenanced lady a hard stare from beneath his well-marked brows and said in his slight, not unpleasing drawl, 'Miss Lucasta has embraced a scholastic career, you say? How commendable! Please give her my congratulations – and of course, condolences.'

He bade a cool and courteous farewell to the sadly flustered lady and sauntered back to his curricle with its coat of arms emblazoned on the silver grey panels of the deep blue paint work. Unruffled as he appeared, he was in fact considerably taken aback. The good lady was, in his opinion, a bad liar. If she was forced to this expedient it could only be that this Lucasta did not wish him to offer for her. Since he could not at all bring the image of the girl to mind, his sensibilities were unaffected. But his pride was hurt. He was piqued, intrigued and could withal appreciate the humour of the situation. His main regret was that he would not after all acquire those delightful schoolgirls for his little sisters.

As an only child of elderly parents, brought up in his stately home in the country, he had missed the company of siblings, and felt an extremely well-concealed envy of the warmth and easy familiarity between brothers and sisters. This lack in his life had been another reason for his acquiescence in his parents' wishes that he should marry and set up his nursery. After his lonely childhood he would enjoy a merry, growing family of his own, a fact that the Marquis's friends, who had heard his sarcastic sympathy for those 'enmeshed in matrimony,' would find difficult to credit.

He directed his greys to his mother's London home in Clarges Street where she was at present in residence. 'It is fixed then, Julian?' she asked. 'Was she not pleased?'

'She was not there, mother.'

'But I do not understand. You had informed the family of your intention to call, and had already obtained the consent of Lucasta's uncle.'

He did not answer her remarks directly but asked instead, 'Would you say that she was an academic sort of girl? Could you, for instance, see her forswearing marriage and worldly advancement to teach in a seminary?'

The Marchioness laughed and one could readily believe in that moment that she had indeed been the belle of her first season. 'Lucasta!' she exclaimed. 'Never! Admittedly I do not know her very well because the family lived mostly in Leicestershire when the children were young. But after she came to town with her parents for her comeout I did meet her a few times. I found her to be unusually attractive, animated and high-spirited. But a blue-stocking? No! Have you no memory of her at all?'

'I am somewhat ashamed now to own that I doubt if I should recognise her if I saw her. But I admit to a little curiosity. You know,' he added as if in extenuation, 'that I have always tried to avoid raising false hopes in the breasts of eligible females, or come to that, the other kind.' As he said this it crossed his mind that the remark sounded arrogant. Perhaps it was. But, he excused himself mentally, it would have been astounding if the experience of being the quarry of so many designing females had not engendered in him a realism that amounted to cynicism.

'I know what it must be,' suggested his mother sagely. 'She is like her aunt Letty.'

'Certainly the aunt I met this afternoon is handsome.'

'Very true. But Lucasta favours her mother more. I mean rather that she may already have given her heart to somebody quite unsuitable, and would rather remain a spinster than marry without love. In that case it is conceivable she might decide to sublimate her natural feelings in a career, as her aunt did in educating her three nieces. The girl would certainly need to earn her keep if she shuns marriage.'

'I see.' The Marquis accepted this, though it left him a little pensive. So a girl without a dowry had rejected the promise of a proposal from one who had everything to offer in the way of riches, estates, consequence and – let him continue to be honest with himself – a degree of looks and address that had fluttered the hearts of many ladies of equal fortune to his own.

He put the problem of Cassy out of his mind for the time being, embraced his mother and drove his curricle on to Piccadilly to call on his friend Byron, with whom he would be a fellow guest at Melbourne House that night. He felt like enjoying an hour of his caustic company, and it was not worth returning to the War Office now that dusk was beginning to fall. Allingham esteemed the poet and frequently lent him money to quieten his creditors. He consoled himself for the small prospect of repayment by considering himself a patron of the arts.

'Evening, Julian,' the star and scandal of London society greeted his friend. He poured a second glass of Madeira from the open bottle. 'You look blue-devilled. What ails you?'

'I am merely indulging in some unaccustomed self-analysis. You know, it surprises me that you still have the entrée to Melbourne House considering your hostess is the mother-in-law of your ex-beloved.'

'So it may. But in fact Lady Melbourne is my greatest friend. We write to each other constantly, chiefly on the very subject of poor Caro, who still bombards me with accusatory letters from Ireland, where she is supposed to have gone to forget me.'

'Accusing you presumably of transferring your volatile affections to Lady Oxford – not unjustly, I imagine.'

'You are hardly in a position to criticise,' the poet pointed out. 'I hear you now have a star of Drury Lane under your protection in place of the obliging Lady Mattingley.'

'For the present, yes.'

'I felicitate you. You know, I was at the theatre yesterday to watch an audition and gave my approval to a delicious little newcomer. I had to take a closer look to confirm my first suspicion. I was right. Legs lovelier than those of La Maris, eyes as blue as the Aegean and jet-black hair. A modicum of talent to justify hiring her apart from the fact that she is a protégée of Sarah Siddons. However, for the moment I have my hands full.'

'So I have observed'

'I am tempted to propose marriage to Annabella Milbanke.'

'Then do so. Anything were better than—'

'My liaison with my half-sister and whole love?'

'Yes.'

'Why do not you marry, Julian?'

'I posed the same question to myself, with the result that I was prepared to fling my possessions, title and worthless self at the feet of an impecunious lady. But she did not want me.'

'Incredible!'

'I thought so too. Perhaps if I could write a poem ...'

'You would appear to have enough to recommend you without bursting forth in rhymed couplets.'

'I am relieved you should think so, for I would find it beyond me.'

'As I would performing the waltz,' Byron returned with a hint of bitterness.

The Marquis, as he took his leave, was diverted by the conviction that, though Byron might not waltz, he would this night, as always, be the cynosure of all eyes, admiring, loathing, adoring and damning.

4

Thea and Grace were consoled over Cassy's departure only by her promise to come home as often as possible and to tell them all about her pupils. In fact Thea declared that, were it not for the expense, she might consider being one of them.

Cassy had found a happy, if humble, home with Louise and John. The latter was, predictably, honoured to have her beneath his roof. He constituted himself her watchdog, and either he, the other jarvey or an appointed representative would collect her from the stage door each evening. She had at first refused, but finally agreed to accept this service as she would otherwise have had to run the gauntlet of bucks who waited there to intercept their favourites, among whom Cassy, owing to her looks rather than her talent, was soon numbered.

She never recovered from the naive thrill and excited realisation, first felt on her arrival at the theatre, that she was performing on the same stage where Nell Gwynne and Peg Woffington had won fame – and royal lovers.

She had, for the purposes of her career, rechristened herself with the simple name Cassandra. As such she was in receipt of comfits and bouquets from gentlemen whom she did nothing to encourage. So Louise's house became a fragrant bower, for being only a member of the chorus she shared a draughty dressing-room with eleven other more or less delectable ladies.

She found it comforting in her new life to be able to keep the little sobriquet of 'Cassy', and thus something of her own identity. She did not frequent the Green Room of Drury Lane, being but an unimportant performer, but she knew that it was the venue of the

28

theatrical great, and those aspiring to greatness, in addition to their friends, admirers and the inevitable Bond Street beaux.

She had soon mastered the new songs and steps and was adequate as both chorister and dancer. But her great advantage in this sometimes frightening new career was that she knew her limitations, and was never too proud to accept help and advice from the stage manager or her fellow artistes.

During the burletta they had to perform a Scottish rigaudon, which was an intricate dance requiring great accuracy and intricacy of footwork, crossing and re-crossing the crossed blades of claymores. This traditional dance, which Cassy had enjoyed teaching her sisters, on the pretext of instructing her pupils in it at the seminary, had originally been performed by Highland soldiers in the seventeenth century. By contrast, there was also a dignified minuet, which Cassy, naturally graceful in her movements, found much easier, if not so stimulating.

Apart from singing and dancing, her troupe greeted, waved farewell to, followed and generally formed an attractive background for the principals of the piece, which became popular enough to last two months.

Cassy's friendliness and lack of conceit soon made friends for her among the other girls who might otherwise have resented Cassandra's refined accent. As it was, Dolly, Tess, Meg and the others would take her aside to practise the steps and choruses that came more readily to them. They accepted good naturedly the fact that she did not accompany them on parties with their beaux, believing her excuse that she was closely guarded by the males of the branch of her family where she lived.

Cassy found it difficult at first to accustom herself to such an overly vociferous audience, members of which stamped, booed, hissed, cheered, shouted encouragement and made loud personal remarks.

The star of the burletta in which Cassy took part had a fine, trained coloratura voice. She had the olive-skinned, dark beauty of her native Spain and a temperament to go with it. The girl had, with an irrational shock, seen the Marquis of Allingham entering the star's dressing-room or escorting her to her carriage after the performance, sometimes in the company of Lord Byron and another lady. The poet had smiled at Cassy once and drawn the attention of the Marquis to her, probably, she thought, because he had seen her audition. In fact what he had said was, 'She is a lovely creature, isn't she?' and the

29

other, with a quick appraisal from those light hazel eyes, had wholeheartedly agreed.

Cassy felt bound to admit to herself that the Spanish singer showed taste in her beau. The tight-fitting coat, knee breeches and stockings obligatory for a theatre visit showed to advantage his long legs with the rounded muscles of the athlete, and square shoulders. He wore a meticulously arranged stock and a fashionable 'Brutus' hair style, and achieved an impression of great elegance without exaggerated dress effects.

'Pepita has the two handsomest men in town with her tonight,' said Dolly, the vivacious copper-haired dancer, wistfully.

'She is after all the mistress of the Marquis,' added Meg, the honey-blonde, matter-of-factly, and Cassy found herself wondering if His Lordship would have relinquished his lights of love if she had married him. She answered her own question in the negative. If he had married for an heir and not for love he was unlikely to have forgone his customary rakehell pursuits – unless, suggested a secret voice, his wife could have made him fall in love with her and held his interest.

She realised with a start that Dolly was talking again, telling them of the rumour that the bad and beautiful Byron was the father of his half-sister's last child. The male sex in general, mused Cassy censoriously, showed a sad lack of particularity in their love-making and yet expected virtue of the ladies to whom they had honourable intentions. She parried smilingly the beseeching speeches of the bucks, with whom she had become notable for her non-availability and nightly escort.

Lord Alvanley, noted man about town, had complained about the fact. 'Julian, this new girl is the sweetest thing I ever saw.'

'Since the last time,' commented his friend sardonically.

'No, you cynic – ever. I have been to see the stupid operatta three times just to look at those lovely legs twinkling in the Scottish dance and see that smile when she calls, "Here we are, sir!" with the other girls during the second act. But she is whisked home after every performance by a hulking great spoil-sport.'

The Marquis had himself been drawn to view two performances of the starring vehicle for his newest in an impressive list of Paphians. This one had lasted longer than others because of the infinite variety of her moods. However, he was just beginning to weary even of them and to experience the onset of the familiar boredom. When this became too overwhelming he would not hesitate to sever the tie, albeit with generosity, diplomacy and decisiveness.

Having noticed Alvanley's vision of loveliness on stage, he had to concede that there was something refreshing about the girl, whose capering and expressive gestures seemed to spring from a spontaneous enjoyment of the proceedings rather than from artifice. He was the more interested when he observed her assured but laughing dismissal of the disappointed bucks, who uttered groans of denunciation of the stolid fellow who waited to collect her, quite impervious to his unpopularity.

The Spanish beauty did indeed stage one tantrum too many and the Marquis's latest affair was thought to have come to an end at much the same time as the production.

When Cassy had received Lord Byron's nod at her first audition she had hardly noticed the gentleman beside him. Such was the usual fate of the poet's companions, unless they happened to have the appearance and bearing of somebody like Lord Allingham. But the second gentleman was nonetheless of enduring fame, and held in firm affection by a generation of theatregoers as the chief comedian of Drury Lane.

His name was Joseph Shepherd Munden and he was to become Cassy's friend and mentor. He had the comic lead as usual in the forthcoming Christmas pantomime, *The Little Glass Slipper*, which was already cast. But, having registered the effect on an audience of Cassy's lissom limbs, he put her forward not only for the chorus line again but also as an additional understudy for the principal boy. Dolly was the present understudy and, though a more experienced dancer and adequate singer, her speaking voice did not carry well and its tones betrayed her lowly origin.

Prince Charming was expecting her first baby and determined, despite the loving protests of her husband, who played Buttons, to carry on with her role if humanly possible in order to make a nest egg for the child, who would have two parents in such a precarious profession. Cassy hoped geniunely that she would succeed, because she liked and respected both the prospective mother and her husband.

But, having been told by the stage manager that Mr Munden had suggested her for a second understudy, she approached the comedian after a rehearsal. He had amused the dancers so much in his character of the fat Ugly Sister that they could hardly perform for giggling. 'You were wonderful, sir,' she told him truthfully, and he was not too

31

spoiled by success to be gratified and thank her graciously. Then she said humbly, 'Thank you for having faith in my ability to take the role of Prince Charming. I wish I had the same confidence in myself.'

'Then, my dear,' said the grotesque lump of womanhood who was in reality a spruce, slim gentleman, 'you shall come home on Sunday and play the part in our parlour.'

'Why, thank you, sir,' breathed Cassy, her eyes shining, and he added, pulling a face like an ogre, 'That is, if those bodyguards of yours let you!'

Cassy laughed, 'Of course they will.'

'Good. Then my carriage shall collect you at your lodgings at three in the afternoon.'

The Mundens lived simply, and, although Joe had a reputation for cheeseparing, Cassy came to the conclusion as she knew him better that his funny little economies entertained him. They told the story at Drury Lane of how he was encountered walking home all the way from Clare Market to Kentish Town with six mackerels impaled upon a stick through their gills because he heard that was where they were most cheaply bought. But as far as she was concerned he and his wife, who had been an actress, were the soul of kindness.

Jessie Munden played the piano for Cassy to practise the uninspired little love songs that Prince Charming was to sing to Cinderella. This occupied an hour or so. Afterwards Joe read the other parts from the script while his wife was Cinderella to Cassy's principal boy.

Then the hospitable couple insisted on their guest staying to supper, which happened to be Jessie's speciality, from her native Cornwall, star-gazy pie.

'You have a splendid cook, ma'am,' Cassy complimented her hostess.

'Lor' sakes, child, call me Jessie like everybody else,' said the buxom lady who still showed evidence of earlier beauty. 'I do as much in the kitchen as the cook's pride will allow, for I was used to enjoy producing something from nothing when Joe and I were struggling.'

Cassy smiled but made no comment. Turning to Joe, she asked, 'Were you always an actor?'

'No, Cassy, I was put to work in a lawyer's office, but it happened to be just off Drury Lane. I used to sneak into the gallery whenever I could, for which I am grateful if only because I had the privilege of seeing the glory that was David Garrick. Then nothing would satisfy me but to try to emulate him. As if I could!' he said a little rue-fully, 'With my funny face!' The ladies had to laugh with him for it was difficult to imagine his rubbery features set in the mask of tragedy. 'Finally, though, I got my chance. But when I wanted to make the audience cry, I made them laugh instead. So here I am, a comedian.'

'The very best in the business,' said Cassy warmly.

Now Jessie asked her guest curiously, 'And what is your story, dear? Joe has told you his. I am no fool and know that you speak like the gentry.'

Cassy liked her new friends so much that she tried to be as honest as she could within the bounds of practicability. 'I lived in the country,' she answered. 'That is probably why I speak differently from Londoners. My parents died in an accident. I have two little sisters who live with an aunt and I have to help in their support. My parents knew Mrs Siddons and she was good enough to give me an introduction to Drury Lane.'

Cassy's eyes had involuntarily moistened when she mentioned her recent bereavement, and Jessie impulsively took the girl in her arms, saying, 'You poor little soul! Joe and I shall become your stage parents!'

So began a friendship for Cassy which was to provide a comfort for her in the many difficulties inherent in her ambiguous situation.

Cassy's only regret was that she had, owing to her enjoyable visit to the Mundens, missed her usual Sunday with her family.

The next week her sisters' customary demands for the latest, preferably funny, anecdotes about her imaginary academy of learning taxed her imagination to the utmost. But another problem was added now to that of the continuation of the school saga. They shared with her their wistful hope that they might be allowed to attend an afternoon performance of *The Little Glass Slipper*, which had opened a few days earlier. The pantomime had been well received, even the frequently savage critics apparently imbued with seasonal good will, though it must have been evident that Prince Charming was a little rounded for a hero of romance.

'Of course you must go, my dears,' agreed Cassy stoutly, for she felt, as her aunt did, that the girls received all too few treats since the death of their parents. The Christmas season could not be a happy one for them this year.

Later Cassy assured Miss Page that she would not only secure three seats for them but also undertake to alter her face so much with *maquillage* that she would be unrecognisable among the other dancers in fairyland and the royal ballroom.

5

Cassy found it difficult to hide her amusement when Grace expounded on the wonders of her first play at their next meeting – the pathetic Cinderella, the lovable Buttons, and above all, the fat Ugly Sister who had made them laugh so much that they were crying real tears. Joe Munden had acted with his usual glorious sense of comedy and mastery of the art of dressing a part.

Thea had a kind word for the dancers too, and told Cassy, 'One of them looked quite like you, but dark and not nearly so pretty.' Her elder sister managed to look incredulous. In fact she had spent a considerable time, to the surprise of her companions in the dressing-room, elongating her eyes, enlarging her mouth with greasepaint and blanching her cheeks with orris root powder.

Thea startled Cassy considerably more, however, by continuing, 'We met the Marquis passing the theatre when we left. He was walking with – you will never guess – Lord Byron, and he took the trouble to stop and introduce us. Oh Cassy, it is a great pity you could not accept Lord Allingham. I could quite easily. But I do not suppose he would offer for a girl of fourteen even though Romeo did.'

'I doubt it, Thea,' Cassy laughed, though she was privately impressed that the supercilious gentleman to whom she had taken such a dislike should have taken the trouble to make himself pleasant again to little girls, this time moreover with no possibility of an ulterior motive.

'He asked how you were enjoying the scholastic life, Cassy,' Grace told her.

'And what did you answer?'

'That you were popular with your pupils and making enough money to keep the home going.'

'Yes,' broke in Thea, 'and we told him that one of the fairies looked exactly like you.'

Miss Page raised her eyebrows humorously at Cassy behind the girls' backs. But Thea had not reached the climax of the recital. 'Our friend the Marquis said that if we would care to see *Mother Goose* he would engage to entertain us and Aunt Letty in his box.' Cassy was amazed by this intelligence, and tried to hide the fact by remarking casually, 'He must have thought you sad rattles!'

'No,' answered Thea with quaint dignity. 'He likes us. He asked his companion if he did not now admire his choice of lady friends and Lord Byron said he did, and that he also liked fairy tales and would be inclined to join the party for *Mother Goose* if he were invited.'

Cassy regarded her sisters with smiling astonishment. 'I think in that case you might be much envied.'

'Pooh!' said Thea, 'I prefer the Marquis.'

It was Grace who concluded the account by saying in a wondering way, 'Lord Byron said something extraordinary.'

'What was that?'

'He said he wished he were ten years old again and in love with Cinderella.'

Cassy was relieved that the prospect of her sisters' visit to *Mother Goose* at another theatre could cause her no complications. But the reported conversation had left her unaccountably depressed. It had suddenly occurred to her that it was unlikely in view of the life she had chosen that she would marry at all. She was a normal woman and wanted the fulfilment a husband and family could provide. Any gentleman she might meet would give her a slip on the shoulder rather than an offer of marriage, and by the time she could retire she would be in her twenties, past her prime, old-callish and maybe even an antidote.

Then her ready sense of humour came to her rescue and her normal optimism returned with a rush as she thought of the colourful career she had embraced and the stimulating people she had met. She smiled at her family in the dazzling way that had endeared her and her mediocre talent to audiences, and which gave life and a lovable quality to her face. Aunt Letty and the girls beamed right back at her as people usually did, and she launched into a colourful story of a school

36

elocution class, which sounded to her own ears like a sketch for Joe to play, but greatly diverted the girls.

The Little Glass Slipper had been running for ten days when Prince Charming succumbed to her very feminine condition and regretfully retired from the role. Cassy was as terrified as she was excited by the possibility of being awarded the part. Both she and Dolly were given an audition, and when she was chosen her triumph was mixed with compunction for her friend, who, but for her arrival, would have automatically won it. But Dolly took it in good part, saying, 'I shouldn't really have cared for it, Cassy, and you speak the lines so much better than I could. Let me not lose your friendship though, when you graduate to your own dressing-room.' Cassy was touched by her friend's magnanimity and kissed her.

She was only too grateful for the training that Joe and Jessie had continued to give her. She put on the tights of the principal boy for the first time, feeling very self-conscious. She had become used to showing her long, slim legs from the knees down, which was daring enough. But this combination of silken limbs with velvet half-boots and frilled open shirt tight over her bosom was a different matter. She tied back the dusky locks of a longer wig with a ribbon. The total result, that of a very desirable young girl dressed up as a boy, was oddly seductive.

She came on to the stage hesitantly in the ballroom scene where the Prince first sees Cinderella. The latter, a pretty actress with feathery fair curls, and a perfect foil to Cassy, realised the other's nervousness and gave her a specially encouraging smile. The bucks in the audience had burst into loud clapping and admiring and highly audible comments on her appearance in the delightfully revealing costume. They were on her side, and her fresh charm and tuneful voice in the songs rehearsed with the Mundens, allied to the golden beauty of Cinderella, enthralled the spectators and drew the most jaded among them into the magic of the fairy story.

Afterwards Joe and Jessie with a host of others came into her star dressing-room to congratulate her, and the beaux were even more deferential and pressing in their invitations. But Cassy insisted, even with Joe and Jessie bidding her celebrate, on going back to her lodgings to share her good fortune with Louise and John, and to recover from the strain of her first leading role. In the event, her disappearance from the midst of her well-wishers on such a night added to her legend, and the bucks made bets amongst themselves as to which among them would woo her from her upright ways, so unusual in the theatre for one who did not profess to be a Sarah Siddons.

The most advantageous aspect of the development for Cassy, apart from the prestige involved, which must be gratifying, was the extra money she was able to contribute to the family funds and the Christmas presents she could not otherwise have afforded. Thea and Grace had warm but pretty new gowns with bonnets and pelisses and Aunt Letty a fur hood and muff. She indulged herself so far as to acquire a new blue velvet cloak bordered with sable and a close-fitting hat to match with a curling ostrich feather on one cheek, an ensemble so becoming that she took great pleasure in sweeping in and out of the stage door in it.

Miss Page had made Cassy a day dress of white kerseymere embellished with Spanish sleeves and pearl buttons and another tucked satin evening gown with tiny sleeves and a low-cut bodice in a shade of blue slightly lighter than that of her cloak. So she felt she could appear to advantage now at the luncheons, parties after the show in the Green Room and other functions to which, as one of the leading players, she was now invited, although she would still only consent to attend them if the Mundens were also present to lend her countenance. Luckily they were popular and enjoyed social life, so that was usually no problem.

Being able to enjoy such gaieties, as well as more intimate gatherings, compensated Cassy greatly for her inability to accept invitations of the ton sent to her by hostesses who had known her parents. Her hours of work precluded these, and she hoped that her refusal to attend such squeezes did not cause offence. In fact it produced comment and speculation until the fantasy of her teaching position came to be generally known.

Cassy could now pay Louise extra for a parlour of her own, which gave her in effect a suite of rooms. She could also afford to pay John the small amount which was all he would accept to convey her home from her ever more frequent engagements after the show. The couple appreciated the addition to their income, but pointed out to Cassy that, now she was a leading lady, she should really move somewhere grander.

But she was unlikely to find lodgings more convenient for the theatre, nor which afforded her the protection which she more than ever needed from the marauding bucks. She was particularly glad of John's stalwart presence when she received two anonymous letters, in ill-written capitals, simply warning her to 'Watch out!' She took them for the work of somebody with a sick mind and supposed all theatre people to be the target of such attentions. She said nothing of the matter to anybody, but the missives left her with a feeling of disgust and ill ease. Louise herself was invaluable in caring for her assortment of perukes, which she kept cleaned and set in different coiffures suitable for any occasion.

However, it was difficult to convince Thea and Grace that, despite the Christmas holidays, it would still only be possible for Cassy to spend a few days at home. She was supposedly earning extra by supervising girls whose parents were abroad and thus had to stay at school. This fabrication could be allowed to account for her lavish presents to the family.

Cassy met Lord Allingham again at an intimate party given by Lord Byron to celebrate the publication of his new poem, *The Giaour*, or infidel. The fact that his Spanish beauty did not accompany him seemed, she thought, to confirm the rumour that the liaison had exploded in a hail of fireworks, being on his side at least one not so much of the heart as of the boudoir.

Beau Brummel was also present, and though Cassy had been introduced to him once at Almack's, she was confident he would not recognise her as a brunette.

Before meeting him Cassy had pictured to herself an over-dressed fop. But she had soon seen that nothing could be further from the truth. He was always fastidiously but discreetly attired. This evening he wore black pantaloons and a dull blue coat. It seemed he had set the mode for dark colours, but it was noteworthy that the Prince Regent, who had brought him into fashion, nevertheless preferred to deck himself in lurid shades and display all his decorations on his coat.

A number of other members of the Carlton House set were at the gathering, which included theatrical people and the sort of society ladies who were known as 'goers'. Cassy reflected with some amusement that she had the opportunity granted to few girls of her birth and breeding to see these elegant Corinthians and exquisites in their more relaxed and careless hours.

The Marquis was laughing at a sally of the Beau's and Cassy could judge for the first time the veracity of her sisters' assessment of him.

They were right of course. When he was not wary of encouraging a *tendre* in a young breast, or misplaced hopes in that of some fond mama, he had a disastrously attractive smile and a warm personality.

She did not realise that he had been watching her too and had come to the same conclusion. As she joked with Joe and Jessie, her face was alive with unaffected merriment at the comedian's drollery. What a piece of artless perfection she was, he decided, when she was not parrying the advances of the town beaux! Yet she displayed her legs in tights. He really must sit through the story of Cinderella just to confirm their reported superiority. Perhaps Byron would come with him since he professed to like fairy tales. His cynical self told him that her inaccessibility was a ruse to attract the highest bidder. Yet some quality in the fair face he covertly regarded made him discount the theory.

He strolled over to Cassy, bowing as he said, 'May I congratulate you, Miss Cassandra, on your success as the charming fairy tale prince?'

'Thank you, sir,' she said, trying not to show the foolish confusion she felt as the cool, light eyes appraised her. 'I did not imagine that you were in the way of pantomimes.'

'Nor am I,' he smiled. 'But I have heard tell of your – charms – from those of my acquaintances who have seen you in the piece.'

She found herself reddening with mortification at the obvious allusion to her legs revealed by the tights of a principal boy. He saw her quick colour and regretted his observation, instinctively compensating for it to the best of his ability by talking to her in the most natural way possible. He spoke of the strange tradition of employing a female to play a pantomime prince, and then drew her out on the subject of Edmund Kean, remarking that Coleridge had said of his performance as Shylock, 'To see him act is like reading Shakespeare by flashes of lightning.'

The Merchant of Venice happened to be one of the few plays she had seen with her parents. In her admiration for the actor whose great artistry was in contrast to his small stature, she responded with equal amiability to His Lordship's disarming friendliness.

'Kean's extraordinary impact on an audience,' she said, 'is achieved even before he has spoken, by the intensity of his black eyes and the impression he gives of power withheld.'

'Yes,' he agreed, directing a quick glance of interest at her, 'Garrick had the same gift. Did you ever see him act?'

'No,' Cassy admitted regretfully. 'My mama said I was too young to leave the schoolroom when he gave his farewell performance. *The Wonder*, wasn't it, at Covent Garden?'

She flushed for the second time, delightfully, he thought, as she realised that the comfortable converse with the unexpectedly civil and attentive gentleman had led her to suggest a kind of background far removed from that likely to be attributed to a female who earned her living in tights.

Although he made no reference to it, the Marquis had not missed Cassandra's unthinking allusion to a refined upbringing. This fact, coupled with her cultured voice, puzzled him. 'Would you,' he asked now, 'join a party I am making up to visit a performance of *Romeo and Juliet* at Covent Garden?' He did not mention the fact that he had already seen the play, but imagined it might entice her. 'I believe your own production will close shortly.'

She was sorely tempted to accept his suggestion, not only because she would dearly love to see Charles Kemble play opposite Mrs O'Neill in the play, but also because she could understand now only too well how the Marquis had so effortlessly charmed her more impressionable sisters. Besides, a closer study of a rake's machinations might further her worldly education.

However, she declined politely, saying, 'You are very kind, sir, but I am not able to join your party.' She felt that a refusal with no excuse offered was the simplest way to avoid another invitation.

His Lordship took her rejection philosophically and observed with a smile, 'Mrs O'Neill has the same colouring as yourself. Are you perhaps Irish too?'

'No,' said Cassy.

'You know, although in my estimation by no means as great an actress as Mrs Siddons, she is so emotional that the women in the audience have been known to sob or faint with her.'

'Really!' said Cassy, awed. 'I hope I should not do so.'

'Why not come and find out?'

'I cannot.'

He continued, unabashed, 'I saw her play Mrs Beverly in *The Gamester*. She had to throw herself on the body of her husband in hysterical despair. It seems that she was so overwrought by the scene that she was still, each time, in the grip of hysteria half an hour after the curtain had fallen.'

'Literally carried away, perhaps,' suggested Cassy on a chuckle.

41

He grinned at her appreciatively and then asked lightly, 'Do you see yourself as an actress of such dedication?'

'I do not see myself as an actress at all so far!' she laughed, strengthening his attraction to her as a person as well as a pretty girl.

'Cassandra is an effective stage name. Is it your own?'

'I have always been called Cassy,' she was able to answer truthfully.

He smiled into her eyes and said, 'Good-bye for now, Cassy. I enjoyed talking to you.' He moved away, and she had the momentary, shaming thought that, were she a straw damsel, she might find him a desirable lover.

The Marquis was saying with rueful amusement to Brummel, 'You know, George, I was wont to consider myself the devil of a fellow. But I have lost the illusion. Two set-downs I have received of late.'

'You don't say, Julian!' exclaimed the Beau with genuine surprise. 'But I can think of numerous females, eligible, or just available, who would consider your addresses in the first case, and your advances in the second, most welcome.'

'You comfort me. But I assure you one lady threw herself into slavery rather than receive an offer from me.'

'Now I know you are bamming me!'

'Not at all. The other spurned my less honourable lures.'

'Plenty of fish, my dear fellow.'

'Admittedly. But I have not been made to angle for them before.'

'I have just the little lady to console you. Let us away to the gallery of the Lyceum tomorrow evening.'

'Let us indeed.'

6

'Have you heard the latest tittle-tattle, Jessie?' said Cassy to her friend one day in the Green Room. 'Lord Allingham, who so lately was insistent upon having more of my company, has now taken under his protection the famous Madame Maris.'

'They say her legs are the most beautiful in London.'

'Better than mine?' she asked, laughing.

'At any rate they have brought her so many lovers that when she was said to have confessed to her husband how many she had had, the *mot* was that she must have a very fine memory.'

'One can't help wondering whether this was an honour he had intended for me. However, it's beneath my dignity to trouble about it.'

But the Marquis was also mentioned in a more creditable connection by her own family. He had kept his word and conducted Miss Page and her sisters to a matinée of *Mother Goose*. The song 'Tippety Witchet', sung by the great clown, Grimaldi, in the pantomime, was constantly carolled by the girls, and they made much of the fact that the attention of the audience continually strayed to their box where Lord Byron sat well to the rear. They had all been entertained to tea at her Clarges Street house after the performance by the Marchioness, who had them singing 'Tippety Witchet' with her. Cassy smiled to herself at the improbability of such a scene, and considered in passing what a ubiquitous presence in her life this Marquis was, without his having any real significance.

More important by far was the fact that she had, owing to her popularity in her first leading role, secured the part of the abigail who is falsely accused of theft in *The Maid and the Magpie*, the next piece to be presented at Drury Lane.

She was more exercised about her ability to succeed in this characterisation since there was no music in the play, and she realised better than anybody that her dancing and singing had compensated before for what she lacked in histrionic talent.

Once again her self-appointed foster-parents, the Mundens, helped her with personal informal rehearsals at home, so that as a result of their guidance her confidence and grasp of the best way to interpret the role increased.

But in the meantime there were the few days' respite for Christmas during which Aunt Letty and her nieces preserved brave faces and some semblance of festive spirit for each other's sakes, whatever their private recollections and regrets.

Two days before New Year's Eve, London was shrouded in impenetrable fog which lasted for a week, so that the year 1813 expired and the new year came in in almost total darkness.

Audiences were naturally sparse at Drury Lane and Cassy was thankful she lodged so near the theatre, when even that short, familiar way appeared like a labyrinth in a nightmare. However by the time *The Maid and the Magpie* had its opening night the fog had dispersed. But the city was shivering in a period of cold that made the teeth chatter and the fingers numb.

Thanks to the Mundens' tuition, her physical appeal and natural exuberance, she made a hit once more, although she was in honesty forced to agree with the critic who wrote that her performance was 'effective more for its artlessness and charm than for any real depth of feeling'. Still, her salary was raised again and with it her ambition to provide a house for the summer where her family could enjoy the fresh air and sea bathing at fashionable Brighton.

However there were more immediate, if contrasting, pleasures to be had in London itself, where the great frost had transformed the expanse of the Thames between London Bridge and Blackfriars into solid ice. Miss Page, Cassy and her sisters sallied forth one Sunday in early February in their warmest garments, faces robin-red with the cold, heads, necks and hands enveloped in wool, to join the merry throng traversing the river by what had come to be known as Freezeland Street. They intended to enjoy the swings, skittle alleys, toyshops and other delights offered in the booths along the Grand Mall which stretched between the bridges.

They avoided the wheel of fortune and establishments for gambling and 'pricking the garter' (they never did discover what this was, which was possibly just as well), patronised almost exclusively by the male sex. But they anticipated their supper by feasting on oysters at a few pence a dozen, pies, brandy balls and gingerbread, licking their fingers and grinning at each other with enjoyment.

Cassy was in the process of doing so after munching a sticky piece of gingerbread when she caught sight of the Marquis examining a bookstall with a devastating young person dressed largely in ermine who, though her legs were invisible, could only be Madame Maris. Lord Allingham, like his companion, succeeded in looking elegant still, despite the weather, in his fur-collared long coat, shining boots and beaver hat worn at a jaunty angle. She was conscious suddenly of her own knitted cap, muffler and childish behaviour.

Luckily he was in profile to them, and she could survey, before they passed on, the two striking faces, the one so aristocratic, the other of an ethereal beauty which nevertheless wore an expression of worldly knowingness which accorded with her record of a precocious love life. Cassy was relieved that neither the Marquis nor her family had glimpsed each other, for the result would have meant embarrassment and explanations for herself. But her fleeting view of the decorative couple had somehow spoiled her outing, and she had to force herself to draw the girls' attention gaily to a hawker of ballads, from whom she purchased the sheet music of 'Tippety Witchet'.

The Marchioness of Allingham had enjoyed the visit of her old friend, Letty Page, and the company of Thea and Grace - just such ingenuous, merry little girls as she would dearly love to have had for her own, had fate not decreed that she should produce but one child, her adored, spoiled and provoking Julian.

Their uninhibited prattle about their elder sister's diverting experiences as a teacher of elocution and deportment made her wish there had been a mistress such as Lucasta at her own gloomy seminary, and quite allayed her suspicions. She was geniunely pleased that Letty and the girls had been able to keep the pleasant rented London house, even if the Leicestershire estates had been sold. She found herself experiencing a new respect for Letty's absent eldest niece, though she still thought it extraordinary that she should prefer to keep herself on a pittance rather than marry the man who was at present laughing so gaily with her sisters.

She was disconcerted by the presence of Lord Byron, who looked at the girls through half-closed eyes as if he had had his fill of juvenile company. But she was by no means as surprised as Letty at her son's unfeigned pleasure in the youngsters, even going so far as to play jackstraws with them after tea.

He had, despite his boredom with conventional society, always undertaken to amuse his much younger cousins, who had installed him as their hero. Indeed his one-and-twenty year old present heir, Thomas, considered him a *nonpareil* and copied his unemphasised good taste to the point of changing his tailor from Stultz to Weston.

Julian had taught Thomas to shoot, to ride, to fence and to hold his liquor. He had introduced him to White's Club and to Cribb's boxing saloon. For all these benefits Thomas's mother, the Lady Anne Furse, was grateful, just as long as her favourite nephew did not lead her son into the more rakish aspects of town life that he frequented himself. The younger cousin's father had been killed at Trafalgar.

But Thomas, like most of the other aspiring beaux of his years, needed no encouragement from his elders to become a habitué of the Peep o'Day Club in Covent Garden, the Green Room at Drury Lane or the Lyceum terrace. He was as handsome as the Marquis, but his features were more rounded, his expression one of eagerness instead of self-containment and his eyes of candid blue instead of enigmatic hazel.

He was presented to Cassy, whom he had adored from a distance during the run of *The Maid and the Magpie*, and was, by no means for the first time but most seriously, struck dumb by 'the incarnation of a dream' as he described her to his mocking but sympathetic cousin.

The latter warned him with the smile that only his intimates knew, 'I assure you, Tom, that you will get nowhere with your invitations. That is,' he added a little wryly, 'I hope not for the sake of my own self-respect since she refused to be included even in a large theatre party.'

Thomas laughed. 'What a facer for you! But one of the *on dits* is that you are dallying with "La Maris", a rather spicier dish but not so sweet.'

'You come late to that choice morsel of gossip. You were going to say that Madame M. must be more to my jaded taste.'

'Well, yes I was, Julian, but of course it is doubtless your duty to take a sweet young thing to wife.'

'I can safely leave the succession to you, cousin.'

'Don't! I would sooner see you with a family. You may be a gay bachelor now, but you will become a sad case if you are still on the town in your middle age like Lord Delverton.'

The Marquis laughed at his cousin's serious face. 'I heed your dire warning, Tom. But you will allow me a few more years before I resemble the disgraceful Delverton.'

'I will freely. Now, how do you suggest I further my acquaintance with Cassandra?'

'You should apply to the Mundens of Drury Lane for an invitation to their house. They would seem to have constituted themselves her guardians.'

'Like Mrs O'Neill's brothers?'

'Yes, and Cassandra is invariably collected from wherever she may be by one formidable fellow or another and wafted firmly away from her followers.'

'Brothers again?'

'Perhaps. But your enchantress is surprisingly well-spoken, although I suppose one can assume that as an actress, if not an outstanding one, she must be able to acquire tones she was not born with.'

'When I pinch her waist I shall be able to judge by whether she says "ow" or "oh!"'

'Optimist!'

Thomas met Cassandra again one Sunday in early spring at Bushey Park. This was the delightful country retreat where the Duke of Clarence, third of the royal brothers, had installed his famous mistress of the last sixteen years, the actress Mrs Jordan. Cassy had driven with the Mundens in their carriage for the luncheon and the afternoon diversion of the woodland, deer park and ornamental gardens, where stage celebrities rubbed shoulders with the more colourful and easy-going members of the *haut ton*.

Cassy had taken a great fancy to Dorothy Jordan, and admired the manner in which she entertained with all the graciousness and dignity of a *grande dame* in spite of her anomalous position. She had borne the royal duke five daughters and five sons and still carried on with her brilliant theatrical career between pregnancies. Cassy also pitied her hostess since, despite their progeny and years together, the relationship could never be considered permanent.

She was laughing with Mrs Jordan in the splendid room where Zucchi had painted landscapes on the walls to rival those outside,

47

when Tom and the Marquis approached them. Like his cousin on an earlier occasion, Tom had the benefit of seeing Cassy in a happy, unguarded moment and was entranced by her dancing blue eyes and the curve of a rosy mouth which showed the sparkle of even white teeth.

Mrs Jordan greeted the gentlemen with her accustomed queenliness, but when she began to present them to Cassy the girl's face became aloof and she said, 'I have already made the acquaintance of Lord Allingham and Mr Furse. Good-day, gentlemen.'

She was about to leave them when Mrs Jordan proposed, 'Why do you two not show Cassandra the garden, as by now you must know it as well as I do.?'

'I shall concede that privilege to my cousin, if I may,' the Marquis told Cassy when their hostess had passed on to greet another guest. 'I escort a lady.'

He was in fact displaying tact and consideration for Thomas. But when Cassy saw that the lady mentioned was the gorgeous Madame Maris, whose famous limbs were revealed through the diaphanous drift of yellow transparent muslin highly unsuitable for a daytime engagement, she felt a hot, unreasonable resentment. 'That will be a pleasure,' she announced, directed her flashing smile at the enraptured Thomas, took his arm with alacrity and turned abruptly away from his cousin.

The young man conducted her to the celebrated topiary walk where peacocks, pheasants and castles had been fashioned from bay hedges. It did not take him long to confirm that Cassandra looked, spoke and acted like a lady, in contrast with the actress Julian currently had in tow. In her sprigged white gown with its demure frills at neck and sleeves, with which she had put on a Norwich shawl and shady hat, she was even more lovely, and naturally so, than she had appeared on the stage.

All this was writ large on his good-looking, uncomplicated countenance. Cassy found herself comparing his overt admiration, frank eyes and boyish smile with his cousin's unreadable regard and the lazy half-smile on the sensual but finely drawn lips. The trouble was that the infuriating, unpredictable older gentleman was, she was forced to admit, by far the more attractive.

'I am sorry,' she apologised to her companion. 'What did you say?'

He smiled at her in mock reproof and repeated his question. 'What role can I look forward to seeing you in next?'

48

'I hope for a part in *The Smugglers' Cave*, a comic opera. I do not know if my singing voice will be considered strong enough for that of the heroine.'

'I haven't heard you sing, but I am told you do so charmingly.'

She looked up at him with delightful frankness and explained, 'I have a true voice, inasmuch as I do not sing wrong notes. That would be too mortifying.' She made a moue of horror. 'But I have not a very powerful one. You know what the theatre is like during a performance, the remarks and the cracking of nuts, the spitting of orange pips in the pit. One simply has to be heard or it is no good!'

He could not help laughing at her accurate observation, and he responded honestly, 'I hope you get the star role. What will you do otherwise?'

'Why, hope for a smaller singing part. There are dances too, and my dancing is adequate if not inspired.'

'You are very modest. Surely confidence in oneself is a prerequisite of success on the stage?'

'Probably it is. But if I can earn a regular income as I do at present for, say, the next five or six years, then I shall be content and can, with luck, retire from the arena.'

He looked at her in some puzzlement. He was so pleasant and unassuming that, as in the case of the Mundens, she would like to have been able to tell him as much of the truth as possible. But she remembered that he was likely to relate what she told him to his cousin, who might put too many pieces of her story together, since he knew her aunt, her sisters and the composition of her family. So she prevaricated by saying simply, 'I am, you see, no Sarah Siddons, but just a person of slender means who wishes to ensure future security with the small talent she possesses.'

Her face was touchingly earnest, and so appealing thus that Thomas wanted to gather her to him and, for a moment, to share his considerable fortune with her. It seemed so unfair that one so young and beautiful should have to pit her wits against fate.

'You have no parents to support you?'

'My parents are dead,' she answered briefly, and was glad of the distraction of a clump of late snowdrops and the sight of a furry-nosed rabbit scurrying across the sunlit glade. She was enraptured with her surroundings and at the same time experienced an unbearable longing for her own lost country home.

She was drawn out of the nostalgia which had suddenly overcome

49

her by the startled exclamation from a young gentleman who was walking towards them, 'How wonderful! Is it really you?' The Villager straw hat, with its lilac ribbons tied beneath the chin to match the flowers on her dress, hid her raven locks.

She looked at the only male of Uncle Matthew's family in Yorkshire, and said firmly, 'I don't think I know you, sir.'

7

Cassy pushed her hat with a graceful gesture further to the back of her head so that sundry curls were visible. Gerard looked at her with momentary uncertainty, then, with a twinkle in his brown eyes that she recognised from childhood, bowed and said, 'Beg pardon, ma'am. You are remarkably like somebody I was used to know, but admittedly some years ago.'

She had regained her equilibrium now and managed to laugh convincingly enough for Thomas. But she was in no doubt of Gerard's knowledge of her identity.

'Forgive me, sir,' Gerard added, turning with a smile to Thomas. 'Remarkable resemblance. But I see the difference now.'

'Quite understandable,' returned Thomas, liking the other's open manner. 'Won't you walk with us if you are alone?' This sacrifice of Cassy's exclusive company proved his natural good nature.

'I should enjoy that. I came here with one of my few town acquaintances, who has deserted me for a female, quite properly. I am lately from Yorkshire. My name is Gerard Loring.'

'I am Thomas Furse, and I shall now present you formally to – Miss Cassandra.'

'Servant, ma'am. What an unusual and delightful name. But you must have another.'

'Naturally. But I am an actress and prefer to be known by the one. My friends call me Cassy.'

'An actress! I am impressed. Are you in a London production?'

'Yes, at Drury Lane.'

'The home of the immortals! I shall make a special point of seeing

51

the performance. Will you acknowledge our acquaintance if I encounter you in the Green Room there?'

'Why should I not, since we have now been formally introduced?' Gerard's eyes quizzed her, and Thomas wondered for a moment if the newcomer had in fact known Cassandra before; whether perhaps she was not quite as strait-laced as Julian thought her. Then he banished the unworthy thought as she drew their attention to the profusion of primroses growing on a grassy bank, and he and Gerard bent to pick her a nosegay.

Cassy saw only too clearly that if her likeable cousin was fixed in London, yet another complication was to be added to her life. There was no alternative but to confide everything to him. But, although he would not willingly give her away, for they had always supported each other in childish scrapes, she had no illusions about his ability to keep his own counsel. Moreover he would ring a peal over her head. Still, it would be comforting to have a male confidant and she looked forward to a coze with him.

By the time the gong sounded for luncheon the two young gentlemen had become friends and Thomas had undertaken to show the newcomer the town haunts he should know, an offer which was received with gratification. Cassy, however, felt faint misgivings on her cousin's behalf, knowing that his allowance could not be generous and his character, though amiable, was not strong.

The way she looked up at Gerard sideways at one point in the masculine conversation made Thomas wonder again all of a sudden about her reputed inaccessibility. He had never had a mistress, but he had to start in the petticoat line some time before acquiring family responsibilities. If she were not an actress, damn it if he wouldn't engage to marry Cassy, so smitten was he. But it would not do. When he knew Gerard better he might elicit some encouraging information, in which case he must develop a strategy.

The trio wandered back through the ante-room to the dining hall which Cassy noticed had, like their former salon in Leicestershire, exquisitely delicate carving by Grinling Gibbons of birds, foliage, flowers and lace. There were apses, as in the other reception rooms, for priceless Chinese porcelain, some pieces of which her Mama had collected with loving care and which had gone, to Cassy's regret, under the auctioneer's hammer.

She went while the guests strolled in from the gardens to examine a vase more closely, just touching the glaze with a finger, and found the Marquis suddenly beside her. 'Do you admire it?' he asked.

'Who would not!' she answered spontaneously. 'I love the *famille verte* porcelain and,' pointing to another specimen in an alcove, 'more, I think, than the *famille rose*.'

He looked at her with attention. 'Where did you acquire your knowledge of porcelain?'

She flushed a lovely carnation pink. What a fair, fine skin she had for a dark brunette, the Marquis thought, and she had learned, with her genteel speech – were it in fact studied – a correct French accent too. A surprising young person.

Conscious of his scrutiny, her cheeks, to her own chagrin, were mantled in colour again, for the gorgeous Maris, whose bosom was two-thirds on display as well as the outline of her legs, was at their side now. 'Cassandra, I shall have to look to my laurels,' she announced with a grin. 'I heard some gentlemen discussing the respective merits of our legs, to my advantage, I fancy. How do you manage still to blush, my colleague? I mislearned the art when I first bared my limbs.'

Cassy, feeling and looking, she was convinced, overwhelmed with humiliation and embarrassment, sought out Gerard for a moment. He was alone, while Thomas had been drawn into a circle surrounding the Duke of Clarence, who was expounding, with his celebrated nautical oaths, his theory of strategy in a sea battle.

'Look, my dear,' her cousin started before she could utter a word, 'You don't flummery me, you know. I've known you since I was in short coats. What's your game? It won't do. Don't know what m'mother and m'sisters would say.'

'Gerard, dear, listen!' she said urgently. 'I trust you, and you must tell nobody, not even your parents, of my deception. I am earning enough now to help to keep the remainder of my little family in decency and respectability, so that my sisters should have a chance of contracting suitable alliances one day, even if I cannot. Don't you see,' she pulled the sleeve of his coat of Bath superfine (an intimate gesture which was not lost upon Thomas, surveying them under his eyelashes from the other side of the room), 'I had no alternative. We could not sponge upon your father. Only Aunt Letty, Louise and John, and Mrs Siddons, who introduced me to the theatre, know who I am, and now yourself.'

'I should not dream of exposing you. You know it. But, dear Cassy, could you not have married? You are the reverse of an antidote, in fact, since I saw you last you have blossomed into a remarkably pretty female. I believe m'father said you had a Marquis at your feet. Did he cry off?'

'No, no, but that is another story.'

'Tell you what. I'll marry you myself – there! M'mother would be delighted. She was always fond of you. I shall have a respectable competence when my great Aunt Dora dies and shan't need a dowry.'

Cassy was touched as much as amused. She looked with affection at her relative, and again her expression was noted by Thomas, now thoroughly jealous. 'How nice you are, Gerard. But you know, dear, that we know each other far too well to fall in love, and nothing else would do, for me at least.'

He looked at her in a new way and said, 'I'm not so sure!'

'Well, I am. I prefer the life I have chosen with all its difficulties. At least I am my own mistress.'

'Take care, my pretty cousin, that you do not end by becoming somebody else's,' he warned her severely.

'I promise you that.'

'Where do you lodge, Cassy? You are not with our aunt, I presume.'

'No, it would create too many problems. I have rooms with Louise and John in Russell Street. They have a hackney-hire business just behind the theatre and I can assure you that they guard my honour and my person as if I were their daughter. Not that I am in any danger, for Joe Munden and his wife Jessie chaperone me when I go about, just as they do today. You must meet them.'

'All right, Cassy. I admire you. My offer still stands, however, if you get tired of this life.' He smiled at her in the old companionable way and she felt a sudden homesickness for earlier days and ways when life was thought to be safe and settled. 'I shall come and see you at your lodgings,' he added, 'I am persuaded Louise and John will admit me.'

'Of course. But no more sentimental nonsense please. I seem to remember in any case that you had your eye on a pretty little neighbour.'

'I have – had —' he corrected himself. 'But she is very young, still in the schoolroom. For the present I am on the town.'

She laughed, 'Well watch that your pockets are not to let. Now, remember, secret as the grave, please!'

He crossed his throat in their old childhood sign and she felt her eyes smart. Thomas by now was convinced that Cassandra had once been Gerard's particular, and that she was entreating his secrecy on the subject.

After the delicious luncheon the guests were free to take their pleasure within at faro, loo or backgammon, or to disport themselves in the fresh air.

Although Cassy had confined herself to weak orgeat, Thomas had indulged himself generously in the Canary wine and sherry sack, which emboldened him to invite the beautiful actress to accompany him outside again, this time for a game of croquet.

He was disappointed to discover that she did not require his guiding arm round her waist to help her play a shot since she had played the game often and with skill on their own south lawn at home. But as she admired the knot garden later with the helpful gentleman she suddenly felt her waist pinched, and, between surprise and outrage, slapped his face hard.

She felt, after her instinctive response, that she had overreacted to his comparatively mild advance. After all she was a guest in an establishment where most of the females could safely be assumed to be ramshackle, or at least broad-minded in the extreme. She looked at the red mark on his boyish cheek with some compunction, and when he stammered crestfallen apologies, accepted them with her most healing smile, and then made some innocuous remark about the birdsong to lighten the atmosphere.

That evening, over a game of billiards at his house in Grosvenor Square, the Marquis inquired of his cousin, 'Well which was it? Did she say "ow" or "oh"?'

'Neither. She slapped my face.'

The Marquis burst out laughing, and after a moment Thomas joined in.

That spring Cassy was kept busy at Drury Lane. She alternated the part of the heroine in *The Smugglers Cave* with the second lead in an operetta called *The Blue Stocking*.

Although still no musical or acting genius, she was by this time looked upon by the management as a reliable performer, who never incurred fines for missing or being late for rehearsals. In addition to this advantage she had, they knew, a big personal following, particularly among the romantic younger gentlemen, not only because her air of innocent allure made them feel protective but because her ebullience and sense of fun appealed to their own high spirits. The ladies liked her too because the wholesome impression she gave them made it more easy for them to identify with her in her joys and sorrows.

Cassy had, naturally enough, numerous opportunities of advantageous, if irregular, alliances in her private life. But she had no intention of deserting the standards her parents would have expected of her or her own ideals. She still clung in secret to the hope of marriage for love. In the meanwhile she was careful to go out only in parties in which the Mundens were included or, occasionally, to spend an afternoon with Mrs Siddons. The great tragedienne was amused and pleased by the small fame of her protégée and took pleasure in parrying enquiries about her background and antecedents from the various gentlemen who, so casually, brought the conversation round to the subject of Cassandra.

For Cassy herself the possibility of renting a seaside house for her family was now a probability. But, on mature reflection, she realised that Brighton was not the ideal choice in the season, when the Prince Regent would be sure to be in residence and holding court at the Pavilion which had grown out of the farmhouse he had once shared with Mrs Fitzherbert, and had then been called Brighton House. His fashionable adherents and those of the Duke of Clarence, as well as those who hoped to break into these charmed circles would make the resort a centre of frivolity, gambling, promenading, balls and assemblies – in short, unsuitable for her sisters.

She and Aunt Letty, after much discussion in which Gerard took his part, came to the conclusion that Worthing would be a better place, equally bracing but quieter, where the girls and their aunt might be expected to find genteel companionship. In fact Miss Page knew of two bosom bows already who would be there.

An advantage from her own point of view was that she would more easily be able to slip into anonymity there than at Brighton when she spent her much needed summer holiday with the family. She knew too that the Marquis, one of the inner circle round Prinny, had his own house opposite the Pavilion on the Steine. She did not doubt that, having now encountered her so often, he could not fail to recognise her if he came across her, as he must surely, in Brighton, with her family and without her wig.

Now that she was a star, Cassy had persuaded Louise to accept part-time employment at the theatre as her special dresser, as otherwise the secret of grandmama's perukes might possibly leak out. So Cassy's exit from the stage door was now chaperoned by Louise, who enjoyed the novelty of this new development, as well as safeguarded by John or his allies.

Shortly after she and Aunt Letty had opted for Worthing, the latter was able to tell her during a Sunday visit that the irksome business of visiting agents would be unnecessary. She had, it seemed, called on the Marchioness of Allingham and found her son there. On hearing of her proposed coastal sojourn with the girls he had kindly volunteered to find them just the right house, and had in fact reported the acquisition of a charming small villa on the seaside, with a garden, and in the right price range.

Cassy did not know whether to be grateful, or irritated by her family's friend taking the matter upon himself. But when she heard that the double programme from Drury Lane was to be transferred to Brighton for a short summer season she was only too thankful that the matter had been so quickly settled. Luckily Louise and her husband were pleased with the chance of a change of air. So Cassy, who could afford it now, took lodgings for herself and the faithful pair in a charming, bow-fronted house with Bristol glass windows in a quiet crescent on the esplanade, engaging the first floor so that the bucks would not be for ever looking into her parlour. John would drive her and his wife to and from the theatre and he was sure to find any amount of casual trade in addition in busy, bustling Brighton in mid-season when Prinny was established there. At weekends she would drive along the coast to Worthing, and everything appeared to have turned out satisfactorily.

8

Thomas was staying at his cousin's Brighton house. He had relished the speed at which Julian's curricle had taken the familiar road from London, the nicety with which the top sawyer had cornered, and the happy anticipation of the gaieties that lay ahead for himself and the young bloods, even though they did not aspire to the Marquis's set.

He knew that Cassy was in Brighton and since she had treated him with her usual natural sweetness and warmth on the occasions they had met since the well-merited slap at Bushey Park he was encouraged to try his luck with her again. She certainly behaved towards his new friend, Gerard, with almost affectionate raillery. Besides, she was a normal flesh-and-blood girl, not an ice maiden, and why should he not be the one to make her realise the fact?

The outcome of this resolution inspired him to intercept her as she was leaving her carriage with her duenna to enter the stage door of the small theatre. 'To prove you forgive me, Miss Cassandra,' he begged her with hat in hand, 'won't you permit me to take you to supper tonight after the performance. I undertake to deliver you straight home.'

She answered sweetly, 'You already have my forgiveness, sir, and my gratitude for your invitation. But I never go out with gentlemen at night.'

'Perhaps a drive to see the beauties of Sussex then on Sunday?' he pleaded, while Louise tried not to show her amused sympathy in her countenance.

'Unfortunately I am engaged every Sunday. But thank you again for the kind thought.'

'With that,' Thomas complained to the Marquis over lunch the next day, 'she managed to remove the barb and all my resentment by smiling at me from those great blue orbs as if she were really sorry not to be able to comply with my wishes. I even managed to accept her ruling with a good grace. Then—' His voice rose indignantly and Julian looked amused. 'What then, cousin?'

'I saw Gerard collect her at the stage door that very same night. They walked together back to the house where I know Cassy lodges – walked!'

'People do.'

'Well, she don't as a rule leave the stage door unless on wheels. But it was a balmy night – I have not finished.'

'Proceed with the drama.'

'He went into the house with her.'

'You having followed them there!'

'Wouldn't you have, Julian?'

'Perhaps, dear boy, at your age.'

'Well, he didn't come out. He didn't come out.'

'Yes, I heard you. So you jumped to obvious conclusions waiting there under the stars. Oh, Tom!'

'Yes, I admit I did and eventually I knocked at the door.'

'Oh, no! Hoping he would open it in his nightshirt?'

'Cassandra's dresser, or duenna, answered the door and when I asked to see her employer she looked surprised. But then she went up and the next thing was that Cassandra was behind her and had asked me in.'

'This is fascinating.'

'She asked me into the kitchen that is, to share a dish of tea with this Louise and her husband, which is what she and Gerard had been doing.'

'Fully clothed?'

'Oh yes. I drank the tea, which I loathe, and Gerard and I walked home.'

'He is obviously looked on as one of the family.'

'I said as much to him, a bit bitterly, I suppose.'

'And his answer?' Julian looked less bored than usual.

'Yes.'

'Yes, what?'

'That is what he said, just "yes". I tell you, Julian, the girl's made a fool of me.'

59

'You needed no help. In any case, I understand that Cassy has known Gerard for many years.'

'Oh, for ever, or rather since a childhood acquaintance in some obscure northern fastness. The reason she denied knowing him at Bushey Park was that she had sought to break all links with that respectable background. That much I elicited from him, but he would not tell me more.'

'Nor should he, if she does not wish it.'

Luckily, not many days after this reported incident, Thomas's attention was drawn to the most divine creature with copper hair who regarded him from beneath her eyelashes as she walked along the promenade at the same time each morning with her little dog. He still worshipped Cassy but knew now it could only be from afar, since she did not countenance a love affair and, even had she wanted it, anything more binding was clearly out of the question. He fancied the owner of the poodle would not be so prudish.

As it happened, from then on, the Marquis, on leave from his military appointment, saw more of Cassy than did his young cousin. The Prince Regent was a patron of the theatre, as indeed he was of all the arts, and a knowledgeable one. Besides attending a performance of the two operettas he entertained the whole theatrical company at his Pavilion on several occasions, at which Lord Allingham was invariably present.

Cassy reflected that it would have been worth commiting the impropriety of becoming an actress if only to see the fat, but still comely, First Gentleman of Europe cavorting with the opera dancers, and instructing his musicians to play the songs he had heard so that he could learn the choruses with their singers.

Henry Holland, the architect, had transformed more than twenty years ago the original farmhouse into a Palladian villa topped with a shallow cupola and with a central rotunda between two wings. But the classical severity of Prinny's favourite home had been relieved by bow windows and delicate wrought-iron work. Since then balconies had been added and an oval room to each corner of the front as well as glass-domed stables and riding house.

Cassy could not make up her mind whether or not she admired the interior of the Pavilion with its Chinese style of decoration, though the canopied ceilings and clear red and yellow lacquered surfaces were arresting. But she could not help being charmed, like her companions, when the Prince Regent produced a sheaf of drawings, like many another ambitious country gentleman. They had been prepared for him by his favourite architect, John Nash, and were for a new home. This new Pavilion would be much grander, even more oriental and, Cassy thought, far too fantastical altogether.

She would always remember the flaring flambeaux and chandeliers bringing to light the dragons on the Chinese wallpaper, the banked flowers, the Prince Regent himself dressed like some exotic mandarin with a chestful of medals and the exhilarating waltz-time music that had feet tapping in their sandals or buckled shoes.

The ladies of the ton came to these festivities, for a royal invitation was not to be disregarded. They looked at the players with curiosity and were sometimes condescendingly civil to them. Cassy was careful not to be cornered by any of them as she could not afford to be cross-questioned, and preferred to lie when imperative only by omission.

She was always besieged by partners because of her fame and her beauty, which had matured with her greater experience of the ways of the world. This night, the one she was to remember best of those at the Pavilion, her eyes were like a sunlit sea and her skin like a pink rose petal from the warmth and excitement of the waltz. She had stopped short of damping her diaphanous pink gown as so many did, but she wore a fashionable *décolletage,* so that the curves of her snowy breasts were visible above the soft material and her arms and shoulders bare except for tiny ruched sleeves edged with rosebuds.

Louise had designed a special hair style for her and the dark ringlets were crowned with a coronet of hair into which were twined her seed pearls, her papa's first grown-up gift.

The Marquis was bowing in front of her, and she could hardly refuse to stand up with him. But she could at least remain silent, as he had during the evening at Almack's when she had taken him in such dislike.

The waltz, she knew, was a development of the old-time dance, the volta. It was so much more intimate than the mazurka, the polonaise or German quadrille where one only touched one's partner's hands, that she could understand the dowagers' objection to it on the score of its temptation to loose behaviour. As she felt the arm around her waist, his hand clasping hers and her bosom pressed to his chest she could not have talked if she had wished. She was whirled into a sensual dream by the man who could have been her suitor. She experienced a weakening and humiliating wish that she could stay

61

clasped so in his arms for ever, and could understand only too well why all those unfortunate females had lost their hearts – and in some cases, she feared – their virtue, to him.

She looked up at last as the music ended and found his eyes looking down at her at the same time, with a hint of a question in them. Then he said peremptorily, 'Come and sit down near the window and let me bring you a cooling drink. You look as bewitching tonight as the fairy queen in Mother Goose, to which I took some young friends not long since. But you must be tired. You have given a performance at the theatre, and have hardly been off your feet since.'

'Thank you,' she said, relieved that she could recover, without his keen eyes upon her, from the confusion into which she had been cast by the unaccustomed feelings dancing with him had produced, from his compliment, and also his reference to the theatre visit with her aunt and sisters. She wondered irrelevantly if he had ever been to see her as Prince Charming.

The scent of summer flowers, predominantly that of the Prince Regent's favourite yellow roses, wafted through the open window by which she sat.

She took the refreshment from him with a smile, saying as he gave her the glass of fruit cordial, and kept a glass of champagne for himself, 'You guessed I did not care for strong drink.'

'Yes. Your image is so wholesome, despite your flamboyant profession, that I could not imagine you doing so.'

'You make me sound like a piece of soap,' she said a trifle tartly.

'A prettily coloured and sweetly scented one then.' He smiled and changed the subject, saying, 'I liked your Spanish dance this evening in the latter part of your programme.'

'Oh, did you come to see us?' She was unaccountably pleased.

'Yes. Like most of fashionable Brighton. Did you realise, I wonder, that the complex rhythm and elaborate heel-tapping of the Spanish type of dance is an expression of bull-fighting and courtship, with the lady clapping her hands for "yes" or "no"?'

'A noisy courtship! I imagine the Irish clog dances, then, are a less sophisticated manifestation of the same thing. Are you interested in dancing, sir?'

'I enjoy the ballet.'

'Taglioni?' she asked wistfully.

'She's a miracle, isn't she? She looks to be all gauze and hair. But I do not mean to undervalue the performance of you and your fellow artistes. Dancing is after all an expression of the joy of living, the Germans stamping and slapping, the Russians squatting, spinning and leaping and of course the clicking Spanish dance you so ably demonstrated.'

'And the waltz, sir?'

'A great innovation. Infectious rhythm and free movement – and it has so many other advantages.' They laughed together, and Cassy thought to herself that he could be an unusually stimulating and delightful companion when he forgot to be bored and indifferent.

She noticed now for the first time that La Maris was present in skin-tight crimson and looking at her conversing with the Marquis as if she would gladly kill her. 'If I felt so jealous,' she told herself, 'I should try not to show it.'

But, as the Marquis rose and excused himself, saying, 'I must not monopolise more of your time', and rejoined the imperious beauty, Cassy was conscious of her own need to hide her feelings. The other woman hooked a white arm through his with a proprietary air and darted a backward glance at her.

But Cassy had no time to succumb to any sensation except that of wonderment. A vast cream satin bulk was before her. She rose quickly and dropped a low curtsey to the Prince Regent, who lifted her up with a podgy, beringed hand and swept her on to the floor. There was a creaking of stays and Cassy feared his damp face might burst into flames with the exertion. But Prinny, as she had heard, was amazingly light on his feet and dearly loved to dance.

The fact that she was the only female of the party from the theatre whom the Prince Regent had honoured in this way could not but be a personal triumph that she could hardly wait to recount to Aunt Letty. She greatly regretted being unable to regale her sisters with a description of the memorable occasion. But she resolved that one day she would make up for her enforced deceit by telling them the whole story of her double life.

For the present the excitement of the moment was enough, and she was human enough to hope that Madame Maris, not to mention the Marquis, had noticed her royal partner. They had – the gentleman with pleasure for her, the lady with envy.

Later during the royal reception, when Cassy had already left, Allingham happened to be in conversation with the distinguished impresario and owner of a chain of provincial theatres and concert halls, Marcus Stanton. He was an influential personage and an amiable and personable gentleman who had preserved his figure and thick brown hair, two advantages which made him look younger than his forty years. 'Hello, Julian,' he greeted the younger man jovially. 'No longer in the army? The last time I enquired of you you were in the Peninsula.'

'A ball in the shoulder put a temporary stop to my military career. But I am still attached to the War Office in another capacity.'

'I am sorry you were wounded.'

'I was more sorry to hear about your bereavement, Marcus. It happened, I believe, while I was on foreign service, else I would have written. Your wife was a charming person.'

'Yes. It is hard on my young daughters to be deprived of their mother.'

'It must be. Where are they now?'

'At the present I have established them with their governess, not a very satisfactory one unfortunately, in the house I have rented here. I have an interest in the production at the Theatre Royal.'

'Inevitably, Marcus! Your influence is wide. I intend to drive myself to Worthing tomorrow to visit two young friends of mine who not so long ago suffered the loss of both mother and father, Sir James Loring's daughters. Luckily they are in the care of a youngish aunt, Miss Page, who is devoted to them.'

The distinguished gentleman said in an odd sort of voice, 'Did you say Miss Page, Julian? Not Miss Lettice Page!'

'Yes, assuredly, because Thea and Grace address her as Aunt Letty. My mother knows her well. Have you met her, then?'

'Yes, long ago. I knew her sister too. I should like to renew my acquaintance with – the family. Would you have room for me in your elegant curricle, Julian?'

'Certainly. I shall be glad of your company. Perhaps some time your daughters might meet my young friends. They are probably much of an age. Write your direction for me and I shall collect you after luncheon.'

'Better still, eat your mutton with me first and meet my little girls.'

'Thank you. I should enjoy that.'

9

With the guidance of Thomas, his new instructor in town ways, Gerard had bought himself a second-hand curricle with a pair of sweet-stepping bays. If his descent on Brighton was not accomplished in the Marquis's time of four hours and fifteen minutes, nor yet the four and a half hours of the Prince Regent, he was still satisfied with his first performance.

His presence in the seaside resort was a comfort to Cassy who, with his arrival, had one person, beside John and Louise, to whom she could speak openly. His frequent appearances with her as an old friend helped her to avoid importunities, while her acceptance of him gave him a standing and reputation as a man about town which it would otherwise have taken him years to acquire.

After the first romantic impulse attributable to the shock of seeing his playmate blossomed into a beauty, he had settled with some relief into a fraternal relationship and kept his sentimental sights on the Yorkshire schoolgirl whose father's land matched with that of his papa.

'Let us go over to Worthing on Sunday in my curricle,' he urged Cassy during the first, oppressively hot week in July when the stuffiness at the theatre had often made her feel faint. 'You will enjoy the drive, and Aunt Letty and the girls will like to see my curricle and cattle.'

Cassy was sure they would be pleased to see Gerard as well as herself, and was young enough to relish the prospect of the fast run to Worthing in the open conveyance.

They set forth on a day of bright sunshine and strong breeze that flicked the sea into curls of foam. Gerard was aware of the envious glances of the bucks as he bowled in great style along the promenade, his tiger more apprehensive, because more knowledgeable, than Cassy, about the capabilities of this ambitious novice whipster.

Despite the sharp bends on the inland road that wound from Brighton back to the coast at Worthing, and the fact that Gerard's efforts to catch his whip above his head, as he had seen the Marquis do, nearly suspended them from an overhanging branch, the trip was enjoyable. The only near-incident occurred when Cassy removed the chip-straw bonnet wreathed in ribbons she had tied under her chin, and grandmama's wig. She arranged her own fair curls as best she could with the help of a tiny mirror from her reticule, and Gerard, glancing at her sideways, guffawed so hard that he only just straightened the curricle in time to save it toppling in the ditch. 'Cassy,' he exploded, 'you would never be recognised in Brighton thus.'

She gave a sharp scream and then snapped crossly, 'That is as may be, but keep your eyes on the road, do! I may become permanently unrecognisable if you land us in the ditch.' She tied her bonnet on once more, concealing her hair for the sake of the tiger, and banished from her mind, as quickly as it had suddenly arrived, the thought of her parents' fate.

Aunt Letty, Thea and Grace exclaimed with pleased surprise at the sight of Gerard and his splendid chaise. They gathered round it, patting the horses, asking questions about mileage and speeds, smiling at the small tiger and generally gratifying its driver.

Then there was the house to admire and approval to be given to Cassy's pale orange muslin with its matching half-pelisse. They had hardly settled themselves in the cosy parlour that faced the sea when Gerard rushed to the window and announced breathlessly that the Marquis had swung his greys to an exact halt outside the door, and was obviously bent on calling on his young friends and their aunt, the most natural thing in the world in view of the fact that the house had been taken at a reasonable rental through his agency. He was accompanied by another gentleman.

The little girls clapped their hands and Grace begged Cassy, 'Don't run away again,' and, becoming a little mixed in her excitement added, 'He did not propose when you did not dispose. You would like him if you knew him. I know you would.'

'I must, darlings, and do not mention my presence,' she said as she ran from the room, calling over her shoulder, 'Gerard, you stay. But be careful, pray, what you say.'

'I can hardly do anything but stay, can I, with my rig outside?' he answered reasonably.

Cassy thought as she reached the refuge of Thea's seaside chamber that this flight from the Marquis was reminiscent of the first occasion he had called upon her at Lowndes Square, except that now she did know him and – yes, she did like him. Furthermore, if a man's touch and voice could, like the Spanish castanets, produce an increased blood beat, she could never have played the role of complacent wife if that had been expected of her.

She distracted herself from this disturbing train of thought by wondering who the second gentleman could be, watching the two tigers below at the heads of their teams disputing their respective merits and, when she tired of this occupation, by browsing through Thea's books. Miss Austen's works were unexceptionable, of course, but she doubted that Miss Page knew her elder pupil had a volume by the notorious Mary Wollstonecraft hidden behind an improving tale. She left it in its hiding place, and picked out, to re-read, the more gothic portions of Horace Walpole's bizarre blood-chiller, *The Castle of Otranto*.

She became so absorbed in the book, which used to belong to her, that she jumped up with a start over one hour later when she heard the sound of voices in the hallway. The visitors must be on the point of departure.

She saw from the corner of the window where a heavy fold of curtain hid her that the gentleman who descended the steps with the Marquis was none other than Marcus Stanton, whom she had met a few times at Drury Lane and once at the Brighton Pavilion. His was, she knew, a name to conjure with in the company of such as the Kembles, Sarah Siddons, Charles Young and Edmund Kean. He was an impresario, with connections in the business and production side of theatres throughout the kingdom. He seemed quite old to Cassy, although personable. He had always treated the artistes with tact and civility and was well liked in the profession. His history was something of a mystery. But it was said he had been an actor, that he was now a rich man and only continued with his dramatic ventures because of his deep love of the profession and to help his recovery from the death of his wife some years earlier.

Cassy understood now that a similar whim that had led the Marquis to escort her family to the pantomime and play jackstraws with the little girls had caused him to pay them a visit at their seaside house. But where did Marcus Stanton fit into the picture?

Thea and Grace came up to Cassy after the departure of the two guests to tell her in hushed tones that she had missed an astounding sight. They fell over their words and interrupted each other. But the gist of the matter was that their aunt's normally composed countenance had become scarlet and then ash pale as she had stared speechlessly at the distinguished stranger who entered at His Lordship's side. The Marquis had greeted her formally and held his hands out to the girls to grasp one each of theirs, looking with a surprised smile at Gerard. But Aunt Letty had given him never a glance and, as if transfixed, had uttered in a voice they had never heard her use before the one word, 'Marcus!'

Eventually she had recovered herself and her social sense enough to bid the visitors welcome and invite them to sit down. From what Thea and Grace could gather from the general conversation afterwards, their aunt and their mama had met the stranger many years ago when they were girls, the latter about Cassy's age, and Aunt Letty a year younger. The gentleman who had caused her such a start had been, then, a humble young member of a strolling company of actors playing in nearby Cheltenham. The Page sisters had persuaded their papa to take them to the theatre, and had met some of the performers, Mr Stanton among them. It was from this time, Cassy deduced, that the ladies had become such adherents of the drama.

Her sisters had been able to glean no further details except that their aunt, though mindful after the first shock of her duties as a hostess, had looked quite unlike her normal self the whole time. The Marquis, it seemed, had happened to mention his intended visit to his friend, and, recognising Aunt Letty's name, Mr Stanton had decided to accompany him and give himself the pleasure of renewing an old acquaintance. Thea had noticed that, although their aunt had kept her eyes for the most part dropped, he had hardly taken his from her face. It was all very strange.

Nevertheless, everything seemed normal when Cassy went downstairs, and though she looked intently at Aunt Letty's comely countenance she could see nothing untoward in its aspect. 'Just look, love,' she said in her usual, nicely modulated voice, 'what the Marquis's mother has sent us. Such thoughtful gifts!' She displayed a tea caddy that was a little work of art in a design of shells and flowers, and which opened to display two divisions, one of which was filled with green tea and the other with black.

'It is quite charming,' Cassy admired the present, 'and just what you will enjoy,' for Miss Page relished, but hesitated to indulge, her taste for the expensive beverage.

'And the Marquis brought us these,' added Thea. Cassy had to marvel at the understanding of their individual bents that had inspired him to present Thea with a pretty box of water-colour paints and the artist's paper to go with it, and an embroidery frame and silks with a page of specimen designs for Grace.

Having duly admired the presents she enquired, 'Aunt Letty, tell me about the other gentleman. I believe you used to know him years ago when you and Mama were young.' It struck her as she asked the question that her aunt had an oddly youthful, uncertain look about her now.

Perhaps her voice was a little too studiedly casual as she answered, 'Mr Stanton was an actor, not a particularly well-known one. Your mama and I were taken as a Christmas treat to see a play entitled, if I recall correctly, *The Duel*, at the local playhouse. I suppose it was not anything great by the standards of Drury Lane. But the fencing was magnificent and' – her eyes seemed to be looking mistily into the past – 'your mama and I were devastated when Marcus – the second lead – was, apparently, run through.' She laughed reminiscently and a little unsteadily.

'Well, my dears, we met this young gentleman by chance while we were out shopping in the town with our old nurse and, shamefully, I suppose, made friends with him while she was buying some needles. You must know that actors were considered quite disreputable in my youth.'

'And still are, as you once warned me,' Cassy put in with some feeling, 'unless they are very great. Then they are more notorious than famous as a rule.' She hastened to add, 'However I understand from what Gerard has told me that Mr Stanton is quite respectable now.'

'So I believe. He came from a good family and had run away to join a band of actors. Our parents would not countenance our knowing him. I think he must have been a far better business man than he was an actor to have done so well! Now, Cassy, here is Gerard coming in from admiring his own curricle and bays again on the pretext of seeing the guests away. Tell us all something of your latest experiences at the seminary, although I am persuaded that Gerard, who was kind enough to collect you from there to call upon us, must have heard them all before.'

Aunt Letty clearly desperately needed a respite from questioning about her acquaintance with their unexpected visitor to inflict this upon Cassy, and her nephew, returning in time to hear, agreed, devilishly, 'Yes, do tell us all about school. I should love to hear again the amusing saga you entertained me with on the journey from that establishment.'

So Cassy was faced with the task of inventing more misdeeds of an imaginary pupil called Mabel, who was very vain, and hoped to secure a duke for husband as soon as she set foot in Almack's.

'Would not a handsome marquis like ours do?' asked Thea seriously.

'Maybe. But I do not think he would be much taken by Mabel, with her carrot-coloured hair, bulbous nose and pea-green eyes.'

The girls were in helpless giggles and Cassy felt that she could safely guide the conversation to their activities in Worthing, and engage Gerard to contribute his account of the small happenings from letters received from home, in his sisters' schoolroom and in their circle of friends in the Yorkshire dales. While he was chatting amiably to the younger girls, Cassy's attention was deflected for an instant by the expression on her aunt's face, a compound of the sweetness and the sadness of recollection.

In fact the lady was re-living the passionate embraces in the copse at their country estate, where she would slip away surreptitiously in the afternoons to meet the dazzling young actor, with whom she had fallen so fatally in love. She heard again, as if it were yesterday, his entreaties to her to elope with him. She did not succumb to the temptation, strong as it was, perhaps because the theatrical company, owing to disappointing attendances, moved on sooner than expected. But, she admitted ruefully to herself, the reason lay more probably in her own lack of the courage necessary to fly in the face of convention and break her parents' hearts by sharing the vagaries and miseries, as well as the miracle of passion, with a youngster who could hardly keep himself in shoes let alone support a wife. She was sure Cassy would not have hesitated in her place.

The girl concerned observed with fascination a slight smile on her lips as the older lady reflected that Marcus had lost neither his looks nor his figure, and had not, from his expression, thought her so sadly changed either. In fact had she known it, he had found his erstwhile love poignantly untouched by the years and as delightful in every way as she had been so long ago. 'Julian,' he said with a whimsical smile as they re-entered the curricle, 'I find I have business to attend to here tomorrow morning, and would be obliged if you would leave me at a hotel and tell my household when you return to Brighton not to expect me tonight.'

'With much pleasure, Marcus. May your business prosper!' He smiled with a gleam of amused understanding and did as he was bid.

When Cassy finally ascended again into Gerard's curricle, which, though she would not voice such an opinion, suffered sadly by comparison with that of the Marquis, Aunt Letty and the girls stood close to say their last *adieux* before she, presumably, returned to school. She noticed just in time that she had left her black wig tossed carelessly on the seat, and sat on it quickly, hoping that the Marquis had not thought to inspect the interior.

After they set forth again Cassy went through the same motions of exchanging perukes, ordering her cousin to keep his eyes to the front. She should have been more careful not to leave this dusky one about for all to witness but, in truth, her life had become of late too confusing, with her two selves jostling each other for precedence, especially when the Marquis was likely to encounter either of them without warning.

She said now to Gerard, 'I am so thankful that Allingham did not observe us entering the house, as he might so easily have done had he driven up a mere twenty minutes earlier. Was he not surprised to see you with Aunt Letty?'

'No, why should he be when I told him I was her nevvy?'

'Oh what a tangled web we weave ...' Cassy felt some disquiet.

But Gerard was more interested in relating to her how impressed the Marquis had appeared with his rig, and that he had pronounced the bays a prime pair. He added, 'We discussed the least possible time in which one could hope to cover the distance between Brighton and Worthing. His was faster, and I just restrained myself from telling him my record would have been considerably better had I not had to consider the sensibilities of a female passenger.'

'Thank goodness you resisted the temptation. You have kept my secret commendably well. But I do wonder what exactly Mr Stanton said to His Lordship when he heard of his proposed visit to Aunt Letty. Do ask him, since I cannot.'

'I shall certainly do no such thing. It is more than enough.' he told her with a grin that belied the severity of the words, 'to convey a lady, who changes her appearance at the wink of an eyelash, without being prevailed upon to ask impertinent questions of my elders and betters. I'll be having word get back to m'father next that I am wasting the ready on actresses.'

They giggled together as they had as children and it must have been that moment of inattention on Gerard's part that caused the mishap. He took a blind corner a shade too sharply and the curricle lurched drunkenly, depositing Gerard, herself and the tiger into a, luckily shallow, ditch.

'Hold the horses!' Gerard barked at his luckless employee, whose worst fears had now been realised, and helped the shocked, shaken but otherwise undamaged Cassy on to the roadway.

It was at this moment that the Marquis's team, unfortunately for Gerard's self-importance but happily in other respects, swept around the bend, avoiding a collision with their conveyance and restive horses with what appeared to them to be uncanny skill. He eased his animals to a standstill, ordering his tiger to hold their heads, and hurried towards the dishevelled and discountenanced small group on the grassy verge.

10

'Are you hurt?' His Lordship asked Cassy sharply.

Out of countenance, surprised but thankful, she gazed up at the apparition and shook her head dumbly.

He and a scarlet-faced Gerard examined the curricle which, looking suspiciously lop-sided, was indeed discovered to have a broken wheel. The Marquis took charge of the situation summarily, saying, 'Miss Cassandra, you had better accompany me.' He told Gerard cursorily, 'I shall send you help from Brighton, which is not above a few miles away. But let us first get your outfit off the road lest it be responsible for another spill.' With some self-control he forbore to comment on the driving which had caused the present one.

Thus Cassy, having quickly and surreptitiously straightened her peruke and bonnet, rode into town beside the Marquis, a privilege many females would grudge her, for he was not, except in rare circumstances, in the habit of taking ladies up with him.

After a while he perplexed her by remarking casually, 'I suppose that Gerard must have delivered and fetched you from a different destination than his own. Did he tell you we had met?'

Cassy swallowed, at a total loss, and simply replied, 'Yes, sir.' So discomposed was she that she prevented herself by a hairsbreadth from adding in a puzzled way that she had thought His Lordship to be in front instead of behind them on the road from Worthing. But she managed to say civilly as a substitute, 'How fortunate for us that you happened to be passing.'

'Extremely,' he agreed drily and elaborated briefly. 'I should not have been had I not had two calls to make at Worthing, the second at a hotel where I kept my passenger company for an hour. If I had not deposited him we should not be so comfortable now.' A little later he added abruptly, 'You should not be driving with an inexperienced whipster in these twisting lanes. You might have been killed.'

He could not know that his warning brought with it the sudden heart ache of remembered loss. She turned her head away to hide the hint of tears. But her painful preoccupation with an earlier accident changed to the more bearable feeling of annoyance as he said, 'You are one of the very few of your sex to ride in my curricle. Ladies are too distracting.'

'Then I shall be the target of much jealousy from your ...' She could not find the appropriate word and he did not help her. But he slanted a disarming grin at her and countered, 'And I from your legion of adorers!' This was said so graciously that she felt in charity with him again, and she was recovered enough from her tumble to appreciate and enjoy the smooth speed and the expertise with which he handled the reins. Contrasting this operation with that of poor Gerard, she perceived in him a master.

Curious glances followed their entrance to the town, and Cassy could well imagine the comments being exchanged to the effect that the unapproachable Cassandra not only accepted the escort of the Yorkshireman, but now sat up bold as brass with the infamous Allingham.

'I believe my cousin Tom told me you have lodgings on the Grand Parade,' said her saviour. 'Will you direct me?'

She did so and thanked him prettily and with geniune gratitude as he helped her down. 'It was an unexpected pleasure,' he assured her and smiled into her eyes in that challenging way he had. 'I promise to send help to the unlucky Gerard straight away.'

She entered the house with her mind in a turmoil, as was usually the case after an encounter with her one-time suitor. She did not know whether she felt more discomfited by being discovered all to pieces or exhilarated by his subsequent company. She abandoned the impossible decision for speculation about the reappearance of the figure from her aunt's mysterious past.

Cassy had every opportunity during the production's short season at Brighton to observe at close quarters the reckless extravagance of the court of the Prince Regent, just as others had done during the state visit to London earlier in June of the Czar Alexander of Russia and King Frederick of Prussia.

This profligacy was particularly apparent when the after-effects of the war against the French and the upheavals of what was in the process of becoming an industrial revolution were causing such distress and poverty. It contrasted, to many shamefully, with the husbanding of resources which had been the hallmark of Bonaparte's meteoric rule on the other side of the Channel.

At the final reception that Cassy attended at the Pavilion that strange summer, Prinny, in his role as patron of the arts, had gathered together painters, poets, and theatre luminaries, many from London. The conversation sparkled like the imported French wine, but Cassy was aware of an undercurrent of more serious discussion concerning the efforts of Napoleon's supporters to rally his followers against his anticipated return.

She was herself a minor star in her own small sphere because of the image she projected of radiant, idealised youthfulness. But she knew intuitively that her success was ephemeral, and all the sweeter because of it. She felt as humble before the great players of the day, such as were present on this occasion, as any stage-struck girl.

When Edmund Kean complimented her on her charming performance in the dual programme at the theatre she thought his resonant and melodious voice was like an orchestra in itself. He fixed his black eyes on her, and so vibrant was his personality that his very ordinary words came as an anticlimax. 'You are a remarkably pretty lass,' said the great man, and the emanation of royal brandy that accompanied the compliment brought to mind the sad whisper that he was ruining his health with strong liquor.

The great actor introduced her to a tall, stately fellow player with regular features whom she would immediately have recognised even if he had not been presented whimsically as 'the ghost of my father'.

Cassy congratulated the two actors in her turn on their much acclaimed *Hamlet*, and, acknowledging her praise with a careless gesture, Alexander Pope in his Irish accent muttered, to her astonishment, 'Had a shocking experience in Brighton last evening.'

'I am sorry to hear it,' said Cassy with concern.

'Invited to dine, Edmund here and myself. But had to leave. Could not support it.' Cassy was bewildered. 'Fellow guest cut her *fricandeau* of veal with a steel knife instead of using a spoon.'

There was a light laugh behind her and Allingham said, 'Don't look so bemused. Alex is the foremost authority on food of his generation.' She looked impressed. 'The gourmands of London and Brighton, like myself, await his verdict on the oyster crop at the start of each season.' The actor looked, Cassy thought, more gratified with this commendation than he had with plaudits on his portrayal of the ghost of Hamlet's father. She was highly diverted.

The Marquis asked Cassy to dance and, as she drifted with him in a dream, she knew that waltz time would always remind her of this place and this man. She closed her eyes as he guided her adroitly round the great ballroom where the musicians fiddled and strummed, myriad candlelights gleamed on exotic splendours and the fragrance of hothouse blooms assailed the senses.

'Do you like dancing with your eyes closed?' came the slight drawl, 'or do you simply want to display your ridiculously long eyelashes to advantage?'

'With my eyes shut I have the feeling of flying,' she smiled up at him, but was secretly glad her lashes were naturally dark in contrast to her fair hair. Did he prefer dark women, she wondered, since his last two prime articles were sultry brunettes? Madame Maris was not in evidence tonight, and she had to remind herself that this fact could have no importance for herself.

'Let us find some seats on a balcony,' he suggested. 'It is so stuffy inside.' She acquiesced, cooling her hot cheeks with the fan she carried on her wrist.

'That is certainly better.' She sighed with pleasure as a soft breeze played upon them. 'Do tell me, sir, is Mr Pope really a food fanatic or just a jokesmith?'

'The former, and treats the subject without unseemly levity! He came to dinner once when my father was alive. But the meal broke up in disorder when Alex announced, "Damnation to your cook, sir. Torbay turbot served smothered with capers is a desecration".'

'Oh no!' exclaimed Cassy. 'I warrant he was not asked again.'

'You are right. Another time, in the Green Room, Alex was musing upon a brace of partridges awaiting him at home. A young actor asked his advice about how to dress his part for a new play. Alex, thoughts on the birds, answered decisively, "With red wine sauce of course".'

Cassy's amused chuckle sounded again, and he said, 'I like to hear you laugh. It sometimes seems to me you have too little reason to do so.'

She looked suddenly shy and said quietly, 'And yet I have a life that many might envy.'

'True. Then my petition to that slip of new moon up there is that it should continue thus for you as long as you want – or need it to.'

'You are – surprisingly kind in wishing on the moon on my behalf instead of your own.'

'Is it surprising in me? You are telling me home truths!'

She coloured. 'I did not mean—'

'You did not. But your remark was salutary all the same. Now here is His Royal Highness bearing down upon us to twirl you round the floor again.' He rose, as did Cassy, and bowed to Prinny.

The heat within after the freshness outside and the scented, heavy body clamped to hers made her giddy and near to swooning. She murmured something apologetic to this effect and shortly, to her dismay, found herself transposed to a stiff, if sumptuously brocaded, sofa in a small saloon and being embraced with enthusiasm by her royal partner.

She heard as from a distance the cold voice of the Marquis. 'Sir, your royal presence is required by your distinguished guests. May I be permitted to relieve you of the care of this lady, as she is obviously not well?'

This firm speech brought the slightly fuddled 'first gentleman' up short. He drew himself up and replied sheepishly, 'I should be grateful. Adieu.' He was gone in a flash of puce satin, and Cassy, darting a rueful glance at His Lordship, was momentarily beyond speech.

'Come,' he said imperiously. 'You must go home. Does your conveyance await you?'

'Yes, sir,' she managed.

'Then I shall escort you to it and make your excuses and farewells for you.'

'You are most obliging, and the fact no longer surprises me,' she said a trifle unsteadily.

'I am obliging when it suits me perhaps, Cassandra. Come along.'

A few days of rain which followed the heat wave resulted in Thea and Grace making good use of the Marquis's gifts. They were busily engaged with them the morning after his visit in the small upstairs room they had labelled their den since they considered themselves too old for a nursery.

So Miss Page was alone in the parlour when a carriage drew up outside and she saw Marcus through the window mounting the few steps in a leap, just as, she recollected fondly, his younger self had taken the stage flight leading to the residence of his supposed beloved.

She straightened hurriedly the curls, which had no trace of grey, under the lace cap and was on her feet looking as calm as she was capable of doing under the circumstances, although her racing heart betrayed her when Grimble led him in. For once the butler had been surprised into a faint inflexion of disapproval as he announced, 'Mr Stanton.'

However unruffled she may have appeared she forgot completely her hastily prepared and casual words of greeting and just ejaculated, 'Oh – oh!' He was not much more sensible, for he dropped his hat when the old retainer tried to take it from him, having failed to stop his impetuous advance into the hall, fidgeted with his cravat and coloured crimson.

When his hat and his composure had been recovered they both burst out laughing and were suddenly at ease. 'Sit down, Marcus, do,' she begged. 'What do you care to drink? There is an orgeat or, I believe, a Malaga wine.'

He held up his hands as if to avert a catastrophe in a gesture which carried her back twenty years. She lowered her head to hide the softness in her eyes. 'Not orgeat, please!' he begged.

When she looked up it was to find his dark eyes fixed upon her in a way that made her say quickly and in businesslike tones, 'Then it shall be the Malaga, even though it is early. Are you staying in the neighbourhood, then? Your second visit is an unanticipated pleasure, if perhaps not very—'

'Not very proper? Then as far as your neighbours, and anybody else is concerned, I must be a long-lost relative,' he decided gaily.

'You have not really changed at all under that mature, distinguished exterior.'

'Neither have you altered. You are just as timorous – and beautiful – as you ever were.'

Goodness! she thought, this is too much. She had not felt so inclined to laugh or cry for no good reason, since that last day in the copse at home when the young Marcus had kissed her wildly and spoiled her for any other suitor.

'Please drink with me,' he said.

'I think I do need a glass of wine to steady me,' she confessed with a quick smile that brought his memory bouncing back over time. 'Tell me, old friend, something of the years that have evidently made the poor boy I once knew such a prosperous man.'

'The key to the puzzle is that I gave up acting. You must admit that I was never very good at it.'

'I shall admit nothing of the sort. You looked wonderful.'

'My dear, you were bewitchingly biased. Anyway, I discovered a talent in myself for directing other people and a natural insight into what sort of production would go, and where. One thing led to another, and particularly to a backer who had faith in me.' He was thoughtful for a minute.

'Then you married.'

'Yes. His daughter became my wife.'

'I hope you were happy,' she said with sincerity.

There was a pause and then he answered her with an effort at honesty, 'It was a convenient marriage, at least for me. She was a good woman. I miss her.'

'I do hope you have children to bear you company.'

'Yes, two sweet daughters of thirteen and eleven years.'

'I am glad. They are much of an age with my nieces.'

'So I thought when I saw your girls. I have installed Marcia and Honor with their governess in Brighton for the season. I am considering transferring them to Worthing where it is quieter. It would be nice if the four youngsters became friends.' Before she could reply he leaned forward and asked, 'Tell me, Letty, why did you never marry? It was not for the want of opportunity.'

She flushed. 'No, it was not. I did not feel that I could accept anybody whom I did not love. But,' she hastened to add, 'do not think I did not have a full and satisfying life with my sister and brother-in-law while they were alive. Now their three daughters are my sacred trust.'

'Was it quite satisfying, my dear?' he asked softly. She did not answer but evaded his eyes, and he added, lightly, 'You have a third niece then?'

'Yes, the eldest.' She considered for a moment of indecision the necessity for duplicity. He had quite likely met Cassandra in London or Brighton.

'Is she married?' he enquired.

'No. Like myself, she does not consider any alliance except for love. She is away from home just now.'

Marcus Stanton put out his hand impulsively and took hold of hers. 'Letty, dear Letty—' he began. Then Thea and Grace came in and he rose and smiled at them.

79

11

The girls looked startled and then glad to see the pleasant gentleman so soon again. He flourished his arm and swept them a deep stage bow, saying 'Ladies!' which made them giggle.

Thea said, 'I thought you were staying in Brighton, sir.'

'I am,' he responded cheerfully, 'but since I find myself a sort of very distant uncle of yours, by intent, I thought I might take a house for my daughters here. They are near you in age and being, like myself, your extremely distant kin, you should all be friends.'

The girls, much taken aback at first at the acquisition of these distant relatives, were none the less approving of the prospect of their companionship.

'That would be nice,' Grace returned for them both, 'for many games are better played with four than two. Besides we have no family near except for Gerard.'

Miss Page darted a look of outrage at the gentleman, but seeing the bland face that met it and the pleased surprise on those of her nieces she gave a little choke of laughter which she changed quickly into a cough. But he had noticed, and his eyes met hers with half-amused apology across the two young heads.

Bless the girls' simple·hearts, thought Miss Page! Matters were getting thoroughly out of hand with Cassy like to arrive any Sunday and soon to be with them on holiday. One would have thought the ever-present possibility of her visit coinciding with that of the Marquis to be enough problem. She caught the visitor's eyes on hers again with an acknowledgement of his villainy and a hope that she should like him for it. From his complacent expression now he must have decided that she did. She must, Miss Page resolved, simply meet and solve each difficult situation as it arose.

However, her new philosophy deserted her completely as she heard Marcus Stanton say to a delighted Thea and Grace, 'I have conceived the most splendid idea!' Aunt Letty looked apprehensive and Thea said with excited anticipation, 'Another?'

'Yes. You shall accompany me to Brighton today to see a matinée. There is a double bill of operettas at the theatre.' He saw their aunt about to demur and added persuasively, 'All quite suitable for young people. My daughters, Marcia and Honor, will be happy to have an opportunity to meet you, and to see again the performance they thoroughly enjoyed. You will like the little leading lady in *The Smugglers' Cave*. She looks not unlike you, Thea. I shall convey you back to Worthing. Do say you can come.'

Poor Miss Page could not immediately see her way out of this quandary. She would not care to watch the look of rapture wiped from the girls' faces, nor to put herself in the light of a kill-joy. So she gave in valiantly, saying, 'That would be delightful. Might we convey a message to my nephew, Gerard, on the way?'

'Naturally,' he agreed with alacrity. 'He shall accompany us to lunch at my house. Put your bonnets on and let us depart with all possible speed.'

The girls changed their gowns and washed their faces in double quick time. But Miss Page decided her morning *toilette* must do. The renewal of an old association made her realise in any case how scanty her wardrobe was. She was bound to use the little time available to write two *billets*, one for Gerard, and, in the event that he should be from home, a second to be handed to the stage-door keeper for Cassy. The star of the production must surely have an understudy, she thought, and then, a little sadly, of what a happy occasion this could have been for her too were it not for the dangers inherent in it.

By a fortunate chance Gerard was at his lodgings, and gratified at an invitation to lunch with such a well-known personage. He took the note from his aunt, but it was not until he discerned the entreaty in her eyes that he realised that some important action was expected of him. When he heard the plan for the two families that very afternoon he grasped the situation quickly, even before reading it, and promised to present himself at the gentleman's house in half an hour, having performed an errand.

Gerard sallied forth into the street ten minutes later, having achieved a precarious version of Lord Allingham's distinctive way with a cravat, which had come to be known as the 'Allingham fall'. He came upon Thomas, on the corner of the Steine, and it occurred to him to entrust a message for Cassy to him, as he looked to be walking in the direction which would take him past her lodgings. 'Well met, Tom,' he greeted him. 'Will you do me a service, since I am bidden to lunch by Marcus Stanton and do not wish to keep my host waiting?' He thought the other looked suitably impressed and continued, 'It is simply to call at Cassandra's house and tell her that her friends from Worthing will be at the performance this afternoon.'

Thomas looked mystified but accepted the commission good-naturedly, not ungrateful despite his earlier failure to engage her interest, for a legitimate excuse to call upon her. But he was unprepared for Cassy's reception of the laconic message.

He told his cousin Julian that evening, 'She said that she regretted that her understudy would have to go on as she felt ill, and must consequently disappoint her friends. I thought this was a golden opportunity to support and comfort her and prove what a generally invaluable fellow I was. But it was not to be. I was sent off on another errand, to tell her understudy, Dolly Mallon, she must take her place this afternoon, putting that poor girl in a devil of a pucker at having such short notice.'

'Poor Cassandra! I hope she is better.'

'Yes! I went back to her lodgings prepared to summon a leech for her, or hold her hand, to be told by her dresser she was already lying down and did not require a doctor. So the effort was to no avail, not but what the understudy is a very lovely girl, if not in Cassy's class. Saw her with her dog before. But I cannot understand why my intelligence should have put Cassandra in such queer stirrups.'

'You should know by now, Tom, that females are inexplicable. Call on Cassandra again, will you, since you are known to her dresser, and see if she is recovered.'

'I did. She had recovered, for she had left for the evening performance.'

'Foiled again.'

'Yes. So I went to comfort the understudy for losing the part again, and offer to walk her dog for her. She improves on acquaintance and, I say, Julian, she is not nearly so unapproachable as Cassandra. In fact ...'

'All's well that ends well. I must abandon you shortly, cousin, for I am due to dine with a military acquaintance hot from Paris.'

'Do you think it is true that Bony's boys are mustering over the Channel?'

'Yes, probably – while Prinny dances.'

'You do not think of rejoining your old regiment, do you, Julian?'

'Not for the present. I can possibly be more useful in another capacity.'

'Anyway,' Thomas added, as his cousin filled his blue enamel and silver snuff box, 'your shoulder injury would presumably not allow of it.'

'It still stiffens. But it does not incapacitate me. I should seek some form of action should war break out again. I am after all a soldier.'

'What would Madame M. do without you?'

'Put up the "to let" sign again. You do not imagine she would wait, like Penelope, for my return!'

'I don't. But I believe there are better bred ladies who would be glad of the opportunity to do so.'

'So you have told me – ad nauseam. Good hunting!' he called over his shoulder as he left for his appointment.

Cassy's short season at the Brighton theatre was drawing to a close. She was looking forward to a rest and was not unduly worried about recognition at Worthing once she had discarded her wigs. Louise had taught her how to arrange her own shining hair in a style totally different from any she had worn before and which was so artless that it was a masterpiece.

She was reasonably sure that Marcus Stanton would fail to connect Aunt Letty's eldest niece with the actress he had spoken to but once or twice, especially in such a different context. It seemed unlikely that the Marquis would think to call again at Worthing now that he was, she had heard, only to stay a short time longer in Brighton.

In the meantime she had been bidden to a late party at his house on the Steine which she was curious to see. Gerard escorted her there, and obviated the necessity of John's services. The gathering was lively since so many notable bucks were present together with a bevy of beautiful ladies, not of the ton, but, Cassy supposed, of the *demi-monde*, included in which, presumably, was herself.

She needed a respite from the dancing some time in the small hours, and drew apart to a smaller salon to sit for a while. The Marquis discovered her there gazing up at the painted ceiling, seated himself beside her and asked quietly, 'Do you like it?'

She considered the blue, starry vault with the cherubim and answered candidly, 'I am not completely sure. It is, I think, the work of Cipriano.'

He nodded approvingly. 'He is all the crack, but I am not convinced that this is one of the best examples of his work.'

'Nor I frankly, sir. But I must compliment you on the Chinese wallpaper in the dining-room.'

'Recommended, of course, by Prinny and ordered from the same source as the hangings in the Chinese saloon at the Pavilion.'

'Your golden curtains against that particular blue are breathtaking.'

'I have, I own, allowed my imagination a little rein here. Such extravagant effects seem to accord with the atmosphere of Brighton.'

'I know what you mean. Is it not the same then in your town house?' she asked with genuine interest.

'No. There the furnishings and draperies are traditional. As for Allingham Park - that, I assure you, is a nightmare of discomfort and antiquity where the winds blow within and without.'

'I am sure you exaggerate,' she protested, laughing.

'If anything I minimise the matter. The kitchens are medieval and there is a mile of corridor between them and the dining-room, so that the food served there is invariably chilled.'

'Now I know you are roasting me!'

'Only a little. I stay there now only when I entertain a house party for the hunting, and for Christmas, which I spend with my mother. She loves the place as it is, and was in my father's and grandfather's time.'

'The gardens must be beautiful. Indeed they are celebrated.'

'Yes, they are. My father's family have always been keen horticulturists and between them have stocked the grounds with rare trees and plants.'

'Do you not share this interest?'

'To a limited extent. If I used the place more I should probably develop an enthusiasm. It needs a family of children to bring it to life. Having been a solitary child, I associate it with loneliness.' He grinned at her suddenly, saying, 'How hypocritical I must sound, trying to wring your withers when really I was, and am, a thoroughly spoiled individual!'

Cassy's look of sweet commiseration changed to an answering smile as she responded, 'Anyway, I am persuaded, with a little planning, the house could be much more livable and convenient for the family and the staff.'

'Are you, Cassy?' he returned lightly. 'Perhaps you will come there one day and give me the benefit of your ideas on the subject.'

'Yes,' she said simply, 'if you ever gave a party there like this one.'

She was aware suddenly of loud voices and laughter in the smaller room where they sat, and the resentful eyes of Madame Maris, whom, in her enjoyment of the homely conversation, she had forgotten. But he seemed oblivious of the curious looks.

'You are young,' she said, to conclude their talk, 'and I am certain you will marry and fill those enchanting exotic gardens with children's happy voices.'

'Cassandra the prophetess!' he smiled.

'But—' she gestured towards La Maris, who was smiling provocatively at a bemused Gerard while glancing sideways at her protector. Cassy realised all of a sudden that she had nearly been guilty of a great impertinence.

Allingham was looking at her with an unreadable expression. 'You think I should discontinue my liaisons if I marry?' he enquired.

'Forgive me,' she said quickly, 'I had no right – I know that, with your consequence – you can choose a wife and still – oh, what have I started?' She put her burning face in her hands for a moment.

'You mean, I think, that a lady who loved me would want my fidelity too.'

'I am sure she should.' There was a little frown between her soft blue eyes. 'I wonder though if such a thing is possible, from what I have observed since starting my career at the theatre.'

'Come now,' he smiled, 'there are many faithful husbands even there, your friend Joe for one.'

She looked contrite. 'I have been presumptuous, sir, and you have been patient.' He took her hand and held it for a moment before patting it in a manner almost avuncular. But no uncle, she reflected wryly, would have left her troubled and trembling from his touch as this disturbing and contradictory gentleman did.

He said now, before joining Madame Maris, who had begun to divert some of the beaux with wittily improper little verses at the piano: 'I should ask Gerard to take you home, Cassy. I fear the proceedings may become hectic.'

She was a little annoyed by his authoritative manner to her, yet touched by his consideration. The dancing had ceased to be merely an excuse for closeness but had turned, in some cases, into overt embraces. Many gentlemen had glazed eyes and the women's voices were becoming shrill. Cassy felt suddenly very young and at a loss. She asked Gerard if he would take her home, as she had a headache, feeling guilty to be dragging him away from an occasion to which he had been so happy to be invited. He went up in her estimation when he complied with her request cheerfully, saying, 'Of course, my dear. This is not for you.'

Their host accompanied them personally to the coach, past the link boys with their torches. He thumped Gerard's shoulder with a sort of friendly approbation, surprising the young man into a pleased smile. He kissed Cassy's hand, and they could hear the singing and music as they bowled away in the darkness.

Dolly, who had been bidden to the Marquis's house at Thomas's instigation, told Cassy the next day that the rest of the evening had been stormy weather, from which she deduced that the assembly had turned into something of an orgy.

12

A few days after her visit to Lord Allingham's house Cassy went to stay in Worthing. She thoroughly enjoyed the cosseting she received from Aunt Letty, who kept her in bed until ten, when her breakfast chocolate was served by her sisters. She was in fact even more tired than she had realised, after the strain imposed by acting in the heat of the small theatre. So weary was she in fact that she avoided the necessity of inventing more Banbury tales about her supposed school by pleading a surfeit of the subject. 'Darlings,' she begged, 'the best holiday for me would be to forget all about it until I have to go back. So tell me all about yourselves instead.'

'Yes, Cassy dear,' agreed Thea willingly, as she and Grace perched on the end of her bed. They duly regaled her with the account of the expeditions on horseback they had enjoyed in company with Marcus Stanton's daughters.

'It was wonderful that the girls came to stay quite near us,' enthused Grace, 'for we all get on so well.'

'Yes,' contributed Thea, 'and when their father is home he has such good ideas for places we can visit. With his escort we are able to go further afield, and it is more entertaining for Aunt to have an elderly person such as herself to converse with.'

Cassy laughed. 'I do not think Aunt Letty would appreciate being called so, for she is still only in her late thirties. Mr Stanton has a youthful aspect and manner too though he must be a few years older.'

'I have to admit,' Thea concurred, 'that I have never seen Aunt Letty in such good looks before. She really enjoyed our visits to the ecastle at Bramber, the wishing well at Fulking and of course to Brighton.'

'Did you enjoy the operettas?'

'Very much, although I cannot imagine why Mr Stanton should have told me the leading player in *The Smugglers' Cave* resembled me.'

'We went again to Brighton,' added Grace, 'to see Madame Tussaud's waxworks, which she has transferred from London for the season. They were very eerie, specially the heads chopped off by the guillotine in France.'

Cassy realised with a shudder, not unsuitable to Grace's observation, how easily she might have been encountered in the town, and changed the subject quickly. 'Do you hire hacks for your riding parties?' she asked. 'If so that must be expensive, but I am glad that you should enjoy yourselves.'

'Oh, no,' Thea assured her. 'Mr Stanton, who is after all a sort of uncle, by intent, has mounted us three as well as his own girls, for the house he has rented has a stable full of horses and the owners told him they would be thankful to have them exercised.'

'Did you say he was an uncle?' asked Cassy sharply.

'Only by very remote relationship,' answered her sister airily.

'I should think it must be,' agreed her elder with private amusement. She was surprised at the rapid development of the friendship between the two families and curious about its possible significance. Was the wealthy widower simply desirous of finding suitable friends for his daughters with an amiable older woman to supervise the quartette, or was he indeed intending to become an uncle by marriage?

However, she kept her conjectures to herself and questioned the girls.

'Tell me, dears, do your riding habits still stand up to inspection? They were very smart, but have you not grown out of them?'

'No,' answered Grace for them both, 'at least only in the length of the skirt and the sleeves of the jacket. We are not fat, you know, like poor Honor whom we are trying to encourage to eat fewer bonbons. Aunt has adjusted the riding habits for us.'

'Yes,' said Thea, 'but to tell you the truth, Cassy, her own green one is sadly shabby. We have urged her to bespeak a new habit. But she laughs and says that as long as she is neat and not actually out at elbows she will do.'

'Um,' murmured Cassy thoughtfully. 'I must see if I cannot add my persuasions to yours.'

Accordingly, when she was alone with Miss Page on the window seat in the parlour, listening to the sea booming and watching the moon's path on it, she brought up the question of the family finances.

Aunt Letty kept the record of expenditure and now she told her eldest niece candidly, 'My love, you have been a wonderful provider. I have only hoped and prayed that you would not need to follow this unsuitable career beyond a year or so. But you were too generous in the matter of this fine house. In addition, you had to maintain your own lodgings at Brighton, and it has all been far too heavy a burden on our combined incomes, even with your star salary. But our outgoings will diminish with our return to town.'

As if to divert Cassy's thoughts from the vexed subject, she added, 'I admire you, my love, for your success, and only wish I might have seen you perform at Brighton. But to do so would have meant more prevarication. As it is I am constantly on the look-out not to drop an inadvertent word that might arouse suspicion.'

'Poor Aunt!' Cassy sympathised with a smile. 'I shall retire from this nefarious profession as soon as I possibly can. But tell me honestly, have you been stinting yourself to help the family, going without replenishments to your wardrobe that you need? If I thought so I should be most distressed. You must, for instance, have a new riding habit, the girls assure me – specially,' she twinkled, 'now that you have an admirer.'

Her aunt coloured faintly, but said with elaborate casualness, 'Thea and Grace are teasing. My habit was extremely expensive and still is quite adequate to the amount of riding I shall do. There will be no opportunity in town.'

Cassy was not convinced, but when she examined the accounts with Miss Page they did indeed confirm that funds were much too low for comfort, or to cope with any unexpected demands on them.

To lighten the depression caused by surveying them Cassy remarked with a humorous gleam, 'There is nothing for it, Aunt. Instead of protecting my virtue so fiercely with the aid of Louise and John, I shall have to accept a *carte blanche* from some gentleman who is plump in the pocket.' She laughed at the other's expression of horror. 'Don't concern yourself! I was only funning. But just consider the triumph if I succeeded, for instance, in attaching Lord Byron. Would that not be something? I often talk to him and I am persuaded he views me with some warmth.'

'I don't doubt it. Do you find him so devastating?'

'I can resist him with ease. But he is certainly an unusually handsome man, with a brilliant mind.'

'Well, my love, continue to resist advances, for I do not despair of your contracting a respectable and happy alliance, when this masquerade is over. You are, if anything more beautiful now, with an added presence and confidence. I am sure, if the Marquis were to meet you again, he would come to propose a marriage of love instead of convenience.'

Cassy responded a little hollowly, 'He does see me quite often, and, I must say, talks to me very civilly.'

'Don't tell me he has—'

'Given me a slip on the shoulder? No, he is much too involved with some other actress.'

'It seems very shocking.'

'Why, Aunt Letty, you as good as told me once that to be a loose fish was natural for a bachelor! I am no longer shocked, for he is only one of many gentlemen of the first stare, married or not, who have some light of love. Men, after all—'

'Yes, dear, I know. But it is regrettable that such facts should be forced on your attention so early.'

'I shall be none the worse for it,' she consoled the older woman, who was looking pensive. It occurred to her then that she had more knowledge of the world by now than her aunt, whose life had been a protected one. In any case, she continued with truth, 'I have met with much kindness in the theatre.'

The ladies retired, Cassy to ponder on ways of improving the condition of the family budget. She had already received offers for autumn productions in London, but the next two months were bound to prove a strain on their purse. She forced herself to stop thinking about the problem for the present. But the vision of a handsome face with light, flecked hazel eyes regarding her, she dared to think, with an amused liking, intruded between herself and sleep.

The immediate question of their financial position appeared to Cassy to be potentially solved by the advent of Gerard, who told them that a certain Romeo Coates was looking for an actress to play opposite his Lothario in Nicholas Rowe's play, *The Fair Penitent,* in a benefit performance in Brighton.

Gerard's disclosure was intended only to amuse his cousins, for the actor concerned was a notorious laughing-stock. It had not occurred to Gerard that Cassy could as much as consider lending herself to the inevitable ridicule of playing with him, however excessively he was reputed to over-pay his leading ladies to entice them to participate in his travesties of the drama.

His announcement was made at a jolly family nuncheon at the Worthing house of Marcus Stanton at which were present Miss Page's family as well as his daughters. It had never crossed the gentleman's mind that Letty's fair eldest niece had any connection with the dark actress whom he had spoken to once or twice.

'Why, who is Romeo Coates?' asked Marcia, the elder and slimmer of the pair of sisters.

'A buffoon, who is a self-styled actor and a crazy combination of vanity and eccentricity, both on stage and off,' her father explained.

'In what way?' enquired Thea with fascination.

'He covers himself with furs all the year round and his buttons, and even the buckles on his knee breeches and shoes, are of diamonds.'

They all laughed and Gerard, his eyes dancing, took up the tale. 'I saw him myself in the park in the carriage he calls a curricle, but which resembles nothing so much as a tea-kettle on wheels. It is painted bright blue and bears his coat of arms.'

'A noble one?' asked Grace, wide-eyed.

'He invented it himself, and very suitable too – a crowing cock. Wherever he goes the street urchins follow him yelling, "Cock-a-doodle-do".'

'How humiliating for him!' exclaimed Miss Page.

'On the contrary, he loves it – so do not waste your pity, Aunt – just as he mistakes the mocking applause and the jeering shouts of an audience for adulation.'

Cassy had been listening with some amusement and much foreboding. She too had heard of this Romeo Coates and, however preposterous a performer he might be, she decided she could support being made to look foolish with him for one evening, if the lowering experience were profitable enough. Gerard should become her temporary agent and make enquiries on the subject.

The hilarious nuncheon came to an end and Marcus Stanton swept the four youngsters off for a drive, good-naturedly leaving Miss Page to have a coze with her nephew and eldest niece.

'How kind Mr Stanton is!' remarked Gerard.

'Yes,' agreed Aunt Letty, 'but he enjoys young company and we will reward him with some adult conversation when he eats his mutton with us this evening. Will you stay, Gerard?'

'Gladly, if you can find me a place to lay my head. I don't much care for driving my curricle at night.'

Cassy, remembering her experience in this conveyance, was relieved, though she had more tact than to say so. Instead she asked him, 'Gerard, do you think that Romeo Coates would engage me as his leading lady in his benefit performance in Brighton?'

Both he and Aunt Letty looked at her askance. The lady was the first to speak. 'You must have windmills in your head. I shall not allow it.'

'Nor shall I,' agreed Gerard stoutly.

Cassy looked at them both with affectionate gratitude for their preoccupation with her well-being. But she continued persuasively, 'The experience would amuse me, and for one evening could cause no great harm.'

'You think not,' countered her cousin derisively, 'when he is the butt of Brighton?'

'Not only that,' added her aunt, 'but supposing Mr Stanton decides to attend the performance. He would surely recognise you now. Although he is due to post into the northern counties, he may take it into his head to delay the trip in order to see what sounds like a theatrical curiosity.'

'Depend upon it. It will be,' declared Gerard, laughing.

'I know, my dears, and for that very reason all eyes will be upon the poor silly star. He will see to that. I engage, should he hire me, to be totally unrecognisable. He will like that, for he must know that I have my own modest following.'

'You have indeed, cousin,' admired Gerard, exuberantly, 'and if it weren't for the fact that I am forced by convention to be ashamed, I should be proud of you.'

Cassy chuckled, but she was pleased by the ambiguous compliment from the young gentleman, whom she finally prevailed upon, despite his and their aunt's misgivings, to go so far as to approach Coates about the matter.

Two days later Gerard returned to Worthing with the tidings that Romeo would pay a whole hundred guineas to secure the support of Cassandra for his one momentous appearance. Cassy could not afford to renounce what sounded like a fortune in their reduced circumstances.

The seats for the performance were already sold out, and rumour had it that Prinny himself would attend. The Brighton wags told each other that the Prince Regent, with his penchant for dressing up, whether in Highland dress or field-marshal's uniform with multifarious orders ablaze on his portly bosom, would bid fair to rival the stage Lothario.

13

As it had not seemed worth while to recall Louise and John from London for the few days of rehearsal before *The Fair Penitent*, Romeo Coates's offering, Cassy had accepted Dolly's invitation to stay with her in Brighton. Her sisters were told that she was to spend a few days with a colleague from the seminary.

She arrived in Gerard's chaise at Dolly's rooms, this time without mishap and was surprised at their lavishness. 'I am glad you like the place, Cassy,' said her ex-understudy, pleased. 'I could not have afforded this in the ordinary way, and am only newly moved here for a holiday. But a gentleman of my acquaintance helps me with the rent, as he likes to visit me now and again.'

Cassy had a fair idea who the gentleman would be, but was sure his innate sense of suitability would preclude his visiting his particular during her friend's stay.

Dolly confessed that she had herself applied for the leading role opposite Coates, whereupon Cassy exclaimed with dismay, 'Oh, my dear, don't say I have spoiled your chances again!'

'If you have, Cassy, I am glad,' Dolly answered, 'for I was dreading the ordeal if I had been accepted, and now my finances are greatly improved, you understand.'

Cassy understood the situation quite well. But she felt a sincere compassion for the girl when she heard for the first time about her early, disastrous marriage to a good-looking, aristocratic French emigré, who turned out to be a deceiver and a drunkard.

'I would decide to leave him,' she said, 'and then when he told me he was sorry and made love to me I weakened and could not go. We started off with plenty of money he had brought from Paris, but that soon went and I was compelled to act in breeches in a booth attached to an inn at Kensington to keep us both.

'Then when our baby son arrived I used to carry him from tavern to tavern to try to get some money out of my husband. By that time I no longer felt anything for him but contempt.'

Cassy was horrified. 'How terrible for you, Dolly! Where is your son?'

'My mother takes care of him in London now that I am earning and can pay her a small allowance. I see them both whenever I can. But my son is five years old now, and I fully intend to keep from him any knowledge of his father's – and mother's misdemeanours. Do I shock you?'

'Not a bit. I have learned too much about life and the lot of women to be easily shocked.'

'My husband, Marcel, is always intercepting me now and trying to get money.' She chuckled suddenly. 'He once got a friend to report his death to me and get the money for the funeral, which I paid up thankfully. I discovered the supposed corpse at the stage door a few nights later roaring drunk!'

The two girls laughed until tears rolled down their cheeks. Cassy thought suddenly how rewarding friendship with a character like Dolly was, and that she would never have met such a vital, if confessedly immoral, person had she not decided to make her way, like her companion, in the only way she could.

'I have decided one thing, Dolly' Cassy said firmly. 'I am going to take you in hand from now on. You shall learn, because you are an actress, to speak like a lady so that you can undertake a greater variety of roles. I shall also teach you to read and write when we return to London, so that you do not need to have a part read and re-read over to you in order to memorise it, as you do now. Will you let me help you?'

'Cassy, I should be for ever grateful,' she rejoined in her expressive but rough voice.

Cassy could hardly believe her eyes when she saw Romeo Coates for the first time descending from his incredible conveyance at the stage door, whither she had been drawn by cries of 'Cock-a-doodle-do' from the street arabs that surrounded him. He advanced towards her, the sunlight glittering on rings, buckles, buttons, brooches and sword hilt. He clasped her to him in an overpoweringly violet-scented embrace. 'My fellow stage idol!' he gushed. 'Come, we will rehearse. Be assured that Brighton will remember us.' In the event he was right.

Coates himself played the 'haughty, gallant, gay Lothario', the role in which Garrick had made theatrical history. But this actor was undeterred by possible comparisons. 'Am I not greater than Garrick!' he announced to the fascinated Cassy, who was to be his Callista. He had experienced considerable difficulty in getting anybody besides herself to act with him. A tall, skinny boy with a whine and a bad cold played Altamont and a man with a voice like the bark of a dog was to be Sciotto.

The rehearsals were a cross between a romp and a country-house charade, except that, in Cassy's opinion, the acting at the latter would have been superior.

On the night, excited reports filtered back-stage. The Prince Regent had gone to London to plan his gala evening at Carlton House, but the Duke of Clarence was in a box with Mrs Jordan. Edmund Kean was in the front row with Byron, Allingham and Alexander Pope; Lady Melbourne was there with her niece, Annabella Milbank, who was directing covert glances at Byron; Beau Brummel had been seen, and also Lady Jersey.

Although Cassy's dressing-room was always full of flowers from well-wishers, for reasons of propriety as well as expedience she had, unlike so many others, never allowed anybody except Louise to be with her in her dressing-room while she was at her toilet. Tonight she, and the secret of her wig, were alone. In desperate fear of recognition should Marcus Stanton be out in front, she had teased and tufted the hair of her fullest peruke into a towering edifice, painted her soft lips into an exaggerated cupid's bow, drawn her eyebrows into thick arches with black pencil and rouged to a hectic flush her normally delicate, rose-petal skin. She giggled at her reflection, vulgar and alien to herself, and then shivered a little as she heard the warning bell for the first scene of this more than farcical representation of a fine old drama.

Lothario was already garbed in white satin, which did little for his solid figure, sallow complexion and general sad lack of looks. He had painted his cheeks a uniform bright pink to simulate the flush of youth of the spirited hero he thought he was portraying.

Cassy found him pathetic as well as ridiculous, but she felt a moment of pure terror as she heard the ironic cheers and crowing that hailed the rising of the curtain. The heat of an August evening in a packed auditorium struck her like a blow. Then, as her leading man ambled laughably and incongruously about the stage, a feeling of unreality enveloped her and a sense of humour came to her rescue. She was not sure whether she was in a nightmare or a comic dream as she supported the rest of the pitiable cast.

The death of Lothario brought blessed relief. Coates writhed in agony and the audience cheered; he staggered and gasped to the accompaniment of more heartening laughter; he dropped on one knee and made the most extraordinary noises. Finally he fell on his back with a resounding whack which shook the stage.

So far so good. The celebrated or notorious in front of the house pushed into Romeo Coates's dressing-room and would have invaded that of Cassy, had Gerard not stood guard stalwartly outside.

Cassy was deathly pale beneath her absurd *maquillage*, her head spinning. She did not stop to change her sequinned gown or to wipe the paint from her face but bundled herself into a voluminous cloak and capacious bonnet, prepared, with her cousin, to run the gauntlet of the curious crowd at the stage door.

Romeo Coates was still holding court within, and she would, had she been in a state to consider the situation coolly, have done better to have waited and slipped out while he was acknowledging what he would doubtless consider the worship of his public in the narrow street. Instead, impatiently waiting for the sad fool, those waiting made do with her, betrayed as she was by the grotesque paint she had omitted to remove.

Gerard did his best to protect her. But jeering faces were pressed up against hers and obscene remarks shouted at her; she was jostled, clutched and pulled hither and thither until she felt her senses reeling.

She thought she heard a peremptory voice ordering the mob to clear a way. Then she fainted, and Gerard told her that the Marquis had gathered her up as she began to fall and that the crowd had backed away as he carried her into a waiting carriage and installed Gerard and himself beside her limp form.

He bore her up the steps of his nearby house as though she were a featherweight. Startled lackeys opened doors and he deposited her gently on a sofa, while Gerard put a cushion beneath her head. The housekeeper was summoned. But before she could arrive Cassy's eyelids had lifted and an expression of relief had crossed the pretty features that not even the garish colours could disguise. She looked up into unwontedly concerned hazel eyes, reached for His Lordship's hand, clasped it and drifted off into unconsciousness again.

She woke some time towards morning to find herself ensconced in a vast Chinese tent bed in a luxuriously appointed bedroom. For a moment she imagined she must have wandered into the Royal Pavilion and gone to sleep as she regarded the red lacquered furniture and the wallpaper whose pagodas and bridges were illuminated by the early sunshine.

A pleasant, plump woman bent over her, 'There you are, deary,' she said comfortingly. 'You will be as right as a trivet now that you have slept. You had a nasty shock.'

'The Marquis—?' Cassy began to question her and then stopped, for her head was aching so.

'His Lordship bore you in here and told me to stay beside you. You are to rest now, which you will do better with your eyes closed rather than looking at all those heathenish colours His Royal Highness persuaded His Lordship to have. But first let me undress you and sponge off that mess you have daubed on your face.'

She obediently suffered the dress to be removed and replaced by a prim nightgown the housekeeper told her the Marchioness used when visiting her son at Brighton. She allowed her face to be washed like a child's, but put a hand to her head when the woman would have combed her hair, saying with an apologetic smile, 'Please, not now, for my head is hurting!'

'Poor child! The Marquis would not allow you to be disturbed last night, and just covered you with the quilt. He has asked the doctor to call later this morning. I am Mrs Farquar, the housekeeper. His Lordship has gone out and will see you on his return. I have never met an actress before,' she added irrelevantly, as she tied the last ribbon on the very proper bedgown. 'Lord Allingham does not usually keep them here.' She put a dimpled hand to her mouth, aghast at her own indelicacy.

Cassy laughed a little weakly. 'You see, without the greasepaint I am much the same as any other girl.'

'But prettier than most,' the lady smiled.

'Mrs Farquar, I was to spend the night with a friend—'

'Don't worry. The young gentleman who accompanied you here with His Lordship promised to bring her word of your whereabouts. Try to sleep again now like a good girl.' This Cassy thankfully did.

When she woke the second time it was to see an elderly gentleman regarding her, as well as Mrs Farquar, who introduced him as the doctor. After a brief examination during which Cassy worried as to whether her wig was straight, or askew and revealing her golden hair, he pronounced paternally, 'You will do now, young lady. Stay where you are for the present and get up when you feel stronger.'

Cassy thanked him but was privately resolved not to trespass on the hospitality of the Marquis any longer. He had been so kind to her already. She would not like him to think that she was presuming on the fact that he had come to her aid. Obviously nice Mrs Farquar judged her to be one of his Paphians.

When they had left the room she smiled to herself and was just about to climb out of the extraordinary bed when there was a tap at the door. She murmured 'Come in,' and felt her heart hammering against the ruffles of the demure gown as she saw the tall form of Lord Allingham. He was dressed for riding in burnished hessians, buckskins and a superbly cut dark coat that sat easily on his broad shoulders.

'May I?' he requested, and without waiting for her permission, placed a chair at her bedside and sat down with a slight smile. For a sudden moment the thought occurred to her that he might be unscrupulous enough to take advantage of her under his own roof. But she did not wish to believe it. He must have read her mind, for he said, 'Mrs Farquar is hovering outside, should you wish to scream for help, and your loyal friend Gerard is downstairs waiting to visit you and to share my lunch.' He grinned disarmingly at her and she was made aware again of the strong and highly regrettable attraction he held for her. 'You looked to be smiling to yourself when I came in,' he said, 'so I hope it means you are feeling much better.'

'Oh, I am. So much so that I had already decided to remove myself from this wondrous bed, to put on my peculiar gown and to thank you, as I do now most truly.'

'Anything I did for you was a privilege. Were you smiling at the bed?'

'That,' and with a sudden rush of mirth, 'the fact that your housekeeper took me for—'

'One of my bits of muslin? In my mother's nightgown too!' His eyes were sparkling with unholy amusement while he thought to himself how paradoxically provocative the high-necked garment was on her exquisite little figure. Her face after the refreshing sleep was enchantingly dewy and youthful above the elderly robe. The beauteous Lucia Maris never looked like this when she awoke.

99

Aloud he simply said, 'She should know me better than that,' which remark set her to wondering whether he meant he would not bring his mistress to stay in his own house, or that she herself did not measure up to his high standard.

His eyes twinkled at her again as if he guessed at her uncertainty, and he told her in a friendly way, 'When you emerge from that admittedly bizarre bed, my housekeeper will bring you your own clothes which Gerard collected for you. We will both be waiting below to drink a toast to your return to health – that is if you feel strong enough to rise.'

She smiled, thanked him again, assured him she did, and, when he had gone, rushed to the mirror to see if her wig was in place. It was, although she had forgotten the chaotic coiffure she had conjured up for herself the night before. What must he have thought of her? If only Mrs Farquar would leave her to her own devices so that she could try to adjust it to a less extravagant and unsuitable style! But her prompt entry confirmed the fact that she had indeed been hovering just outside the door during His Lordship's visit.

The housekeeper, however, having buttoned Cassy into a simple, lavender-sprigged gown, did accept her assurances that she could do her own hair. She was not, after all, a lady's maid, and the delightful actress's head, looking surprisingly like a bird's nest, was beyond her capabilities to put in order.

So Cassy snatched off the offending wig, wishing dear Louise were present, and did her best with it with the aid of nimble fingers and the silver-backed brush and comb she found on the toilet table. As a result of these efforts the two gentlemen awaiting below surveyed her, the one with cousinly approval, the other with admiration.

The two drank her health in canary. But Cassy, fearing a recurrence of the headache, refused it in favour of the milder refreshment she in any case preferred. She had not, however, expected a scolding after the gracious toast.

'Now Cassy,' started the Marquis sternly, 'why were you so addle-brained as to lend yourself to the piece of foolishness last night? We expected it of Romeo, and went there to mock him as he deserves. But for you ...'

She coloured unhappily and looked at Gerard as if for inspiration. But that young gentleman, whose carefully contrived stock still failed to approach that of his host, merely looked uncomfortable. There was nothing for it but to tell the truth, since she could hardly inform somebody who had rescued her from, at the least, unpleasantness, that her reason was no affair of his. So she blurted out, 'I needed the money and Mr Coates was very generous.'

The hazel-flecked eyes rested on her thoughtfully. Then he asked quietly. 'Did your previous earnings not suffice?'

Gerard looked even more embarrassed, and, unthinkingly, stammered, 'I would - have helped.' Then seeing His Lordship's eyes resting with a hint of disapproval on his face, he coloured, and wondered if the older gentleman had read confirmation in his outburst of the romantic interest the whole of Brighton doubtless suspected him of having in Cassy. But the Marquis said simply, 'I am sure you would, Gerard. You are very proud, Cassy. That is why I reproached you. You cannot have relished your experience.'

She felt the sudden sting of tears and looked down before she could meet that quizzical regard. 'I did not, sir, but it was worth it.' She did not add, as she might, that to the monetary gain was to be added one step further in her acquaintance with one whose wife she could not now be, and to whom she would never be anything else.

She forced herself to take a lighter tone and soon had her two companions laughing at her description of Romeo Coates's stage directions to his fellow players, which could be summarised in one order - 'Leave the centre of the stage to me and never stand in front of me.'

After the delicious meal, Gerard said he would conduct Cassy home in his curricle.

'Then do, my dear boy, convey her with care,' begged the Marquis with a humorous inflection that reminded Gerard of the mortification of their meeting on the Worthing road. However, there was no doubting the fact that he was a complete hand, as witness not only his handling of the circumstances of the spill with Cassy, but the awkward situation last night. He did not appear to have any evil designs on Cassy either, which was fortunate.

Their host helped her on with the redingots of twilled silk which moulded her slender waist, and she arranged her bonnet herself with great care over her head.

14

Cassy had thought of asking Gerard to stop at Dolly's lodgings so that she could bid her friend farewell. But she changed her mind, since it occured to her that Thomas, knowing her to be absent, might well be in residence. Not for anything would she discountenance either of them. Dolly deserved a little happiness, and she would not easily find a nicer protector than Thomas, unless it be the Marquis himself. But 'nice' was perhaps hardly the correct epithet to apply to His Lordship. She wondered if La Maris found him as contradictory as she did herself. She experienced an irrational pang. This weakness must be overcome. She engaged Gerard in animated conversation until the feeling passed.

Gerard drove Cassy to Worthing as carefully as the Marquis had bidden him and, her sisters having been invited to tea in the garden of their friends' house, he was able to share with his cousin the fun of watching Aunt Letty's expressions as she was told of the play and the events that followed it – merriment, distress, thankfulness and specu-lation, in that order.

After the departure of Cassy and Gerard the Marquis requested his tolerant and devoted steward, Tibbs, who had served his father be-fore him, to bring the port. As His Lordship did not usually partake of this libation at midday Tibbs hazarded a guess that something had upset him. But his employer was not so much upset as amazed at the emotions a girl could produce in one supposedly immune.

He drank slowly and very thoughtfully, eyes gazing – whether into the past or the future Tibbs could not know. But he watched his master, to whom he was much attached, out of the corner of his eye. Surely His Lordship could not have lost his reputedly stony heart finally to a woman of the theatre, however ladylike and delightful her aspect.

After a while Tibbs saw, with some relief, his employer rise decisively from the table, cold sober, shake his head and murmur, amusedly, 'What a coil!'

The hundred guineas solved the immediate financial difficulties, and Cassy was able to enjoy the rest of her short holiday in the bosom of her family, which seemed to have extended to include Marcus Stanton and his daughters. But they all dealt so well together, and he apparently accepted her as another adopted niece, that she was quite content it should be so.

It transpired that he had indeed witnessed the singular performance of Romeo Coates and his unfortunate fellow players at Brighton. His description of the action from the point of view of the audience made her laugh inordinately, and she was delighted that the girls should share the fun.

After their return to London Cassy was offered the lead in a revival of Sheridan's *The Rivals*, and she was glad of the chance to prove herself as an actress at Drury Lane, in the part of Lydia Languish. She hoped subsequently to appear there with her dear Joe Munden in this year's Christmas offering, *Harlequin Hoax*.

She settled back in her lodgings with Louise and John as soon as rehearsals started, and now Dolly came to her twice weekly for elocution lessons, and to practise her reading and writing, in all of which she was proving herself an apt pupil. She was still the understudy, but, at Cassy's request, the management would give her a leading role once her diction was improved.

Rehearsals were going well and she was enjoying the companionship to be found in the Green Room, the luncheons with a merry crowd at Dubourg's in the Haymarket, visits to the Pantheon pleasure gardens, and suppers at Grillion's or the Clarendon, where the great chef Jacquard reigned supreme.

Outside these fashionable centres, as at Steven's Hotel and Long's in Bond Street, could usually be seen thirty or forty saddle horses or tilburys with the occasional cabriolet, and Cassy knew that Lord Byron, the Marquis of Allingham, Beau Brummel and their coterie were frequently of the carousing company there, when they did not join the racy, mixed society of the theatrical sets.

Cassy always brought Georgie, the child named for the Prince Regent, a toy or some fondants. She marvelled that his father could bear to leave such a sweet wife and child. But Dolly would have a successful future in the theatre if she could learn to speak correctly, or, as she described it herself, 'in a la-di-da' manner. As young Georgie was now sharing his mother's lessons in reading and writing, rivalry produced rapid progress.

The only cloud on the horizon of Cassy's present full and challenging life was a new succession of menacing notes. The first, received shortly after her return, read, 'Why should you have fame and fortune?', which puzzled her by its pointlessness. The next announced, 'An eye for an eye and a tooth for a tooth', which meant even less since Cassy could not recollect that she had been the cause of anybody losing an eye or a molar. Taken metaphorically, she supposed she could be thought responsible for Dolly losing the part of Prince Charming in *The Little Glass Slipper*. But she and Dolly were firm friends, and the other girl was intelligent enough to realise the advantages of improving her education and thus her earning potential. The third contained but one word, 'Beware!'

Cassy tried not to think about these sordid missives, and to regard them as what she was still sure they must be, the product of a misguided practical joker. But they left her depressed and preyed on her mind. She was tempted to confide in Gerard. But that volatile young gentleman had already enough to tax his powers of discretion regarding Cassy without giving him more secrets to keep. Besides, what could he do to guard her against possible danger of so unspecified a nature?

But there were festivities ahead to divert Cassy's attention from the ravings of a deranged person. The Prince Regent was to give a fête for two thousand at Carlton House. The Peace of Paris had been signed on 30 May and the occasion had been intended originally to be a peace celebration. But preparations for it had taken so long that it was decided that peace was a circumstance to which the public had become accustomed. So the point of it had been changed to centenary celebrations for the accession to the throne of George I, founder of the dynasty, combined with homage to the Duke of Wellington. However, nobody really minded what the excitement was about as long as the joyful events actually took place.

The great John Nash had been commissioned by Prinny to provide gay buildings of a temporary nature for the occasion as additions to Carlton House. In St. James's Park Nash had built a Chinese bridge over Charles II's long canal, with a huge pagoda in the middle and pavilions at each end.

Regent Street, the gracious thoroughfare that he had planned for his patron to link up Carlton House with Regent's Park, also bore witness to his art and to the Prince's own vision of a beautiful London. The old crossroads had now given way to a circular point called Regent's Circus, and the new shops along the streets leading from it had fronts with delicate curves to repeat the circus effect.

Cassy was flattered to be invited with other artistes, like the Mundens, to the gala evening at Carlton House. She was secretly also delighted to be included in the party formed by the Marquis of Allingham to foregather at his Grosvenor Square residence and attend the festival together.

The Marquis welcomed Joe, Jessie and herself, and then greeted Lord Byron, who came just behind them with a lady on each side of him and a resigned look on his face.

From rueful remarks passed by the poet it emerged that his one-time love, Caro Lamb, had arrived helter-skelter from her Irish retreat on the news of his possible nuptials only to find Lady Oxford in possession of his person and his parlour. Since both ladies remained, Byron had brought the two. Cassy and Jessie were vastly entertained by the looks of venom exchanged between the slender Caro in well-damped white muslin and the mature Lady Oxford, whose opulent curves were encased in amber satin. Of the impervious object of so much feeling, Jessie said in an undertone to Cassy, 'He really is "The Corsair" himself!'

Jessie was looking her best, like all the women present, in ruffles of cream lace, and she complimented Cassy on her soft silk robe of an unusual pale peach shade in which her lovely shoulders and arms were revealed as being of almost the same delicate shade and texture. Her wig had been arranged in soft curls with a ringlet falling softly on her left shoulder.

Many of the gentlemen were as colourful as the ladies, Edmund Kean in a peacock blue tail coat over his white knee breeches, Byron in his favourite olive green and Joe Munden in rich burgundy. But the Marquis succeeded in looking, to Cassy's mind, the most notable of all in black and white.

It was to be expected, however, that the Prince Regent would outdo his guests in magnificence, and when their particular party descended from their cortège of carriages and was escorted past the colonnade of the palace and the pacing guards, expectations were confirmed. His royal purple coat was of velvet, his knee breeches violet and the decorations on his chest sparkled like the stars which shone above the royal park.

Chinese lanterns hanging in the tall trees, as well as the moonlight, illuminated the lawns as the guests strolled in the balmy, scented air of a late summer evening, Cassy with the Marquis beside her. He appeared to have constituted himself her partner, and even if it were only because of the absence of his paramour, she could not help feeling a private satisfaction.

The supper room was hung with golden silk, and gold and silver fish swam through a marble channel of water down the centre table.

After the supper there was, inevitably, waltzing, and Cassy had no thought of the morrow as she danced with the Marquis under the great chandeliers of the royal ballroom and later walked with him arm in arm beneath the stars in the fairyland outside the palace, where a hundred violins filled the night with melody.

Cassy, as part of her sweet exaltation, was glad she was, temporarily at least, not of the ton. As one more shameless actress she was free to dance with the Marquis time after time as she had done so unabashedly this evening, and to wander, oblivious to the stares of those that recognised her, with the same tall gentleman's hand in hers.

He steered her at last to a rustic seat in an arbour where the flowers matched the pale moon and wafted their cloying fragrance to them.

Cassy gave a great sigh and her companion raised an interrogatory eyebrow and asked, 'Was that a sad or happy sigh?'

'Oh, happy. I shall always remember this evening, even when I am old and grey.'

'My dear, you said that as if you thought that there would be no more such evenings for you. And I am sure, on the contrary, that there will be many.'

She smiled up at his unwontedly serious look and said, 'But it is for Cassandra to foretell the future.'

'Nobody believed the poor girl when she foretold the fall of Troy.'

She laughed. 'No, they didn't! How frustrating for her! But I did see a happy future for you. Do you remember?'

106

'Very well.' He looked at her intently. 'I hope, Cassandra, that you obtain your heart's desire.'

'Oh, I shall not get that particular thing, but I shall make a satisfactory life without it.'

'Cassy, Cassy, I wish I knew what was in your mind,' he said with the gleam in his eyes that she watched for now. Then he remarked lightly, and the gleam changed to a wicked twinkle, 'You have chosen a lovely and most unusual colour for your gown. It matches your skin and makes you look as if you had just risen from your bath. You see!' He laid a finger over a narrow ribbon shoulder strap and the soft skin next to it. She felt her cheeks redden and her skin where he had touched it seemed to burn. He smiled, kissed her hand and drew her up, saying, 'Now let us go and watch the fireworks near the bridge.'

In the display they saw the incandescent ships of Trafalgar, and Wellington's profile. The pagoda in the middle of the ornamental bridge poured forth showers of rockets. Suddenly, to the horror of the watchers, the tower burst into flames and a man leapt into the canal and lay sprawled on a floating stage, followed by the crack that signified the collapse of most of the pagoda. Women screamed, and Cassy, overwrought as she was by the excitement and emotions of the evening, buried her head on His Lordship's shoulder and sobbed.

His voice was as unhurried as ever. 'Stop it, Cassy. There is nothing to be done. The man is being recovered, though I fear it is too late for him.' He led her away from the crowd, which watched now for the most part in motionless fascination, to where it was quiet and dim.

'Sweetheart,' he said, 'you are ruining my coat. Look at me.' She did so, trembling, her eyes swimming. He dabbed her face dry with his silk, Cologne-scented handkerchief.

'What did you say, sir?' she asked.

'I told you to stop drenching my coat,' he said teasingly. He took her damp face between his hands and kissed her lips as if experimentally, then tenderly and then deeply. He drew her yet more closely towards him until their arms were round each other tightly, and they kissed again.

She could feel his heart beating against her and came suddenly to her senses. He must think her by now yet another easy conquest from the theatre. Perhaps this was how one received a slip on the shoulder. But he smiled very tenderly and said, ' "Sweetheart" was what I said. Let us find the Mundens and see if they are ready to leave the festivities.' Still holding her hand he drew her towards the palace.

Joe and Jessie, tired and surfeited, were only too pleased to accompany them. He directed the driver to Cassy's abode, where the light in the window proved that Louise was waiting up for her as she insisted on doing despite the girl's protests. The Marquis accompanied her to the door, bowed formally and bid the highly impressed Louise a polite good-night.

'There you are at last, Miss Cassy, looking as if you were moon-struck. Come and drink your milk. What a handsome gentleman!' She peered at her, hoping to draw her charge into a comfortable prose.

But Cassy, bemused, returned, 'I am so tired, Louise. I shall tell you all about it in the morning.'

Before she slept she touched her mouth with a finger, seeming to feel yet again the soft, insistent pressure of his kiss.

She was forced to face the ironic fact that she loved with a mature passion the man who might have been her bridegroom, had she wished it. But she knew now that by accepting his dutiful addresses she would never have come to know the real person as she felt she did now.

She understood only too well how it was that a woman of her despised profession might accept his temporary protection. She would not do so herself for such a course would offend every precept she valued. But marriage to him being out of the question, the temptation of belonging to him completely, even if only until his fancy wandered further, could be all too seductive.

She understood how Dolly, fettered as she was by a disastrous marriage, and so much in love with Thomas, could welcome the joy and completion of her association with him. He was charming and considerate, but the end of the affair was implicit in the beginning. When he married he would deal generously with her.

Cassy thought that she would flee the city were she able, and the pleasurable pain of seeing the Marquis again. But the play was to open at Drury Lane in September.

15

The Rivals was reasonably well received and Cassy's performance in it praised by some. She was popular with the critics as well as the audience. But she was bound to agree with the one who wrote that her interpretation of the character failed to measure up to the performances of the great actresses who had taken the part of Lydia Languish in the past. But she was particularly grateful, after her experience with Romeo Coates, not to have been the target of scoffing comments.

The Mundens had arranged a supper party for Cassy and friends at the Clarendon. Jacquard had excelled himself with his creations of *boeuf tremblant, matelote* of eels, larded guinea fowls, *peu d'amour* and other masterpieces.

Cassy's spirits were effervescent. The play looked to be a tolerable success and her supper companions, including Lord Allingham, were congenial. Merriment was occasioned by Lord Byron's rejection of all the splendid dishes in favour of hard biscuits and soda water.

'But you do not appear to be fat,' puzzled Thomas.

'Perhaps not now. This is a healthy day. I like to live by extremes.'

'One had noticed the fact,' commented Joe with some amusement.

'I sparred with Jackson for exercise this morning, and with Julian, who has learned his punches too well from the *Emperor of Pugilism!*' He smiled at Allingham. 'Fencing and play with the broad sword never tired me half as much.'

She glanced with surprise at the Marquis. She knew he had been a soldier, but his apparent prowess in the ring added another dimension to his image.

The object of her thoughts smiled at the eccentric poet. 'Your other extreme is of course your membership of the Hell-Fire Club.'

'Whatever is that?' enquired Cassy.

There was a general laugh and Allingham told her, 'It is not so much a club as a way of going on – members indulge in desperate, romantic, blasphemous revels continued loudly and obstreperously into the night, followed by fencing, shuttlecock, the practice of marksmanship – shall I go on or do you see the scene?'

'I could hardly fail to,' she laughed, and Byron grinned deprecatingly, and changed the subject in the abrupt way he had.

Having bowed to Edmund Kean and Charles Kemble, who were at another table, he stated positively, 'Kemble performs the role of Hamlet. But Kean *is* Richard III.' Others at the table took issue with him over the remark and Cassy saw the eyes of Lady Oxford fixed on the poet.

Dolly had a small part in the play, and she was vividly happy to have been included in the party tonight, with her lover smiling and attentive beside her.

Alexander Pope, who made one of their party, had, as was his habit, kept quiet out of respect for the sacred rite of eating. Jacquard himself had emerged at one moment from his domain to enquire anxiously about the *boeuf tremblant*. Pope considered the matter, then gave his verdict – 'Perhaps a little, just a very little, too *tremblant*.' Jacquard nodded his high-capped head as if in confirmation of his worst fears.

Gerard, the new man about town, had discovered what he described as 'a prime piece of goods'. She was a gorgeous red-head, who was a principal dancer at Covent Garden. She simpered up now into his young, ingenuous face like the eighteen-year-old she had not been for many a year. Cassy could not like her and looked at her cousin with affectionate concern. But perhaps he would settle down the better as a country squire with his pretty neighbour if he first experienced the bitter-sweetness of love, city style.

Meanwhile, in a quieter circle, Miss Page was as confused, uncertain and conscious of as many racings of the blood and thumpings of the heart as her eldest niece – emotions of which she had long since ceased to consider herself capable.

She was re-established now with Thea and Grace in the London house and lessons had started again. They had all been sorry to leave

Worthing, the gallops over the Sussex downs, the outings and the sociable meals with their new friends. Marcus Stanton had settled his daughters back in town too, preparatory to setting forth on a further provincial tour followed by a sortie into Europe, now the war was over, in search of ideas and contacts in his particular field.

So, a period that had brought back with it the rush of sweetness she had known in youth had been succeeded by quiet resignation. She supervised her nieces' education and the household, occupations long accepted as providing a sufficiently satisfactory life. But these had now become strangely flat. How could she have dreamed that, at the advanced age of seven-and-thirty, she would be longing for the tones of a man's voice which she had first heard declaiming some nonsensical lines on a stage some twenty years ago; that the inadvertent contact with this person when he lifted her down from her horse would have set her trembling. She had even in this ridiculous condition of second flowering fancied that his heart beat as hard as hers did, and that his regard was one of tender wonder.

Thea and Grace found their dear aunt surprisingly strict these days in the schoolroom and were as confounded by the energy with which she organised a frenzy of house-cleaning. Still, as Thea remarked to Grace, 'Grown-ups are incalculable.' Grace looked at her elder sister with some respect: She had not come across that word before. But Thea who was literary, obviously knew it meant Cassy's absent-mindedness and faraway look when not recalled to the ordinary world of family talk, as well as their aunt's vagaries. Thea herself had heard the adjective applied to the deliriously diverting and devastating Lord Byron, whose appearance and reputation had caused her to struggle through some cantos of *Childe Harold*. She had not understood all, but had been stirred by the sound of the words.

Two visitations in one week gave Miss Page food for thought. The first was a morning call from the Marchioness of Allingham. Letty was pleased to see her old friend, while being as always wary of questions concerning Cassy.

After affectionate greetings the older lady declared, 'Letty, your sojourn at Worthing may have been dull, for I am persuaded it is a lamentably dreary place. But the sea air has brought a glow and sparkle to your looks I have not seen for many years. Where are your little nieces?'

'In their schoolroom, in the throes of doing the sums I have set them. Gratiana manages them with ease though she is younger, while

111

poor Althea is in despair at the sight of a numeral, as was Lucasta. But Althea can already compose a pretty sonnet while her sister is almost illiterate!' She was conscious of running on about the attributes of her nieces in an unaccustomed way as if to ward off more references to Worthing and her holiday there.

But Her Ladyship's attention had been diverted by the mention of Cassy. 'If she does not shine at figures one would not have thought a scholastic establishment the most suitable background for Lucasta.'

'One would be justified,' agreed Miss Page hurriedly, 'were it not that she teaches only ladylike accomplishments such as elocution, deportment and dancing.'

'Yes, I remember now that you told me so. She would shine at such subjects, she is so graceful and has a particularly pleasing speaking voice. I hope she does not give instruction in the waltz. I know it is much in vogue, but I cannot accept the propriety of circling the ballroom clasped to a gentleman's breast.' She shuddered, but added smiling, 'I am forced to admit that my son finds my disapproval antiquated.'

'No, I am persuaded that she does not teach the waltz, just the quadrille, the cotillion and,' searching for inspiration, 'a little Greek dancing, I believe.'

'Quite unexceptionable. Why do I never see her? She must have some free time, and I like to think I was her dear mama's friend.'

'My sister loved you, as I do,' Miss Page assured the gracious lady in all sincerity. 'But I fear the headmistress is something of a slave driver, and as Lucasta is unusually well remunerated for her services she does not care to cavil at the lack of vacations.'

'I hate to think of the poor, pretty dear being forced to earn her living thus,' deplored the Marchioness.

'So do I,' said her aunt truthfully. 'But she seems content, and though I would prefer her to marry, she is most independent and swears she will only do so if and when her heart is engaged.'

Lady Allingham sighed and Miss Page looked at her curiously. 'I wish her heart were engaged with Julian, for I am of the opinion that he and little Lucasta would deal splendidly together. He tells me he considers rejoining the colours, for he thinks that Bonaparte must reappear and require another drubbing before his ambitions are finally thwarted. You can imagine how that makes me feel! Just the one child, and he spends his spare time racketing after actresses and other dubious damsels. That is perhaps only to be expected as a phase. But I do not think he is happy, Letty. If he married he might renounce his military leanings and take over the management of his estates. At the least I might have the joy of a grandchild as consolation were he to perish.'

Miss Page understood and was sorry for the older lady whose fine hazel eyes, inherited by her son, were wet. But before she could speak words of comfort the latter added, 'I want all of you, Lucasta included, to spend Christmas with us at Allingham Park. Julian always panders to me by coming there for a day or so over the festive season. He took such a liking to your younger nieces and I feel certain – call it a mother's instinct if you like – that should he and Lucasta have the opportunity of making friends in a natural way my dearest wish might be fulfilled. Should it not, I shall still have the pleasure of your company.'

Miss Page was at a loss after this appeal. She could not hurt her friend by an outright refusal. But Cassy had already told her that she hoped to procure the feminine lead in *Harlequin Hoax*, in which case it would hardly be worth her while to post into Oxfordshire, even if it were not for the probability of instant recognition by the Marquis and his mother.

However, it was still October and much could happen between now and December. So she temporised. 'How lovely that would be, Maria, and how kind of you to ask us. I shall certainly bear your invitation in mind and mention it to Lucasta at the first opportunity.'

After the Marchioness had left, however, and on mature reflexion, Miss Page resolved not to tell her nieces about the invitation. She would not like the younger two to be disappointed at her refusal, and she feared that strong-minded Cassy might try to persuade her aunt to accept it. Apart from a disinclination to be away from London and her eldest niece at Christmas, she dreaded the necessity of telling her old friend a further string of untruths.

Later that same week Aunt Letty was hearing her nieces recite alternate verses of *The Lady of the Lake* by Prinny's literary favourite, Sir Walter Scott. Thea put a considerable amount of expression into her words for she loved poetry. But Grace, who did not, stumbled over the lines and delivered them in such a wooden way that her aunt showed irritation. 'You could do better than that, Gratiana, if you did but try,' she snapped.

'I am not Cassy!' said her youngest niece pertly.

'What do you mean by that?' asked her aunt sharply, suspecting for the moment that the little girl had guessed her sister's secret.

'She teaches elocution, doesn't she!'

'Yes of course, dear. I have the headache this morning and I suggest you both get out your drawing pads and see if you can copy this vase of chrysanthemums, while I go and take a posset.'

The girls looked at each other significantly. There was no doubt that their dear, mild and lenient aunt had not been at all herself lately. She suffered from unaccustomed indispositions and was changeable and irritable. They dreaded that she might be really ill, and resolved to put their fears to Cassy when they saw her at the week-end.

Miss Page felt ashamed of her impatience. She should by her age have learned to curb it, and had thought to have done so until quite recently. She had been lucky to have had a happy home with her sister and, even after the tragedy, to have been able to keep her nieces with her. She must exercise more self control.

A coach drew up outside as she drank the draught on the parlour window seat and the cause of her uncertainties and dissatisfactions mounted the steps in his quick way. As Grimble opened the door she put her hands to her flaming cheeks as if to cool them. But they were still a becoming rosy colour as Marcus Stanton was ushered into the parlour. She had thought him departed on his travels and the surprise made her voice shake a little as she exclaimed, 'Marcus, you are here!'

He laughed boyishly. 'I hope you do not mind. But I have come to ask your advice, my old friend – who looks this morning so very young.'

This sort of remark did nothing to calm her nerves. 'Really, Marcus!' she said with a small smile.

'Should I spare your blushes? But you were already pink as a rose when I entered. I thought to find you closeted in the schoolroom.'

'My nieces are drawing, and I have allowed myself an interval. How can I serve you?'

'My governess has been called home to a sick mother. She is no great loss. But with my imminent departure I cannot leave Marcia and Honor to the possibly far from tender mercies of a new one, even if I had time to go through the procedure of discovering her. I must send them to the seminary where Cassy teaches. Is that not a sound notion?'

He was looking at her for approval and she could think of no way but one to extricate herself from yet another of the quandaries that so constantly confronted her.

114

She took a deep breath. 'No, Marcus. Cassy tells me that the standard of education there has dropped. You see, the headmistress is to retire and, I suppose, has lost interest. There is even some question as to whether the school will stay open.' She was conscious of burbling, but he looked disappointed until she said, 'Would you not rather in such circumstances let them come to me to share lessons with Thea and Grace. I believe that your daughters still have their nurse and a staff to take care of them at home.'

The face that seemed to her to have become but more handsome with time beamed at her, and he put his hands out for hers. 'I would never have asked this of you, Letty. But it is difficult to tell you how relieved and grateful I am for your suggestion. My little girls will enjoy the company of their friends, and I rejoice that you and they should get to know each other even better. You see – but now is not the time; I think you read my mind, and heart.'

She dared not admit to him, or to herself, that she did, for fear of being mistaken. But, now that she had committed herself, there was an oddly sweet satisfaction in being able to have his children, part of him, under her guidance.

'I shall inform you of the fees I shall pay you, for you are still a green girl about business and are like to cheat yourself.'

She could not deny this, and was aware that, practically, the supplementary money would help them all and put less of a burden on Cassy. Her nieces would derive positive benefit from a little competition in their lessons.

She thought he was going to kiss her hand, as was his custom, before he left. But instead he kissed her on the brow. She gasped and while her mouth was still open he kissed it quickly, saying, 'I cannot be sorry for leaving you even more adorably flushed than when I arrived. My daughters will be here on Monday at nine. I shall return to spend Christmas with them and you and your nieces too, of course, before sailing to the Continent. Au revoir – my dear one.'

He was gone and so was Letty's headache. She felt much relieved, and guilty as a result that she had already decided to refuse Lady Allingham's invitation. She returned to the classroom in a trance-like state and praised extravagantly the vases of flowers drawn by her nieces. They were somewhat surprised since their conference concerning their aunt had, they thought, prevented them doing themselves justice.

They were delighted with the news of the addition of their friends

115

to their classroom. 'But won't the extra work tire you and give you more headaches, Aunt Letty dear?' enquired Thea solicitously.

'Why no,' answered her aunt. 'I am feeling much improved already.'

She did look better too, thought Grace. Thea was right. Grown-ups were – whatever the word was. She had forgotten it again.

16

Cassy in Russell Street suffered – an apt description as it happened – another visit. She was ensconced one afternoon with her feet up on the sofa in her small sitting-room. She had been reading with gratification the much-improved exercises provided for her correction by Dolly and Georgie. She had decided with a degree of amusement that she was at last justifying her own description of herself as a teacher.

Louise scratched at the door and announced a lady, with the faint air of disapproval, which she was so good at expressing, to give the lie to the description. Cassy rose to greet the red-headed beauty to whom she had taken an instantaneous dislike when she had met her escorted by Gerard at supper at the Clarendon Hotel.

There was no doubt, Cassy thought on closer inspection, that she was a piece of perfection. Her abundant, shining hair crowned a face whose alabaster complexion was illuminated by calculating but admirable green eyes. She was puzzled by the unexpected arrival until the visitor, whom she guessed to be some five or six years older than herself, explained her purpose.

'I have come to talk to you frankly, Cassandra, since our circumstances must be somewhat similar, though I have my own establishment with my personal maid.' Her hard eyes took in the clean, comfortable, if simple, room with an air of disparagement. 'In case you had forgotten, my name is Sybil Lane. I am a ballerina, appearing just now at Covent Garden. I dance the principal role in two of the short ballets.'

Cassy, looking at her lissom figure, could well believe her. But she

117

wished her caller could realise that such vivid loveliness as she possessed were better displayed against a less ornate background than the violet velvet pelisse with gold frogging and the hat, also of lilac, with too many ribbons and flowers. She had the impression that the other wished to impress or outdo her. It was also a pity she had to speak at all, since her voice, from its high pitch and coarse accent, was bound to spoil the first impression.

She sat down at Cassy's suggestion and continued, in startling fashion, 'It is about Gerard.' Cassy's face stiffened. 'Oh, don't poker up. It is common knowledge that he has been your beau and still dances attendance on you whenever you call the tune. But it would seem you now have the Marquis of Allingham as your protector. Don't bother to deny it. I saw you look at each other at the Clarendon. I want you to leave Gerard alone. He is in love with me and pays me regular calls.' And allowances, thought Cassy realistically. 'But he thinks he still owes some allegiance to you' – the green eyes flashed – 'and I won't have it!'

'Allegiance?' echoed Cassy, astounded by the outburst. 'Yes, perhaps, that of a friend of many years' standing. But I swear to you, Sybil, that he has never been romantically involved with me.'

'I don't believe in friendship between men and pretty young females,' stated the red-head definitely. 'I want him to stop coming to see you.'

'Then you must tell him so,' responded Cassy coolly. 'I shall certainly not reject his friendship, which is all he feels for me. If you do not believe that you must solve your problem in your own way. Now, if you will excuse me—' She rose to see the unwanted guest to the door.

'For all your ladylike airs and graces you are no better than I am!' was the parting shot. 'And, from your whereabouts,' she looked at her surroundings again, 'not even as good.'

Louise returned after Sybil's departure, bringing Cassy's tea as an excuse to vent her feelings. 'There's a brazen one for you,' she said. 'She almost knocked me down as she strutted past me.' Cassy had not known whether to be diverted or disgusted by the conversation. But now she laughed. 'She doesn't know any better, Louise. She wanted me to stop Mr Gerard coming here or escorting me out.'

'Your very own cousin!'

'She wasn't to know that and I could hardly tell her. But she is decidedly ill-bred.'

'Surely, Miss Cassy, she is not Mr Gerard's style!'

'Well, Louise, I have discovered that the women that gentlemen fancy when they are on the town are not usually the style they marry.'

'I should certainly hope a fine young gentleman like Mr Gerard would have more sense than to take that one to wife,' Louise sniffed.

'I am quite sure he would,' said Cassy. But in this she was to be proved in error.

She was wryly amused to find that Gerard must have taken heed of the strictures of the woman who was, she guessed, his first amour. He came to see Cassy and her family at the house at Lowndes Square on Sundays but rarely now came to her lodgings or to the Green Room as he was used to before the advent of Sybil. When she did see him he was abstracted, evidently taking his love affair to heart. Remembering the red-head's predatory gleam and seductive looks she could appreciate his preoccupation whilst missing his companionship.

Because of his defection she omitted to confide in him, as she would doubtless otherwise have done, that an anonymous letter of a more explicit character had now reached her.

It had read, 'If you do not want your family to know your shame, meet my emissary outside Mr Wickes's Gold and Silversmiths in the Haymarket, *alone* at three of the clock this Thursday. Bring twenty guineas in your reticule and pass it over. No more shall be heard from me.' Again the writing was in capital characters and decorated with blots as if the quill had been dipped in a standish whose ink had thickened and run dry.

Cassy felt a chill. Whoever her blackmailer was, he must know of her background and her need to keep her identity secret. Only Sarah Siddons, Gerard, Louise and John knew that she desired to keep her aunt's and her sister's lives quite separate from, and unsullied by, her connection with a profession which was despised even by those who greatly enjoyed going to the play.

The Great Sarah, Edmund Kean and a few others were received perhaps, but even these luminaries were looked upon as somewhat in the nature of alien creatures. It was rare that a gentleman married an actress, and in such an event both would have to overcome much prejudice.

Cassy made her own decision, for she did not want to worry the Mundens, who had already done so much to help her. She would keep the sinister assignation and see who the blackmailer's emissary was. She could come to no harm in a public street. As for the money, she could not and indeed would not pay it, for she was not so bird-witted as to think that the demands would end with payment of the first.

She decided to walk from Drury Lane on the fateful afternoon, though to do so unaccompanied was to invite stares. It was a bracing autumn day with sunlight and scurrying clouds and she would have enjoyed the exercise had it not been for its cause. She had purposely dressed in the least conspicuous way she could devise, in a dark brown pelisse and bonnet to match with a deep poke that shadowed, if it did not conceal, her face.

However, the Marquis, walking briskly across Regent's Circus towards the same small street, saw the slight figure and neat attire with an appreciative eye, which changed to a frown when he recognised Cassy's charming features, set as they were with purpose.

Her thoughts elsewhere, she did not notice the elegant figure in the pale pantaloons and corbeau-coloured coat of superfine until she saw him walking towards her, and marked sub-consciously his military bearing and gait despite his appearance of a Bond Street beau. She flushed, as she always did with surprise or embarrassment, a fact that never failed to annoy her. However His Lordship found this endearing and enquired amicably, 'No escort, ma'am? May I remedy the lack?'

'Oh— oh,' she stammered. 'No, it is not at all necessary.'

'And I do not think it at all suitable for a lady to jaunter about town alone,' he countered with seriousness beneath his teasing tone.

She answered quickly and with dignity, 'I am not jauntering, sir. I have a - destination. Furthermore I am not a lady. I am an actress, as you well know.'

He smiled at her so that she felt her skin warming to colour again as he responded, 'For me you are both.'

'Thank you, sir,' she tried to say lightly, but she was in fact grateful for his words. 'You are gracious. I should appreciate your escort just as far as the Haymarket.'

'The Theatre Royal?'

'No.' Having no time to fabricate a falsehood, she told the truth, 'I go to the jeweller's at the corner of Panton Street.'

'Mr Wickes, under the sign of the King's Arms and Feathers. Indeed he has taken many of my guineas too.'

Trinkets for your lights of love doubtless, decided Cassy with a stab of something alarmingly like jealousy.

'Not for adornment for yourself, I imagine,' she said aloud, and smiled a little.

'Well no,' he rejoined. 'I am glad to see you can smile by the way, for you looked at first to be suffering from an overwhelming melancholy. Now let us walk together, for I am bound for the little shop beside Mr Wickes, where I buy my snuff.'

In truth she was grateful for his company and almost inclined to confide in him, until she remembered the special reasons why she could not. They passed the little theatre, then Dubourg's, the Hotel de Paris, the oyster bars and the Orange Coffee House, and finally, at the sign of the Rasp and Crown, the Marquis raised his hat, promising to look for her when he had completed his business, and disappeared into the small shop, whose owner bowed low and immediately produced, from among the many mixtures, His Lordship's special sort.

While the wizened shopkeeper filled his snuff box and a supplementary jar, the Marquis went to the doorway to see if Cassandra was in the jeweller's shop whose royal charter dated back to the time when George III was Prince of Wales.

But as Cassy arrived she was far from considering the impressive record of the place designated as her rendezvous. She hovered outside, looking at the gleaming pieces mounted on velvet. The next moment a seedy-looking fellow in a coat of cut that had become shabby, and with a dissipated countenance that yet retained its fine features, took hold of her arm roughly. 'Hand over the money and you will hear no more of the affair,' he rasped in a voice that held a vestige of some indefinable accent.

Cassy gave a suppressed shriek and pulled away. But as the other put his arm out towards her again the Marquis was suddenly at her side and the fellow ran down an alley-way beside the swinging sign of the Orange Coffee House.

Allingham drew Cassy's arm through his. 'You are shivering,' he said. 'Let us walk quickly, as I suspect you do not plan a purchase here today.'

'No, I don't,' agreed Cassy in a low voice, not far from tears. 'I wish I could explain. But I – can't.'

'I regret the fact,' commented her companion, 'because you are distraught and I should like to stand your friend. By that, my dear, I mean somebody you can trust – you understand?'

'Yes,' said Cassy, and was grateful for the frank way in which, she realised, he was informing her that he would not offer her a *carte blanche* with his friendship, and for the comfort of the pressure of his arm and his company, when she was so shaken.

'I would like to confide in you,' she added, 'for you have already proved yourself a friend. But my problems concern others beside myself.'

'I see. What about Gerard? Can you not enlist his aid?'

'Gerard,' she twinkled up at him now, 'is lost in love with another actress, not with me, whatever the tattlemongers might have said.'

'I never took him for your lover, if that is your meaning,' said the Marquis airily. 'Too callow by half! But he is, or was, a good watchdog. Don't tell me his particular is the fair – or should I say, flaming – Sybil!'

'I fear it is. But I suppose he must be allowed his youthful adventures.'

'Yes, grandmama,' assented His Lordship, 'but he has found himself over-rich fare.'

Cassy was glad to be able to laugh again. 'Then I hope he may soon suffer from indigestion. There is such a sweet young neighbour at home in the country, who is only waiting to grow up enough to marry him.'

'Is there indeed!' said the Marquis with a glint of amusement. 'Lucky Gerard!'

Cassy recovered herself enough to add, 'At least he tells me she is.'

She sometimes marvelled that she had never quite given herself away to this very astute gentleman. Then it occurred to her that he never asked her any awkward or direct questions. Probably he was not interested in her sufficiently to do so, except as a pretty girl to kiss in the dimness of a scented garden.

Now she said, 'Please do not trouble to accompany me home, I am all right now, and it must be out of your way.'

'It is. I was going to pay my tailor and then to the War Office. But the former can wait until the morrow to receive the unaccustomed bounty of pay within the sennight, and I find walking on such a day preferable to sitting at my desk. I hope, after your encounter with that ugly customer, you will not jaunter, or otherwise walk abroad alone again.'

'I shall engage not to do so, nor to pity your tailor who is, I believe, Weston.'

'How would you know that?'

'Because your cousin Thomas told Gerard so when he enquired. He also mentioned that he had taken his custom from Stultz where my – where a friend of mine used to go.' She had so nearly said, 'my father' that it was clear that the shock had addled her wits.

'I must be flattered, I suppose, to be the subject of discussion,' he responded easily. 'The Prince of Orange has lodgings over Stultz, you know, while he is waiting to pay his addresses to the Princess Charlotte. But the *on dit* is that she prefers the handsome Prince Leopold to the Dutchman.'

When they arrived at Louise and John's house Cassy looked up at her tall companion. 'I accept your offer of friendship,' she said, 'and I thank you.'

'You need not. Just bear in mind that a friend can be trusted. You know my direction. If you need me I am at your service.'

Having gained the privacy of her room Cassy threw herself into a chair and considered the afternoon. The frenzied look of the shabby man who had accosted her outside the jeweller's had engendered in her a sort of disgusted pity as well as fear. She was convinced in her own mind that he was the actual blackmailer.

Then she thought of the Marquis who was to be a friend and nothing else. It was, after all, perfectly acceptable to love one's friends. Unfortunately she was convinced that she had by no means heard the last of the blackmailer, and that this particular friend could not be asked to help her.

17

It was a relief for Cassy to be with her aunt and sisters on the next Sunday, their gay young voices distracting her from the matter preying on her mind, as they told her about the welcome invasion of their schoolroom. They were so full of the jokes they had played on each other, and of comparisons between their respective school marks that they forgot to ask her the usual barrage of questions. For this she was grateful, as in her present anxious state of mind it would have been difficult to find satisfactory answers.

When they were alone, however, Aunt Letty told her concernedly, 'You look so tired, my dear. You have been working too hard again, or not getting enough sleep. Which is it?'

'I am a little weary,' Cassy admitted, 'because now that *The Rivals* only runs a little longer we already have rehearsals in the mornings for *Harlequin Hoax*. Luckily my part in the pantomime does not require much study, and the songs are simple and catchy. I suppose,' she said with a smile, 'that I must arrange to be ill one afternoon so that the girls can attend a performance. I really could not go through all that daubing of grease-paint again. But what of you, Aunt? Do you not find teaching four pupils twice the trouble of two?'

'Strangely enough I do not, for the rivalry between them stimulates them to greater efforts.'

'I am glad. I agree that the money their father is paying is a boon, so absurdly generous as it is. He must be in love with you!' Cassy had been funning, although she had long suspected Marcus Stanton of a stronger feeling than admiration for her aunt. But she was unprepared for the fiery blush with which her sally was greeted.

'Oh, poor dear!' she cried contritely. 'You and I both have this stupid complexion that colours up for the least thing. I was only teasing. But,' she added thoughtfully, 'might he perhaps have a *tendre* for you? It would not be strange.'

Aunt Letty had regained her calm and answered with a smile. 'I shall be honest with you, Cassy. I do think he may be considering a proposal of marriage. I do not delude myself that he has not felt the need of a second mother for his daughters. But were that all ...'

'Is it not then, dearest of aunts?' enquired Cassy with seeming innocence.

Miss Page looked down, as bashfully as a young girl. 'I do believe he finds me – attractive to him still.'

'Still, Aunt Letty?'

'We were very much in love with each other twenty years ago when we were young. I had not the courage, I am ashamed to say, to go against the wishes of my family and face the ignominy of marriage to a player.' She put out a hand impulsively to Cassy as if to beg her pardon.

'I am not sensitive on the subject, I assure you, Aunt Letty, and I do understand.' But she thought privately that she herself would, in her aunt's place, have faced the ignominy. She took the outstretched hand. 'And then?'

'Then he went away, and I never found another whom I could love.'

'Then you do love him still,' said Cassy triumphantly.

'I never stopped doing so. But there will be little time for romantical scenes since Marcus will be away in the north until shortly before Christmas and in the New Year he is for Europe. Let us not discuss the matter any more lest you set me blushing again. Please, Cassy, do not mention the subject in front of the girls. It would quite destroy my authority.'

Cassy said reproachfully, 'As if I would!' and added ruefully, 'More secrets!' But she did not tell her aunt that the secret weighing most heavily upon her at the moment was the latest anonymous note she had received which commanded her, since she had not paid up, to renounce her role in *The Rivals* or 'take the consequences' – whatever that might mean.

Gerard arrived later in the highest of spirits and engaged in his usual cousinly chaff with the girls. He would not stay beyond four o'clock as he announced that he had an engagement for the evening. Cassy had no doubt of its nature, and hoped the disillusion would not make Gerard suffer too much when his ballerina found a protector with more wealth, more address and more consequence, as one day she undoubtedly would.

All three of us, Aunt Letty, Gerard and I, are in love, she reflected with wry amusement. To her, love seemed like a see-saw, pitching one between bliss and misery. At the moment Gerard was at the high end, and she wished sincerely that her dear aunt might always stay there. Dolly too would suffer bitterly when Thomas married, as was inevitable, and she wondered if her friend's present happiness would have made it all worth while.

Thoughts of Dolly made Cassy wonder for a moment why she did not relinquish her part in *The Rivals* to her understudy for the last two weeks, and take a rest before the pantomime started. But to do so would be to obey the order of a mad man, and what might he demand of her next? Besides, a player who deserted the cast without strong reason would be suspect in the future. She shivered suddenly.

In spite of her disquietude Cassy enjoyed the rehearsals for *Harlequin Hoax*, for Joe Munden's clowning in the pantomime extended to his periods off stage and laughter was never far away.

However, one evening during a short period alone on stage in the course of *The Rivals*, a full bottle was hurled at Cassy's head from the front of the pit. It burst harmlessly at her feet, splashing ale on the boards. The culprit, she was informed later, had flung himself out of the fire exit from the theatre before he could be apprehended. She realised that she could have been hurt had the missile met its mark, and that it was not the impulsive action of a playgoer enraged by a poor performance. The audience had been appreciative, laughing when they should. She was competent and well-liked. The assailant must, she felt sure, be the writer of the notes, expressing his displeasure at her disobedience to his instructions.

She carried on with the performance after a minute as if nothing had happened and was consoled by a personal ovation at the end of the play. There was general indignation back stage. But Cassy made light of the incident.

However, she still had Louise to face in the dressing-room. She was in tears. 'Miss Cassy love, she wailed, 'what would your lovely mama have said? You might have been killed if the bottle had hit your head. This life is not for you. It must end.'

'Well it will, Louise,' she said calmly, putting an arm round the dresser's shaking shoulders, 'just as soon as I can see things at home the way my mama and papa would have wanted them. Now, hush up, do, and tidy this peruke for me before I face the stage door.'

She did not know whether to be pleased or dismayed when the Marquis and his cousin Thomas arrived at her lodgings the next morning before she left for rehearsal. She received them in Louise's seldom-used downstairs parlour, for it was her policy never to entertain gentlemen, even, for appearances's sake, Gerard, in her own sitting-room above.

'Cassy,' began Lord Allingham sternly, 'this is the outside of enough. Dolly told Tom that there was a deliberate attack on you last evening.' He looked at her appraisingly, noting her unusual pallor and heavy eyes. 'You are to tell us what is going on and what we can do to help. It is obvious that you have an enemy, but not why.'

Thomas nodded his head vigorously. 'Cassy, please be sensible.'

She sat down abruptly. 'You are both very kind. Since you ask it, I shall entrust you with the information in confidence, that I have been receiving threatening anonymous letters.'

'Can you tell us why?' asked Thomas.

'No I cannot,' said Cassy, 'because I do not know.' She was determined to repay their gesture by being as honest as she could within the inevitable limits. 'But, among nonsensical warnings, two were explicit. When I encountered you, sir,' she addressed the Marquis, 'I was on my way to see a so-called emissary of the writer to whom I had been ordered to pay a sum of money in order to protect – my name – from scandal. Needless to say I had no intention of paying, even if I could. But I thought I might recognise somebody.'

'And did you?' His Lordship looked at her intently.

'No, the fellow you saw was nobody I knew, though I have assumed that he was the actual blackmailer. Recently I received a missive warning me of an unspecified danger if I did not immediately give up my role in *The Rivals*. None of it makes sense to me, I promise you.'

'The latest threat least of all,' agreed Thomas in a puzzled manner.

Cassy managed a smile. 'You comfort me. I was persuaded I could not have been so offensive in the part, or I would have received notice to quit before now.'

'I think you should leave the cast,' said the Marquis decisively.

'There are only a few weeks of the play to run, sir, and I should consider myself craven if I gave in to intimidation at this juncture.'

Lord Allingham regarded her with a frown between his brows. 'Cassy, Cassy,' he complained, 'what an over-independent and foolish young lady you are! Did you at least keep the letters? Where and how were they delivered?'

'No, I am afraid that I considered them filth and destroyed them. They came by ordinary mail to my lodgings. They were written in capital characters on cheap paper.'

'So,' said Thomas, 'there is no help there in tracing the sender. Cassy, if you will not retire from your role before the end of the run, will you promise to let us know if you receive another threat?'

'I do promise it. I feel much more comfortable now that I have shared my fears with – two friends. Now I must hurry to rehearsal, else my pay will be docked.'

'My curricle is outside,' said the Marquis. 'I shall deposit you at the stage door on the instant.'

So Cassy arrived at the rehearsal promptly, and Joe, having heard like all the rest of her ordeal, made it his business to chase the shadows from her face with quips and drollery. Dolly was especially sweet and suggested, considerately, that she and Georgie should forgo their lesson which had been arranged for that afternoon so that Cassy could rest.

'I shall lie down a while, Dolly, before the show. But bring Georgie round as usual for an hour first. I enjoy having you both.'

Dolly's improvement in speech was remarkable, and she had been given a small speaking part in *Harlequin Hoax* which should lead to bigger roles next year. She was deeply grateful to Cassy for her guidance. But the latter considered that Dolly's own efforts had been praiseworthy, and that her association with the aristocratic Thomas had probably also effected a faster rate of progress, since the actress was a natural mimic. It was a happy Dolly who brought her handsome young son to Cassy's sitting-room that afternoon, the only gentleman, as his mother told him with a grin, who was honoured by admission to this inner sanctum.

When after the departure of her satisfactory students Gerard arrived to commiserate with Cassy after her shock, she told him, as she could not the other gentlemen, the complete truth of the matter.

'The whole business does not begin to make sense,' he summed it up. 'I can only assume that somebody has taken the trouble to follow you to Aunt Letty's house and make enquiries about your relationship with a respectable family. But the attempt to make you renounce your present role seems pointless. However, I personally will be greatly relieved when you give up this pretence. I wish I had seen more of you lately. It might have deterred this madman if you had at least the appearance of possessing a protector. But, you see ...'

'Don't bother to explain, Gerard,' Cassy said. 'I understand perfectly well that Sybil would not appreciate your attention to a supposed rival.' She had no intention of mentioning his mistress's visit. Why should she disillusion her cousin so soon in the character of his love and darken the glow in his eyes?

But she was riveted by his next words. 'Cassy, you will be my friend and champion me with m'mother and m'father. I intend to marry Sybil. How could I not! But they will not easily accept the fact. You have seen her, so you know how utterly perfect she is, and I can assure you that her mind is as lovely as her appearance.'

Cassy was thunderstruck. She knew Sybil from observation and repute as an unscrupulous schemer, and Gerard as an ingenuous and credulous young gentleman, inexperienced in dealing with her type. This marriage must not take place, not just for the sake of his family and the suitable neighbour with whom his married life would be potentially happy, but also for his own. However, adverse criticism of his beloved could only antagonise him.

'Have you actually offered for her and been accepted?' she enquired.

'Oh, yes. Is it not above all things wonderful?'

She answered his transports by saying drily. 'You must do what you think right, dear cousin. But oblige me, if you wish for my support, by taking time to think. Remember that you do not inherit your competence until you are twenty-five. I hope you mean to be quite open with Sybil, who is indeed beautiful, about your means and circumstances. Remember she earns a good salary, with the likelihood of more. Can you be sure she is prepared to give up all this to become the wife of a moderately prosperous country squire?'

She knew that suggestions about his duty to his lineage and consequence could only incite revolt. So she concluded kindly, 'I ask you only not to act hastily. Whatever you should decide, you know I shall wish you happy.'

He looked somewhat deflated but could find no cause for annoyance in her mild and reasonable homily. He went away with his eyes still blinded by the light of love, and Aunt Letty told Cassy the following Sunday that Gerard had brought his intended bride to see her. 'What a brassy piece,' was her description of Sybil, very similar to the words of Louise. 'It is not that she is of the theatre. I am hardly in a position to criticise that. But were she the daughter of a duke, which she so

129

patently is not, I should not care for her. Nor, I noticed, did Thea or Grace. She could hardly bother to address them and they were quite silent in her company.'

'I can imagine,' answered Cassy with feeling. 'I am of your exact opinion. I hesitate to interfere and risk a breach with Gerard, but I shall take counsel with a friend, and see what can be done to show my misguided cousin his beloved in what, I am persuaded, is her true light.

'I hope the consultation may produce results. But it would do no harm were I to write a letter to your Aunt Sophie suggesting she summon her son home on some pretext, in the strong hope that he may find there the means to mend a broken heart!'

18

Cassy decided that there was only one person who could advise her what to do about Gerard's disastrous attachment to Sybil, and that was the Marquis. He had, after all, offered her assistance together with his friendship and, though he did not know that Gerard was her cousin, he understood him to be a friend of long standing. So she sent him a *billet* by John requesting him to oblige her by calling on her at her lodgings.

He arrived the following afternoon and, in her gratification on Gerard's account for his prompt response to her summons, she could ignore the fact of her own gladness to see him. She had the desire, irrational in one professing to be self-sufficient, to cast her troubles on his broad shoulders and, worse still, herself upon his breast.

She contented herself, however, with saying, 'Sir, I am happy to see you. I need your advice.'

'It is yours for the asking, and my friends call me Julian.'

'Yes. What am I to do to prevent Gerard from marrying Sybil?'

'You put the question succinctly. I shall answer as concisely. You leave the matter to my direction. What a chawbacon the boy is! We start by forming a merry party, six of us perhaps – you and I, Dolly and Tom and the lovers – to go to Astley's Amphitheatre tomorrow. There is a late performance we can attend after your respective productions end. You may enjoy the entertainment in addition, I hope, to achieving your object.'

'Indeed I shall, for I have never been there and I hear that it is famous fun, sir – Julian.'

He threw back his head and laughed. 'You make me sound like

Sir Galahad. We shall collect you and Dolly from Drury Lane and then proceed to Covent Garden for the – flaming foe. Any more threatening letters?'

'No, I am glad to say.'

'Good. Until tomorrow then.'

Cassy could not help looking forward to the next day, even if the expedition were but a means of executing a plan, until she reminded herself that, if it succeeded, Gerard must be hurt. She wished that, just this once, she could appear with her own corn-gold hair.

But when she emerged from the stage door with Dolly they looked, thought Tom and the Marquis, as handsome a pair as could be found. Dolly's vivacious face was framed by a dark green velvet bonnet to match her cloak. Cassy wore the matching hat and pelisse with sable collar of the particular soft blue which so sweetly flattered her eyes.

But when the carriage arrived at Covent Garden to collect the third couple it was clear that these two were outshone. Sybil was resplendent in a raspberry-pink cape and hat with a long plume curling on one cheek, as if to claim her ability to wear with triumph a colour that few red-heads dare. Gerard, beside her, looked, Cassy thought, part proud, part embarrassed and very much the boy. A diamond flashed on the dancer's left hand which, thought Cassy, Gerard could ill afford. She looked magnificent, but Cassy spared a rueful thought for the effect such an apparition would have on Gerard's very proper parents.

She caught a gleam of amusement in his eyes as the Marquis looked at the approaching couple and then at Cassy's face. She asked herself, not for the first time, how he succeeded in laughing with eyes alone.

When the greetings were over, Sybil took obvious stock of her rivals, deciding with evident satisfaction on her own supremacy. She tucked her arm through Gerard's possessively as they entered the vehicle.

'I am so pleased at the prospect of seeing the wonders at Astley's,' exclaimed Cassy unaffectedly.

'Did you never go there before?' asked Thomas surprised.

'No, probably because I was a country child. Since my removal to town the opportunity has not presented itself.'

'I remember the first time I saw a circus parade,' said Dolly, smiling at the memory. 'I was very small, and I pushed through the legs of the people in front to watch the great Sergeant-Major Philip Astley himself in military uniform, and mounted on his famous horse,

Gibraltar, leading the procession. I can still see in my mind's eye trumpeters, circus riders in costume and, in the rear, in a small conveyance a so-called "learned pony", distributing handbills.'

'I recall the same,' laughed Thomas, 'and my amazement that an animal could be so perfectly trained.'

'Better still,' contributed the Marquis with a reminiscent smile, 'was the sight of Philip Astley with Billy "his little learned military horse" riding together like two old cronies in a hacking cab.'

'Oh no!' protested Sybil, giggling loudly.

'Oh yes! I remember informing my father that I wished to be a breaker and trainer of horses too.'

'What did he say?' asked Dolly, amused.

'He took me to Astley's to see Billy dance, feign dead, jump through hoops, ungirth his own saddle, wash his feet in a pail of water, play hide and go seek, calculate, set a tea table, lift a kettle of boiling water off the fire and make tea for the company.' He took a deep breath and there was general laughter.

'Did that not dampen your ambition?' asked Cassy.

'Not at all. I practised for hours at home with my own pony. But he was a slowtop and the results were not encouraging.'

She laughed, and His Lordship was out of all reason pleased to see the cares lifted from her face, even temporarily. 'So you gave up?' she enquired.

'Yes, with regret. Having failed so dismally as a breaker and trainer of horses I decided to be a circus rider instead.'

Thomas groaned in simulated suffering. 'I remember that phase only too well because you tried to persuade me, tot as I was, to stand beside you on your poor pony.'

'How unkind in you,' Cassy chuckled, highly diverted.

'You cried craven!' the Marquis accused his cousin.

'Wisely, because after you had fallen off twice you decided to stick to hunting.'

'The Astleys were favourites of Marie Antoinette, I believe, when they performed in Paris,' Gerard told them.

Sybil's attention had been engaged by the mention of Paris and she said now, longingly, 'How I should love to go to France!'

'Would you?' returned the Marquis as if much struck. 'I am engaged to go there for a spell after the New Year,' and, with what Cassy thought of as a devil of mischief in his eyes, added, 'Come with me then.'

'You don't mean it, sir?'

'Of course I do.'

Cassy looked with compunction at her cousin whose eyes were fixed on his beloved with incredulity. Sybil gave him a sidelong glance and patted his hand with a roguish look, saying, 'Well, sir, if I am not on my honeymoon before that time I shall be sorely tempted!'

The carriage had arrived now at the Amphitheatre at Westminster Bridge, which had been burned to the ground but had now risen finer than before from the ashes. They were ushered into a box. The Marquis, to Cassy's chagrin, until she recalled the fact that he was obliging her, seated himself very close to Sybil, making gallant play of arranging a shawl around the shoulders of her daringly low-cut gown of raspberry red embroidered with flowers in *gros de Naples*.

On a stage hugely enlarged and backed by mechanically adjusted platforms that rose one above the other, companies of horses 'died', plunged into cataracts, leaped battlements and scaled mountains. The noble animals were the undoubted stars of this part of the programme with the riders as supporting players. Cassy's eyes sparkled with excitement as they enacted the battle of Salamanca, Alexander the Great's triumphs and an assault by Cossacks. But she was aware of Sybil's fiery hair brushing Allingham's lean cheek as she turned to smile at his murmured remarks. Her face was flushed, Cassy thought, not perhaps without some bias, to much the same colour as her gown.

Only Gerard seemed not to be enjoying himself, and his cousin began to feel a trifle guilty about her own agency in causing his distress. The next moment, as she saw the red-head fluttering her eyelashes at the Marquis and the green eyes devouring his face, she was rendered more confident that his present humiliation was worth while and, a little wryly, that she had presented her problem to an expert at dalliance.

However, Sybil, desirous of retaining Gerard's attachment while relishing the flirtation and possible prospect of a more profitable prey, darted dazzling smiles at the bewildered boy from time to time and leaned over his shoulder to let him sip from her champagne glass during the interval.

Cassy appreciated Allingham's thoughtfulness in ordering a tray of tea to be served in addition. She noticed that the dancer's voice was becoming shriller and her countenance rosier.

'Gerard,' said the Marquis, 'I hear that this enchanting - red rose - is to grace your northern fortress. Shall you like it, my lovely,' turning back to Sybil, 'living among the turnips as a squire's wife?'

She hiccuped, said 'Pardon!' and then replied on a burst of laughter, 'I had rather go to Paris with you,' casting a sideways teasing glance at Gerard, who, though unsure of her real meaning, was by now sadly disenchanted.

He took no heed of the celebrated arielist, who had the rest of the party gasping as he wheeled a boy in a barrow from stage to ceiling and back again. Then Sybil was uttering shrieks of merriment as she leaned from the box to watch a supposed member of the audience insist, in pretended drunkenness, on riding in the ring. But Cassy's amusement at the spectacle as he threw off innumerable coats and waistcoats was spoiled by her sudden realisation that Gerard had slipped away. Finally the adept performer let his trousers descend, to the delectation of the laughing onlookers, whipped off his shirt and appeared in impeccable equestrian costume.

Cassy was so distracted by visions of Gerard's possible desperate reaction that she barely noticed that the rider was performing a feat of great difficulty, as Thomas informed them in an undertone. He bestrode two horses galloping side by side.

Sybil slept with her head on the shoulder of the Marquis during the coach ride back. She had appeared not one whit disconcerted by the disappearance of Gerard which caused Cassy such forebodings. Dolly and Thomas snuggled together and exchanged opinions about the marvels they had seen. 'One night, Julian,' suggested the latter, 'we should take the girls to Sadler's Wells.'

'Certainly, if Cassy would like it.'

'What and where is it – Julian?'

'It is a delightful rural garden near Clerkenwell with fountains, clipped hedges, shell grottoes and temples. You can drink the waters there, medicinal but unappealing to me personally, and take tea or other refreshments. There is also a show ring where can be viewed tumblers, rope dancers, acrobats and such. It is worth a visit.'

'Indeed it sounds so,' agreed Cassy, with her thoughts straying to Gerard.

By now they were arrived at Sybil's house, where the Marquis, having failed to awaken her, carried her with a look of comic resignation, up to the door where Thomas knocked. The woman who appeared in answer stood aside for their entrance in a remarkably matter-of-fact fashion. A little later they emerged laughing and rejoined Dolly and Cassy, who could not help joining in their mirth.

'Poor Gerard!' remarked kind-hearted Dolly. 'Both he and his faithless betrothed will have heavy heads in the morning.'

'Tom and I will push ourselves to discover his whereabouts,' said the Marquis hearteningly to Cassy. 'It will not hurt him to become jug-bitten, and you need not fear that he will do away with himself, as, from your expression, I collect you do! Tom, you are more the sufferer's age. You shall lead me to the dark dens to which you doubtless introduced him. Here you are at home, Cassy. I am pleased you can accomplish the passage to your door on your own two feet.' At the door he kissed her hand, and said, 'Don't worry!'

Gerard, sheepish, sick and sorrowful, called on Cassy the next afternoon. 'What a dunderhead I have been, cousin!' he exclaimed without preamble. 'I thought Sybil to be so perfect, so precious that I could do no other than make her my wife, lest I lose her. But I saw last night she was not at all what I had thought her.'

'I am so sorry, Gerard,' Cassy ventured on delicate ground.

'You will hardly believe it, but at first when I saw her behaviour, I wanted to do away with myself.'

'I am so glad you thought better of it.'

'Yes, so am I. It seemed to me she was not worth it.' Cassy smiled to herself. 'I was disgusted and disillusioned by Allingham too. It seemed unkind in him to say the least, seeing that he, who could have anybody, should seem to steal my love.' Tears of self-pity and the aftermath of a libidinous night came to his bloodshot eyes. 'But, you must know that he and Tom searched for me through the night until they finally found me at a club – whose very name should not sully your ears for all that you are an actress.

'In fact, the more I see of the world of the theatre and its ways the more I wish you would leave this life. Already it will be difficult for you to attend parties of the ton unrecognised. If you leave your return to the polite life much longer it may become impossible.'

Cassy was irritated as well as amused that Gerard's disappointment in Sybil should have made him so censorious and self-righteous, with little justification on his side. She thought him ripe now, if his mama sent for him, for a pure romance with the pretty neighbour. In retrospect he would consider himself the devil of a fellow on account of his London adventures.

'Did the Marquis and his cousin join you in—?'

'Drowning my sorrows? Certainly they did, though I think

136

Allingham must have a head and constitution of iron. While Tom and I were weaving our ways to bed he was bound for the War Office, appearing quite his normal self. I wonder now if he was not bent on exposing Sybil to me in her true colours, for he must be too old a hand to want her for himself! But oh, Cassy ...'

'Yes, I know,' Cassy cut his new lamentations short hurriedly. 'You will be the wiser for your experience.'

'I am already, in the ways of wickedness.' Cassy found it difficult not to laugh, since she guessed by now that he was enjoying these melodramatics. Instead she asked, 'Did the Marquis mean it when he said he would go to France in January?'

'Apparently. But not with Sybil I am sure. Cassy, what a *parti* you let go when you refused his suit!'

'I never waited for his declaration. That is very different.'

'Well, he will not make one now. You can depend upon it.'

'I do, Gerard, and I appreciate your concern. Forgive me now if I rest a while. I did not sleep for long and must look presentable for the evening performance. Let me see you again soon.'

'Of course. You know, Cassy, I consider travelling north soon on a repairing lease.'

19

The next afternoon Cassy, accompanied by Louise, sallied forth to Bond Street to do some early Christmas shopping. The charming, if expensive, custom of exchanging gifts had been introduced to England from Germany by the Duchess of York, wife of the brother of the Prince Regent nearest in age to himself.

The fine trees above the low wall separating Burlington Arcade from the street wore their autumn colours and there was a nip in the air. She had passed Long's, Steven's and the Three Pigeons inn before she was attracted to the display in a bookshop window. There were Fanny Burney's *Eveline*, Miss Austen's *Pride and Prejudice* and the newly published *Waverley* by Sir Walter Scott. Byron's poems were on view and also the latest work by William Godwin, which was supposed to be full of shocking notions which would overthrow society and abolish marriage. She smiled to think what her aunt would say if she presented this treatise to Thea, who was interested in new ideas, and entered the store to buy the unexceptionable *Waverley* instead.

Next, with Grace in mind, she browsed through the piles of sheets in the music shop next door. Her youngest sister played the piano well already, and the girls often sang together. She came away with an armful, including *Tom Bowling* and *The Jolly Young Waterman*, which were all the rage, having been written by the prolific Charles Dibdin whose sea and soldiers' songs had helped to keep up the nation's morale during the French war.

In a picture shop she was pondering over the rival merits of a series of prints by Hogarth, when she heard a warm laugh behind her, and turned to find Mrs Jordan examining the series of *The Harlot's Progress.*

'Cassandra!' she exclaimed with pleasure. 'It is too long since we met. Do you not think these delicious?'

'I do,' admitted Cassy, 'and those others, *Marriage à la Mode* and *The Rake's Progress* also. Do look at them. But since I seek a gift for a gently nurtured female' – it was Aunt Letty in fact – 'I think I should be safer with these flower prints. Do not you?'

'Without a doubt. But as I do not have to be so nice I shall buy some of these hilarious pictures for Bushey Park.'

Cassy noticed with some amusement that Louise regarded the easily recognisable actress and courtesan with awe and alarm. But the maid in attendance on this merry, fashionably clad woman was clearly proud of her position.

'Cassandra, you shall come and drink tea with me at the Clarendon, where I am staying.'

'Thank you. I should like that, ma'am.'

'I told you to call me Dorothy, as all my friends do.'

She swept Cassy with her into the nearby hotel, with the abigails bringing up the rear. She dispensed Bohea in her private sitting-room, and regaled the girl with enjoyably scandalous stories about her theatrical and amatory career.

Afterwards she patted Cassy's hand and said, 'So you see, my dear, that I have achieved success the hard way. I will tell you candidly that I was a trifle prejudiced against you because you were a protégée of the high and mighty Sarah's. That woman never did approve of me.' With due regard to the difference in their attitudes Cassy could quite see why. 'But when I got to know you I thought you an unassuming, sweet child who should be gracing a gentleman's house instead of the boards.'

'I shall never be an immortal,' Cassy admitted with a laugh. 'But I do not intend, all the same, Dorothy, to take up with any gentleman who does not care to marry me.'

'I do see. That is why I want you to come to Bushey Park again with Joe and Jessie on Sunday. It is beautiful before the autumn leaves go, and I have an idea.'

Dorothy's manner was so earnest and persuasive that Cassy felt she could not well refuse. Besides, her curiosity was aroused. So she promised, took her leave and, with a tight-lipped Louise, retraced her steps along Bond Street.

Lord Allingham was about to enter Long's and stopped to say, 'Good-day, Cassandra. I am glad to see you have a duenna.' He smiled at Louise who regarded him with equal approval.

'Have you been buying bonnets?' he enquired, seeing the parcels Louise carried.

'No, Christmas presents, and taking tea with Mrs Jordan who entertained me with the story of her early life. It was quite absorbing.'

'That I doubt not!' He looked at her almost, she thought, with disquiet.

'I am bidden to Bushey Park again on Sunday with the Mundens,' she said now.

'Then I shall see you there.' She felt a wave of pleasure. He asked finally, 'Is all well with you?'

She realised that he was referring to the anonymous note and was glad to be able to answer, 'Thank you, yes.'

A glory of russets, golds and tawny reds met their eyes at Bushey Park. There was the usual collection of theatrical personalities and other notabilities. But this time Cassy really felt that she belonged to the colourful throng.

But she had hardly had time to seek out her friends among the guests when Dorothy Jordan said apologetically to the Mundens, 'Forgive my taking Cassy away from you. But I particularly want her to meet somebody.' There was a purposeful look about her hostess that indicated to the girl that the coming presentation had something to do with the mysterious conversation at the Clarendon.

She was confronted by a gentleman who might be in his late thirties. He had fine, manly looks and a dignified bearing and she recognised him even before Dorothy mentioned his name as Charles Young. He was a leading player at Covent Garden, where he had recently triumphed as Cassius to the Brutus of John Phillip Kemble, Mrs Siddons's famous brother.

He had, she knew, the reputation of being a great gentleman as well as a great actor, and she found herself liking him immediately. He said pleasantly, 'I am very glad to know you, Miss Cassandra. I hope you are happy in your comparatively new career.' He looked at her as if he really meant it and Cassy responded frankly, 'Most of the time, I am, sir. But I am still fresh to acting and have much to learn, unlike yourself and Mrs Jordan.'

'Graciously said!' he smiled. 'But one must have a streak of grim endurance, I think, to survive in the theatre, specially as a woman. I wish you every success, if you want it!' His eyes seemed to tell her without words that there must be a more fulfilling fate for somebody as unspoiled and innocent-seeming as herself.

Charles Young took Cassy in to luncheon, and drew her out in a manner devoid of flirtation or flattery about her hopes and prospects in the theatre, offering her sound advice. She enjoyed his company, and when Lord Allingham came up to them after the meal she was about to introduce the two gentlemen when she heard the actor say, 'How are you, Julian? Quite recovered from your wound, I hope.'

'Perfectly, thank you.' The Marquis turned to Cassy with a smile, saying, 'I was privileged to see Charles's *Hamlet* at the Theatre Royal, Haymarket just before my regiment was ordered to Spain.'

'What an extraordinary occasion it was for us too!' recalled Charles Young amusedly. 'Colman, the guiding genius of that theatre, who gave me my first chance in London was in the King's Bench prison for debt. We were uncertain of receiving any payment at all. But eventually I am glad to say that we did.'

The Marquis left them laughing and sauntered off to join a faro bank while Cassy's attention was claimed by the Mundens and Alexander Pope.

The actor told Cassy at parting, 'I shall look forward to our next meeting.' It was said formally but his smile was warm, and as their chaise rolled down the tree-lined avenue Jessie raised her eyebrows at the girl in comical questioning and brought the over-ready colour to her cheeks.

'I am not surprised to see you blush,' said Joe with a grin. 'It is the first time I have seen Charles take notice of a female since his poor young wife died.'

'Oh, did she? How very sad! Had they been married long?'

'No,' Jessie answered her question. 'He married a lovely girl called Julia Grimani who had played Juliet to his Romeo some ten years ago. Fifteen months after the wedding she died having their son.'

The tragic and romantic story made Cassy think of Charles Young with kindness in spite of her conviction that Dorothy had brought them together for the well-intentioned purpose of match-making.

She found herself wishing that the Marquis, with his touch that set her blood racing and his kiss which promised yet greater rapture, had not succeeded so successfully in destroying her interest in other men.

She must have looked pensive as she thought of the parallel case of Aunt Letty, who could never be content with second best, because Joe and Jessie rallied her with their cheerful nonsense and the rest of the journey was spent laughing.

20

Now that Lord Allingham was her avowed and proven friend, Cassy no longer cavilled at making one of his party even when the Mundens were not included. She realised that his passion on the night of the festival at Carlton House was but the natural response of a normal man when a desirable girl threw herself, as she had, into his arms. She was more reprehensible than he, and they had both suffered from a species of moon madness.

Since that time he had shown her no further lover-like attentions nor any inclination to be so much as alone with her. On the contrary, he treated her with an easy camaraderie that might almost have been chilling had it not been accompanied by consideration and kindness. If he had a current mistress she did not appear with him in public. So, when he invited her to join a party for supper, a promenade or, more recently, to accompany Dolly, Thomas and himself on an expedition to Sadler's Wells, she agreed willingly.

But Dolly, lying with her lover on a fur rug before the fire late at night, was intrigued. 'Dearest,' she said lazily, 'Julian has kept a succession of beautiful women, has he not?'

Thomas continued to stroke her rippling hair as he rejoined, 'I can certainly bring to mind a number of high-flyers. Thing is m'cousin tires of them quickly.'

'As you will one day of me.'

'I cannot envisage it.'

'I know you cannot.' She smiled up at him fondly in the firelight. 'Our lives must one day take different courses, and I am grateful they should converge now for a while. I shall never reproach you, Tom. You have been so good to me.'

He was moved and, unable to find an answer, kissed her glossy head. Looking into the flames she added, 'Your cousin is ever mindful of Cassy's welfare, yet makes no demands upon her. It is difficult to fathom his motives. He would not marry an actress, would he?'

'I cannot conceive of it.'

'At the same time Cassy would never take a lover. If she would have, I am certain you would have sought her for yourself.' She looked up quizzingly through her long hair into the handsome young face.

He pulled a russet tress reprovingly and returned, 'To think what joys I might have missed with you! But I freely admit, love, that Julian's behaviour is not a little puzzling.'

They were not the only ones who found it so. When Cassy would entertain Aunt Letty with an account of her activities since their last meeting that lady would wonder at the number of times the name of the Marquis arose. He had been with her on this occasion or that; he had escorted her here or there. Finally she said, 'Lord Allingham is so assiduous in his attentions that I cannot help wondering what he wants of you. It cannot be marriage now that you must be considered to be beneath his touch and he must know you would not—'

'Of course he knows I would not—' Cassy laughed. 'He has a selection of obliging females to choose from both in and out of theatrical circles. Perhaps he simply finds me less of a widgeon to talk to than some others. I have more of his company for the present since he is, I understand, between mistresses.'

'Cassy!' expostulated her aunt.

'Well, you know his reputation as well as I do. But I confess to enjoying his companionship now that he does not wish to offer for me to please his mama.'

Miss Page looked sceptical. 'To relish the attentions of a distinguished, polished man of the world is one thing. But take care you do not discover him to be too disastrously engaging.'

'I shall try to heed your warning,' she returned non-committally.

The Sunday of the proposed trip to Sadler's Wells dawned cool and cloudy, but by the time the Marquis, as promised, had arrived to collect her in his curricle the sun was shining. He had warned her to dress warmly, and so she wore a woollen travelling pelisse of green with a close velvet collar and a snug bonnet in the same material to secure her peruke.

Dolly was already esconced next to Thomas in his own curricle behind that of the Marquis, and differing from it in its colour combination of black and yellow. She had been inspired, charmingly, to wear a warm black cloak and yellow hat to complete the scheme.

Both gentlemen, noted top sawyers, wore many-caped coats that reached to the tops of their boots and carried spare whip heads through their lapels. The other members of their party were to make their way to 'the Wells' by coach.

Louise and John came to see them all off with some misgivings. But the Marquis called down as they set off, 'I promise to bring her back safely. Have no fear!'

'I must be doubly honoured, Julian,' Cassy told him with a twinkle, 'to be taken up beside you for the second time. Perhaps you do not find me distracting.'

'I shall not,' he smiled, without removing his eyes from the road, 'if you refrain from making provocative remarks.'

So she settled to enjoy the exhilaration of the breezy drive to Islington, acknowledging yet again his skill as they swept fast but safely round the twisting lanes carpeted with the last of the fallen leaves and lined with thick hedges of briar and holly. She was impressed by the split-second precision with which he passed a stage coach on a narrow portion of the road, in his nonchalant confidence seemingly unaware of the mere inches to spare between the conveyances. It crossed her mind that his tiger must have an exciting time of it. But when the greys finally drew to a steaming halt at their destination and the small person jumped down to hold their heads, it was clear that he possessed complete faith in the Marquis and had lost not one whit of his composure.

Although it was only mid-morning, the enclosure was already full of yellow-bodied post chaises, whiskys, tilburys and curricles, with postilions and ostlers going about their duties. Their faces whipped by the wind, joking and laughing, the quartet went into the comparative warmth of a marquee where the speciality of the Wells was being served, as well as, and in their opinion greatly preferable to, the spring waters. It was a steaming negus, made with wine, hot water, oranges, lemons and sugar. They raised their mugs to each other and then strolled with the other townsfolk who were gathered to enjoy a day out. They surveyed the caged lions and tigers with their pungent jungle whiff, the magnificent school of horses in their stables and the pen of little yapping dogs which would comprise another act.

In a booth a gypsy woman, her swarthy brow adorned with a chaplet of coins, and wearing a veil and jacket of barbaric colours was waiting to tell fortunes to the credulous. 'Let's go and have our palms read,' urged Dolly, her eyes sparkling with anticipation.

The Marquis and his cousin crossed her lined palm with silver and Dolly pushed Cassy forward first. Did she, the latter wondered, really want to hear her future foretold, even if she would not really believe it?

However, by now the gypsy was intent on the small, soft palm, tracing Cassy's life line with a dark finger and turning her hand this way and that. She looked up into the girl's enquiring face and an expression of surprising sweetness irradiated her lined features. 'Whether or not you will be pleased I do not know, but you will exchange fame for a lasting love, crisis for calm. I see four children.'

Cassy thanked her, smiling if unimpressed, and Dolly took her place. There was a longer pause this time and the gypsy looked intently into the girl's bright brown eyes before she said, almost unwillingly, 'The reverse is true for you. Fame like a flame, but the embers of a lost love.'

'Fame!' echoed Dolly, paying attention only to the first part of the prognostication.

'Yes. Something I do not see in many palms. Now, the gentlemen?'

They both shook their heads emphatically and the girls, thoughtful, heads close together, preceded them out of the tent.

Outside they met the Mundens, who had come by coach and were regarding the cage of lions. To Cassy's surprise, her new acquaintance from Bushey Park, Charles Young, accompanied them together with a boy of about eight years. Cassy was pleased to see him again and he turned to introduce his son. But seeing the boy pressed against the bars he said sharply, 'Stop that,' and explained that a child had recently had his arm so badly mangled that it had to be removed.

The ladies shuddered, the boy backed away and made his bows to the newcomers with a pleasing expression that resembled his father's.

'Would you like to visit the gypsy, Jessie?' asked Dolly.

'No, my love!' the other laughed. 'I know my fate, and here he is beside me.' Joe pulled one of his whimsical faces and patted her cheek affectionately. Cassy fancied that Dolly looked, for the fraction of a second, a trifle wistful.

They all decided they were hungry and went in search of some lunch, stopping on the way to reserve the sixpenny seats in the numbered, roped-off portion of the great top where were usually to be found the people of fashion. Elsewhere the seats were threepence. Lunch consisted of another speciality of the Wells, suckling pig cooked on a spit and roasted chestnuts. Jessie and Dolly wished to try a glass of the famous mineral water, which was claimed to be a sovereign cure for rheumatism. But they pulled such faces on doing so that the others had no intention of following.

Afterwards, in the big circus tent, Charles Young sat at one side of Cassy and his son on the other with the Marquis beside him. Mr Young talked to her like the intelligent person he obviously thought her, first about the little theatre in the Haymarket's valiant fight to keep going in spite of its load of debts, and then concerning the likelihood of an unsuccessful outcome to the war being fought against the American colonists who wanted their independence from the mother country.

Cassy again found him sensible and likeable and responded animatedly. But she was also conscious of the boyish laughter at her side at some of the Marquis's observations, and reflected momentarily on the easy way he had with youngsters. He would, she thought, be a charming father, and then mentally chided herself for being sentimental. She turned her attention firmly to Mr Young, whose theory about the apparent failure of the American campaign was that the conventional tactics of the King's men were no match for the wily rangers and other defenders fighting on and for their own soil.

Now the circus was about to start and the boy, another Julian, leaned forward eagerly in his seat to see the parade of noble horses, the turbanned Indian boy riding an elephant and the tumbling clowns. Cassy, in her own enjoyment of the sight, nearly came out with the fact that she wished her younger sisters could be with her. She was distracted from the blaring of the brass, the beating of the drums and the colourful array by new doubts about their future conjured up by her passing thought of Thea and Grace.

If, she mused, Aunt Letty did in fact marry she would inevitably have her own establishment and the responsibility of her stepdaughters. It was, even, not beyond the bounds of possibility that she might have children of her own. Cassy would not dream of foisting herself and her sisters permanently on Marcus Stanton, any more than she would have on Uncle Matthew.

It became, she reflected, even more important for her to save enough money through her own efforts to make herself and her sisters independent, however often they might go to stay with their aunt and her new family. Aunt Letty deserved her late flowering of felicity without the burden of additional complications.

Cassy had a slowly growing, small account at the bank now and should by the end of the winter season be in a better financial position. She realised only too well that she must make money now, while her looks, health and stamina remained. She was under no illusion that her acting powers would gain parts for her were these three assets to fade.

By that time, Thea at least should be ready for her debut. She pictured again suddenly her own first appearance at Almack's and, with some amusement, the tall exquisite whom she glanced at sideways now as he laughed at the child's excited asides.

'I conjecture that your thoughts must be worth at least a golden guinea,' remarked Charles Young, turning to her. 'How many miles away were you?'

She laughed and answered apologetically, 'I had gone off into a reverie which would be a dead bore to hear about. Now the show has started and I am firmly back in my seat next to yours at the circus.'

'And I am glad to have it so,' he responded simply and with no apparent attempt at gallantry.

They sat enthralled while the lion tamer, dressed in his scarlet uniform, had the animals crossing over and marching, and then put his head in the mouth of one. The clowns doused each other and those of the audience nearest them with water and frequently lost their trousers. The little dogs they had seen in their pen burst balloons and sat atop trotting ponies. Seals balanced balls on the tips of their velvety noses and Madame Saqui, whom Cassy remembered seeing at Vauxhall gardens in the summer, mounted the tight rope in all her splendour of spangles and tinsel, ostrich feathers surmounting her head, and performed her special sideseat bouncing and the most graceful jumps and steps.

As they left the tent and returned to their respective conveyances Cassy noticed the boy patting the greys attached to the newly washed curricle of the Marquis. 'Why don't you ride beside His Lordship and I can take your place in the carriage,' she suggested to him impulsively. 'I am sure you would enjoy it.' The boy's shining eyes were reward enough and Lord Allingham gave a smile of assent.

'I am sure he would too,' agreed Charles Young, pleased for his son.

'Let us all meet at my house for supper then, as long as you do not anticipate a meal to tempt the fancy of an Alexander Pope. My son and I eat simple fare.' So it was agreed.

Cassy sat in the carriage in the child's place, and the obvious rapport between Charles Young and their young friend brought as much gratification to the expressive faces of Jessie and Joe as, the girl was persuaded, it would have afforded Mrs Jordan. She must be careful not to give the impression, simply because she found him conversable, of a willingness to co-operate with the well-meant intentions of her friends.

21

Naturally enough the two curricles had arrived at the house, at the other end of Baker Street from where Mrs Siddons lived, well before the carriage. As Cassy, her friends and their host entered the house they heard shouts of what sounded like a lot of children at play. Mr Young led them into a big downstairs play room where the Marquis and his cousin were seen to be crouched on the floor with no regard for the knees of their light-coloured unmentionables. They were directing a battle with the lead soldiers that his son had hurried to present for their inspection.

Even Dolly had been pressed into service to move the pieces, appointed as she was to Tom's headquarters. But it was clear that the Marquis and his namesake formed too powerful an adversary for them and the boy shouted to his father, his face pink with excitement, 'Oh, Papa, Lord Allingham is a complete hand. Such a campaign as we are waging! You would not want us to stop until the battle is won!'

The newcomers could not gainsay him, and it was clear, to their amusement, that the adults on the floor, with the possible exception of the good-natured Dolly, had no intention of abandoning it.

So, with a laugh, they left the battlefield. The ladies deposited their outer garments and Charles Young looked with approbation at Cassy's white kerseymere gown, high in the neck and long in the sleeves, whose very simplicity accentuated her pretty figure.

The appointments of Mr Young's house were, apart from the framed showbills on the wall of his earliest successes in Bath, like those of any gentleman's establishment. But Cassy was surprised to see a parasol on the stand in the hall and a woman's shady hat.

Charles Young must have seen the direction of Cassy's eyes for he said quietly, 'I hope you will not think me morbid. But although my beloved wife has been dead these last nine years, I like to keep some of her things about the house. They seem to bring her a little closer, and her spirit is a benign influence. I hope I do not embarrass you.'

Cassy felt her eyes moisten with sympathy, for he spoke so simply and sincerely that his remarks did not appear macabre, as they might otherwise have done. 'May I show you Julia's portrait?' he asked.

'Please do.'

He drew her into a small room where, over the carven mantlepiece, was the likeness of a most beautiful young woman with speaking, lustrous eyes and dark ringlets. She seemed truly to look down with kindness at them. Cassy touched his arm and exclaimed, 'How lovely she is!' Then she was surprised at herself for having spoken of the pictured girl in the present tense. But in some way, perhaps because her husband wanted it so, her presence seemed to pervade the house.

'Now let us join Jessie and Joe,' he suggested more prosaically, 'and I shall order some wine – unless you would prefer tea.'

'I would, please,' admitted Cassy, and Jessie was found to be of the same mind.

The four warriors came in from the play room as the tea was being served and Mr Young hastened to reassure the gentlemen with a smile that they were not expected to partake of it, saying, 'I have a good sherry or a creditable Madeira.'

'You relieve my mind,' said the Marquis with an answering grin, adding exultantly and with a comradely glance at his young second-in-command, 'We won the battle. The enemy was powerless against our skill.'

'That is not quite fair,' protested Thomas. 'Had you agreed to continue the fight we would have come about. But I am forced to own that my junior officer' – with a merry smile at the laughing Dolly– – 'was definitely not up to yours.'

She pouted prettily at him, the little boy looked pink and pleased and the evening continued to be agreeable, with Charles Young deprecating unnecessarily the simple but perfectly cooked supper. Young Julian had been allowed to stay up with his elders as a special concession and was full of questions for the Marquis, whom he looked upon now as his special property, about his days following the drum in the Peninsula as a captain of the First Dragoon Guards.

Lord Allingham, with a look of apology at the ladies, told him briefly something of the campaign, speaking of Sir John Moore and of Wellington with respect and affection and talking with familiarity of such places as Albuera and Corunna. He recounted some of the lighter episodes of overseas service, such as being blinded by smoke in a Portuguese cottage from the fire burning in a hole in the middle of the floor, and the skill with which they learned to catch chickens.

'Is it true that wives accompanied the soldiers into battle?' asked Dolly with interest.

'Yes, certainly, as far as they were allowed.'

'And camp followers too, I believe!' she continued and then darted a guilty look at the child, whose presence she had momentarily overlooked.

However, the Marquis answered, 'Inevitably. Personally I am against females being allowed at the battle front at all. Soldiers are well able to look after themselves and batmen do the essential chores for the officers. Women are just a responsibility and a nuisance.'

'You are quite right, sir,' agreed his namesake stoutly, which made them all laugh, since it was clear by this time that the boy was prepared to accept any observation of his hero's as gospel truth. 'You sold out, sir, did you not?' the child enquired of him now on a note of regret.

'As far as my command was concerned, yes. But I am still in the Army on what you might describe as special duties, which may involve me in some foreign travel in the future. Now, let us change the subject to one of more interest to the ladies. Come, Jessie, you choose one.'

While Jessie chose to speculate about the Princess Charlotte's possible choice of bridegroom, Cassy wondered whether Lord Allingham's military commitments would lead him into any future arena of war. Although he could never be for her other than a friend, the thought that he might again be in danger was nevertheless intolerable.

Although Cassy realised that she had been introduced to Charles Young by those good-naturedly trying to foster a match, she could not find it in her heart to discourage his friendship. He made no special effort to attach her but was always pleased to join her when he came across her in the club-like atmosphere of the Green Room at Drury Lane, or at some theatrical occasion. Eventually, however, he invited her, with some diffidence, to accompany himself, his son and a nephew of the same age on an outing to Primrose Hill.

They travelled there in a comfortable tilbury, and Cassy enjoyed watching the boys swishing through the brown leaves and running races, while she walked more sedately with Mr Young. While they watched the flight of the boys' kites into the sky of flurrying white clouds on blue, her cheeks tingling in the brisk breeze, her companion told her something of his own background.

'I was at Eton,' he told her, 'when financial troubles at home cut short my education. My father had taken to bad ways. I should not care to elaborate to one who is so clearly a lady as well as an actress.' He smiled at her gently and she was grateful for his courtesy.

'Anyway I and my younger brothers decided to take our mother away and charged myself with her support. In my spare time from clerking I did odd jobs in a theatre, for I had always fancied myself as an actor.'

'With some reason!'

'Thank you. I finally took the part of an absentee performer and acquitted myself creditably enough to receive an offer from the theatre in Edinburgh. There I met and was befriended by Sir Walter Scott, who is still my friend. At last I came to London, to the Haymarket, where I played Hamlet, and then Romeo.'

'And then you married Juliet, who was your dear Julia.'

'Yes, my dear, and I shall be perfectly frank with you. I do not think myself capable of being in love with another woman. So what I intend to say to you now I hope you will not take amiss.'

'I undertake not to do so,' promised Cassy, who guessed what was to come.

'It is because I like and respect you, and fear for you in the hard profession that, for your own reasons, you have embraced, that I offer you, not my heart, but my hand and my loyalty. No, don't speak yet.' His head was lowered. 'My son needs a woman's influence and my house a mistress. I realise you cannot care for me. But, by becoming an actress, you have, knowingly, restricted your opportunities of a grand, or even of a respectable marriage. Am I offending you?'

'No, sir,' said Cassy truthfully.

'I should like to take you away from such a fate as I feel might befall you, to keep you from wearing yourself out in a life that can destroy a woman. I do not want you to answer my proposal now, next week or even next month. I would prefer you to consider it at your leisure. Think of me, if you will, as a last resort and, whatever you

153

decide, always your friend. Oh, what a speech!' He smiled at himself and looked a little uncertainly at her.

Cassy had tears in her eyes. 'A last resort! How could I think so little of you as that? I am deeply honoured, and promise to think about your suggestion. Oh, look! Julian has entangled his kite in a tree.' Her cheeks were rosy now with emotion as well as the autumn air. But Charles Young was so adroit at leading the conversation back to ordinary topics that she was soon quite comfortable with him again. She could not imagine being able to bring herself to marry in such a case, but at least she could do him the courtesy in return of not rejecting his suit out of hand. His friendship she valued already and always would.

Charles Young was playing the role of Petruchio at Covent Garden when Cassy received the last and most terrifying note of all from the anonymous letter writer. It read simply in large black characters, 'Too late!' She was tempted to go for advice to him or even to the Marquis. But she well knew that they would both try to prevail upon her to abandon the play which was due so soon to conclude its run, or at least to report the matter to the police. But her reasons for stubbornly insisting on playing her part still applied. In any case, what could the Bow Street Runners do to protect her from a menace so nebulous? The result of applying for protection must be a lot of questioning and resultant publicity that she could not in her peculiar circumstances afford. So she kept her own counsel.

However, she must have showed her fear and disquiet for Dolly asked her before the performance if she felt unwell. Cassy laughed off her friend's concern, but took care to add a little rouge to her pale cheeks and to get Louise to chafe her icy hands before she went on the stage. But nothing untoward took place during the show.

Cassy and Louise left the stage door together as usual and the familiar hackney awaited them. The driver, as was habitually the case with John and the other jarveys, had a scarf muffled round his mouth and his cap well down over his ears against the biting November cold. It was not until they were seated in the warm interior that Louise asked through the curtain, 'Is that you, John?' There was no response. But since they were already drawing towards the house she shrugged her shoulders.

As they came to a stop outside it the driver climbed down, opened the door of the hack, pushed Louise roughly out and, as Cassy in a sudden panic went to follow her, shoved her back into the conveyance and turned the key in the lock. She flung herself at the other door, but that was already secured. The unknown driver was bearing her off at a terrifying pace into the unknown.

She screamed, without much hope, from the small window and, soon realising its pointlessness, set herself instead to watching for landmarks. Unfortunately the night was dark. But she saw the sheen of water and assumed that they must be by the river. She knew that they crossed a bridge. Then there was just a labyrinth of streets which she could tell were in a mean part of the city by the faint glimmer of candles in the windows. She tried to still the sobs that racked her and to force herself to remain calm. If she could achieve this object she must at least be at less of a disadvantage when confronted by her captor.

At last the vehicle slowed down and the clip-clop of the hooves sounded at a walking pace. Her kidnapper unlocked the door and pulled her out into a stinking pitch-black alley. He held one of her hands in an iron grip and when she started to scream hit her on the cheek, saying, 'Shut your mouth or I shall gag you. Anyway, nobody comes here at night.' A rat scuttled across her path and she stifled a cry.

He pushed open a shabby, creaking door and dragged her up some rickety stairs. Through a mist of tears she saw a dirty room containing a wooden upright chair, a truckle bed and, incongruously, a shelf above it filled with finely-bound but mildewed books. There were makeshift curtains of blanketing at the windows.

He bolted the door behind them, lit two tallow candles and threw her on the bed. Oh, God, she thought, surely this could not be an attempt at violation by a maniac? Then she recalled the letters and decided that there must be some form of reasoning behind them. He sat down on the only chair, took off his cap and removed the scarf from around his face.

It was no surprise to recognise the individual she had last seen in the Haymarket before the Marquis's sudden arrival had put him to flight. She blinked back her tears and studied him curiously.

He must have been a fine-looking young man once, and there were still vestiges of good looks in the straight profile, curling black hair and pale blue eyes in which the pupils looked as small as pinpoints. Where had she seen eyes of that curiously light blue before? His face was veined, grey-looking and prematurely lined, his figure well-shaped but too thin and the muscles slack.

155

He snarled at her with a sudden fury that twitched his mouth, 'Stop staring at me like that!' There was that trace of a foreign accent again. He added, 'You might just as well take off your bonnet and cape. You will be here some time.'

She shivered with a mixture of chill and terror and said shakily, 'It is cold in here. I prefer to keep my cloak on.' She took off her bonnet, mindful as ever, despite the straits she was in, not to upset the wig.

'As you like,' he replied indifferently. 'Now we will talk.' She noticed his hands shaking as he turned to pour himself the remains of a colourless liquid from a bottle on the battered mantleshelf. He was a drunkard, she decided, and possibly, judging by his eyes, addicted to laudanum too. Then, all at once, she recalled on whom she had remarked those distinctive light eyes, in that other case clear instead of bloodshot. Combined with dark curls, they contributed to the captivating charm of little Georgie who was named for the Prince Regent. 'You're Dolly's husband!' she said.

'Yes. You are quick as well as pretty and talented.'

'Surely Dolly—' she began in distress.

He cut her short. 'Dolly is not in this with me. She is taken up with her fancy buck and spares not a thought, nor a guinea, for her starving husband.'

Cassy felt an overwhelming relief combined with shame that she could, even for a minute, have suspected her friend of being an accomplice of her husband. Her panic subsided fractionally and she realised that this contemptible, depraved creature, whatever his sick reasoning, desired money and not her virtue. 'If you had not brought your beau along to stand guard the time you came to meet me, and had paid up, this need never have happened to you,' he added truculently.

'Until you had spent that money on gin and gaming and needed more.'

He looked at her malevolently out of those striking eyes that must once have fascinated Dolly and told her, almost defensively, 'I come from a distinguished family in France and was not used to, nor trained for, earning a living. But I secured some parts in plays that called for a foreign accent. I was considered to have potential and I was very handsome.'

She looked at him dispassionately after this childish boasting and retorted, 'You still possess the bones of good looks. It is only excess that has spoiled them. You have a fine, resonant voice and, as you pointed out, a slight, not unattractive accent, however perfect your English phraseology.'

'I had an English governess,' he answered matter of factly. Then he surveyed her with something like admiration. 'You have courage, little lady, for that is what you are, aren't you, a lady? Your voice has the natural refinement that my wife apes when she rejects my reasonable demands for a portion of her income, for keeping out of her and the boy's life.'

'What do you know of me that you should threaten to disclose my identity?'

'Nothing unfortunately,' he admitted with surprising candour. 'But when Dolly told me you were a real lady and must have run away from home for reasons best known to yourself, it followed that you must have something to hide. So I surmised that a few threats might produce the goods. Dolly is irrationally attached to you, else she might not have refused to borrow money from you to give to me, which she ought, all things considered.'

'Why ought she?' asked Cassy, mystified.

'Because you got your chance through influence, while Dolly had to struggle from the gutter. Then you took the part of Prince Charming which was rightfully hers and which would have established her as a leading actress. She would in that case have been able to support a husband who conferred distinction on her by endowing her with the noble name of de Mallon, famous in my country before and after the Revolution.'

'Could you not return to your own country and your inheritance?'

'If I had the wherewithal – not that the members of my family spared by La Guillotine have much remaining to them. But they might be more generous than my wife. Tomorrow, however, she will have a chance to prove herself in your role before the production ends, and then will qualify for the part you might have had in *Harlequin Hoax*. She will be the more eager in such a position to pay me off and forget my involvement. She is too besotted with her lover to ask him for money to compensate me for the loss of my conjugal rights.'

'You forfeited those by your evil ways long ago,' Cassy told him, feeling calmer until she saw the murderous glint in his eye.

'That is enough! If you do not agree to relinquish your roles in both productions I promise to disfigure your lovely face badly enough to make their loss inevitable.'

'But—' she started desperately.

'No buts. You are my prisoner and shall remain so as long as it is necessary to accomplish my ends.'

'You are to be pitied,' Cassy said, understanding the situation now. 'You are still young and could easily become presentable and even personable again. You could yet make your way on the stage with the right introductions – as you truthfully remark that I did. I would engage to help you. That would surely be better for you than battening on women.'

He looked at her narrowly and for a moment she thought that her words had softened him. The thought of the irreparable harm to her budding career his plan could cause, if it were successful, made her add appealingly, 'I work because I need the money.' She did not add that, without her salary over the next season, and her contribution to the housekeeping, her family could not keep the house. The less that he knew about her personal circumstances the better.

But he laughed contemptuously, snatched her reticule and took from it the two guineas she always kept there in case of emergency. He took his empty bottle and snapped, 'Stay there. I have to go out.'

He locked the door after his departure, presumably to replace the bottle of spirits, and she found herself laughing uncontrollably and hysterically at his admonition. She had already confirmed that the small, barred window let on to a sheer drop of two floors on to the cobbled yard. She could hardly kick down the thick door either. The trap was sprung.

22

Cassy began to weep hopelessly and with a feeling of utter desolation. Then she forced herself to overcome the rising tide of despair and, more out of an effort of will than any real interest, went and examined the stained books on the shelf. They were the choice of a cultivated person, mostly in French but a few in English. She recognised the names of François Villon and Voltaire among the former and of Christopher Marlowe and Spenser among the latter. Finally she shook the dust off a volume of English verse and searched in it, hoping, in her extremity, for the comforting contact with her dead mother of a poem by Lovelace.

With blurred eyes she read in the yellowed pages the familiar lines of 'To Althea from Prison', then those less well known of 'To Gratiana dancing and singing'. She thought longingly of the happy days when her family was intact.

Re-reading the poems she knew so well deflected her thoughts momentarily from the inevitable opening of the door, but soon her kidnapper returned with a new bottle and poured himself a glass. She wondered if he intended to feed her in captivity or let her starve.

While he concentrated on the liquor Cassy's hand went to her foot, tucked as it was beneath her on the rickety chair. With the strength of desperation she rose, hurled herself across the room and hit him over the head with one of her little boots. The blow could not have been hard enough to hurt him seriously. But that, combined with the alcohol, served to infuriate him so much that he punched her face, cursing in French as the contents of the bottle spilled. He took her arm and twisted it viciously until she felt an agonising pain and everything dissolved into merciful blackness.

She did not hear the stampede of feet on the stairs nor the battering against the door. She did not see Lord Allingham, his cousin Thomas and Dolly enter the room. The two men grasped the gin-sodden creature while Dolly hurried to where Cassy lay, blood on her face and her arm in an unnatural position. 'Marcel!' Dolly sobbed. 'How could you, even you!' She attempted ineffectually to wipe the blood off Cassy's bruised face. 'She is not dead!' she cried now in relief, and the Marquis rasped out at her assailant, 'How badly have you hurt her?'

Sobered by shock, he answered defensively, 'She is but stunned, I think. I hit her face not her head. Her arm may be dislocated but I doubt if it is broken.'

Lord Allingham's face was contorted with fury. 'You shall await His Majesty's pleasure for your crime. Tom, help me to tie him. Then stay with him until I secure the services of the Law. I must get Cassy to my home and under the care of my own doctor as quickly as possible. For the sake of all, this matter must be handled with discretion.'

But now Dolly burst out, weeping uncontrollably. 'Julian, I beseech you not to have him imprisoned.' Her face was suddenly ugly with tears. 'He is the father of my son, and long ago I loved him.'

The abject creature tossed the rest of the glass of gin into his mouth and looked at his wife with alcoholic remorse and, just possibly, a trace of genuine emotion. 'I loved you too, and little George. I still do. I am not beyond redemption.' He turned to the Marquis, whose face was unrelenting and whose only consideration was for the unconscious girl, begging, 'Give me a chance!'

Dolly said, 'Marcel, I promise to pay you a guinea a week while I am earning. For this you must promise not to try to see myself or our son again, nor to demand money by any other means.'

'I accept,' he said, 'if you will only let me go.'

The Marquis looked at Dolly's husband with hard eyes, and heard Thomas add his deciding plea to hers. 'Leave it like that, Julian. It will be better for Dolly – and Cassy.'

'So be it then,' the other agreed with obvious unwillingness. 'Come to my house in the morning, and I shall have legal papers drawn up there for you to sign. Personally I would rather see you in prison. You can thank your unlucky wife for your escape.'

They carried the injured girl carefully between them to the carriage and put her on the seat with her head on Dolly's lap.

An hour later the Marquis, having already dispatched a footman for the doctor, laid Cassy tenderly on a bed in his house. He looked fearfully at her chalk-white face with its cuts and discoloured patches.

While Thomas paced below, the doctor finally arrived accompanied by the footman, who passed him over to a disconcerted Tibbs. The butler remembered seeing the same young person put to bed on an earlier occasion at his employer's Brighton residence. Could she, he wondered, be subject to fits? This time the actress looked as if she were dying. Would she perhaps have some connection with the recent low spirits of his moody, changeable but respected master? His Lordship must indeed be smitten by this woman of the theatre, who had been painted like a clown on her arrival at the Brighton house. He shook his grey head regretfully.

The doctor waited for the Marquis to leave the room and then, with Dolly still present, examined his patient. He felt her head very gently and then, more to Dolly's consternation than his own, for he had been told his patient was an actress, he removed the black peruke and revealed short-cut golden hair. There was no swelling on her skull. Then, glad that she was still unconscious, he manipulated her right arm gently, deciding that it was dislocated and severely bruised but not broken. He gave the limb a skilful jerk which straightened the displacement but brought her round with a shock of pain.

'Dolly!' Cassy cried. 'Thank God! What happened?' Then she added on a rising note of hysteria, 'My wig! Dolly, replace it – please!'

'Be quiet, young lady,' the doctor hushed her, wondering privately that this child who looked as innocent as his own daughter should wear false hair, act, and be one of the notorious Marquis's lights of love. She was said to have fallen downstairs, and he could only conclude that, if this were true, one of His Lordship's celebrated orgies had taken place. 'You are in a better condition than might have been expected after your accident, and lucky to be so. Now let me feel your pulse.'

Since his patient's head was undamaged and she was fast becoming dangerously agitated over her peruke, he allowed the other woman to obey her plea and put it back. Then he requested Dolly, whose tear-stained beauty proclaimed her another Paphian, to fetch a glass of water from the pitcher on the night-stand and then administered a

161

soothing draught. He applied arnica to the bruises and suggested to her companion that his patient should be undressed, with care for her painful arm, and allowed to sleep.

When he had left the room Cassy said with desperate appeal in her voice, 'Dolly, the wig! Keep my secret!'

'You know, Cassy love, that I would never do or say anything to hurt you. So don't worry about anything. Just rest.' The sick girl sighed and closed her eyes.

The Marquis was awaiting the diagnosis with his cousin below. The doctor tried to combine a disapproving countenance with professional pomposity. However, His Lordship was impressed by neither and demanded a clear-cut description of the patient's condition without medical jargon.

'She is suffering from severe shock,' the doctor responded with offended dignity, 'her arm is not broken, but there is extensive swelling and bruising which must cause pain. She is in no condition to be removed from here.' He could not now disguise a note of regret. 'I presume Your Lordship can procure a female relative or other competent attendant for her, as she will require considerable care.' He tried to look stern again but dropped the attempt in the face of the Marquis's haughty glance.

'Certainly. My old nurse has been asked already to look after her, and my housekeeper will also help.'

'Good. I have given the – unfortunate lady – a powder to sedate her and induce sleep.'

'You will come tomorrow then.' It was an order, not a request. A footman, who wore blue and grey livery with buttons of silver embossed with the Allingham arms, lighted a flambeau to escort the doctor to his gig.

After his departure Dolly appeared, saying, 'She is too unwell to do more than accept the fact of her safety for the present, without questions.' She looked at His Lordship with a hint of her old roguish smile as she enquired, 'Have you by any chance one of your mother's bedgowns here too?'

'No,' he answered her look with a similar glint, 'for my mother has her own establishment in town. I do, however, possess a garment – which I was intending to present—'

'Quite!' said Dolly demurely, and soon, with inner amusement, saw the unprotesting Cassy dressed in a transparent confection of lace and ribbons in blush pink, which she was persuaded would bring an expression of yet greater disapprobation to the doctor's face on the morrow.

The Marquis had in fact had a consultation with the devoted Tibbs, talking to him with the special smile that charmed his staff as well as anybody else on whom he cared to bestow it. 'Would Mrs Tibbs take over the sick-room for the present? You may accept my assurances that the lady upstairs is gently born and virtuous, even if appearances may have been to the contrary. I am sure that – nurse,' he smiled again at the butler, whose wife was used to tend him from babyhood, 'will oblige me in this.'

The old man smiled back in relief and nodded his head, saying, 'I do not doubt it, Your Lordship. She will like to have charge of somebody again, and would do anything for you.'

'Yes, bless her! Tibbs, I rely entirely on your ability to ensure discretion and silence on the subject outside this house, from the rest of my household.'

'You may, sir. I shall summon Mrs Tibbs right away.' He and the Marquis's old nurse had their own quarters on the premises. Mrs Leggat, the housekeeper in Grosvenor Square – Mrs Farquar stayed to supervise the maintenance of the Brighton house – had already undertaken with alacrity to relieve Mrs Tibbs when necessary.

Shortly after, the Marquis, accompanied by his old nurse, quietly scratched on the door of the room where Cassy now lay. Dolly let him and Mrs Tibbs in with her finger to her lips. He trod softly to the big four-poster where the injured girl slept, and looked at the tumbled dark hair and discoloured face above the frivolous bedgown with, Dolly thought, an expression on his face that she found impossible to read. They tip-toed out, leaving the large, motherly woman sitting in proud custody of her patient.

They joined Thomas in the library, where the Marquis accepted the brandy his cousin had poured him, having first given a balloon glass to Dolly and bidden her drink it. She was looking pale and shaken but said, nevertheless, 'Julian, let me stay with her, tonight at least. It were better than a stranger.'

'You are near collapse yourself, Dolly,' he countered, 'and must take over Cassy's part tomorrow. You need some sleep. Nobody could be more reliable than my old nurse. So you need not be anxious.'

'I suppose you are right, Julian.'

'I know I am, Dolly. Tom will take you home now, and deliver a *billet* to the stage manager to the effect that Cassandra has been taken ill. Are you still of the same mind concerning your renegade husband? Are you sure you can afford this sum?'

Thomas interpolated quickly, 'She shall not be without the means!'

She smiled gratefully at her lover and said, 'Yes, Julian, it is the best.'

'Then come to me here in the late morning and I shall have my lawyer in attendance. Go now, my dear, and you, Tom.'

'I heard you tell Tibbs that Cassy comes from a genteel background, Julian,' his cousin said as a parting shot. 'I always suspected it and I was sure of it when she slapped my face!'

Cassy had, on her first awakening from unconsciousness, suffered such excruciating pain that she was, while thankful for deliverance from her captor, quite incurious as to its means or her whereabouts.

She awoke the second time with a whimper as her face throbbed violently: her arm sent the message of countless shooting pains to her brain and she felt a vertigo when she tried to keep her eyes open. But before she closed them again she had seen an elderly, concerned face above her own and a soothing voice that recalled her comfortingly to childhood said, 'There, there, little one! Drink this draught and the pain will be eased.'

Cassy let the woman support her head while she drank obediently. She wanted to ask who had brought her to this soft bed, whose house this was, and the kind person's name. But when she tried to speak, the effort was too much for her, and she just smiled gratefully and drifted off to sleep.

Marcel de Mallon, cousin of a French *comte* whose head had rolled while the crones knitted beside the guillotine, was admitted to the house in Grosvenor Square the next morning. Tibbs regarded this scion of a noble house as if he should have used the tradesmen's entrance. But his heritage as well as his short, promising stage career enabled the Frenchman to walk with the dignity of bravado into His Lordship's study. However, this did not survive the icy appraisal from the gentleman behind the Buhl *escritoire*. De Mallon's eyes dropped and he shuffled his feet on the Turkey rug.

Dolly sat in a chair and the Marquis's man of business, hovering at his side, cast a glance of distaste at the newcomer and laid a document before Lord Allingham. The latter perused it with care and then explained its significance to Dolly, whose reading standard was not yet up to the exercise, saying, 'In return for your allowance of one guinea weekly your husband will undertake not to annoy, molest, intimidate or try to obtain extra money from yourself or your son. Do you have any questions?'

She shook her head, avoiding her husband's eyes. The Marquis passed the document to him without a word. The latter looked as if he might say something, then his face reddened and he wrote his name. He looked at the Marquis, who had witnessed the signature as well as the lawyer, and said, 'Believe it or not as you choose, but there is some humanity in me. I am sorry – for everything. Tell me please, how is the lady whom I hurt.'

'She will recover,' Lord Allingham answered shortly.

'I am glad.' He gave a quick glance at Dolly, whose eyes were still lowered, bowed stiffly and left the room.

The Marquis rose, took Dolly's hand and drew her to her feet. He took out his cambric handkerchief and handed it to her with a slight smile. 'Dry your eyes! Will you go and see Cassy before you leave?'

'Yes, of course, Julian. What did the doctor say about her this morning?'

'He pronounced her improved, but much in need of rest and quiet. He thinks she was already very over-tired and run-down.'

'I am not surprised.'

'Ask her please, if she will receive a visit from me later.'

'Of course, and thank you, Julian, for everything.'

Mrs Tibbs had been relieved by the housekeeper, who bobbed a curtsey as Dolly took her place in the chair beside Cassy's bed. The invalid smiled up at her friend, looking less bemused but with the livid marks still shockingly conspicuous across the pallor of her face, and the shadows of suffering beneath her eyes. 'Dolly dear,' she said in a quiet voice, 'You have discovered my guilty secret. But I trust you implicitly with it!'

'You can! But your own hair is so lovely that you must have strong reasons for disguising it. When you are stronger you may feel like telling me them. How do you feel, Cassy?'

'A little better. I know Lord Allingham has the nuisance of me again, but how and why I was rescued and brought here I hope you will tell me.' She paused a moment, evidently finding it tiring to speak – 'You will take my role, Dolly?'

'Yes. But your part in *Harelequin Hoax* awaits your recovery.

Luckily you have rehearsed it. There was consternation at Drury Lane when word of your serious indisposition arrived. I am entrusted with kind and loving messages from everybody.'

Cassy was moved as well as relieved that her part in the pantomime was safe. 'And poor Louise? She knows I am all right?'

'She does now. Oh, Cassy,' Dolly's eyes swam with tears, 'it is so dreadful that it was Marcel who treated you so!'

Cassy cut her short, putting out her uninjured arm to take Dolly's hand. 'You have been the greatest sufferer. You will always be my dear friend. But – I am so confused.'

'I am not surprised. Marcel is luckily not a very accomplished criminal, especially when foxed, which is most of the time. In the darkness he attacked John with a club hard enough to stun him as he went to enter his hackney carriage preparatory to colllecting you and Louise from the stage door. Don't worry, John was not much hurt. Louise found him in the yard and when she had brought him round they returned together to Drury Lane.

'As luck would have it Julian and Thomas were with me in the Green Room. I did not doubt that Marcel must be the culprit, for he had waylaid me several times, threatening me with grim reprisals if I did not obtain money from Tom or you. He harboured a particular grudge against you, Cassy.'

'So I discovered, and from his point of view it must seem justified.'

'Nothing can excuse him! Thank God I remembered the name of the sordid alley where he lodges, if not the number. Within a surprisingly short time we were in Julian's carriage, and he was himself driving it like the devil through the dark streets. I thought we must surely overturn. But he is really a *nonpareil*. We saw the hack outside the house where you were held. The street door was open. The place seemed deserted, but luckily you gave a cry of alarm. The two men began to kick the door down and Marcel, realising all was lost, let them in. I thought Julian would throttle him when he saw how you had been treated, and he wished to hand him over to the Law. But my entreaties saved him from prison.'

'I am glad for the sake of Georgie and yourself,' murmured Cassy, and closed her eyes.

'That is all, except that I am charged by Julian to ask if he may pay his respects to you later when you feel more the thing.'

'How could I not wish to see him, to express my gratitude – again! Please convey it also to Tom. Dolly, I shall think of you tonight. My

166

wishes and prayers will be with you. Go and rest now before the performance, but before you do, try if you will to tidy – my hair – for I naturally do not want my nurses to attend to it.'

Dolly did as she was bid with some skill; Cassy gave a little smile of satisfaction and drifted off to sleep again as her friend closed the door softly behind her.

23

The Marquis looked down with compunction at the fair fragile face, and with involuntary appreciation at the rounded perfection of form and pearly sheen of skin displayed by the indecorous blush-pink confection.

Long, dark lashes fluttered open, blue eyes gazed into inscrutable hazel ones, and then smiled as the latter narrowed into a friendly glint.

'Sir,' Cassy started, and amended, 'Julian ...' She chuckled a little weakly. 'Sir Galahad rather, for you are always coming to my rescue and again I must thank you.'

'Must you? Well do so by joining me in a glass of wine. The doctor recommended it for you as a strengthener and stimulant.' He made a gesture to Mrs Tibbs who came forward to support her patient, having first wrapped about her shoulders a grey shawl which, Cassy surmised, must be one of her own. She was glad of it, having only just become aware of her diaphanous apparel. 'To my rescuer!' she said, valiantly sipping, and trying not to screw her face up with distaste.

He toasted her solemnly but with an imp of mischief in his eyes now. 'To the damsel in distress I invariably carry back to one or other of my beds.'

Sinking back with relief on to the pillow she rejoined amusedly, 'How shocking it sounds! This bedgown too ...'

He had the grace to look a trifle embarrassed, but answered airily, 'Just a little thing I found I had about the place. Now, tell me, how do you really feel?'

'Oh, weak as a kitten, but I shall be quite stout by the morning and able to rid you once more of my troublesome self.'

'Not troublesome, rather, say, diverting. What did I do for excitement before Cassandra entered my life?'

'I have theories on that subject,' she answered with a glimmer of amusement.

'Do you indeed?' he smiled. 'Then you had liefer keep them to yourself. Now please banish everything from your mind but the need to rest. Could you take a little of the beef broth for which my chef is famous?'

'Later perhaps.'

'Very well. But be thankful that I do not force gruel upon you.'

After he had bowed and promised to give himself the pleasure of another visit that evening, she reflected wryly that, had her adventure taken place on the stage of Drury Lane, it must have ended in a love scene. Instead, here she was ensconced for the second time in a bedroom of his while he treated her with the teasing kindness of a long-time friend, if not even of an uncle. He seemed to have forgotten entirely the wild passion that had once blazed so fiercely between them. However, she was forced to assume from his reputation that such amorous interchanges must be for him mere commonplace. Even so, she concluded on a little splutter of mirth, he could, however great a libertine, hardly jump into bed beside the injured girl he had rescued. The giggle turned into a tiny whimper which brought her nurse hurrying to dispose her sore arm more comfortably.

She must not, she decided, before drowsing again, dwell on this unseemly subject lest, in her weakened condition, her temperature soar. Why, when she was so comfortable with him as a friend, did she simultaneously experience this stirring of the senses at his approach; this vibration of her being to the deep tones of his voice as a violin to its musician? She was aware that a real lady should not be thus affected by a gentleman, and feared that she must instead be, simply, a woman.

Cassy did not know what time it was when she opened her eyes again, but the room was dark, curtains drawn, and the firelight flickering on light oak panelling and illuminating an area of the white fur rug and silky carpet of subdued blues.

In the high chair by the bed sat a woman who rose as the invalid's head turned towards her. Then the voice of her dear Louise said softly, 'Miss Cassy, love, you was so still I kept bending over to make sure you was still breathing. I was that worried!'

Cassy clasped the warm hand with her good left one and exclaimed, 'Oh, I am so glad you came! You will tell Aunt Letty that I am safe and that she is not to fret!'

'Of course. I have already sent word to her. Now let me look at what that sinner did to your sweet face. May the Lord forgive him, for I cannot. Your arm was hurt too, that nice Mrs Tibbs tells me.'

On the night table was a tinder box with its piece of flint steel and small quantity of charred linen rag, and a silver snuffer on a little tray. The dresser lighted the candle there, and those in the silver sconce on the toilet table, the *escritoire* and either side of the fireplace.

'Yes, Louise,' Cassy confessed. 'I fear that I ache everywhere. But there is no irreparable damage. I am sorry that you have had so much worry on my account.'

The dresser brushed away a tear and answered in heartfelt fashion, 'All that matters is that you are safe with His Lordship.'

Cassy gave a faint, incredulous smile. 'You actually approve of my installation in a gentleman's house?'

'I would not if I were not sure he means only well by you. Mrs Tibbs assures me he would never harm a lady, and he must know by now that you are just that, actress or no. She says as how he has sterling qualities he tries to hide sometimes. She should be able to judge since she had charge of him since he was in his cradle.'

Cassy had to smile. 'I see you have made a friend. I did not know that Mrs Tibbs was Lord Allingham's old nurse. But she certainly cedes place only to you in taking care of me.'

'I am that relieved in my mind, as otherwise I must have moved here!'

'What nonsense! I hope to return to you tomorrow anyway, and you should certainly not leave poor John after he has suffered such an unpleasant experience. How is he now?'

'Quite sound save for a bump on his head and the mortification of being bowled over without the chance of a mill. He sends his condolences and respects. Now, Miss Cassy dear, where you procured the immoral thing you are wearing I know not! But just let me change you into one of your own ruffled nightgowns. I have brought such possessions as I thought you might need, not knowing how long you might have to stay under His Lordship's roof.'

Cassy was grateful to be rid of the offending blush-pink item, but her pallor was more marked and she could not help drawing in her breath as her injured arm was placed within the full sleeve of her own pretty but proper garment.

Louise wrinkled her brow in sympathy. She bathed Cassy's face and hands gently, quickly removed her wig, brushed the spun-gold hair and arranged one of the other perukes that she had brought carefully over it. 'I have brought all your wigs in this locked hatbox, Miss Cassy,' she said. 'I shall put it in the big cupboard here and the key in your reticule. I shall be back tomorrow to help you. But this evening I have promised to attend Dolly Mallon at Drury Lane, for she is that nervous! I can at least help her on and off with her costumes and greasepaint. She is a good lass, if not a lady like you.'

'She is also my dear friend. I am so pleased that you are going to support her this evening, Louise, for it will be an ordeal for her to play the part for the first time. Don't delay now, for you have left me quite clean and comfortable. You were so kind to come and so clever to think of the box of wigs!'

After accepting Louise's final exhortations to be good and get well soon, Cassy's eyes traversed the agreeable chamber without moving her head, which pained if she did so. She reflected that, while possessing all that was needed for a lady's occupation, the room with its striped hangings of olive green, mid-blue and white and lack of frivolity proclaimed itself the choice of a bachelor.

Mrs Tibbs entered, bearing the celebrated beef broth, which she insisted on spooning into Cassy, who had difficulty in accomplishing such a simple task herself with her left arm. 'I did not know till Louise told me,' the girl said with a smile, 'that you were His Lordship's nurse.'

This remark opened the floodgates of affectionate reminiscences about the lonely, spoiled, headstrong small boy who still kept her devotion when he had become the outwardly haughty gentleman. Cassy was touched, and glad of the sidelights on her host. But she was beginning to be dismayed at her own feelings of exhaustion and its attendant near-tearfulness which took the place of her anticipated recovery.

The Marquis subsequently paid her another brief visit, looking intently at her and informed her, 'I am to accompany Tom to Drury Lane tonight. You would think it was he and not Dolly who was to play your part for the first time!'

She smiled up at him with an effort and said, 'I am glad. Give her my love.' She thought he looked magnificent in his burgundy velvet tail coat, creaseless grey pantaloons and cravat arranged tonight in a 'waterfall'. She watched his departure with a certain wistfulness, and the room which had come to life with his presence was suddenly chill and depressing.

Mrs Leggat, on duty now, had just prepared Cassy for the night when that same gentleman tapped softly at the door. He asked his housekeeper in an undertone if Cassy was awake and could receive him. He regarded her extremely flushed face with inner perturbation, but said casually, 'The performance went well. Dolly spoke the part as nicely as you had taught her. But I fear she is not as great a success in it as you were, and there were some cries of "We want Cassandra" from your admirers!'

Cassy tried to smile at him gratefully and to speak. But she saw his handsome face through a mist of fever, and her head was aching and her damaged arm throbbing so much that the effort ended in a grimace instead. She felt his cool hand on her forehead and his touch this time was merely comforting.

Finally she brought out thickly, 'You are back early.'

'Yes. I came to tell you of your pupil's creditable début, and had intended to go forth again for a game of faro at Watier's. But the weather without is so inclement that I cannot be bothered to leave home again tonight. So should you or your nurse need me' – he looked significantly at his housekeeper, who nodded understandingly – 'I shall be at your disposal.' He picked up her good hand and kissed it lightly. 'Take your sleeping draught now and try to make that over-active mind of yours a blank!'

It was strange, Cassy thought, as she closed her burning eyes, that the mere presence in the house of Lord Allingham, admitted rakehell though he might be, was sufficient to quieten her anxieties and give her a sense of security.

24

Cassy slept in snatches during which she was beset by jumbled, upsetting dreams. At one time she was led up the aisle to be married to a Romeo Coates who awaited her dressed in pink-spangled tights like those that Madame Saqui had worn on the tight-rope at Sadler's Wells. Then she was being booed and pelted with fruit and bottles by a great crowd standing in a theatre. She tried to dance, but her slippers slipped on skins and pulp and she collapsed in a heap of spattered tulle, to the vociferous delight of the audience.

She woke up towards morning crying and muttering in a delirium, and Mrs Leggat rang for a servant to request the Marquis's presence. It occurred to the housekeeper that her employer looked almost as elegant as he did by day as he entered the chamber a surprisingly short time later wearing a long, corded velvet dressing-robe in deep red with black satin lapels. 'Sir,' she said worriedly, 'she is wandering in her mind and her hands and forehead are burning. I have tried to calm her, but without success.'

He looked at the hectic colour in the girl's cheeks and said, 'You were right to call me. Be so good as to inform Mr Tibbs that he should dispatch a footman forthwith for the doctor, and then ask Mrs Tibbs to relieve you while you get some sleep. I shall stay with the patient meanwhile.'

She curtseyed and departed to do his bidding, darting a final, compassionate glance at the small figure in the big bed.

When the housekeeper had gone the Marquis looked into Cassy's heavy-lidded eyes and captured her fluttering hot hand, holding it fast

173

in his. Her grasp tightened, her muttering ceased and she spoke for a moment quite rationally. 'I am glad you are here.'

He looked down at her face with a question in his eyes. Did she know to whom she was speaking, or was he simply a fatherlike figment of her feverish wandering? Whatever the answer, it sufficed for the moment that his presence and touch seemed to quieten her. So he sat beside her and held her hand silently until the doctor arrived with Mrs Tibbs on his heels.

He confirmed that the girl's pulse was tumultuous and her temperature soaring. 'I am not surprised at this delayed reaction,' he said. 'But, contrary to the opinion of many of my colleagues, I do not believe in blood-letting unless it is really necessary.' He turned to the concerned Mrs Tibbs, 'When she is restless sponge her with cool water and try to soothe her feverish fears. I shall administer a posset to bring down the temperature and a dose of laudanum to alleviate her pain and induce sleep. We must hope that nature will do the rest.'

He looked less disapproving and more human now as he told Lord Allingham, 'I cannot know what this lady's life has been of recent months, Your Lordship. But when she recovers I would strongly advise you to persuade her, if you can, to take a long rest.'

The Marquis caught his old nurse's eyes on him as if in mute appeal, and he held her glance, looking years younger as he grinned, 'Do you think I can't, nurse?'

'I think you can do most things you set your mind to, Master Julian – Your Lordship,' she responded with a demure dimple in her cheek.

The doctor smiled at the Marquis with some commendation, remarking, 'I see that my patient is in good hands. I shall call again later in the morning.'

He bowed himself out and Lord Allingham, to the surprise of his old nurse, took Cassy's hand again and held it gently until her eyelashes were lowered on her flushed cheeks and her weak threshing resolved into a deep, drug-induced sleep. Then he laid her hand softly below the coverlet, rose and smiled at Mrs Tibbs, who spoke to him as comfortingly as she once had to the child with a childish woe, 'Don't you fret now. I shall take care of the little love for you, and see her well.'

He passed his hand affectionately over her head in its starched cap and rejoined, 'I know it. But I shall be at home still in case I am needed.'

Cassy's fever abated slowly, but the extreme weakness remained so that she was amenable to Allingham's orders to remain as his guest for the present. Her head gradually ached less and the bruising was fading from her face.

Finally she overcame her lassitude enough to allow one or other of her devoted nurses to help her to the high wing chair where she would sit for an hour at a time. By this stage she determined to make, what seemed in her convalescent condition, to require a superhuman effort, the decision to remove herself from the Marquis's house.

In spite of her demanding role, Dolly visited Cassy whenever she could spare the time and was at last told the strange story of her friend's double identity. But she was charged not to divulge the secret to a soul, even, or particularly, to her beloved Thomas, who would find it difficult to keep it from his cousin. Others, including Charles Young, who had enquired for her, had been told that she had gone away to recuperate to an undisclosed address.

She was sitting in the comfortable chair before a crackling fire now. A lacy white shawl was round her shoulders and a fur rug over her knees. She and the Marquis were playing backgammon, a game which he had newly taught her and at which she could now beat him once in ten times. He was home so often of late that his staff was agog with speculation, though none of them would have dreamed of mentioning the matter outside the house. His companionship was for her a disturbing joy to which she dared not allow herself to become too accustomed.

She acknowledged defeat in the game with a pout that was half a scowl and announced, as she had resolved to do, 'Julian, it is time I left your house and returned to Louise and John. You must be the subject of so much gossip below stairs!'

The Marquis contrived to look affronted. 'There is, as you well know, no question of your returning to your lodgings yet awhile. If you are not comfortable here I must find you an alternative place to convalesce. As for servants' tattle, it is of no import. Does the possibility of it worry you?'

'No, not for myself, for you ensure that there is always a female in the anteroom and the door left open when you visit me. Besides your staff would never discuss your business outside the confines of your house. They are quite devoted to you.'

'Yes, despite my lamentably wild ways, I do believe they are,' he agreed as if in sudden realisation.

'I think your ways cannot have been so wild recently,' she smiled up at him shyly, 'since you have been so considerate in keeping me company.'

'Is that such a hardship for me, do you think?' he asked her quite seriously.

'You make me feel that it is not just so that I can be quite easy about being here, where I am content and cosseted to pieces. But I must force myself to get upon my feet again, lest I lose my part in *Harlequin Hoax*. You understand, I know, how important it is for me to keep it.'

'I know that you feel it is. But the doctor has ordered you to rest completely for at least two months to avert a serious breakdown.'

'Oh, no—' she began, distressed.

'Do not put yourself into a taking. I realise that you are concerned about the loss of income. But you must allow yourself to be guided by the doctor, who has stated categorically that your health would not withstand a knockabout pantomime season with daily matinées as well as evening performances.'

Certainly the prospect filled her with dread in her weakened state. But she answered a little desperately, 'Not now, I agree. But within a week.'

'Cassy,' His Lordship started now, and his face was unwontedly earnest, 'do you truly consider me your friend?'

'None better,' she responded with fervour.

'Then I shall take upon myself the privilege of a friend and lend you the money to enable you to take the rest so necessary to your future health. Perhaps you have relatives you would like to visit.'

If this was meant to be a question Cassy did not answer it directly but said instead, 'Julian! I am bewildered. You go too fast. If, as a long-term policy, it is expedient to obey the doctor's decree, I suppose I must. Because you are my friend I would accept your loan, as I have already accepted so much else from you, as long as I felt sure I could pay it back after the New Year.'

'Why should you not? I spoke to Charles Young recently. He would like you to act with him when you are quite strong in a re-issue of the popular play, *Remorse*, by Samuel Coleridge. I should not, you must know, foreclose by demanding payment in kind, even if you were tardy in repayment – unlike the best villains at Drury Lane.'

She laughed a little embarrassedly. 'No, how could you, being the sort of person you are?'

176

He looked at her with an odd little smile. 'Oh, I could, Cassy, I could very well, believe me. But I would not.'

She coloured, recalling again as she looked at his firm mouth the feeling of its pressure on hers. 'How is Mr Young? Did he tell you if little Julian still wants to be a soldier after your stirring tales?'

He laughed. 'I dare say the boy will follow in his father's footsteps and become one of the gentlemen of the stage in every sense of the word, although at present it seems that he wishes to be presented with a pair of colours as soon as he is old enough. Charles was most anxious about your welfare. I wonder,' he said lightly, 'if he is in love with you.'

'Never!' Cassy assured him sincerely. 'Poor man, he is still in love with the memory of his wife.'

'That is all very well, but such sentiment makes a poor bed companion,' countered the Marquis frankly, 'and does little for the boy.'

'True,' concurred Cassy thoughtfully, deciding to ignore the first part of his remark. 'It cannot be easy for him without a mother.'

'I thought Charles might have offered for you, since I believe you went on some expedition with him and his son.'

'He did.'

The Marquis raised an interrogative eyebrow. 'And—?'

'He asked me to consider his proposal at my leisure and not to give an answer for the present. He said I should think of marriage with him as a last resort. Such humility from so fine a gentleman was affecting.'

'Have you considered his offer?'

'A little.'

'And what conclusion did you reach?'

'Only that, perhaps, if I were no longer of use, elsewhere - such an alliance might prove of mutual advantage.'

'I see. Somehow I was under the impression that you would only marry for love.'

'So was I. But ...' She was silent, unable to explain to the handsome gentleman whose hazel eyes regarded her so intently that, since she could never have him for her husband, there could, for her, be no question of a love match. Avoiding further discussion on this dangerous topic, she asked, 'Is it true that you are bound for France after the New Year?'

'Yes, probably towards the end of January. I am to pursue some enquiries about continuing Bonapartist sympathies and investigate the possibility of a further outbreak of hostilities.'

She shuddered. 'That could not happen surely, after so many years of war and such a short period of peace? The Congress of Vienna ...'

'Attempts an arbitrary resettlement of powers, my dear, pandering to princes, but failing to solve any of the real problems.'

'What a sad thought!' After a pause she looked at him with her direct blue gaze. 'I shall accept your offer of a loan and give you my pledge upon it.'

'If you wish, though that is not necessary,' he said indifferently.

'I shall also take your advice and relinquish my part in the pantomime to Dolly. I shall return to Russell Street at the end of this week, and when Louise has repacked for me there I shall go to stay with – relations – for a while.'

'Good,' he applauded her decision briskly, but made no comment on her last words.

Cassy said, to change the subject, 'Would you not normally have been established in Oxfordshire by now, for the hunting and shooting?'

'Probably. I usually take a party to Allingham Park about this time. But this year my duties have kept me at my desk in the War Office.'

She hoped that this explanation was the truth. She would not like to be the cause of his sacrificing his sporting pursuits, as he already had so many of his other activities in order to keep her company.

'Then I have benefited,' said Cassy sincerely. 'Am I not allowed to thank you—'

'Certainly not without running the risk of being a dead bore,' he said, and then added surprisingly, and as if on impulse, 'but you could show your gratitude in a practical way.'

'Only tell me how,' she offered warmly, realising only after that she might have been a trifle rash.

'By returning here on New Year's Eve for the masque, as my guest of course. You should be well enough by then.'

She opened her mouth to speak and then closed it again without finding a suitable response to his preposterous, impossible and tempting suggestion. This costume ball was, she knew, not merely a raffish theatrical occasion but an annual society event.

He grinned at her sympathetically and said crisply. 'I shall send an invitation to you through Louise, who will doubtless know your direction. My carriage will collect you from Russell Street on the night.'

He went on to talk of other things, but Cassy was acutely conscious

178

that she must appear rag-mannered not to have confided to him at least the name of the relations she had mentioned, and their place of residence. But he seemed, in fact, oddly incurious. Perhaps, she thought, he preferred not to enquire too exactly into the private lives of theatre people. Yet he wanted her to attend the masque at which it must be assumed that his mother and other members of his family would be present. She decided to think more about this apparent contradiction, and how she would deal with the matter of the invitation, later, at Aunt Letty's, when she felt more the thing.

Allingham did not refer to the ball again during Cassy's last week under his roof. She was sad to think that this surprisingly happy interlude had now reached its conclusion. She would miss the Marquis. But now that she was becoming stronger daily, and her arm usable, her natural spirit of independence made her wish to be under her own roof, even though she knew that this would in the next months largely be supported by this reputably ruthless rake, who had been so good to her.

Miss Page, Thea and Grace were overjoyed to have Cassy home, supposedly recovering from a careless fall at the seminary. Aunt Letty had been fretting about her inability to visit her sick niece at Allingham's house, even though Louise had kept her informed regularly of the patient's progress. So she was all the more appreciative of this chance to enjoy her company and make a fuss of her. Cassy for her part was glad to relax with her dear family and to further her acquaintance with Honor and Marcia, who were, though they did not yet know it, soon to be part of it.

25

It was not until the third evening after Cassy's homecoming that she and Miss Page had a chance to talk privately. Up to then the schoolgirls had monopolised the newcomer by day, and the first two evenings she had been so tired from the effort of removing first from the Marquis's house and then from her lodgings that she went to bed as early as the younger girls did. But, at ease now before the fire in the small parlour, Cassy and her aunt could fill in the gaps in each other's knowledge of events since their last meeting without the necessity of keeping a strict guard on every word.

Miss Page sipped her coffee and said, 'When your Uncle Matthew wrote to tell me of his pleasure in Gerard's betrothal to their little neighbour, he asked me why he had seen no announcement of your forthcoming marriage in the *Morning Post.*'

'In that case it would be better to make no comment at all on the subject when you write felicitations, rather than to commit untruths to paper.' Cassy looked at her aunt commiseratingly. 'What a trial I am to you!'

'Never that, my love. But I admit that I should wish to be able to convey happy tidings of you to him. I blame myself, oh so bitterly, for ever permitting this masquerade.'

She looked suddenly so distressed that Cassy said firmly, 'You had no alternative and must not have vain regrets, for I do not.' Then, to distract her, she hastened to relate in her own droll manner the story of Gerard's abortive romance with Sybil.

Miss Page, faintly shocked at the outset at the unsavoury episode in her nephew's life while he was acquiring a little town bronze, ended up by dabbing the tears of merriment from her eyes. The girl had employed all her talent for mimicry to describe the ballet dancer's last rendezvous with Gerard and his friends and the cool way in which the Marquis had despatched her.

'Certainly your life is never dull,' Miss Page declared finally, perhaps to reassure herself. 'When I think of your encounter with that villainous Frenchman and how it might have ended! Would it overset you to tell me the whole story of it now?'

'Of course not,' said her niece, and launched into the recital of her capture, rescue by the Marquis and his subsequent care of her.

After hearing it Miss Page asked wonderingly, 'Cassy, could Allingham by any chance have fallen in love with Cassandra the actress? It seems so singular that one of his reputation should have gone to such lengths to save you and then to make you well and yet ...'

'Not expect to make love to me?' Cassy thought fleetingly, and with some guilt, of the evening in the gardens of Carlton House, the kisses that, if never to be repeated, were unforgettable and impossible to regret. Aloud she said, 'He is too much the gentleman, whatever the gossips may say, to have done so when he had given me the protection of his house and his own staff to take care of me. But, to reply honestly to your question, I myself know not, for he is – enigmatic. Sometimes I wonder, like you, if he might just possibly, and with the utmost reluctance, have developed a small *tendre* for Cassandra.'

'With reluctance?'

'Naturally, for I am persuaded that he suspects that I come of genteel stock. He is perceptive enough to realise that I have no desire to discuss my background, and sensitive enough not to ask me questions about it. But he certainly realises by now that I would never consent to become his mistress.'

'Could it be that he has recognised you as Lucasta?'

'Definitely not, for how could he do so when he never knew her?' She laughed reminiscently. 'The one occasion when he danced with me he looked anywhere but at my face. But, oh, Aunt Letty, I confess that I might have been in a great quandary while actually living in his house, for I would never have contrived to conceal my yellow locks without Louise's and Dolly's help. How thankful I was that I was not suffering from a head injury! As it was, the doctor discovered that I wore a wig. But dear Dolly cajoled him into keeping my guilty secret from the Marquis on the grounds that he prefers brunettes, and that I was quite desperate to keep his affection. This served, she told me, but to confirm his contempt for women of the theatre.'

'What a pucker! Then you confided in Dolly?'

'I had no choice and cannot be sorry for it for I know I can trust her. In fact it is something of a relief to have one other person in my life as Cassandra to whom I can talk without subterfuge.'

'Then I am glad.'

Miss Page was silent for so long that Cassy said, 'You are very pensive.'

Her aunt looked up with a slight frown. 'I was thinking – I suppose it could not be that Allingham intends to offer for Cassandra, player though she be?'

Cassy looked startled and then coloured hotly. 'Such a thought had not occurred to me. He would have more consideration surely for his family. But I own that I find one thing strange ...' It was her turn to hesitate.

'What, dear?'

'The fact that he desires, nay, almost demands, that I attend the New Year's Eve masque at Allingham House. This is, as you know, not one of his theatrical, *demi-monde* occasions, but an event to which the ton will be invited and at which his mother, and doubtless other of his relations, will be present.'

Miss Page raised her eyebrows. 'That is certainly a surprise and a poser, for, if you went, we could put no dependence on his mama not knowing who you were.'

'Are you so sure that she would recognise me? Just consider that she could not have seen me more than twice since I grew up and that we are all to wear fancy dress. I'm an adept at *maquillage*, as you know, and I could try to avoid a close confrontation with her.'

Miss Page looked at her niece intently, and said, 'You want to go, Cassy, don't you?'

To the older woman's dismay Cassy's eyes were suddenly brilliant with tears and she said in a strangled voice, 'I don't know. I don't know what to do.'

Her aunt went and kneeled beside her, taking her in her arms as she had so often comforted the child Cassy. She said positively as she stroked the golden head, 'You are in love with Allingham, naturally.'

She had not expected an answer, but while her niece struggled to regain control of her emotions Miss Page came to the conclusion that, were she sure that the Marquis returned Cassy's love, she would not hesitate to acquaint him herself with the facts of their deception. But how could she be sure?

Cassy had recovered herself and, though she did not attempt to deny her aunt's words, she quite clearly had no intention of proceeding further with the painful subject. Instead she asked conversationally, 'Will you post north with my sisters for Gerard's wedding in the spring?'

Miss Page accepted Cassy's lead equably and replied, 'Possibly. But it is difficult to commit ourselves to the journey so far ahead of time. Much can happen before then.'

'Yes,' agreed Cassy a little mischievously now, 'like the reappearance of Mr Stanton. Do his daughters have news of him?'

'Yes, he writes to them regularly from various towns where, he told me in my own communication' – she blushed and lowered her eyes – 'he is engaged in theatrical ventures preparatory to embarking on his continental tour. He intends after it to ...'

She paused and Cassy prompted her curiously, 'What does he intend, Aunt Letty?'

'To sell them all as successfully established going concerns.'

'Really? I wonder why.'

Her aunt answered in a rush, 'Because he wishes mé to be his wife and is aware that the theatre connection would not do. He said he could afford now to be a country gentleman, which is what he was, after all, born to be. He explained that he was writing to ask for my hand to spare me the pain of rejecting him verbally twice.'

'And will you reject him?' asked Cassy, eyes twinkling now.

'Oh, my dear, as if I could!' Miss Page laughed, but her face was mantled with colour. She looked at her niece a little apprehensively. 'Marcus told me that, if I would accept him, he would wish nothing more than to have my nieces, all three of them, living with him and to be allowed to do as much for them as he would for his own daughters.'

'How good he is! I wish you joy, dearest of aunts, and rejoice in another happy ending. But to make Thea, Grace and myself a charge on him is as unthinkable as it would have been to plant us on Uncle Matthew.'

'With the difference that Marcus is a rich man.'

'I realise that, and also that my sisters should stay with you, if you would like it, until their schooling is complete. But you must – I know you must – see that we ought still to be financially independent. They could not accept dowries from your husband any more than I could.

If I myself were to have married a rich man who wanted to accept responsibility for them that might, I suppose, have been different. So, Aunt Letty, the situation is not changed as regards the necessity for my earning as much as I can during the next few years, even if it means appearing from time to time with poor Romeo Coates!' She laughed, encouraging her aunt with an affectionately quizzical look to share her amusement at such a ridiculous notion. In fact, though, she knew that in the event that she was unable to secure another profitable role she would not hesitate to make a fool of herself in public again. She had not mentioned Allingham's loan, as Miss Page did not yet seem to have realised the implication of Cassy's loss of the pantomime part on the family finances. Time enough to tell her about that later.

Miss Page sighed and said, 'There is nothing to be gained from talking any more about it now. You may, I hope, eventually come to think differently. Who knows, perhaps ...'

But she apparently thought better of whatever she was about to say and changed it to a peremptory, 'Bed, Cassy. You look worn to a frazzle.' But as her niece obediently kissed her good-night, she felt no great confidence that sleep would come easily to either of them.

Louise brought a letter to Lowndes Square on a bitterly cold morning during the first week in December. When she arrived, Cassy was giving the four girls a dancing lesson with the dual purpose of warming them up and of giving Miss Page a respite from the classroom. The latter made the old servant drink a dish of tea with her while the lesson was still in progress. The rhythm in quadruple time of a gavotte could be heard, accompanied by girlish laughter and Cassy's intructions to them at the pianoforte.

Louise looked amused, and then she became serious as she said, 'It were the Marquis of Allingham what left this for Miss Cassy, ma'am. Said as how he would call again for an answer.'

Miss Page looked distracted, which caused Louise to dart her a look of sympathy, the more so when she asked in some puzzlement, 'Did His Lordship not enquire for Miss Cassy's direction?'

'No, nor wouldn't, even though he has proved her friend. He knows better than to ask questions as I'd never answer. If I'd of taken all the guineas the great gentlemen and bucks have offered me to satisfy their curiosity about Cassandra I'd of retired long ago and John with me.'

Miss Page laughed and said sincerely, 'Bless you, Louise, for your loyalty. How is John, by the by, after his misfortune?'

'Right as a trivet. Ah, here's Miss Cassy.'

The girl greeted her dresser affectionately and took the *billet* with a heightened colour. Miss Page said briskly, 'Why don't you take Louise in to pay a visit in the schoolroom while you read your letter and see if an answer is required.'

Cassy drew Louise into the adjoining room, returned to read the short missive and then handed it to her aunt. Allingham had enclosed an invitation to the costume ball and announced that he would himself call for her in his carriage at nine o'clock on New Year's Eve. He hoped that she was recovered in health.

'I shall go, I think,' said Cassy, avoiding her aunt's eye.

Miss Page, dismayed and bitterly opposed to her niece's decision, said with unusual asperity, 'That is mere bravado on your part. You could easily cry off without causing offence on the grounds that you are not yet quite strong. Besides,' she added with intentional, and most uncharacteristic, cruelty, 'you must know that you would never have been bidden to such an event were you not to be in fancy dress and presumably unable therefore to be so easily identified as Cassandra.' Cassy said nothing, and Miss Page continued rather desperately, 'Most dangerous of all for us is the fact that Lady Allingham is sure to pay special attention to any lady in whom her son is seen to display a marked interest.'

Cassy was on the defensive, for she recognised only too well the force of her aunt's arguments. 'I agree with all you say,' she said with an appeal in her voice. 'But since there can be no future for me in my association with the Marquis, I can afford to act – indifferently – with his mama. It would indeed be unfortunate if she took a liking to me and so hoped that his attachment would lead to the marriage she wishes for him. I could always disappear, like Cinderella, into the night if the situation became too difficult for me.'

'Oh, Cassy, Cassy, what a heedless, obstinate girl you are!'

'I know I must appear to you to be so. But I do want very much to see the New Year in – with him.'

Miss Page was moved unbearably by the sparkle of tears in the girl's eyes and gave up the struggle. Instead she smiled valiantly and said, 'Then it is settled. You will stay at Russell Street on the night of the ball. It remains but to decide on what you should wear.'

Cassy said lovingly, 'Thank you, dear Aunt Letty. The challenge will be to look beguiling, and as unlike both Lucasta and Cassandra as possible.'

'Marie-Antoinette in a powdered wig perhaps?'

'No, because the light colour of it would be reminiscent of Lucasta.'

'The Queen of Sheba?' Miss Page strove for a light tone.

'Coal black, was she not? The greasepaint would need to be excessive and would likely run in the heat.'

'I have it. A Chinese.'

'You have indeed.' Cassy's eyes lighted up. 'That is an inspiration, for Louise can arrange one of the wigs in a sleek, lacquered style which will make me look different for a start. A complexion coloured subtly olive-amber and eyes well narrowed will, I am convinced, effect the complete transformation – oriental but vastly becoming.'

'Do you hope to borrow a Chinese robe from the theatre?'

'Yes, because the wardrobe mistress at the Lane is good-hearted and is Louise's bosom bow. I have the very gown in mind, slit at the ankles, with a tiny, upstanding collar and lovely embroidery.'

'It sounds most suitable,' said Miss Page in a bright manner that hid her heavy heart. Was there to be no end to deceit, she asked herself dispiritedly. This latest variation on the theme was, it seemed, to be a masquerade within a masquerade.

Louise was given a letter, thanking the Marquis, accepting the invitation and agreeing to his arrangements. She promised to get in touch with her friend and colleague at Drury Lane immediately, and to see that the Chinese robe was in good condition.

In the event Christmas was a happier time for Miss Page and the Lorings than the previous one had been. Their grief over the fatal accident to their loved ones had, inevitably, dimmed a little with time. Marcus Stanton and his daughters spent two days with them before going off to stay with his in-laws when Boxing Day was over. If Miss Page's radiance had not ensured a festive spirit at Lowndes Square the high-spirited charades, dancing and sing-songs devised by Cassy and the actor turned impresario would have done so.

Cassy left for her lodgings the day before NewYear's Eve so that she could pay Dolly and Georgie a visit and also make sure that the Chinese costume that Louise had secured for her fitted and looked as perfect as possible.

The Marquis duly called for her, and Cassy complimented him on his own costume, surprisingly enough for one of a noble house, that of

Oliver Cromwell. But the severe black suit with a deep white collar and Puritan headgear over his own smooth dark hair gave a new and attractive aspect to his good looks.

He in turn stared long at the girl whose lovely figure was so strangely seductive an the high-necked clinging robe of yellow silk embroidered with jade green and vermilion dragons. Her hair might have been painted on and the artistically achieved change in her skin tone and slant of her eyes made her seem excitingly eastern and different. 'Clever Cassy!' he said. 'How exotic and beautiful you look.'

Cassy's heart lifted at his praise and she felt sure that an evening that had started so favourably would be one to remember. She was to be proved right.

Although it was such a short distance from Drury Lane to Grosvenor Square Cassy enjoyed riding in the silver-grey coach which carried a coat of arms on each door panel. The horses drawing the conveyance were a glossy black with harnesses of polished black leather and crested silver. Cassy, in her evening cloak, delighted in the padded upholstery of the interior, with its silver lamps and silken cushions. 'I think that this carriage was originally a pumpkin,' she declared, 'and those splendid steeds mice from Cinderella's kitchen.'

'Then do not, pray, disappear at the witching hour.'

Her elongated eyes looked mysterious to him as she said, 'I do not - plan to. But, tell me, Julian, how did you contrive to come for me this evening when you must be expecting so many guests?'

'Because escorting you is preferable to standing in a receiving line, a role that my mother and elderly uncles enjoy and play to perfection.'

Cassy felt a stab of fear as he mentioned the Marchioness. 'And shall I also stand to be presented?'

He tucked her hand in his arm. 'By no means. My eastern princess will appear from nowhere.'

She felt an overwhelming relief. As they arrived at Grosvenor Square some latecomers were still descending from their conveyances and crossing the red carpet, lighted by the flambeaux of the link boys. But the receiving line within had dispersed, although Cassy realised that she would eventually have to be introduced to Julian's mother. However the meeting was achieved briefly and comfortably. The lady's hazel eyes looked at her without recognition but with smiling admiration as her son said in his lazy way, 'Mama, you have not yet, I believe, made the acquaintance of my Chinese princess, Cassandra.'

The gracious lady, to whom Cassy found it impossible to act

'indifferently', but only as her natural self, was obviously not a regular playgoer, for the name meant nothing to her. 'Oriental royalty with blue eyes!' she said amusedly, pressing the girl's hand. 'You look entrancing, my dear. Let me have a chance to know you better when we do not have such a squeeze.'

'That would be the greatest of pleasures.'

The older lady looked after the handsome couple speculatively. Such a pretty-mannered girl, she thought, and refined in spite of the *maquillage* essential with her costume. Perhaps this time ...

When the ordeal of meeting the Marchioness again was over, Cassy was able to survey the ballroom with a sense of enchantment. It had been draped in pastel satin to resemble a pavilion at a tournament, and the ladies' perfumes and the hot-house blooms delivered that day from the Allingham country seat emanated a heady sweetness. Cassy saw Harlequins and Columbines, ancient Britons, Roman senators and Greek maidens. But, thankfully, she noticed nobody she knew from the free and easy circle she had frequented since she had become an actress. The very few whom she recollected from her London season would never connect the little Lucasta with Julian's delectable flirt who was dressed so seductively, Chinese style. Had Thomas not been in the country to share the festive period with his family and had Lord Byron not been within a day or two of his wedding, things might have been different. As it was she was besieged with requests for dances from gentlemen wearing the feathered hats of Tudor gallants, crowns of laurel leaves, bishops' mitres and even cockaded helmets.

But, without neglecting his duties as a host, Allingham danced with her as often as he could, particularly if the music was in waltztime.

'Is that not an Italian coffered ceiling?' she asked at one time as she twirled round in his arms, her head thrown back in enjoyment.

'Yes, the result probably of somebody's Grand Tour. I had forgotten,' he added outrageously, 'that you really only became acquainted with the bedchamber.'

'Wretch!'

He took her into the sumptuous supper and she intercepted a smiling glance of approval from his mother, who was the centre of a group at the other end of the room. Cassy felt both gratified and guilty.

'Your mama is delightful,' she said.

'Yes. I believe that she likes you too.'

'But would not, I fear, were she to know who I was.'

'Possibly not,' was the indifferent answer, which told her nothing of his feelings on the subject.

'You have her eyes, but otherwise ...'

'I am said to favour my father. Shall I show you his picture in the gallery?'

He drew her through an anteroom where one or two couples were sitting, and into a dimly lit, deserted gallery. He held a lighted sconce up to the portrait of a tall courtier with a splendid physique who regarded her with the moody expression she had sometimes seen on his son's face.

'Yes,' she said, 'you do resemble him.'

A sudden draught blew out the candles he was holding. The Marquis returned the sconce to a marquetry table and, in the gloom, they both turned, as if it were the most natural thing in the world, into each other's arms. He held her tightly against the whole length of his body. She felt his lips, as on that long ago evening, searing hers and her mouth opened beneath them. She was not sure whether it was his heart or hers that she could hear thudding.

They were both trembling and murmuring broken endearments. As his arms drew her yet closer she felt a shaft of desire shoot through her body which made her try to pull away just because she so ardently longed for yet closer union. But he held her against him still, whispering, 'Sweet, beautiful Cassy, I want you so.'

She touched his lips tenderly with a finger. He drew her to him again, kissed her hard and said, 'Let us return to the ballroom, Cassy, before I forget that I was born, at least, a gentleman. You can never leave me now.'

She looked up at him, puzzled by his words and shaken by his lovemaking. She accompanied him back to the dance, where they stayed apart for propriety's sake until the music was stopped just before midnight so that champagne could be served. She waltzed with him then in the first dance of 1815, and his closeness was almost more than she could sustain without revealing in her face for all to see the truth of her love.

An hour later the guests sat or stood in clusters round the ballroom while a dance troupe, engaged as a surprise diversion by the Marchioness, who liked the ballet, pirouetted before them.

The dancers were like snowflakes, light as gossamer, their white-clad legs a pattern of perfection. But the most arresting of them all was Sybil, the redhead from Covent Garden.

Cassy kept as far back from the dancers as she could, and watching the suddenly thoughtful face of the Marquis, guessed that he too was taken aback by her unanticipated presence and its reminder of reality.

As Sybil finished the dance she sank into a smiling curtsey, looking at the Marquis alone, and it occurred to Cassy that she was under the impression that she had been engaged to entertain his guests at his own special request. He bowed coldly and then his eyes sought those of Cassy in instinctive anxiety for her.

The ballerina's green ones followed the direction of his glance and her face became suddenly ugly. 'Oh, Your Lordship,' she shrilled, 'so, Cassandra is here! I did not know you introduced your doxies from Drury Lane into polite society, even in disguise.'

Allingham strolled with magnificent aplomb to Cassy's side, raised her cold hand to his lips and smiled into her eyes. Then he turned to the dancer and said in icy tones, 'How dare you speak thus of the lady who will do me the honour of becoming my wife!'

Cassy's eyes were like blue bruises in her face. The Marchioness and her relations looked shocked and bewildered and the guests peered questioningly from one to the other of the protagonists in the drama, some with compassion for Cassy, others with delight at a new scandal.

Allingham shepherded the entertainers into a small room for refreshments and then gave a sign to the orchestra to strike up the music. With a bow to Cassy, he swept her once more into the waltz. The sudden babble of comment had stopped in the face of their host's aloof bearing and forbidding expression.

Cassy danced impeccably, like a marionette, avoiding the eyes of the man she could only love the more, and respect, for his chivalrous gesture. When the waltz was over she murmured an excuse and slipped away.

26

Cassy found a basin and scrubbed her face clean. She fetched her cloak, and, knowing already which door led to the back garden, went through it and round to the front of the house. There, shivering with the cold of the early hours of the morning, and total misery, she confirmed by questioning one of the jarveys that the waiting hacks had been ordered for the entertainers.

'Oh, good!' said Cassy brightly. 'Then I may wait inside. The chief dancer is my friend, and it is *so* cold!' She gave him her most bewitching smile and he opened the door of the vehicle for her with alacrity, saying, 'Y'ore right, missy, proper perishin' it be for the first day of the new year.'

'You!' Sybil cried in amazement as she came out of the house, waved the lesser dancers to the other carriages and saw Cassy. Then she climbed in beside her and slanted a look at her compounded of defiance and shame.

'Yes, Sybil, here I am. You have had your revenge and now you must help me.'

The ballet dancer looked with sudden compunction at the white pinched face and said, 'You really love the cove, don't you! I'm sorry now I said what I did, but I was bitter against you for losing me Gerard. Not that I don't have a much superior prospect in tow now. How can I help you?'

'By finding me a place to stay.'

'Seems as if the proud Marquis is stuck on you too, the way he spoke up, in front of him mother too. So why run?'

'Because I *do* love him, too well to marry him under the

circumstances. I was a fool to go at all tonight. I was warned against it but I wouldn't listen. The thing is that I cannot return to my own lodgings because he will possibly seek me there.'

'Then, if you insist on being so addlebrained as to run away, you can stay for a few days in mine, on account of I have an assignation. Look here's the key, and you can explain to the landlady when you see her. She's a good sort and broad-minded. Has to be, I reckon.' Sybil gave her gamine grin. She kissed Cassy impulsively. 'We'll drive there now and I'll take the hack on to my gentleman friend's house.'

'Thank you,' said Cassy bleakly. 'One more thing. John and Louise will worry, so will you leave a note through their door, or desire the driver to do so? But do not call or they will ask awkward questions.'

'Nor I wouldn't anyway, for that dresser-cum-landlady of yours has a way of looking down her nose I don't care for above half. Here, write on this.' She took a crumpled theatre programme from her reticule. 'I'll see it gets there. Meantime, Cassy, use whatever you fancy in my wardrobe for you won't care to face the day looking like a – Pekingese.' She giggled at her own joke.

Cassy scribbled a few words to say that she was staying a night or so with a friend and did not trouble about Louise's inevitable puzzlement when she had so many more far-reaching problems. Aunt Letty would not be anxious for the time being since she had expected that Cassy would stay at her lodgings for a few days in order to acquaint herself with any theatrical opportunities that might be in the offing.

She crept into Sybil's room without disturbing the landlady. Her temporary retreat was lush but, inevitably, in execrable taste. However, Cassy was too exhausted by the activity and emotion of the evening to notice. She sank gratefully into the mauve and yellow draped bed whose headboard had been painted, inexpertly, with cupids, and went fast asleep.

She woke to winter sunshine streaming in the grubby window and felt much restored. Then she remembered all that had happened the night before and wept into the pillow. Finally she blew her nose, wiped her eyes and made up her mind.

She would send a note to Charles Young's residence asking him to receive her the following morning and, if his offer of marriage still held good, without love but with mutual respect, she would accept it. As his wife she would be able to work in the theatre until such time at least as she could pay off her debt to Lord Allingham. That was one service that she could never permit her bridegroom to perform for her.

She had already faced the fact that, unmarried, she could not act in public, both for her own sake and Julian's, not to mention that of his charming mother, until the scandal concerning herself and him had died down. So it seemed, sadly, that she might never now achieve the independence that she had coveted for Thea, Grace and herself. If not, she might just as well relinquish them to the care of Aunt Letty and her new husband, and make herself useful to the widower and his son. Perhaps, she thought now in bitter self-examination, she had been guilty of false pride. She would in due course trust Charles Young with the truth about herself. But for the present she must continue to wear her dark wigs, however inconvenient, so that Lucasta and her family might never inherit the taint of Cassandra's indiscretions.

Cassy considered the riot of colour that constituted Sybil's clothes and found, to her relief, a dove-grey dress and matching pelisse that fitted and became her. With it she could wear the wide poke bonnet she discovered, which hid effectively the sleek black hair that looked so wrong with day wear.

Her first and most pressing errand must unfortunately be to Russell Street to obtain the collection of wigs so essential to her that were at present in Louise's charge. She had no desire to suffer her dresser's cross-examination and recriminations, since she thought it likely that the Marquis, if he cared for her, would have made enquiries about her there. However, she could see no alternative to calling at her lodgings in a hack and hoping not to be observed by anybody who knew Cassandra.

In the hall she encountered Sybil's landlady, very stout but with a pleasing merry countenance that must once have been pretty. She accepted Cassy's presence amiably, saying, 'Going out in the cold, are you? Come into my parlour first and drink a cup of chocolate and eat a piece of my seed cake in the warm. I'm slack at the present as my other lodgers are away for the holiday.' Cassy could not help recalling with amusement Sybil's boast that she had her own establishment and maid.

She was grateful, for she found that she was hungry, and she thanked the kind woman in her sweet way. She felt better able afterwards to face the trying time ahead.

Louise greeted her with relief, but demanded sternly, 'What are you up to, Miss Cassy? Your message didn't tell me nothing sensible and

His Lordship was that worried about you when he came here this morning. Where did you get those clothes?'

'I borrowed them. Now, dear Louise, if you love me, pack up my things quickly in my valise, and let me have the precious box of wigs. While you do so I must write a *billet*.' But as she sat at the desk her dresser hovered over her and Cassy warded off more questions by saying, 'No, don't, I pray, ask me anything further now, for I do not wish you to be forced to tell lies on my behalf. Be sure that I shall let you know, as soon as I do myself, where I shall be.'

'As you say, Miss Cassy,' the dresser said, but her face was expressive of wounded feelings and Cassy kissed her, saying, 'We shall see each other again very soon. Do hurry now, for I have to pay the driver of the hack for waiting.'

Within ten minutes she had written a brief note for Charles Young, saying that she would call upon him late the following morning, had hugged Louise, and had returned to the hack with her few possessions. She felt relief that Russell Street seemed to be deserted, irrational joy that Julian had been concerned enough to call. The jarvey dropped her *billet* for her in the actor's letter box and she wondered, with sudden overwhelming depression, what the morrow would bring.

Cassy asked Sybil's landlady, who had taken a fancy to her, to chaperone her on a morning call to Charles Young. The good-natured woman quite understood that there were occasions when a lady might wish to visit an unattached gentleman. She was pleased to act propriety, to enjoy a break from routine and to take a ride in a hackney cab.

Charles Young came forward to greet his guest, taking both her hands in his. 'Here you are, my dear,' he said with his celebrated smile. 'I am glad you have brought your duenna. What can I order you?'

'Nothing, thank you, sir.'

'I was in the Green Room at Covent Garden last night when Allingham was enquiring for you. He seemed to have lost you!' He gave her a quizzical look that had a hint of wistfulness in it.

Cassy flushed. 'I have reasons for not wishing to see His Lordship. I have come to you because – because—'

'To tell me perhaps that you will accept my offer of matrimony – or that of friendship? We will be honest with each other, won't we?'

194

She cleared her throat, looked down at her hands and answered, 'The former, if you please.'

He looked at her downcast face hard and then spoke very seriously and gently. 'I would have taken you gladly to wife, my dear Cassandra, knowing that I could command only your liking and loyalty. In return I would have offered the same sentiments. But I am not prepared to marry a woman who loves, and is loved, by another man. You do love Julian, don't you? He certainly appears, from his distraught air, to care deeply for you.'

She could only lower her head, nod speechlessly and blink away the tears.

'I shall not ask you what makes you want to escape him, and come to me. But I am honoured in your trust. I should like to substitute sincere friendship for a, possibly, disastrous marriage. Will you let me help you?'

Charles Young lifted her face with a hand under her chin and Cassy looked at him, ashamed. 'You are very good and I do not deserve even your friendship. But I am grateful for it. Lord Allingham has been forced, you see, because of scandal, to announce his betrothal to me. I could not marry him thus, whatever our respective feelings. Somehow I must contrive to earn enough money, both to repay him a debt, and to help my family. Had you accepted me as your wife – and I do not blame you for not doing so – I should have insisted on working for the time being. I would not—'

'I know by now what you would not do, Cassy, and that is be beholden to any man, except one day, I hope, the husband you love.' There was an expression of faint sadness on his face. 'Do you want a part in a play?' he added in a matter-of-fact tone.

'Unfortunately I cannot take one – though I am grateful for the offer – until the conjecture and gossip about Lord Allingham and myself are replaced by another *on dit*. But I shall be glad if you will suggest some place where I can sell the pearls my parents gave me. They should fetch enough to enable me to pay my debt to the Marquis, help my family and still keep myself in some simple style. The pearls are – rather good ones,' she ended in a small voice which seemed to her host quite pathetic.

He answered simply. 'I see. Then the best thing you can do is to sell them to me and redeem them at once when you are in a position to do so.'

'Oh no! Why should you do this for me?'

'Because I would prefer to hold them for you rather than that you should incur another debt. I have excellent surety.' Cassy brushed away another humiliating tear. 'Then, thank you, sir. What more can I say? I do not know how much exactly they are worth.' She drew the string from her reticule.

'My dear girl, these are exceptionally fine. You·should not carry such jewelry around with you. I shall deposit them in my safe.' He moved to draw aside a portrait of Sarah Siddons and withdrew from a compartment in the wall what seemed to Cassy a sum of money vastly in excess of what she had expected.

'I am sure that is too much, sir.'

'I am equally convinced it is not. Do you wish me to send Allingham the amount you owe him rather than to approach him yourself?'

'Please, if you would be so good.'

'Then write down the exact sum. Where can I find you, Cassy? What do you intend to do?'

'I do not know exactly. I consider posting north to relations. But I would rather not burden you with a secret that I should prefer to keep at the moment. Will it do, sir, if I undertake to let you know in due course?'

'It must, I suppose. But I am concerned for you, Cassy. I wish I could have kept you safe with me. But—'

'Oh, I understand,' she replied hurriedly. 'Tell me, sir, how is your son?'

His eyes lit. 'Very well. I have found him a young tutor whom he likes.'

'I am glad. Thank you once again for your kindness.'

'And you for your confidence in me. You are not going in a hackney cab with that money on your person. Wait while I call my carriage for yourself and your maid.' When he had summoned it he said, 'I shall engage to have the sum I have deducted conveyed to Lord Allingham. Would you like my note on our transaction?'

'Oh, no,' she said, 'your friendship is enough.'

'Then go, my dear, and God be with you. Let me know should you ever need me.'

'I promise.'

Charles Young ushered Cassy into the conveyance to the great interest of her temporary chaperone, who, having been regaled with ratafia and biscuits, was in the mood to find the gentleman yet handsomer than she had thought him on the stage. 'Fancy you knowing him!' she marvelled. 'He is splendid!'

'Yes,' said Cassy and changed the subject. 'Thank you for accompanying me this morning. Will you mind if this coach drops us at Bond Street? I have some purchases to make there. We can take a hack home.'

'Let us by all means stroll down Bond Street,' the landlady concurred with satisfaction. 'Before I lost my figure I was well known among the beaux.'

'I can well believe it,' said Cassy truthfully, and in some amusement. As she had not wanted Charles Young's coachman to deposit them at her companion's house and subsequently perhaps be able to divulge her present whereabouts, Bond Street was the first point that had sprung to her mind. She thanked him for his services as they alighted there.

But by the time she had been bowed to by 'Skiffy', or Sir Lumley Skeffington, painted, powdered and in pale blue satin, as well as by other dandies, much to her companion's edification, she had begun to regret her decision.

She was about to hail a passing hack when a voice hailed her from an elegant brown and gold closed carriage with emblazoned doors. As the horses were reined in at the curb at the occupant's bidding she saw with pleasure the maturely beautiful countenance of Lady Oxford, framed in a close-fitting bronze velvet hat with curling ostrich feathers. 'Join me, Cassandra, my pet,' she begged. 'I have not seen you in an age. Come home to luncheon with me and let us indulge in a girls' coze.'

Cassy decided quickly that this invitation was the solution to the risks incurred of recognition by the Marquis himself, or a friend of his, in this fashionable thoroughfare.

She climbed into the grand coach followed with enthusiasm by her chaperone, who knew a great lady when she saw one. Arrived at the town house, Her Ladyship's housekeeper took the duenna in charge and the accredited beauty sat Cassy in a comfortable chair and insisted on her taking a glass of wine. 'You look pale,' she said with some concern. 'Have you been ill? I have been abroad in Paris, which is now so gay again, and was only home to spend Christmas with the children. I am out of touch with London. Byron is married, you know,' she added with seeming irrelevance.

But Cassy understood perfectly the connection between this remark and her former intelligence. 'Poor Byron!' she remarked.

'You should have rather said, poor Annabella!' corrected her Ladyship. 'He will lead her a fine dance.'

Cassy could not help considering, with unwonted cynicism, how singular society was. This woman could remain a leading hostess of the ton, although her numerous progeny were known, from her family name, as 'the Harleian Miscellany' owing to the uncertainty of their varied parentage. But then she had never been in, nor married into, the theatrical profession, however much its members might divert her.

Her hostess asked, 'Are you in a play at present, Cassandra?'

'No. I was in fact ill, ma'am, as you surmised, and shall probably take a rest in the country.'

'Be buried alive more like,' shuddered her ladyship.

Over luncheon she was struck by inspiration. 'Cassy,' she announced, 'our meeting today was surely meant to be. Come back to Paris with me as my social secretary. You can arrange my routs and masques and write my invitations and formal notes. I cannot pay you as much as you could earn at Drury Lane. But I promise that your duties would not be arduous. Just wait, Cassy, till you see those French uniforms and fashions!'

The girl laughed outright. 'You make it all sound quite entrancing, ma'am, and if I thought I could be really useful I would be greatly tempted.'

'You would be invaluable. It is a good recipe for enjoying life to fall whenever tempted! Now, if only you could master some of the lingo, which I cannot seem to do ...'

'In fact, ma'am, I do speak French quite well.' She recalled in time that she should not confide in her prospective employer that she had received the benefit of lessons from nursery days onwards from Aunt Letty, who spoke the language beautifully. Instead she explained, 'I had a friend who helped me to learn it.'

'There, I knew this arrangement was predestined! You must come! When can you be ready?'

Lady Oxford was used to having her own way, and the fact that she achieved it with charm and graciousness was to her credit. Cassy accepted her fate, which was a more agreeable one than the visit she had contemplated to Gerard's family, with its necessity for further falsehoods. She knew that she could not, for the present, face the well-deserved reproaches and inevitable distress of Aunt Letty, and intended to write an apologetic but reassuring letter to her as soon as she was quite sure of her future movements.

So she said, 'I can be ready any time, ma'am. I presume that you do not count on an indefinite stay in Paris. I do not have many gowns in town.'

'Oh no, I shall simply reside there until I tire of it,' the lady answered insouciantly. 'We shall have suitable toilettes for day and evening made for you there. The modistes are real artistes, and much cheaper than my Veronique here in London. We shall have such fun!' She squeezed Cassy's hand and completed the transaction by saying, 'Will you be packed and ready the morning after next when we will drive to Dover and take the packet?'

'Yes, certainly. But may I rely upon your discretion until our departure, for I have reasons for not wanting it generally known where I am bound?'

Her Ladyship chuckled. 'I guessed it, my dear. You have far more romantic reasons for wanting to run away than ill health. The cure for one man is another one. Of that I am convinced. I shall be as silent as the sphinx.'

Cassy and Sybil's landlady were driven back by Lady Oxford's coachman and deposited a short way from their destination. The girl, her flagging spirits raised at the unexpected prospect of foreign travel, said in her sweet way to her companion, 'You were so good to come with me today and lend me countenance, I must leave you the day after tomorrow.'

'I was glad to be of service, and I enjoyed my day out. Don't think I did not realise right away that you are a lady, whatever queer starts you may be in. I shall be glad to help you any way I can before you go.'

'Thank you. I would appreciate one service very much. Would you undertake to have an important letter delivered for me after I leave, and,' she smiled at her confidingly, 'keep your tongue between your teeth about my movements since we met?'

'Never doubt it!'

Cassy spent much of the following day teaching herself to dress her own different wigs as quickly and artistically as Louise did. After continued trial and error and much practice she felt that her efforts were creditable. She must always remember to keep the hat box containing them locked, and she was thankful for the fact that her prospective position in Paris would hardly entail her having her own abigail.

Cassy wrote affectionately and at length to Aunt Letty. She enclosed the greater portion of the money she had received from Charles Young and informed her simply that she had obtained temporary but respectable employment out of town. She apologised for any anxiety she had caused and promised to write very soon again.

The landlady accepted only with the greatest reluctance the small cash present that Cassy insisted on giving her. At the front door she saw the girl off to her new life with a fond embrace and a demand to see her again on her return from her journey.

27

The packet from Dover was crowded, but Lady Oxford's party had their sleeping accommodation reserved below. Cassy felt a little queasy as the boat dived into the deep troughs. She heard the crying of children, the screeching of seagulls and the whinnying and stamping of horses battened into the hold. Then she forgot all this in the sheer novelty and excitement of the experience.

When she had accepted Lady Oxford's suggestion, she had in her confusion of mind momentarily overlooked the fact that Lord Allingham had mentioned a trip to France some time towards the end of this month. Later she had comforted herself with the knowledge that he would be on a military mission, and had not specified Paris as his area of operations. She would probably be on her way home before his arrival, and even if she were not, would hardly be likely to meet him socially in her capacity as a superior sort of domestic employee. The object of her flight from him would be spoiled immediately if they were seen together, and she controlled the tremor that even the remotest possibility of an encounter with him produced. Whether he thought of her with anger, pity or contempt she could not know. She directed her thoughts rather to the casually amused way that Lady Oxford had listened to her account of the débâcle at the masque at Allingham House. She had not dreamed of entrusting her kind but loquacious employer with the secret of her real identity.

As the craft approached land she was already leaning curiously over the rail to see the huddle of houses and the sails of a ·clipper in the harbour loom into view through the morning mist. A bell clanged to alert passengers, who like her employer were still snoozing, and a rousing voice called 'Calais in five minutes. Calais!'

There were crowds of people meeting and greeting each other in a gabble of French and English. Then Lady Oxford's party was on the road to Paris.

She drew Cassy's fascinated attention to the Tuileries Palace, whither Louis XVIII had returned in triumph, remarking, 'He was accompanied by the niece they call "Madame Première". Very fubsy-faced she is too.' Cassy giggled. 'But the couple were welcomed with a mass of white cockades and paper *fleurs de lys*. Mind you, their popularity was short-lived.'

Next she showed Cassy the obelisk in the Place de la Concorde where Robespierre, Charlotte Corday and poor Madame Première's mother, Marie-Antoinette, were guillotined. 'She was not fubsy-faced,' admitted her informant of the queen celebrated for her beauty. 'But her popularity was even more short-lived than her daughter's.' She gurgled at her own macabre joke and Cassy, half shocked and half amused, gave a peal of laughter. But she was relieved when the Ile de la Cité reared its Gothic cathedral spires in mid-Seine and they left behind them the scene of past horrors. Then there was Nôtre Dame, where, she was told, Napoleon had been crowned Emperor by Pope Pius VII just eleven years before.

Lady Oxford's rented house, belonging to a noble family who had lost their fortune, was in a quiet, select boulevard, and was a gem of continental elegance.

The bedchamber designated for Cassy delighted her, for despite the greyness without, it gave the impression of being flooded with sunshine. The hangings of the casements and the huge canopied bed were of intricately looped and festooned golden yellow satin embroidered with *fleurs de lys*. The ceiling was one of Cipriano's better achievements, more successful, Cassy decided with the sudden pain of remembrance, than that in Lord Allingham's Brighton house. It was painted in the tender pale blue of a sky in spring with white puffs of clouds. The furniture was in delicately wrought gilt and marble and the Aubusson carpet in pastel shades – the yellows and blues predominating. Cassy's spirits lifted. It was surely better to be unhappy, if she must, in such very charming surroundings.

In point of fact it transpired that Cassy had little time to dwell upon her private woes. The French capital was full of English visitors, who had rushed across the Channel to compensate themselves for their incarceration in their damp isle during the war.

The ladies bought supple satins, gossamer laces and ring velvets that had not been available at home for years. They copied the French dress styles and the coiffures, like the fascinating 'la victime' inspired by the guillotine.

The dandies had come to look at the French ladies, and the more sober-minded gentlemen to open up business again and to study the political climate. With them were the returned, aristocratic French emigrés.

The result was a giddy social whirl in which Lady Oxford's *petits soupers*, *ridottes* and masques were, with Cassy's aid, among the most notable.

The indolent beauty soon came to rely on her social secretary's natural flair and energy. The girl's ever increasing fluency in French enabled orders to be transmitted, and their execution more easily supervised, in a household of hired French servants and a handful of English ones who had accompanied them from England.

Cassy had expected, and desired, to stay in the background. But Lady Oxford, suffering from an aching, if inconstant, heart over the defection of Byron, demanded her young friend's lively companionship. She was also astute enough to realise that the girl's loveliness, grace in the dance, willingness to sing or help organise charades and masques made her own entertainments the more popular with the younger beaux and ladies of fashion. She had, besides, developed a real regard for Cassy.

The latter had never confessed to her friend and employer the depth of passion that she, most unfortunately, felt for the Marquis. But, having heard the drama of the New Year's ball Lady Oxford strongly advised Cassy to take him as her lover if the opportunity arose but still to follow her sound advice to marry into the French aristocracy. She appreciated the fact that the girl's stage career had rendered her ineligible as a bride for any English nobleman, but thought that her stage background would not have the same significance abroad.

Cassy, in fact, already had a suitor, the Duc de Lange, who came calling upon her the morning after their first meeting straight from duty at the Tuileries Palace. He was wearing the epaulettes of a captain of the Royal Guards, and he tossed his shako and sabre *briquet* on a padded elbow chair before sinking on one knee and entreating 'la belle Anglaise', to marry him. He was large, bewhiskered, likeable and an excellent marriage prospect.

'Take him,' counselled Lady Oxford when he had departed after begging Cassy not to dismiss his suit summarily but to think on it. 'Just consider,' Her Ladyship pointed out persuasively, 'that once safely married to him you can have all the amours you fancy.'

Cassy feared to offend her friend by an admission that marriage on such terms was not for her. She reflected with inward amusement that, though her hostess spoke with affection of her husband, she had never yet seen them together. So she made an airily evasive reply.

She wondered sometime if she could, or even cared to, cope with the eventual struggle to re-establish herself on the stage after so long an absence. There would be so many eager newcomers waiting for auditions. With the urgent need to maintain her sisters gone she might be tempted to find a post abroad in a real scholastic establishment. Her French was fluent, her German adequate and lessons in singing, dancing and elocution presented no problem to her, even if spelling and arithmetic did. She smiled to herself. It would be ironic if, in such a way, she should return to being blonde Lucasta, and thus turn the fabrications about her imaginary academy into fact.

Some days later Cassy was attending a ball at the hôtel of a Marquise of the Bourbon family when she saw with consternation the painfully familiar figure of Dolly's husband, Marcel de Mallon, at the far side of the room. But in contrast with her last view of him, he was now resplendent in snowy cravat, silk knee breeches and a pale satin coat. He looked sleekly well-nourished now – at Dolly's expense, she thought with contempt – and strikingly handsome in a shifty-eyed, weak-mouthed fashion. If he had in fact repaired his fortunes, as seemed likely, Cassy had every intention of preventing her friend's further sacrifice of a regular portion of her hard-earned income.

As her one time captor danced gracefully past with an exquisitely gowned lady, she slipped into a small side parlour to avoid detection. The sight of him had affected her with a powerful revulsion.

But having discovered by discreet enquiry that he was a great favourite with the ladies and considered an eligible, rich bachelor she felt even more indignant on behalf of Dolly and Georgie. However, she realised that, failing more evidence against him, she must give him the benefit of the doubt. It was just possible that, having re-established himself in France, he intended to send for his family and make reparation.

She was destined to learn more of him a few days later. This time she saw him at a crowded musical evening at a country house in the Bois de Boulogne. Cassy avoided his vicinity for fear of being forced to confront him. But his glance had passed over her without recognition. In white batiste with rosebuds at her shoulder and a new Parisian coiffure she would not at first sight remind him of the desperate actress of his London adventure.

But Cassy kept de Mallon under surveillance and she noted that he was flanked during the recital by a number of other dandies, including the son of the house. She remarked, without attributing significance to the fact, that they were, by nods and unobtrusive signals, seeking an opportunity to escape the performance and be private. This was in itself hardly surprising since young gentlemen were notoriously unenthusiastic about the efforts of elderly amateur musicians. Cassy, motivated by instinctive suspicion, murmured to Lady Oxford that she wished to fetch her shawl. She was arrested as she went to the powder closet by the hum of male voices from the half-open door of a small salon. She lingered unashamedly outside it long enough to distinguish the voice of de Mallon among the others.

She heard a list of what sounded like provinces and the strength of their respective forces and a heartfelt 'Vive Bonaparte!' hurriedly hushed by the others. When Cassy, carrying her shawl, passed the door again it was closed and she could discern only a murmur of conversation.

She returned to Lady Oxford's side and was so abstracted that the latter had to repeat an observation twice before her young friend heard her and agreed, with a quick smile, that the Beethoven sonata had been excellently rendered on the pianoforte.

'I believe you are not at all musically inclined, in spite of your sweet voice, Cassy,' the older woman teased her.

'I am sorry, ma'am. It is not that,' Cassy apologised. 'I was just pondering ...'

'On the Duc de Lange's proposal, I hope.'

Later in the musical programme Cassy noticed that the conspirators were once again at the back of the room. Her thoughts were still on the implications of what she had heard. It appeared to bear out the contention of the Marquis that there was a new tide of pro-Napoleon feeling. But it seemed extraordinary that the heir to a noble title such as their host's son and other well-bred Frenchmen should be plotting action to support the exiled Emperor, should he escape from Elba.

Cassy asked herself to whom she could convey the intelligence. She decided during the polite, if relieved, applause that greeted the conclusion of the last piece that she would, during the supper that was to follow, try to discover and memorise the names of the seven or eight other gentlemen present with de Mallon at the meeting.

She achieved her object by tactful enquiries here and there, and her experience of learning lines stood her in good stead in the feat of memory required. As soon as she returned to her luxurious chamber she sat at the marble-topped writing desk and, in the soft illumination from the cut crystal candlesticks with their drops and pendants, drew out paper, quill and crested blotting book. She painstakingly inscribed the names she had learned and what few details of provinces and numbers she had overheard.

Her task completed, she resolved to sleep upon the problem of the best person to approach with information that might be of importance. This must obviously be an Englishman, since it was painfully clear that the loyalties of any Frenchman, however aristocratic his lineage, must be in doubt.

The question was solved for Cassy the very next morning in a disquieting way. Lady Oxford entered the morning parlour where the girl was writing invitations to their latest function with a mischievous expression on her face. 'My love,' she exulted, 'Allingham is here, waiting on you in the morning salon.'

'No!' Cassy protested involuntarily. The revealing colour flooded into her face and then she paled.

Her Ladyship looked at her with some surprise and then said, 'If you feel so strongly, I shall afford His Lordship ten minutes of my company while you compose yourself and invent a speech of dismissal. I must own that I wish that fascinating wretch were here on my account.' The good-natured lady bestowed her affectionate, half-mocking smile on Cassy, who had recovered her wits enough to thank her.

The girl changed into a particularly becoming morning dress of high-necked honey-coloured crêpe and she entered the saloon with all the composure she could muster to greet civilly the unwelcome, but longed-for guest, who regarded her steadily from eyes that had become, once again, unreadable.

He was still dressed for travelling in buckskin and hessians and, after bowing to Cassy, accepted without comment Lady Oxford's excuse of household duties to leave the couple alone.

As she closed the door with a last curious backwards glance he said politely, 'Forgive my attire, ma'am, but I have ridden direct from the Pas de Calais.'

'But not to see me, sir, I trust,' she said with equal formality, though she felt an unmaidenly desire to throw herself into his arms. 'I collect that you were due in any case to come to France.'

'Yes. But when I heard from that fop Skiffy that Cassandra had been seen talking to Lady Oxford in Bond Street I discovered your trail, decided to follow it and to fulfil my military obligations earlier than planned.'

She said with deep reproach in her voice, 'You were rash and most unwise to call upon me here. I came away precisely so that our names should no longer be associated. My present employer is only one of many members of London society who have settled here for the nonce and who would appreciate food for future speculation about us.'

'I see. I wonder what article of value to yourself you had to sell to be able to pay back so promptly my small loan to you?' His mouth tightened, but he said suddenly in the old way, seeing the shadow of sadness in her face, 'What is it, dear? Was the thought of betrothal to me so repugnant that you must needs flee at all costs?'

She could not answer for the lump in her throat and the smarting of her eyes. His voice hardened. 'I see it was. But I still think you must marry me and give up this way of life, which is most unsuitable for you. I offer you my hand and name, Cassy, and undertake to make no physical demands upon you if that is what you would prefer.'

She looked at him, her face suffused with lovely colour. 'You must know by now that it would not be at all what I would prefer – that you are far from – repugnant to me. But my answer must remain the same.'

'I cannot force you to the altar,' he returned disdainfully. 'I presume you have found somebody who suits you better here in France. Marriage to a Frenchman would certainly be a solution to your difficulties, since you do not want me.'

Hurt pride made his voice and face flinty, and Cassy was brought up against the realisation that, despite the fact that he had once whispered endearments and owned to desiring her, he had never actually said that he loved her.

Now she cried in desperation, 'You do not understand!'

'I think you have made your sentiments quite clear. Please make my adieux to your hostess.'

But, when he would have swept out, Cassy detained him with a supplicating hand. 'Please do not go – like this, and be – so angry,' she said in a breaking voice. 'I shall still think of you always with the gratitude you dislike and as – my friend.' She paused. 'Besides, I must tell you something important that might have some bearing on your business here.'

He looked surprised, but waited while she described succinctly the appearance of de Mallon in the city and the snatches of conversation, implying Bonapartist allegiance, that she had heard in the house in the Bois de Boulogne the previous evening.

His attention was diverted from their personal relationship and he asked urgently, 'Do you recall any of the names of the men who were present at the meeting? The house you mention is on my list of possible Bonapartist strongholds. But investigation into those you heard talking might well produce valuable information.'

'Yes,' she answered quickly, relieved to be able to recompense him in some way at least for the wound she had been forced to deliver, if only to his *amour propre*. 'I discovered and memorised them all and wrote the list as soon as I returned here.'

'What a girl you are!' he commended her, and she was thankful for the return of a vestige of warmth to the expressive voice, which was capable of such tenderness as well as harshness.

She ran upstairs to collect the list and he watched her with new respect while she added names of provinces and other details in case they might help to complete a picture. 'The month of March was also mentioned,' she added diffidently, 'and somebody, I don't know which, said, "Vive Bonaparte".'

He looked thoughtful. Then he smiled slightly. 'Accept my gratitude in return for yours.' He hesitated, seeming unsure of himself for once, then asked, 'Shall you stay in Paris long?'

'I had thought to remain away from England until the scandal of Cassandra and the Marquis is superseded by another. Then I hope to return without shaming either your family or myself.'

'No suitors here, then?'

She was stung to retort quickly, since the notion that he might think her unsought was somehow intolerable, 'On the contrary, I have had one offer already and need not despair of receiving others.'

There was a glimmer of amusement in the flecked eyes as he

rejoined, 'I never really doubted it, my dear. Shall you accept one and become a pillar of Parisian society?'

'No!' she said emphatically.

'Do you hold the whole male sex in such dislike?' he asked in sudden curiosity.

'Of course not. But,' she added with honesty, 'I have an attachment already.'

'Oh! Is your affection unrequited then?' His eyes were enigmatic again.

'It does – not signify.'

He looked at her, nonplussed, then rose to take his leave, saying, 'We shall doubtless encounter each other again here though I avoid squeezes of the *beau monde* whenever possible. I promise not to seek you out again. But I am, as ever, at your service.' He looked at her as if he would have spoken further, then bowed a little ironically and left, leaving Cassy a prey to conflicting emotions, those of the joy and reassurance that his proximity brought with it, and of a most profound depression.

Lady Oxford bustled back, and seeing Cassy's distraction remarked sympathetically, 'He has quite put me into a flutter too. He is, next to Byron, the most attractive rake I ever met.' She continued, clearly with the kind intention of diverting Cassy's thoughts, 'Allingham told me that Byron rode north to his wedding on the second day of this month like a man to the guillotine. How I miss him, Cassy!'

The girl felt bound to commiserate with the incorrigibly romantical lady. 'Never mind, ma'am,' she drew herself out of her preoccupation to say consolingly, 'just think of the hearts you have broken here.'

Her hostess giggled like a girl but replied with commendable honesty, 'Not as many as you have, love. Now don't say you are going to desert me just when we are dealing so comfortably together. You cannot be made to marry Allingham, though' – she looked pensive – 'I might be much tempted.'

Cassy had to laugh. 'No, I won't leave you yet, ma'am, if you still like to have me here. You have treated me so kindly.'

'Good. Then that's settled. Besides,' she concluded to Cassy's surprise, 'I expect one of my daughters tomorrow. She is newly out of school, just seventeen and an engaging little thing. You will be a companion for her.'

28

The girls took to each other right away. Agatha was a doe-eyed, brown-haired child with her mother's famed figure on a smaller scale. Otherwise she must, Cassy thought, resemble whoever her father might be.

However, she had a serious turn of mind and a romantical nature. Cassy enjoyed the recent schoolgirl's wide-eyed wonder, and Agatha appreciated the older girl's ready sense of humour and matter-of-fact, critical approach to the social whirl in which she suddenly found herself somewhat at a loss, if delightfully so.

They had been companions for more than a week when, exchanging laughing reminiscences over the fulsome compliments from a pair of French beaux at a *ridotte* the evening before, a surprising conversation took place.

'You are a real jokesmith, Cassy. You take nothing seriously, even your suitors. You have so many of them, in spite of the fact that, unlike me, you are not an heiress!'

Cassy was amused, but hastened to caution her, 'Do not, I beg of you, announce the fact that you are rich or you will become the prey of every gazetted fortune-hunter in town. That is a danger to which I am not myself exposed.'

'You could not think I would be so vulgar as to tell anybody I am my father's sole legatee.' But then Agatha qualified the assertion ingenuously, 'I have only told one special person.' She looked all of a sudden joyful and at the same time guilty.

'Which person?' questioned Cassy sharply.

'I should not have told you so much if I did not trust you, and I shall not divulge the gentleman's name even if – if you put me on the rack.'

'Which is unlikely, since I don't possess one. But why did you tell this special person of your expectations? Did he ask you? I know your mother does not talk of them. In any case you have only just left school. You can expect far more suitors than I have, some with fortunes equal to your own and with no inclination, as a consequence, to hang out for a rich wife.'

'Yes, Cassy, but you are not sentimental yourself and you cannot comprehend what it is to fall quite hopelessly in love.' Her velvety brown eyes were damp and Cassy was quite appalled at her revelation. 'You think I am not up to snuff,' Agatha continued earnestly, tears hanging on her long eyelashes, 'but I recognise a noble spirit. He told me he could never have been an aspirant to my hand unless I had told him I loved him as much as he loves me.' The tears fell, and, seeing her fumbling, Cassy silently handed over her own kerchief.

Agatha mopped her eyes, blew her pink nose and still contrived to look as lovely as only the very young can under such testing circumstances.

'I do sympathise, dear,' Cassy assured her. 'I may fun, but I am not heartless. Tell me, is this poor but chivalrous gentleman French?'

'I – I do not wish to say more, Cassy, because it would be unfair to make you keep secrets from my mama.'

'As you wish,' Cassy conceded the point. 'But I am not being cynical, only practical, when I warn you that fortune hunters do not necessarily announce themselves as such.' She tried, with an affection-ately teasing expression, to get the other girl to smile.

Instead, the pretty, soft mouth puckered, and she protested. 'Oh, but you do not know him!'

'Very true. Now let us walk together with your maid to the Champs-Elysées and see if we can discover ribbons of the exact lavender of your new gown.'

Cassy did not raise the question of Agatha's beloved again. But, without betraying her confidence or appearing officious, she was vigilant on her innocent and inexperienced friend's behalf. She had herself gained knowledge of the world, sometimes bitter, both in London and Paris, and this frenetic society of the newly restored monarchy and its adherents was a heady atmosphere for a country girl like Agatha. Her worldly and frivolous mother, fond though she might be, was, Cassy thought worriedly, hardly the ideal guardian.

Cassy saw Lord Allingham only infrequently, although he was always eagerly sought after by society hostesses. Apart from his usual boredom with entertainments of the *beau monde* he was heavily involved in official duties. His absence, Cassy thought a little ruefully, was just as well for both their sakes.

But her treacherous heart smote her none the less when she caught sight of him one morning escorting a gorgeous female into the milliner's establishment patronised by the fashionable female world.

'What distinguished looks Lord Allingham has!' remarked Agatha, 'and I surmise he is about to spend an unconscionable amount of money on a *chapeau* for his lovely companion.' She smiled up at Cassy, inviting her to share her innocent amusement. She was surprised to see a shadow on her friend's face, but reassured by the answering smile that quickly followed it.

'I am sure of it too, Agatha. Will you help me to choose a new reticule? This one is sadly shabby.' Lady Oxford insisted on providing Cassy with a generous salary for what her social secretary considered trifling services. But when she protested, her patroness feigned offended feelings. She was thus able to replenish the limited supply of clothing she had been able to collect from Louise's house with some new and stylish Parisian ensembles.

She was glad to be seen wearing her olive green Russian mantle, pelisse and cap edged with ermine when she and Agatha encountered the Marquis on their return along the fashionable street. He doffed his hat and his eyes flickered over Cassy with obvious admiration as he passed. But he did not stop to speak. It would not have been at all the thing to do so in any case in view of the fact that he would then have been forced to introduce his presumed present particular to them.

Cassy could not help appreciating the humour of the situation in her own case. Lady Oxford had, charitably, seen no point in telling her daughter more about her companion than that she was, owing to her parents' untimely demise, in reduced circumstances. There was in any case a tacit understanding between the older woman and her companion not to discuss the latter's theatrical career in front of other people.

The high point of the season was an invitation from the Duc de Bourbon to a ball at his vast barracks-like palace, which was stiff with sentries.

But within its austere walls Cassy and Agatha drew in their breaths in wonder as their eyes were dazzled by the sumptuousness of their surroundings and their ears ravished by the sweetness of a hundred violins.

The Duke himself who, rumour had it, wanted to marry a London courtesan who had conquered his heart during his exile, was bluffly blond and plumply handsome.

The nobility of Paris was present *en masse* as well as the more distinguished foreign visitors, including, for once, the Marquis of Allingham. Cassy, prejudiced perhaps, found he put the more flamboyant gentlemen in the shade in his trim, steel-grey coat with its silver buttons, which fitted so sleekly over his wide shoulders.

He danced with various society ladies, including Lady Oxford, who had him laughing at one of her sallies. He stood up with Agatha too, gazing wearily over her brown head as he had once done with Cassy at Almack's in what seemed another age. He did not approach Cassy, who half hoped and half feared he might, but took into supper a royal duchess whose amber velvet ball gown made no pretence of hiding anything but the points of her opulent breasts and whose ink-black eyes devoured his handsome countenance.

Over the *filets de perdrix à la Lorraine,* the caviare and the Savarin cake in Kirsch syrup, Cassy, with a feeling of unreasonable desolation, tried not to cast covert glances in his direction, but to concentrate on her self-imposed task of watching Agatha's reactions. But although the girl, at her prettiest in white with scarlet ribbons, was radiant with pleasure and excitement, Cassy could not see that any particular gallant had attached her, or that her behaviour towards the Hussar officer with the encrusted epaulettes who had escorted her into the supper salon was expressive of anything but a mild flirtatiousness.

But although Agatha caused Cassy no disquiet at the Bourbon ball, at home her moments of elation alternating with melancholy like sun and rain in April were alarming. While still professing the deepest friendship for Cassy, she would make the flimsiest excuses to go off alone, except for her young French maid. But Cassy had no greater opinion of this duenna's steadiness than of that of her mistress. She would not demean herself by questioning either the abigail or the coachman. But such were her misgivings that she would by now have voiced them to her employer had she not given her solemn promise to the younger girl not to do so.

One sparkling day, when the wind whipped the ladies' skirts into full-blown tulips, Cassy finally decided to follow Agatha and her maid on a morning shopping jaunt, purported to be a quest for a surprise gift for Cassy's imminent birthday.

The latter, unaccompanied, hoped she would not be seen by anybody who might recognise her, and shake her hard-won respectability. She wore an old woollen cloak and enveloping hood, which she was confident that Agatha would not have seen. She walked at a discreet distance behind the hurrying girl who, in support of the truth of her story, was indeed making for the most frequented shopping boulevard in the vicinity.

She and the animated maid, who roused Cassy's suspicions by casting theatrical glances over her shoulder, disappeared into a bookseller's shop. Cassy gave a quick peep through the diamond-paned bow window and saw, to her incredulous dismay, Agatha's sweet face, tremulous with emotion, gazing into the tenderly smiling visage of Marcel de Mallon.

Cassy retraced her footsteps rapidly, repelling curious looks with a quelling air, and was thankful when she gained her objective without recognition. She was aghast and bewildered by the object of her friend's first love, which, even though probably a passing fancy, could leave only disillusion in its wake.

Cassy sat in the buttoned yellow velvet chair in her chamber, with her blue eyes unseeingly on Cipriano's painted ceiling and her thoughts in chaos. How could her enemy aspire to Agatha's hand, even to gain a fortune, when he already had a wife and child? Even he could not hope that a bigamous marriage would remain for ever undiscovered. Both the Marquis and his cousin as well as herself knew of his domestic background. So what did he hope to win by this role of humble adorer? A love affair was one answer, but Cassy doubted that an unscrupulous man of the world who had opportunities of numerous amours would trifle with such a very young girl if money were not involved. But how did he hope to gain his objective?

Her ruminations were interrupted by a scratching at her door, and the entrance of Agatha herself who, holding a parcel in full view, said she hoped Cassy had not been dull during her absence.

The older girl looked at the younger with compassion for her artlessness and for the suffering she must inevitably experience. She forced a smile, replying 'Indeed I have. Go and take off your bonnet, hide that pretty packet and play me at backgammon.'

Agatha pouted prettily in pretended petulance. 'Only if you let me win one game. You are too crafty by half.' Cassy thought wryly that she would have to become more than half crafty if she were to bring this business to a satisfactory conclusion.

Lady Oxford and her daughter joined Cassy at her bedside for her birthday breakfast in early February of chocolate and croissants. Her employer gave her an ermine tie to go with her fur-trimmed cap, and Agatha presented her, imaginatively, Cassy thought, with Rousseau's controversial work, *La Nouvelle Héloïse*.

Cassy felt a rush of gratitude and affection for the two ladies which she tried, haltingly, to express. Their kind thoughts made up in some part for the absence of her own dear ones. Her pleasure was complete when Lady Oxford said, 'We will all three go to the Opéra this evening. Fillipo Taglioni is staging short ballets in which several members of his large and gifted family are taking part. Even his little daughter, Marie, is said to hold promise of greatness though she is not yet twelve.'

'How wonderful!' said Cassy. 'I have heard that the mite can already cross the stage in a few bounds without as much as a footfall being heard by the audience.' She looked forward eagerly to the treat.

Lady Oxford had provided suitable escorts for the girls and herself and it seemed to Cassy ironic that all three females would have preferred other, if less suitable, companions. As things were, she was herself squired by her erstwhile suitor, the Duc de Lange, impressive in his uniform, who had, to her relief, settled for an affectionate friendship. He was always amiable and entertaining and his frequent presence protected her from other, less welcome attentions. Agatha had a pink-faced young fellow officer of his in attendance and her mother another, scarcely older than the other two, yet visibly smitten by her autumnal beauty.

The audience at the theatre was brilliantly attired and determined, as the hum of excitement showed, to enjoy the occasion after so many years of war and austerity. Most people rose respectfully to their feet when the massive King Louis appeared in the royal box with Madame Première, the Prince de Condé and their recent host, the Prince de Bourbon. But Cassy noticed that there were those who ostentatiously failed to leave their seats.

One of the Taglionis danced the title role of the princess in the main ballet. Cassy would have recognised the vision of loveliness with almond eyes and high cheekbones that she had seen with the Marquis in the Champs-Elysées, even if Agatha had not in an undervoice drawn her attention to the fact. Although she managed to nod at the girl with a smile, her own jealousy shamed and shocked her.

During an interval, while the gentlemen in their box poured them pink champagne, she scanned the audience for Lord Allingham. He was not visible there, although, she reflected with irrational resentment, he might well be in the ballerina's dressing-room.

However, her eyes lighted upon the comely face of Marcus Stanton which broke into a spontaneous beam of delight as he caught sight of her. He excused himself at once from the party he was with, and with a friendly gesture made his way from the stalls to visit her.

Cassy felt a wave of warmth, for the friendly gentleman who loved and would marry her dear Aunt Letty was the nearest thing here to her own family even if he could not know it yet. She held out her hands to him and made him known to her companions, although, not surprisingly, he had already met Lady Oxford with Lord Byron in London.

Cassy thought that he looked at her for a moment in a puzzled fashion. But then at her invitation he sat down and talked comfortably to them all. Finally he turned aside to Cassy and complimented her on her deep pink satin gown with its overdress of net that made her look, he said, like one of the roses that bloomed in the summertime in his English garden.

He was evidently curious about Cassandra's presence in Paris, but sensitive enough to keep his questions until the morrow when he undertook, with Lady Oxford's permission, to wait upon her at home.

Cassy realised that Marcus Stanton was unlikely to have heard the scandal about the actress and the Marquis as he had not been in London since the New Year. He slipped away as the curtain was about to rise on the next ballet. But the unexpected meeting completed Cassy's enjoyment of her birthday.

When he came to call the next morning Agatha had left on a so-called shopping expedition with her maid, and her mother was making one of her almost daily morning calls. Cassy had already decided to acquaint him with the facts of her double life as much for Aunt Letty's sake as for her own comfort. He was not so much horrified as, predictably, Cassy thought, diverted by the story.

'Poor Cassy!' he said, laughing, 'To think I did not recognise you suffering in Brighton beside Romeo Coates! I realise now why we saw the understudy instead of the star on the afternoon that I escorted both our families to the theatre there. Come to think on it, I could have sworn I had seen you before when I first met you at Worthing.

Then I put it down to your resemblance to your dear mama as a girl. Oh, what a poser I have given my Letty!'

Once again Cassy had emphasised the lighter side of her masquerade and of her association with Allingham. But so understanding was he that she found herself telling him about the drama of the costume ball too.

He looked concerned, but said, 'I think better of the Marquis for claiming you as his betrothed, knowing what a high stickler his mama is. She would not have been pleased with the naughty trick played by Lucasta, even had she known who you really were. But you are a girl after my own heart.' He was thoughtful a moment, then he continued, 'I suppose one of these days theatre folk will be considered respectable, but not in my generation, nor yours. That is why I intend winding up my connection with the profession before I marry Letty – that is, if she has not changed her mind,' he added, apprehensive as a boy.

'I don't doubt that she will marry you, sir,' Cassy assured him with a wide smile.

He looked pleased and said, 'Thank you for your vote of confidence. Do you sometimes miss the theatre, Cassy?'

'In some ways. I presume I shall in due course return to it, although ...' She did not finish the thought but asked instead, 'Will you not miss it yourself?'

He had looked concerned at her words but now declared, 'Like the devil! I shall have a sweet compensation, however, and wish you may yourself be as lucky some day. We will discuss our shady pasts then, Cassy, like the reformed characters we will be. Are you going to marry that fancy French Johnny who was casting ardent glances at you last night?'

'No, for I do not love him,' she answered frankly.

Lady Oxford bustled in now in time to hear Cassy's last statement, and cried gaily, 'Welcome, Mr Stanton. Were you asking my foolish Cassy about the excellent opportunity which she has refused? I must admit that I have found marriage most convenient myself and cannot understand her attitude. I was never so free when I was unattached as I am now.' She was clearly unconscious of the comic singularity of her sentiments and, although her listeners forbore to comment, the laughter in their eyes was irrepressible.

Lady Oxford now told her guest warmly, 'You must come to dinner after my return from a two-day visit to friends outside Paris. I would not leave my little daughter if Cassy were not here to bear her company. When do you leave, and whither are you bound next on your tour?'

'Not for another week, ma'am, and I go then to Vienna, where, with the Congress in full progress, the theatre is enjoying a boom.'

'How I envy you!' Her ladyship sighed. 'I believe the city is – incandescent – with life. The Duke of Wellington is representing the Prince Regent at the talks there, is he not? I am informed that his staff officers must be able to dance well and to be acceptable socially.' Her eyes were the dreaming pools of a young girl.

'Yes, Wellington has replaced Castlereagh at the Congress,' Marcus Stanton confirmed, and added rather drily, 'I hope his officers acquit themselves as well strategically as in the ballroom.'

He wrote down his direction at the request of his hostess, and took his leave from her. Cassy saw him to the door, and he promised her quickly to respect her confidence, but to call again to show her a letter which he had received from Miss Page. 'Your aunt gives news of the girls' progress, but mentions only that she has not seen Lucasta recently. I naturally assumed that she was working over hard in the seminary!'

They smiled at each other like conspirators and on that happy note his visit ended. But when Agatha returned from her outing a cloud was cast on Cassy's enjoyment of the morning by the look of exaltation on her face. She marvelled that Lady Oxford was not more observant of her daughter and wondered whether she should not herself tell her hostess her fears. But the older woman was so full of plans for her departure that afternoon that Cassy decided to wait until her return – a decision which she was to regret.

29

Cassy watched her young companion that evening as closely as she could without arousing her suspicions. She decided that her vivacity over their simple game of cards was excessive. She ventured to remark, 'You are in alt tonight, Agatha.'

'Do I seem so, Cassy?' she replied quickly. 'If so, 'tis just that it is fun to be seventeen, in Paris and to have a friend like you.' She gave Cassy's shoulder a little squeeze, saying, to the other's disquiet, 'You would never turn against me, would you?'

'No,' averred Cassy staunchly. But her heart misgave her. It sounded ominously as if the girl had decided to throw her bonnet over the windmill, perhaps in her mama's absence.

While Agatha pondered her play Cassy made a desperate resolve. Dolly's husband must be confronted and threatened with exposure if he did not relinquish his designs. But where would she find him? She had discovered already, with thankfulness, that he was not on her employer's invitation list. She could not enquire for him about town without causing comment. She was forced at this juncture to own to herself that she would in any case be much too frightened to face him alone.

She came to the reluctant conclusion that there was only one possible course, and that was to enlist Lord Allingham's aid. He not only knew de Mallon's record and potential for evil, but also, doubtless, his whereabouts, as a result of his presumed investigations into the background of the Bonapartist supporters listed on Cassy's paper.

After Agatha had won the game Cassy told her she must fetch a half-written letter which she had left in the morning parlour. She found the Marquis's direction in her employer's book, and quickly sent a footman there with a *billet*, on the pretext of having overlooked an invitation card.

She asked him in the missive to kindly call upon her at ten o'clock the next morning, when Agatha should be engaged in her lesson on the pianoforte, for which she showed talent. The lackey returned with the information that His Lordship was from home, but that his man expected him later. Much later, Cassy supposed sadly.

Nevertheless he arrived to see her on the hour the next morning, meticulously groomed as ever, and asked with anxiety, 'What's happened, Cassy? Something serious, I must presume, for you to summon me here!'

They could hear the strains of one of Mozart's works played with some ability, as she told him of her fears for Agatha.

'Could you not simply tell the silly widgeon what you know of him?' he asked logically.

'No, although that is what I should do if she would only confide his name to me. But,' she smiled at him a little wanly, 'Agatha told me she would rather be put upon the rack than divulge his identity, for fear I might be prevailed upon to inform against her. I only discovered the horrid truth by following her to a rendezvous in a book shop.'

'Oh, Cassy,' he grinned at her with the half-admiring mockery that she loved and had so missed at their last, strained interview, 'what a rash and reckless girl you still are!'

'Only when I have to be,' she defended herself, suddenly irrationally happy.

'Which seems to be most of the time. Anyway, I intend to handle this matter myself. As you guessed, I do know his address. Your intelligence about the Bonapartists has been of great use, by the way. Do you trust me to frighten off de Mallon without your help? There is no need for him to know of your connection with the matter, now that you are living down your – our – lurid past.' He smiled a little sardonically.

'I do trust you to handle him – all the better without my help,' Cassy assured him with the utmost sincerity, 'and—'

'No, don't thank me,' he warned her. 'As a matter of fact it assuages the wound to my vanity to be of use to you at least in something.' If only he had said even then that his feelings had been hurt instead, she might so easily have weakened, confessed her love and begged him to marry her after all, and to perdition with his family's feelings.

But now they were in the hallway and the butler's faintly disapproving mien made his lordship say with a wicked gleam, 'He clearly suspects me of coming to ravish you in his employer's absence.'

'Oh!' she coloured furiously, 'you really are—'

'A wretch? So you have told me. I shall write to you the result of my confrontation with the villain. It were better for your reputation than my calling again.'

He was gone and Cassy looked after him with regret and longing.

That evening a note inscribed with her name and marked 'Private' was handed to her. It read:

Ma'am,
The outcome of my meeting with the subject of our discussion was as satisfactory as anticipated. Shock and chagrin were followed by announcement of expected divorce and dubious protestations of genuine devotion. Subject undertakes to take necessary steps to end association and own presence here.

Your Admirer

The laconic communication was typical of its writer, and entertained Cassy as much as it relieved her mind. Now she must watch Agatha like a hawk to save her from humiliation. She felt an unwise inclination to treasure this dry letter in the strong, literate hand. Then she quickly and resolutely destroyed it.

That same evening a far more flowery script was to be seen on a *billet* delivered to Agatha, and borne by her trembling hands to be read in the privacy of her chamber. Cassy, forewarned, went up to her own, adjoining bedroom, prepared for what was soon to be heard, racking, heartbroken sobs.

Cassy hurried in and gathered the girl in her arms, saying nothing until the sobs subsided to a shudder. She drew her on to a *chaise longue*, patting her as she would a hurt child.

'He writes that he must go away because he cannot bear to be in the same city as me when he knows I can never be his.' Agatha buried her damp face on Cassy's shoulder.

'Come, love,' Cassy said in a comforting voice, 'lie on your bed and your maid shall bring you a posset.' There was nothing else to say, least of all the truth, that time and another, worthier love would mend her heart.

Cassy could not sleep any more, she was sure, than Agatha in the next chamber. She had known the joy, pain and grief of love herself and was consumed with helpless pity.

Thus, later, she heard the creaking sound of the heavy oaken hall door being opened stealthily. Then there was a footfall outside her window and, peering out in consternation, she could just discern Agatha alone, starting to walk hesitantly, and looking to right and left, as if uncertain whether to hail a fiacre or to go on foot along the dark, mud-spattered boulevard.

Her indecision gave Cassy time to throw her cloak and hood over her nightgown and draw on her stoutest boots. She flung herself down the stairs and into the street.

She ran after Agatha the length of their road and round its far corner, in time to see her turn off again. She finally reached her halfway along a narrow, inelegant street.

As Cassy came running up, panting, two exquisites, slightly foxed, stopped simultaneously as if in surprised pleasure to find two such young and pretty *filles de joie* at their, presumed, disposal.

But before they could utter a word a languid voice assailed them in perfect French, informing them amiably but definitely that the ladies were under his escort. 'Baste!' answered the one without rancour and they called 'Bonne nuit' as they continued on their genial unsteady way.

'Julian!' Cassy exclaimed. 'Thank God you chanced along this street.' By now she had her arm round the girl who, possibly regretting her impulse to join her beloved, had seemed as much relieved as bewildered to perceive Cassy and Lord Allingham's approach from opposite directions. She had a small bundle under her arm and the Marquis looked at it and the girl's face with understanding and a flash of compassion. 'Come along,' he said briskly. 'You ladies should not be out alone, as you have just, doubtless, realised. Let me escort you home.'

Cassy smiled thankfully and Agatha allowed herself to be drawn along wordlessly, her face piteous. His lordship conversed lightly about the state of the streets, asking no questions. The candle lanterns were alight outside the house and the butler, in hastily donned livery, already peering anxiously down the street. He was one of the English staff and when the Marquis told him firmly, 'The ladies are out a little late but, as you see, not unescorted,' he glanced quickly at Agatha's woebegone expression and returned calmly, 'Yes, sir. Miss's maid will be glad to see her returned.' There was an inarticulate cry from the back of the hall and the French girl in nightcap and dressing robe ran to her mistress with words of reproachful endearment and led her, unresisting, upstairs.

The faintly disapproving butler of the previous occasion actually smiled now and said, 'There will be tea and biscuits in the small salon in a few minutes, Miss Cassy. I am sure her ladyship would wish you to partake of some, sir, being such a raw night.'

Cassy said, 'Yes do come in and talk to me a little, Julian.' She was not conscious that his Christian name had twice come unbidden to her lips since their fortuitous meeting, nor, till they were seated before the rekindled fire and she had begun to undo her cloak, that she was still in night attire.

But he had noticed her natural use of his Christian name with a softening of his eyes, and then burst out laughing when he saw why she began hastily to button the garment again. 'Oh, Cassy,' he said eventually, 'how bored I was till I met you! This is not the first time, you may recall, that you have entertained me to tea in your nightgown.'

She blushed fiercely but answered pertly, 'Were you a gentleman of the first stare you would have pretended you did not notice it.'

'But then you knew I was not!'

'What a lucky coincidence that you should have been walking along that particular horrid street!'

'Not so coincidental except for the timing. I had been to see if our mutual enemy had kept his promise to vacate the rooms. He had. So the poor child was spared a mortification. But then I am persuaded you would have contrived something even without my arrival on the scene.'

'Surely he could not have hoped to carry through a bigamous marriage?'

'No. I gathered that he had two alternative schemes. The first was to seduce Agatha and then confess all, trusting her enslavement would induce her to wait for the divorce Dolly must be all too pleased to grant him. The second, once the girl had eloped with him, was to persuade her father – whoever he is – to buy him off.'

'Unspeakable!'

'Indubitably so.'

'Do you know where he went?'

'I suspect de Mallon has gone to act as messenger boy for rich Bonapartists who, it seems, used to pay for his intelligence from London. Be assured that he is being watched.'

'Surely Napoleon is well guarded on the island of Elba?'

'My dear, who knows at this time what partisan elements may be anywhere? That is the trouble when you have a country divided. As you now realise, allegiance to King Louis is by no means an integral part of wealth and breeding.'

'It is all most confusing. Anyway I shall confide enough to Lady Oxford to prevail upon her to send poor Agatha away for a change of scene.'

'That would be wise, since even the servants here must know by now about her recklessness.'

'Julian, I forgot to tell you, Marcus Stanton was at the Opera House the other night. Was that not famous?'

'Yes, you must have been pleased to see somebody with whom you share experience of the theatre. Does he stay long in Paris? I should like to see him.'

'He leaves for Vienna next week.'

'A pity he could not take Agatha with him. There would be plenty of gallant dancing partners there to distract her.'

'If only it were possible, that would be just the thing.'

'I must go now, or that more tolerant butler may begin again to question my integrity.'

'Now he would not. But it is late, or early. I shall, I promise, not attempt thanks, but just say, "very well met". Good-bye, Julian. Good luck.'

'How final that sounds. Good luck to you too, my dear.' Hazel eyes looked deeply for a moment into misted blue ones. Then he lifted her hand to his lips and said, 'Rather, au revoir.' Cassy shook her head mutely.

She retreated wearily to her chamber. On the way she met the little maid tip-toeing out of Agatha's room, and to her questioning look she answered by putting her hands beneath her cheek in the gesture of a sleeping child. 'Bonne nuit et bon jour,' Cassy smiled. She was too tired to cogitate on her friend's immediate future. But, cheered by the comfortable interlude and her renewed camaraderie with the Marquis, she was soon asleep herself.

Marcus Stanton paid her a second visit the next morning to read her Aunt Letty's last letter on the pretext, to the butler, of having forgotten his gloves. With a deprecating smile he omitted its introduction and conclusion. But he told her of the girls' scholastic progress. They were reading *Mansfield Park* together and Marcia and Thea could play piano duets prettily. Jemima the cat had produced six adorable kittens in Miss Page's best summer straw. There had been a cold snap, but nothing like the great frost of last winter. They had not seen Lucasta recently, which was regrettable. But she was doubtless busy. At this Cassy looked at him ruefully and he smiled back with friendly complicity.

She felt a great wave of nostalgia on hearing the homely account. Seeing her companion's sympathetic expression she hastened to say, 'It is stupid of me to hanker after home when I have such a full and diverting life over here.'

'But it can never be the same as being with your own,' he nodded. 'I know, for I get lonely myself, my dear. I shall be glad to get this tour over and return home – to Letty.' He looked at her with a faint trace of appeal and some embarrassment.

Cassy found herself reassuring him for the second time, and liking him the more for the need. 'I do not doubt that all will be just as you would wish, sir,' she said. 'In the meantime I dearly wish you could take two temporary daughters on your further travels.'

She had not seriously contemplated the possibility of removing Agatha and herself from Paris under his protection. She was, rather, idly thinking aloud. Her young friend was still asleep, but she feared the sense of desolation which would face her when she awoke. However, he answered quite seriously. 'If you were one of the temporary daughters I should be only too pleased.'

'Would you really, sir?' she asked, struck suddenly by a real possibility. 'You see, Lady Oxford's daughter has had an unhappy experience here.'

'A romance gone awry?'

'Yes. I should so like to get her away to fresh surroundings.'

'Why should you not then both accompany me? There could be nothing lacking in propriety in the arrangement, specially since I am all but your uncle!'

'If only the fact were generally known! I must admit it sounds an ideal solution.'

'Think about it, then consult with your hostess and send me word. I leave by carriage in two days. We would be two weeks on the road to Vienna, but would put up at comfortable hostelries. I have business in Strasbourg, Stuttgart and Munich and you would be able to visit the theatres and the concerts there. I don't doubt that Lady Oxford would know of a lady who could accommodate you in Vienna, and if not, I have friends there myself who would be sure to welcome you both.'

'Then I shall discuss our plan with her. I should not care to leave her if I did not know she expects company from England. I am convinced that Agatha would benefit from the change, and that I should enjoy it all very much.'

'Good. I await your decision.'

When Agatha came downstairs she seemed to Cassy to move as if in a dream. She had refused her breakfast and now bespoke her carriage. Cassy asked if she might accompany her for a drive, but was told politely that she would prefer to take just her maid. 'You do not mind, do you, dear Cassy?' she enquired anxiously, pulling at her friend's sleeve feverishly. The latter, looking at the white, pinched face with lavender shadows beneath the big eyes, forced herself to smile warmly, and say, 'Of course not, dear. But come back soon and bear me company. I am a little homesick today.'

Cassy realised that Agatha was bound for de Mallon's lodgings, but knew that she must let her go and learn the worst. The knowledge that he had left without leaving a direction would be painful but salutary. She would preserve a romantic memory without the bitterness that would have accompanied the revelation of his perfidy.

Nevertheless Cassy waited on tenterhooks for her friend's return, visions of a small body floating in the Seine before her eyes. However, despite the even deeper sadness on her face, Agatha held herself on her return with a certain youthful dignity. She would have refused nuncheon had Cassy not threatened to fast with her and thus constrained her to eat a few mouthfuls.

Lady Oxford arrived home in the early afternoon with gifts of hand-painted fans for the girls. She was so full of the delights of her visit and in such a glow of beauty that Cassy suspected she might have found a replacement for the dreadful and delightful Byron. However, she stopped her chatter in full spate to look with sudden concern at her silent daughter. Her Ladyship might lack for sense but never heart.

She bade Cassy accompany her into her peach and duck-egg blue satin-draped boudoir before she had her nap, saying peremptorily, 'Tell me, Cassy. Is Agatha unhappy or is she sickening for something?'

'The former, ma'am. She fell in love with a man whom I know, from the theatrical world, to be a dangerous criminal and fortune hunter. He has been scared off, so let me not weary you with the details.'

'I suspect a ruse of my resourceful Cassy's! Thank God for it! But the sight of her poor pale little face quite oversets me. What do you think can be done for her?'

'Well, ma'am, I know we could both accompany Mr Stanton to Vienna. I would not have suggested it if I did not know you have house guests due, and would not be quite alone. I think Agatha should have a different environment and he would, he told me, be grateful for our company.'

Lady Oxford was unwontedly thoughtful. Then she smiled at Cassy. 'You have thought it all out, have you not? But,' she admitted, 'the idea has much to recommend it. Why you young people have to take love so seriously, though, I do not understand. When would you leave?'

'The day after tomorrow.'

'So soon? I had not thought to lose you both so quickly. But perhaps it is better so, for hurried preparations for the journey will occupy poor Agatha's mind.'

'I hope only that she may accept the suggestion, ma'am.'

'I wonder whether Mr Stanton would dine with us this evening, if he will not object to being invited at such short notice.'

'I am sure he could not under the circumstances.'

'Then let me write a note to be conveyed to him forthwith. In Vienna, you know, you could both stay with my old friends the Prince and Princesse de Polignac. He is an eminent royalist and she enjoys young company and is bound to be in the middle of the social merry-go-round.'

Marcus Stanton duly arrived for an informal dinner in answer to Lady Oxford's apologetic and gracious missive. At first Agatha was shy and too preoccupied with her own disappointment to be anything but speechless. But it was soon seen that, as the father of daughters, he had the happy knack of drawing out young females, and she was eventually asking civil questions about his proposed journey.

He told her about the remarkable astronomical clock on the

cathedral at Strasbourg, and that he hoped to attend a performance at the Opera House in Vienna.

'I associate Mozart with Vienna,' Agatha volunteered listlessly. 'I am very fond of his music.'

'So am I,' agreed Marcus Stanton. 'Just consider that the composer was a child phenomenon, who published operas and performed in public at the age of six.'

There was a trace of animation in her face now. 'I would never have believed it!'

'His genius never lapsed. Yet he was carried to a pauper's grave in Vienna while only in his mid-thirties.'

'Oh, how sad!' exclaimed the girl, struck obviously by the sudden suspicion that hers was not the only tragic case.

So, after accepting the kind gentleman's invitation, it was eventually an Agatha with a vestige of colour in her face, and not such a pallid, lovelorn maiden, who went, with Cassy, through the flurry of preparations for the journey.

30

When Cassy and Agatha set forth in Marcus Stanton's unostentatious but commodious carriage, they bore with them Agatha's little maid to attend them both, and an assortment of rugs, foot-warmers, muffs, hoods, scarves, brandy flasks, comfits, and anything else that Lady Oxford considered essential to their comfort.

She had embraced them both with tears in her fine eyes and the girls were saddened at leaving her, as well as their two very different loves.

But Marcus Stanton soon contrived to make them merry. The driving was sometimes tiring, but, much travelled himself, he knew at just which inn they could be most agreeably fed and accommodated. The road had been kept open by necessity because of the heavy traffic between the French and Austrian capitals. During the first days they traversed the valleys of the rivers Marne and Moselle, scenically delightful, even in winter.

Cassy found that her aunt's future husband improved on acquaintance and was glad of the opportunity to establish such an easy relationship with him. Without being loquacious he kept the girls from being dull, telling them the more amusing anecdotes about his travels, but otherwise keeping the conversation firmly on general subjects and away from personal and theatrical talk.

The astronomical clock at Strasbourg was every bit as fascinating as their escort had promised. They spent an evening at the theatre there watching a production of Molière's *Les Femmes Savantes*, which, though a strain on Agatha's limited French, was acted with such comic felicity of gesture that she enjoyed it anyway.

They all stayed with professional friends of Marcus Stanton, and the covert glances directed at Agatha by the eighteen-year-old son of the house brought a sparkle to her eyes that proved, to Cassy's satisfaction, that she was not too heartbroken to appreciate masculine admiration.

In Stuttgart, the pretty town on the river Neckar with its hilltop castles, they watched a circus which Agatha relished more as it provided no language problem. But Cassy was reminded by it of a certain memorable occasion with Lord Allingham at Sadler's Wells.

At Munich Agatha was enchanted by a performance of her favourite Mozart opera, *The Magic Flute*. By this time Cassy judged that, but for the occasional soulful look, she was restored to the cheerful child of their first meeting. In her own case the distractions and diversions prevented thoughts of the Marquis recurring quite so frequently. But she feared, like her aunt before her, that she was a hopeless case.

The last ten miles of the journey were a race with the snow, and flurries floated out of a steel-grey sky as they entered Vienna.

The Princesse de Polignac greeted the girls and Marcus Stanton with heart-warming pleasure in spite of her surprise. 'How delightful!' she exclaimed in her prettily accented English. 'We have so many visiting dignitaries that the presence of two such young and lovely English misses can only increase the popularity of my husband and myself.'

In her letter to her friend, introducing the two girls, and requesting her to receive them, Lady Oxford had described Cassy merely as Agatha's companion. She was so obviously of a good family that her hostess assumed her to be simply one of the legion of unfortunate damsels forced by adverse circumstances or penury to become governesses or something similar.

The Princesse, no beauty, but vivacious and charming, begged Marcus Stanton to call just as often as his friends in Vienna and business there could spare him. He promised to do so, bade his charges an affectionate farewell and departed in a whirl of snow and smiles.

At the time of the Congress Vienna was, as Lady Oxford had foretold, a city of magic. It was thronged with crowned heads, ministers, ambassadors, officers in the brilliant uniforms of many nations and fashionable ladies who did their utmost to outdo the gentlemen in splendour.

Whatever the result of the interminable, dreary deliberations,

230

romance, excitement and glittering gaiety flourished in the midst of them. Living as they were in the temporary home of a French nobleman, whom they found to be amiable but much engrossed in political and social life, Cassy and Agatha were at the hub of it all.

Agatha, inevitably, had an ample wardrobe. But, while Cassy was glad of the extra clothes she had bought in Paris, she was forced to become even more adept at altering a fichu, a sash or some ribbons to add variety to her more limited choice of attire.

The girls were waltzed off their feet, treated to gallantries in broken English and invited to every sort of function, from evening assemblies and balls to promenades and drives. The opera house and theatres were packed nightly, and the different performing companies gave Marcus Stanton plenty of scope for securing new acts and artistes for his English chain of theatres. His easy, amiable manner had already made him a favourite with their host and hostess, and on the few evenings when they were not otherwise engaged, they were happy to accept his invitations to the play.

After five days in Vienna, however, he decided he must take leave of his new friends and proceed, as planned, to Budapest and thence home to England. However, the Prince and Princesse would not hear of their guests going with him, as they would have been welcome to do. Indeed life had become so vivid for the two girls, with little time for recollections and regret, that their host and hostess had no difficulty in persuading them to stay in Vienna until they could all four travel back to Paris together after the Congress was over.

So the two friends thanked Marcus Stanton for all his kindness and entrusted to him, discreetly, letters to Miss Page and Agatha's mysterious male parent. They both enthused on paper about their well-being, the kind hospitality they were enjoying – and omitted in both cases to mention that they had left their hearts behind in Paris.

With the advent of her decorative young guests, the house of the Prince and Princesse with its pretty gilded and moulded ceilings and pastel-papered rooms became, as Lady Oxford's home had in Paris, even more popular with sprigs of the Austrian nobility, as well as with younger staff officers.

Cassy was a particular asset as she could, although loth to put herself forward, be persuaded to play and sing ballads in French, English or the German in which she was becoming ever more fluent. In fact she was already conversant with the songs that had been specially composed for an amateur production of *Cinderella* that their aristocratic young Austrian friends were to produce at the Palace of Schönbrunn shortly, even though she had been offered, but declined, a role in it.

Cassy and Agatha were invited to the Imperial Riding School by their most regular escorts, a merry minor princeling of the Hapsburgs and a dashing young cavalry captain, respectively, to act the part of languishing damsels of the Middle Ages while their 'knights' took part in an ambitious medieval tournament which became the talk of the city.

During the course of this stirring event Cassy, wearing a becoming coif and wimple and a trailing robe, caught sight in the entourage of the amusedly watching Duke of Wellington, a familiar chiselled face. Lord Allingham, she saw with a shock that distracted her attention from her champion on his fiery steed, was in uniform. She darted a look of startled interrogation at him and he inclined his head in her direction with a small smile.

Agatha, similarly transformed into a medieval maiden, seeing the direction of Cassy's glance, asked surprisedly, 'Is that officer not the Marquis of Allingham?'

'Yes,' answered Cassy. 'I do not know why he should be in Vienna.'

'And in uniform!'

'Well, Lord Allingham has been on sick leave, you know, but has never severed his connection with the army,' Cassy replied with assumed indifference. 'Now just look how my gallant knight has vanquished his foe. What a crack-brained and dangerous exhibition it is to be sure, Agatha!'

'Oh yes! It is difficult, is it not, Cassy, not to be happy here in this capital of pleasure.'

'Yes, love.' Cassy squeezed the younger girl's hand affectionately. 'You are less cast-down now, are you not? Life still has a great deal to offer.'

'Oh yes. I suppose I should be grateful to Lord Allingham for preventing me, though he could not realise it, from committing a great indiscretion the night he encountered me – and you – in the Paris street.'

'Yes!' agreed Cassy emphatically, refraining from adding that he had already averted that possibility even before their nocturnal meeting.

Inevitably Cassy saw the Marquis during the next weeks at the grander social occasions to which he accompanied his celebrated commander-in-chief. He was never present at the more youthful festivities. She could, she knew, not expect him to call upon her or even seek her out at any function, but she was illogically chagrined when he did not do so.

He spoke to her eventually in a draughty corridor as he was about to enter the card room in the palace of an Austrian nobleman. She could hear the cribbage calls behind him, 'Thirty, ace in place. Twenty-six, five's a fix.' He leaned against the wall and regarded her, approving, she felt, her white muslin gown which she had refurbished with pale orange threaded ribbon through the puffed sleeves and very low-cut neckline.

She felt her fingers clenching at the unexpected confrontation and noticed that he looked even finer in the regimentals, which set off his wide shoulders, slim waist and long, well-muscled legs.

'I know of no lady who blushes as becomingly as you, Cassy,' he told her with a twinkle. 'Are you not cold in this draughty mausoleum?' She was conscious suddenly of her daring décolleté, all the crack though it might be.

'I am on my way sir, as it happens, to fetch my wrap,' she answered formally.

'I collect that my name was Julian when you poured me tea in your nightgown at our last meeting,' he pointed out, his experienced eyes caressing her creamy curves involuntarily.

'You look so very grand that such a familiarity seems disrespectful. Besides we might be overheard. Please satisfy my curiosity regarding your reason for being in Vienna.'

'Of course. I came to report my findings in France to Wellington, on whose staff I find myself. I am, regretfully, forced to participate in all the dull discussions. I did not hope to have the pleasure of encountering you yourself in one more capital city even though we may only converse in an empty corridor. I surmise that you accompanied Marcus Stanton and the lovelorn lady.'

'Yes, his departure seemed a heaven-sent opportunity to transpose her, and she could hardly go alone with him.'

'Tell me, did my prescription of Congress dancing improve our young patient's condition?'

'It has proved just the thing.'

'And you? Is your Austrian prince no more acceptable than your French duke?'

'Neither more nor less,' she replied with dignity. And then added anxiously, 'You do not expect a resumption of warfare, I hope!'

'At present we do not know what to expect, Cassy,' he answered frankly, and with that reply she had to be content, as he bowed to her and entered the games room.

A party was arranged by the Prince and Princesse de Polignac to visit the Opera House for a production of *Figaro*, and it was on this occasion that Agatha made the acquaintance of a newly arrived young English diplomat, Sir James Wayne, who was to do more to complete her cure than all the other beaux.

Later she told Cassy, 'Sir James talks much more sensibly than the others, and loves Mozart's music as much as I do. I feel I have found a friend.'

He called by permission, ostensibly on the two girls. But Cassy had no illusion about his true interest, nor anything but gladness for her companion. As she saw the serious young eyes gazing into each other's over a plan to hear a mass of their favourite composer at St Stephen's Cathedral she perceived an incipient romance that could well lead to an enduring relationship.

When she talked to Lord Allingham for the second time it was at a *petit souper* given by her host and hostess and hospitality made it necessary. She mentioned in passing Agatha's new friendship.

'Sir James Wayne? Yes, I know him,' he nodded. 'Rich as Midas with excellent career prospects.' Then he added, irritably, 'Do you never think of yourself, Cassy?'

'Why yes. I think that I am so very lucky to be here where history is in the making.'

'What sort of history, I wonder?' he responded moodily, and then asked abruptly, 'How long do you intend to stay here – is it not time you considered returning home?'

'I should not like to abandon Agatha yet and cannot for the time being – make plans for myself. I must allow more time for the disgrace attached to our names to be forgotten in London.'

'Oh, that is of no import to me. I suggested a remedy which you could not accept. So,' he looked at her, frowning, 'take care of yourself, Cassy, since you will allow nobody else to do so.' Then he claimed the attention of his hostess to compliment her on the entertainment.

31

A week later Vienna was covered by a thick blanket of snow, which had been presaged by flurries for the last few days. The crisp white sparkle of the city and its woodlands only added to the enchantment engendered by its activities.

A great cavalcade of sledges had already been commanded for the conveyance of the players and guests to the performance of *Cinderella* at Schönbrunn a few days later. Cassy and Agatha, who had been invited to it by their particular Austrian beaux, were looking forward to the unusual occasion, though the younger girl would have preferred the escort of her music-loving diplomat.

He and Agatha attended many of the same functions and he would talk and dance with her whenever the occasion permitted, but the young couple were being circumspect. Agatha had learned the lesson of discretion, and their extreme youth augured a sensible period of courtship without over-hasty decisions.

Two days before *Cinderella* was to take place, the prince who had jousted for Cassy's favour at the tournament arrived with the tidings that the lady who had been chosen to play Prince Charming had been taken ill of a putrid fever. 'Please,' he begged, 'Cassy, *liebling*, come to our rescue. The dialogue is so simple and sparse that you could learn it in a day and you already sing the songs better than she did. Play the part to save our friends from despair. They have worked so hard to make the evening a success!'

Cassy could hardly resist such an appeal, specially when the Princesse added her entreaties to those of the young Austrian. It would be churlish and ungrateful in the extreme to refuse to help. The assignment should present no difficulty and would in the ordinary way have been a pleasure.

However, she realised with apprehension that to appear at a large, cosmopolitan gathering in the role in which she had made a success in London was to court speculation and comparisons.

So she accepted the challenge with strong misgivings, hoping that the Marquis would not be present at Schönbrunn the next evening to deplore her indiscretion.

After a period of frenzied concentration on the small amount of dialogue that served mainly to introduce the songs and ballet, followed by intense rehearsal, her Austrian friends gratefully pronounced their saviour a first-class prince.

Wrapped in her warmest clothes, Cassy found the trip by sleigh drawn by jingling horses exhilarating, and Schönbrunn, surrounded by snow-laden pine trees, like a palace in fairyland. Within, the flagged halls were warmed by blazing log fires and later the shadows were chased away by a myriad candle lanterns and oil burners.

While she changed into the blue and gold doublet and hose of Prince Charming she felt a return of the old thrill, even though this was only an amateur production. Her fellow players had taken her to their hearts, specially the gentlemen, who surveyed her lovely legs with approbation.

So the absurdly pretty prince in the auburn wig and feathered cap started the opening song with gay confidence, and Cinderella was inspired to excel herself opposite her dashing hero. The pantomime was played to a hall packed with people, who received it with stamping and cheers. An excited Cassy accepted congratulations afterwards in her makeshift dressing-room and the tributes of her numerous admirers.

As she was dressed again in her high-necked gown a taller figure appeared at the doorway and a deeper voice cut across the babble of conversation. 'Come along, Cassy,' said the Marquis.

It did not occur to her to disobey the stern voice and, with perfunctory farewells, she drew on her outer clothing and followed him, seemingly without her own volition, through the hallway out into the snow. At last he turned to her and said coldly. 'I had not thought to see you in tights again. Do you, after all, crave notoriety?'

He could not know all the circumstances and Cassy was aware of the unfairness of his slashing words. Yet she found herself lowering her head wordlessly against the attack like a scolded child.

Footmen with flambeaux illuminated the sledge that waited in the courtyard, which had been cleared of snow. He handed her in, tucked a fur rug up to her chin and said, 'Since you care nothing for your reputation you will not object to my open escort.' Then they sped silently, except for the jingling harnesses, into the faintly glimmering city.

Lord Allingham accompanied her up the steps towards the front door of the house. Then, before she could touch the bell-pull, he put both his arms round her, imprisoning her against a wall. He kissed her several times savagely until her senses were swimming and she was languorous with longing. Then she recalled herself abruptly, wrenched herself from his grasp and slapped his face hard. He looked at her, one cheek crimson, saluted her mockingly and said, 'Good-bye, Cassandra.'

She ran headlong upstairs, grateful that her host and hostess were still, with Agatha, at the palace. She hurled herself on the bed, weeping uncontrollably. She must, somehow, find a way to leave Vienna, where she might at any time encounter again the loathsome, insulting Marquis.

When Agatha scratched at her door Cassy pretended to be asleep. The next morning she parried questions about her precipitate departure from the palace with excuses about an attack of faintness and her unwillingness to cut short their enjoyment in the reception that followed the pantomime. She accepted the congratulations of her host and hostess, and of Agatha, politely, and, though they glanced curiously at her closed, pale face, they decided separately that she must be expected to suffer a reaction after rising so gallantly to the occasion.

For Cassy the immediate problem was how to remove herself from Vienna, whence she could not travel unescorted; then how not to offend her kind hostess, supposing she could achieve her object. Moreover, she did not wish Agatha to feel in duty bound to accompany her, when she was so enjoying the particular friendship of Sir James.

It took all Cassy's dramatic ability to enable her to fulfil her social obligations without comment during the next two days. But while she laughed, flirted and danced, her mind was busy trying to devise a means of escape once more from the man she loved, who had treated her with the contempt he must have felt she deserved.

She thought sadly of her flight from him to Drury Lane, and then of her departure from Allingham House with the dancer Sybil. This last recollection made her think in desperation of the English dance company at one of the theatres. Marcus Stanton had told her of the regret its members felt at the prospect of leaving Vienna, where they had found protectors or lost their hearts. Perhaps, if she mentioned his name, they might let her join them. But before Cassy could embark on an adventure she must regret, fate took a hand in her affairs.

The girls were taken by their host and hostess to an evening reception in honour of a visiting field-marshal, no less a person than the Prince Regent's younger brother, Edward, Duke of Kent. When she was presented to the lady with him she realised immediately that she had already made her acquaintance with Lady Oxford in Paris. She was, Cassy recalled now, a Madame St Laurent, who had lived with the royal duke for the last five and twenty years. She was so quiet and unassuming that her liaison with the balding gentleman, whom Cassy recognised from the cartoons, had assumed an aura of near-respectability. In the happy-go-lucky atmosphere of both Paris and Vienna she was in any case accepted socially without question.

When Cassy curtseyed and smiled at her in her charming way the elegantly dressed but homely lady said immediately, 'I remember you well, my dear. One does not easily forget a girl with eyes that smile as yours do.'

'What a nice thing to say, ma'am,' said Cassy unaffectedly.

'It is true. Come sit beside me, *chérie*, and tell me what you are doing in Vienna besides, I don't doubt, breaking hearts.'

'Not that. But certainly this city is stimulating and diverting. I am a house guest of the Prince and Princesse de Polignac.'

'Yet, in spite of your smile and all those distractions, you seemed to me at first sight this evening to be a trifle wistful.'

'You are very astute, ma'am.' Tears rose unbidden to Cassy's eyes at the words, and she was surprised into honesty. 'It is just that I am anxious, for personal reasons, to leave this city.'

Madame St Laurent asked simply, 'Where do you wish to go? You are a long way from England – or is Paris your home?'

'I don't much mind. My home is in London. But when we met in Paris I was acting as Lady Oxford's social secretary and companion.'

'I see.' How comfortable this lady was, Cassy reflected. She just accepted facts without probing deeper into the reasons for them. Then she astounded Cassy by saying, 'Do you care to come and stay with me in Brussels? Our visit here is over and I leave with the Duke of Kent for home the day after tomorrow. I should be glad of your company, since His Royal Highness bides only a few days before proceeding to London.'

Cassy gazed at the kind, plain face, hardly daring to belive her good fortune. Madame St Laurent laughed and ventured, 'Your face is so expressive, my dear, that I can see you would like to come but there are difficulties in the way. Let me know tomorrow, for we leave here the following morning.'

'Thank you, ma'am, most sincerely,' said Cassy. 'You have exactly guessed the situation. I hope I may come, and am persuaded I should enjoy your company a great deal' – a statement which she believed to be the truth.

Later among the distinguished company on this momentous occasion, she saw the Duke of Wellington, attended, among others, by Lord Allingham. The latter stared at one point straight at Cassy with a puckered brow, as if he would approach and speak with her. But to her relief, his attention was drawn elsewhere by his commanding officer and Cassy took the chance to sit beside the Princesse de Polignac on a sofa where she was momentarily alone.

She decided then and there that there was nothing to be lost by being forthright. So she told her amiable hostess of the invitation to Brussels and her inclination to accept. 'I have had such a wonderful time with you, ma'am,' she added. 'But Congress could continue indefinitely, and in Brussels I would be near the packet for home.'

The Princesse took the girl's hand. 'I understand,' she assured her, 'but we shall miss you. I know you have become unsettled recently, that something has gone wrong for you. Perhaps a change of scene will do you good, just, as Agatha confided in me, it did for her. You do not intend to take her with you, I presume?'

'Oh no. I know she is in good hands and that you will deliver her back to her mama in due course. Besides, I am sure she would prefer to stay.'

Her hostess laughed. 'No doubt about that while young Sir James is here. They make a charming couple, if a little on the earnest side. You realise of course that the household you join is an unconventional one. But I believe the situation is accepted with equanimity in all but the most elevated strata of Brussels society.'

'I shall not aspire to those, ma'am,' smiled Cassy, secretly amused at the thought of her flamboyant, if virtuous past.

She was thus able to confirm her acceptance of the new invitation right away, and she marvelled at the kindness she had met since leaving Allingham House. It did not occur to her that her ready friendliness and pleasing personality brought with them their own reward.

She parted reluctantly from her little friend Agatha, giving her a note of thanks and explanation to deliver to Lady Oxford when she should return to Paris. Her round of regretful leave-takings achieved, she kissed her host and hostess on both cheeks in the French fashion and joined the royal, if somewhat irregular, cortège.

32

Cassy occupied the second carriage with Babette, the pleasant elderly lady's maid who was part of the entourage. Cassy was relieved, but unsurprised, that she was not constrained to be in the company of His Royal Highness during the many hours they spent on the road. He struck her as being fierce and formidable, although he was civil enough to her.

However, she was bound to acknowledge the luxury of their conveyance, the royal arms on the gilded doors, the solid gold appointments and the pomp with which they were received at their various stops. She was in fact treated like a visiting princess, and wished her travelling clothes could contribute to the illusion.

It was already March when the party arrived at the small château set in its deer park and ornamental gardens on the outskirts of Brussels. The very next day news was delivered there by special messenger that Napoleon had escaped from Elba and was making for France. So the royal duke left even more hurriedly for duties in England, kindly bearing with him a letter for Miss Page which Cassy had written.

There followed a period of uncertainty and rumour. They heard that the Vienna Congress had broken down and that Bonaparte had landed at Cannes. On March 10 he was at Lyons and a few days later he was joined by Marshal Ney. Napoleon had, it seemed, then taken over the Tuileries, and the so-called 'hundred days' had begun.

For Cassy, as well as for Madame St Laurent, it was a time of anxiety. With so much of France rallying to Napoleon she feared a confrontation between the French and the English in which the

Marquis, whom she sometimes hated but always, lamentably, loved, might be involved. She found herself wondering what he might have said if he had succeeded in speaking to her at the reception for the Duke of Kent, and recalling the shameful ecstasy of those last kisses that were intended as an insult. She hoped Lady Oxford and her other friends would be safe in Paris.

In fact, Lord Allingham had determined to apologise to Cassy for what he realised in retrospect was an unforgivable exhibition. He learned after that evening at Schönbrunn that Cassy had been persuaded against her better judgment to act as substitute for the ailing Prince Charming, and had only complied with the request, out of her usual thoughtless good nature.

Although he had tried to rationalise his relationship with this girl, as was his way, the Marquis seemed quite unable to do so. She had dealt bitter blows to his pride by rejecting his suit on two occasions, even though the proposals might have been unromantic. He had admired as much as resented her independence of him.

His senses had been stirred by her appearance in stage costume, particularly the offending tights, yet he was indignant that other men should be given the opportunity to find her similarly desirable. He found her touching, tantalising, admirable and audacious. She was in his blood and, he feared, his heart. He could not forget her even when pressing military events occupied his time as they did now. Damn it – she had escaped him again!

In London Miss Page had been startled and intrigued by a letter from her errant niece delivered by a footman in royal livery. The Duke of Kent had kept his word to Cassy. The recipient read with a mixture of exasperation and amusement that she was now in Brussels as the house guest of another lady, who was even more unconventional in her life-style than Lady Oxford.

Her niece wrote that she realised that the news of Napoleon was disquieting, that she promised to return home soon and that she remained her devoted Cassy. Thea and Grace, while still kept in ignorance of their sister's stage career – now in abeyance – had been told that she was abroad as a sort of governess-companion to Lady Oxford's daughter. They envied her the feminine equivalent of what sounded like a Grand Tour.

Aunt Letty herself had been overjoyed by the return of Marcus and by his first-hand news of Cassy. She was immeasurably relieved that she need no longer deceive him about her eldest niece. She was to go north with him and the girls to attend Gerard's wedding, and meanwhile there was the pleasurable task of viewing a selection of country houses for sale sent to them by the agents.

Cassy and Madame St Laurent enjoyed one another's company and the latter's only regret was her strong conviction, derived from her royal lover's parting words, that Cassy should be sent back to England before Brussels was ravaged by war. Accordingly she persuaded her to accept the escort home of a Belgian diplomatic couple leaving for duty in London some time in June.

Cassy was bound to agree. But meanwhile the younger set was bidden to the château to meet her, and she discovered that her hostess's connection with royalty made her invitations welcome, in the more worldly circles at least. So the golden May days drifted by with drives along the leafy boulevards to the Place Royale to view the Palais de Justice, horseback riding, rowing on the ornamental lake at the château – and the endless discussions concerning Napoleon and his possible plans.

By June, when the roses were in bloom in the château gardens, the Duke of Wellington's headquarters was established eleven miles south of the city. The advent of his staff officers, who had broken so many hearts and marriages in Vienna, started yet another social whirl. The same cosmopolitan hostesses, who liked always to be at the centre of events, had established themselves in Brussels, as well as numerous officers' wives.

Cassy realised that the Marquis of Allingham was, most probably, at the headquarters. So, for fear of meeting him, she began to decline invitations whenever it was possible to do so without causing offence. Her hostess accepted her pleas of headache or other *malaises* with her usual unquestioning placidity. But the kind lady was by no means obtuse, and she knew well enough that the disorder from which Cassy was really suffering was a severe fit of the dismals. Whether this was caused by the threat of war or a passing, unrequited infatuation she had no intention of enquiring. But she hoped that the surprise presence of the Duke of Wellington, with whom she had considerable influence through her high-ranking royal lover, together with some of his most attractive staff officers, at her coming garden party might help to distract the English girl.

Over an early nuncheon on the appointed day Madame Laurent said, 'Let us hope that Babette can conjure me a respectable coiffure to go with my new blue afternoon gown. What shall you wear, Cassy? Mind it is not the same colour.' Her brown eyes twinkled.

'I thought my primrose muslin, ma'am,' said Cassy, who would not have dreamed of refusing to take her share of the responsibility for making her kind friend's afternoon reception a success.

'Good, that will make a nice contrast. Would you for once like Babette to arrange your hair?'

Cassy smiled gratefully. 'That is sweet of you, but you know that one of my funny foibles is to prefer to fiddle with it myself.'

'To very good effect too, I am bound to admit. I sometimes wish that I too could be independent of my maid, for we often disagree about what suits me, and she is so very opinionated. Before you retire, Cassy, just run and make sure that Henri has picked enough strawberries.'

Cassy went to see the gardener as requested and then repaired to her room to get ready. With the high-waisted muslin with its square neckline and tiny puffed sleeves she wore a shady chip-straw bonnet that tied under her chin with matching ribbons. Her hair was curled sweetly beneath it, and her eyes seemed larger than ever in the lovely face that showed unaccustomed hollows and pallor.

However, this same countenance became mantled with colour as she saw later a party of British officers, among them the Duke of Wellington, arrive and become absorbed among the pretty girls whose gowns fluttered like butterflies across the smooth lawns.

Shortly after Madame St Laurent had presented Cassy to the debonair Duke, who looked, most deceptively, as if attending such functions was his only preoccupation, she saw Allingham making straight for her in a determined manner.

She felt that she might faint and also that this afternoon's encounter seemed like an uninterrupted continuation of the last time she had seen him, when he had looked as though he wanted to approach her. He was frowning in the identical way, but his face was oddly uncertain as he bowed before her. Hazel eyes looked deeply, unsmilingly, into blue ones. 'Was I so offensive that you were forced to run away again? If so, I am deeply sorry, Cassy.'

She could not for the life of her think of one thing to say and dropped her eyes to avoid the appearance of staring at his dear countenance.

'Do you forgive me?' he asked now very softly.

'I must, since you ask it. But tell me one thing truthfully. Were you aware that, when I left Vienna, I had come to stay with Madame St Laurent?'

He tried to look abashed. 'I own that I made a point of discovering the fact.'

She looked as stern as she was able in view of his nearness. 'Then, what I shall not forgive is your presence here today. I do not understand why you should seek me out again, as you did in Paris, when I gave up a promising and profitable career, and left my own country, to give the tattle-mongers a chance to forget us, and to make your self-sacrificing offer of marriage an irrelevance!'

'Quite a speech! I see that you do have it in you to become a second Siddons. As virtuous too.' His voice had regained its asperity.

'How like you to jeer at me! It would suit you if I were not virtuous, I don't doubt.' She was trembling with a mixture of emotions.

'Oddly enough it would not. You jeered first – at my desire to marry you and accused me of – banishing you.' His lips twitched suddenly and his eyes glinted. 'Oh, Cassy, Cassy, come, let us be private if you do not wish this *tête à tête* to arouse interest. Madame St Laurent requested that you show me the rose garden.'

'Why?'

'Because I desired her to do so.'

She glared at him and they strolled, well away from each other, to the garden where the roses were Henri's justifiable pride and whose fragrance reminded them both, separately, of the heady scent of Prinny's yellow favourites one evening at his Brighton Pavilion.

Cassy bent her head to examine a perfect pink specimen and to hide her damp eyes. He said in a voice that sounded suddenly unsteady, 'I did not mean to distress you, as I did at our last meeting.'

'And I did not intend to jeer at your proposal. But to announce your betrothal to an actress ...'

'What do I care if you are an actress?' She stared at him with the beginning of an incredulous smile. 'I want *you*, you little fool – oh, not as my mistress as I thought at first – but as my wife.'

Her smile grew wider. 'But the family ...'

'To the devil with the family!' He pulled her behind a trellis heavy with white ramblers, pushed back her hat and kissed her fiercely, then very tenderly on each eye and her pretty nose.

245

Her arms stole round his neck and his regimental buttons against her were a delicious discomfort. Her heart was ricocheting round its cage.

'You are a perverse, provoking and unpredictable female, and I love you to distraction,' he said against her cheek. 'God and Napoleon willing I shall make you mine, whatever your scruples and however you may try again to escape me. Say it!'

'Say what, my very dear?'

'Why, that you love me, of course. You never have.'

'But I have often wanted to. You are the haughtiest, most high-handed wretch of my acquaintance, but I love you with all my foolish heart. Will Napoleon be willing, do you think?'

'I know only that we are forced to give him a final drubbing. Go back to England, please, as soon as possible. Wait for me. You should have an escort ...'

'Madame St Laurent has arranged my departure with a diplomatic couple of her acquaintance. So do not worry.'

'Not worry about you, Cassy? I fear that to do so has become a habit. Shall I write to you again, care of Louise?'

There was a smile lurking in his eyes and Cassy wanted that very moment to tell him everything. Then the Duke of Wellington, some other officers and a bevy of admiring belles came into the rose garden. They were swept up into the merry company and did not have the opportunity to talk alone again. But Julian would, Cassy knew, be at the Duchess of Richmond's ball the night after next, and so would she, and could confide everything to him then. Would he, she wondered, like her hair fair when – back in England and together at last – she reverted to being only Lucasta?

But not long after Madame St Laurent's last guest had departed, the Belgian diplomat arrived to say that his wife was fearful to stay in view of the grave news. If he was to escort the English miss, she must be ready to accompany them on the next morning's packet.

Cassy tried several times, but did not succeed in putting her whole strange story in a letter to Julian. Finally she decided that there was nothing for it but to wait to relate it until he could see for himself the truth of it, and the love, in her face.

She did not hear until much later that the Duchess of Richmond's ball had been interrupted by a messenger bearing the Duke of Wellington intelligence of the defeat of his Prussian forces at Ligny. It was the eve of the battle of Waterloo. The hundred days were over.

33

Aboard the packet Cassy's companions talked so constantly of their certainty of imminent bitter fighting in the vicinity of Brussels that she stared blindly at the grey, heaving water, seeing nothing but his face and seeming to hear, not the wild wind and waves, but the sound of gunfire. The Belgian diplomat drew her into shelter, saying concernedly, 'You are quite wet. It is an unpleasant beam sea and I hope you do not feel unwell.'

She had barely noticed the motion, so intent was she on her own thoughts. 'No, I am all right,' she said, 'but thank you, anyway.' So, with a last worried look at her face, he hastened back to comfort his wife whose lips were set and eyes closed in silent endurance.

At home, three days later, *The Times* proclaimed in banner headline, 'The War is Won.' Napoleon was banished to St Helena. But, among the rejoicings came the news of heavy casualties. Cassy, like the Marchioness of Allingham, waited for news.

Lord Allingham's official report bore witness to the fact that he was a liaison officer between Wellington – riding on the slope above the smoke of battle in his grey caped coat, a telescope under his arm – and the war arena. It was a dangerous appointment.

He made mention of the screams of wounded men and horses, the shocking noise made by the hail of British bullets against the breastplates of Kellerman's and Milhaud's *cuirassiers* and the suffocating smoke and smell of burnt cartridges. He wrote that it was impossible for the soldiers in the squares to move without treading upon a dead or wounded comrade.

The battle, which had begun at mid-morning, was finished by night-fall with a general French retreat, British and Prussians in pursuit.

But all these facts were only recorded in Lord Allingham's journal later when he recovered the use of his hand, for he broke his arm and several ribs when his horse was shot beneath him.

Aunt Letty and the girls greeted Cassy rapturously, and only interrupted their questions about her travels and distinguished friends for the time it took to recount the progress of their lessons, their friendships and the little domestic details they thought, correctly, she would want to know.

When Cassy was alone with Miss Page she described, without the more intimate details, her various meetings with the Marquis, and amused her with descriptions of some of the more indecorous aspects of life on the Continent.

Finally she said shyly, 'Aunt Letty, dear, Julian wants to marry me.'

Miss Page contrived to look startled and delighted at the same time. 'Which of you?' she demanded absurdly.

But her niece, who could do nothing to stop the tide of crimson rising to her cheeks, understood the question perfectly. 'Cassandra.'

'Glory be! What about his family?'

Cassy's eyes were brilliant. 'He consigned them to the devil.'

The two ladies laughed helplessly and then Miss Page kissed Cassy and said fervently, 'If only Julian is safe, and if only my friend Maria can bring herself to forgive Lucasta for having been Cassandra! Oh, how simple life will be when you are but one person!'

'Yes, and if only Julian himself can pardon my deception! Have you thought, Aunt Letty, that he may abominate blondes and find Lucasta as much of a dead bore as he did the first time he was constrained to dance with her?'

'Stuff! He has fallen in love with the person you are, just Cassy, and neither with a Drury Lane player nor a milk-and-water miss whom his mama wanted him to marry.'

'I only hope you may be proved right,' said Cassy a trifle doubtfully, and led the conversation to her aunt's own plans, an easy achievement since it was a theme close to her heart.

There was, Cassy learned, to be a quiet wedding, which was what she and Marcus both preferred, at the local church of St James in Piccadilly. Then they would drive north to spend their honeymoon in the Lake District.

It was suggested that, while the newly married pair were away, Marcia and Honor should be installed with their old nurse and housekeeper at Silverdale, the country house in Berkshire which they had finally chosen. Miss Page could hardly wait to show it to Cassy, for it had a river running through the grounds, stocked with trout, a stable of hunters and hacks which the girls could ride and a large flower garden. However, she had, quite rightly, thought that Cassy would like to stay in the London house with her sisters until her aunt's return from her honeymoon, when it would be relinquished. It would be time enough then to discuss her nieces' immediate future.

Cassy, content though she was for the time being to be with her family again, felt as though suspended in a vacuum halfway between heaven and hell. The heaven was the memory of the kisses and the declaration in the rose garden; the hell was the uncertainty of Julian's safety.

During this period of plans and preparations Cassy spent as much time as possible with her sisters, for though they were glad of their aunt's happiness, her coming marriage was one more upheaval in their young lives.

But she made time to visit Louise and John and also Dolly, who was now playing a summer season in *Wild Oats* at the Haymarket Theatre and was considered a star.

She wore the dark locks of Cassandra on these occasions to avoid having to make statements about the future for which she was not yet ready. She postponed calling on the Mundens until such time as she could do so without prevarication.

When Cassy went to Dolly's old lodgings she was redirected to a charming small house in the same neighbourhood. She was welcomed with cries of delight by the actress and her mother. Georgie was still at the high-class day school to which his mother could now afford to send him. Cassy congratulated her friend on her lavishly decorated new home which, though she might not herself have chosen such strident colours, was proof of the actress's present prosperity.

'How good it is to see you,' said Dolly, 'and looking more beautiful than ever. Tell me everything that you have been doing.' So, since Cassy also wanted to hear about her friend's rise to stardom and about the casts for the forthcoming productions, the girls prosed until the very last moment before Dolly had to leave for the afternoon performance.

Cassy had described the incident in Paris concerning Marcel de

Mallon and Agatha. 'Depend upon it,' Dolly had declared disgustedly, 'he would have destroyed the girl, milked her of what money he could and then blackmailed her as the price of her reputation. I know him!'

'So do I!' Cassy shuddered. 'Did he ever ask you for a divorce?'

'No. The one guinea allowance still gets delivered to the London address, where I dare say he keeps a light of love.'

'Then surely you should discontinue payment?'

'Probably. But truly, Cassy, I can afford it, and it is worth it not to be troubled by him. I should not care to marry again. I prefer my independence. I have bought this house myself. By the way, what news of Julian? Tom told me he was at the battle at Waterloo.'

'Yes. But I have no word. Has Tom heard anything?'

'I don't believe so. Still soft on the handsome Marquis, Cassy?'

The other coloured. 'Was it so obvious?'

'Only to me, because I know a piece of good acting when I see it, even if it is only the role of indifference. Good luck to you, pet. You deserve it.'

Georgie, taller and showing every indication of his father's good looks without their weakness, came in from school, hugged Cassy and persuaded her to stay a while to admire his new lesson books while his mother left for her dressing-room.

While she was doing so Thomas arrived, greeted Cassy exuberantly but without surprise and said to Dolly's mother, 'Our girl finds she has forgotten her reticule. If you will get it I will take it back to the theatre for her.' So the affair still flourished, Cassy thought.

She asked now, keeping the anxiety from her voice, 'Have you heard aught of your cousin Julian since the battle, Tom?'

She thought he looked a little embarrassed. 'Oddly enough, yes, just today. He has sent word to his mama through a returned brother officer that he is recovering from a broken arm and ribs. He hopes to be with her soon and' – Thomas flicked a glance at Cassy – 'has become betrothed to a Belgian girl.'

Cassy's smile was fixed. 'I see,' she said in a calm little voice and then turned to Georgie, kissed him and said, 'Your work is much improved and I am proud to have been your first teacher.' After that she remarked casually to Thomas, 'You must find London very thin of company now that it is so warm.'

He looked at her gratefully. 'Yes, the Brighton road is full of carriages and curricles again. I hope to be on it myself soon. Ah, you found the reticule. I must be away.'

'I am glad your cousin is getting better,' Cassy said as he took his leave of them. 'When you see him give him my best wishes for a speedy recovery, and wish him happy.'

Outside the house Thomas squared his shoulders and felt a release of tension. Thinking of Cassy's gay smile, he knew that she could not be as besotted about Julian as Dolly had suggested.

Back at Lowndes Square, Cassy told Miss Page Tom's news as soon as she could be alone with her. Shocked and dismayed, her aunt moved towards her. But Cassy put up a hand appealingly and said quietly, 'Don't, dear! After all, what is there to say? Just let me alone to – assimilate the facts. I shall be all right.' Miss Page gave a gesture of helplessness as she watched her niece's slim figure receding up the stairs.

In her chamber Cassy lay, dry-eyed, on her bed. She went back in memory to her last meeting with the Marquis and those words of his that had been engraved on her mind. 'God and Napoleon willing, I shall make you mine.'

Had he thought better of his intention, declared in a moment made sentimental by the threat of danger and the scent of roses? Had the full enormity, for himself and for his family, struck him with sudden force and made him change his mind?

Her hot eyes regarded, without seeing them, the water-lily pattern of the bed curtains while she reflected that a handsome wounded officer must have found many females to flutter over him in Belgium. Everybody knew that a man weakened by illness was easy prey.

There was a cold weight of misery on her, making her feel numb and the whole of life grey. However, she went downstairs to supper, talked with animation to her family and ate everything on her plate quite without tasting it. She continued to go through the daily motions of living, joining in the girls' talk and fun, as if she were watching from outside some other person doing these things. All three of Miss Page's nieces entered into the excitement of the wedding. Conversation centred on the hang of a hem, the tilt of a hat, the colour scheme of the large salon in the new house and the plants to choose for a herbaceous border.

Miss Page, however, was far from reassured by Cassy's outwardly normal appearance and behaviour and she shared her misgivings with her husband-to-be. 'She is eating her heart out in secret, Marcus, and once all the bustle is over I fear for her. Nobody knows better than I do how bitter the reaction from a lost love can be.' She looked at him with a little reminiscent smile.

'Except I, my love,' he corrected her. He looked suddenly abstracted, then said after a minute, 'You know, Letty, the whole business seems to me a hum, and knowing Julian as I have for some years, not at all what I would have expected of him. Rake he may be, but he was always straightforward. When we are married, and he can be presumed to be recuperating at Allingham Park, would you care to pay a bride visit there?'

'Oh, Marcus, how well you understand! That is exactly what I would most like.'

When Aunt Letty returned from her honeymoon there was a girlish glow to her cheeks and a glad light in her eye to accompany her stylish new toilette. The sisters' new Uncle Marcus found it difficult to keep his eyes away from her.

By contrast Cassy's face, though determinedly cheerful, looked wan. 'You have been working too hard,' the new Mrs Stanton accused her.

'No, no, 'tis but the heat. I am quite well.'

But her aunt was under no illusion. Nevertheless the special dinner that Cassy had planned was a success and, after thanking her for looking after everything so well, and Louise and John for their stewardship, the Stantons repaired to their town house to spend the night there and make sure that all was well. Grimble would accompany them to the new house in Berkshire in due course to reign over the staff there, and the cook and the maid had agreed to go too.

As arranged, the Stantons arrived back at Lowndes Square the next morning to confer with their eldest niece about future plans. They looked, thought Cassy, with approval and faint surprise, even more pleased with themselves than they had the day before.

'Pander to me, my dears,' Aunt Letty said winningly to her nieces, 'and change from those dresses into the gowns that Marcus brought you. We shall have a celebration today.'

Smiling and intrigued, the sisters did as they were bid, for it was impossible to gainsay their aunt in this delightful mood.

Cassy doubted that the enchanting white confection that had been her own present was quite suitable for day wear. But she had to admit as she brushed her golden hair into ringlets before the long mirror that it was vastly becoming.

She had hardly returned downstairs when the sound of horses drawn to a halt was heard outside the house. From the casement of the morning parlour she saw the familiar face and form of the Marquis ascending the steps and experienced such a shock that she flew upstairs to hide once again in her chamber. But her one terrified, wistful glimpse had been enough to tell her that he was thinner, paler and out of uniform.

'Welcome, Julian,' said Marcus Stanton. But his wife contented herself with kissing her guest on the cheek with an expression of smug satisfaction.

He bowed elaborately to the two little girls, dressed up in their new finery. 'How chic you look!' he said with his gleaming smile. They were pink with pleasure both at seeing him again after so long and at his compliment.

'Do you think that Lucasta is disposed to receive me now?' he asked them and they noticed with astonishment that his voice was a little unsteady.

Thea pondered the point and looked at her aunt for guidance. But that lady simply smiled serenely, which was no help.

However Grace, who had observed her eldest sister's precipitate flight, said firmly, 'No, I do not think she is disposed.'

With that, to their consternation, their aunt gave Lord Allingham a nod of the head upwards and said with equal decision, 'Her door is the second one on the left.'

The Marquis mounted the stairs and they heard him call loudly, 'Cassy, do not bolt the door. I have regained enough strength to carry you, but would prefer not to be forced to break it down.'

As she emerged wrathfully he gathered her up, disposed her over his stronger shoulder and went easily with her downstairs again.

Cassy struggled furiously in her captor's grasp. He gave Thea and Grace a conspiratorial wink. They looked quickly at their aunt and uncle, saw that they thoroughly approved of the episode and so, taking their cue from their elders, danced up and down and clapped their hands.

Cassy was bundled unceremoniously into the curricle, the tiger leaping behind with a wide grin. The Marquis took the ribbons in one hand and flicked the horses to a start. Then they were going at such a spanking pace that she could not have jumped out without doing herself an injury.

'Let me go, sir,' she cried on a sob of rage.

'Never! This is an abduction.'

'I beg your pardon?'

'You need not.' He drew the curricle skilfully to a stop and, before

253

she could elude it, had put his one good arm round her tightly and kissed her hard.

Breathless and totally bewildered, she yet managed, for the second time, to slap his face.

'Not so good a blow as before,' he said, but was forced to blink all the same. 'So Cassandra is Lucasta, "that bright northern star".'

'That comes from Lovelace's poem!' she exclaimed in spite of herself. Then a sudden bitter suspicion assailed her. 'Did you know who I was all the time?' If so, she reflected, his desire to marry the actress Cassandra was neither so affecting nor so courageous.

'No, I did not, although for a very short while in Brighton I began to wonder. You resemble Thea and even Gerard a little. Then I dismissed the notion as absurd since I could not believe that your aunt would permit such duplicity. Now I realise that, though charming, she has never been any match for your wilfulness. I did not know you so well then.

'When you consented to stay in my bed in London' – he grinned at her wickedly – 'I had no further doubt that you really were an actress of genteel background but small means. Then you disappeared, and reappeared in households of dubious reputation. Lucasta would have gone home long before, or I thought she would. But then I never really knew Miss Loring either.'

'Nor shall you now.'

'That would be a pity, for she is not only a gorgeous blonde – and I have always had a weakness for fair women – but also brave, independent to a fault, resourceful and a little stupid.'

'Stupid!' she echoed, as surprised as she was incensed.

'You must be, surely, Cassy, else you would never have believed that I would declare my intention of marrying you one month and become engaged to another female the next. The Stantons did not credit it. You cannot know me very well. But we will remedy that, my darling.' Cassy felt a rising, incredulous gladness. 'Young Thomas, who only half listens to anything he is told, drove me to the country to recuperate and remarked that he might have misled my friend Cassandra.'

'Oh, Julian!'

'You may well say, "Oh, Julian!" Luckily my mama was so overwhelmed that I had survived Waterloo and been restored to her that she, if most unwillingly, accepted my avowal that I intended to marry somebody who had performed on the stage.'

'Poor Lady Allingham, she must have been horrified!'

'I do not doubt that she was, but she put a good face on it mostly, I sincerely believe, because she remembered you at the costume ball and how pretty behaved you were before the drastic *dénouement* by the terrible Sybil.'

'Who tried to make up for it afterwards.'

'Did she? You surprise me. Anyway, just picture to yourself my mama's relief when your aunt and new uncle arrived to discover for themselves if I were a scoundrel, and then completed their mission by telling us the story of your double life. Now stop talking!'

'But you have scarcely given me an opportunity to say a word!'

'Then do not.' He kissed her again, this time with her full co-operation, until, as in Vienna and again in Brussels, she felt weak from wanting him.

'Would it hurt your poor ribs if I put my arms around you?' she asked at last.

'I am prepared to risk it since we are to be married today. No, do not move them, for your arms feel very comfortable there. I was going to say, when you tried to interrupt me, that we will drive to Grosvenor Square now, where my mother is waiting to accompany us to church. Your family will join us there and Marcus will give you away. I wish you to wear your own mama's pearls, which are Charles Young's wedding gift to you, and this diamond and sapphire ring, which I will now place on your finger.

'After the wedding we will return to our town house and stay there for a few days, and nights, quite unchaperoned until we have decided where to spend our honeymoon. When we return Thea and Grace will live with us, for I want sisters. I await your objections.'

'But I have none, Julian - dearest.' Her eyes shone like the sapphires on her finger.

'Just as well,' he said brutally, 'for, as I may have mentioned, this is an abduction.'